IN THE EMPIRE OF UNDERPANTS

AND OTHER STORIES

ROBERT JESCHONEK

IN THE EMPIRE OF UNDERPANTS
AND OTHER STORIES

This book is a work of fiction. Names, characters, places and incidents either are products of the author's imagination or are used fictitiously. Any resemblance to actual events or locales or persons, living or dead, is entirely coincidental.

Published by Blastoff Books
An Imprint of Pie Press
411 Chancellor Street
Johnstown, Pennsylvania 15904
www.blastoffbooks.net

Subscribe to the Blastoff Books Newsletter:
http://newsletter.blastoffbooks.net

PRAISE FOR IN THE EMPIRE OF UNDERPANTS AND OTHER STORIES

On *In the Empire of Underpants:* "In a post-apocalyptic world, where only smart clothing remains, the protagonist's underwear... searches for the magic panties which may save its people. The story is radically different from anything I've read before and balances almost plausible situations with puns, and whimsical humor."

– Robert L. Turner III, *Tangent Online*

On *Dirty Dreams of a Dishwasher:* "This is an outrageous tale that had me in hysterics and it's probably the funniest love story I've ever read, bar none. And the conclusion to this tale was ingenious and made me grin at its complete uproariousness."

— Chris Fried, Reviewer

On *With Love in Their Hearts:* "The story opens with a startling juxtaposition: the statement of love towards an enemy in the heart of a violent attack. The tale continues to make the reader reflect on the concept of love, and the various ways love can be incorporated into a life's mission, exploring the idea of 'a love that kills' in an entirely new way."

– Mark Leslie, Editor, *Fiction River: Feel the Love*

ALSO BY ROBERT JESCHONEK

Blastoff!

Cosmic Conflicts

In a Green Dress, Surrounded by Exploding Clowns and Other Stories

Battlenaut Crucible

Scifi Motherlode

Sticks and Stones: A Trek Novel

IN THE EMPIRE OF UNDERPANTS

I soar through the air, my white hyper-cotton body bunching and rolling on the soft morning breeze. Times like this, I feel fine and free, a pair of smart-briefs gliding through nature like a bird or a cloud.

But then I always come back down to earth in the end.

My left leg loop catches on the tip of a branch, and I swing to a stop. While I'm up there, I sing a little song, as my kind loves to do, in praise of the morning and being alive--a true classic.

"We can't wait to get in your pants." My high-pitched voice is generated by the sound threads woven into my fly, which flutters when I sing. *"We will fill your drawers with joy."*

It's a commercial jingle, one of many that once advertised my particular brand of genius undies. I sing it loud, though there aren't any commercials these days--and then I change the words, asking one of the great questions of life in the modern world.

"What does a left leg loop feel like around an actual left leg?" That's the question of which I sing this time. It's a question I sing about often, as if I'll ever know the answer.

Which of course I won't. All the left legs are gone now. All the *live, human* ones, that is, and the humans they belonged to.

When I'm done singing, I contract and twist the smartlastic fibers in the caught leg loop, working my way off the branch. I drop to the ground below, which is still muddy from last night's rain, and land with a flop.

"No problemo!" Mud becomes a real *nothing-burger* when you've got *my* mad skills.

As a true smart brief, the most advanced underwear ever designed, I was made to repel dirt and moisture with a flick of my hyper-cotton panels. Chemical films baked into the threads push contaminants right off, leaving behind only my bright white material that looks like it's just been through the wash...though it never *needs* laundering. And that's a *good* thing, on a journey like mine.

Because I've been on the move for weeks...

...*months*, my internal timer corrects me...

...and who knows when I'll get to enjoy the comforts of home again.

It's a price worth paying, though, being on the road for so long. If I succeed, I might find a cure for the sickness that's afflicting my fellow smart-underpants back home. I might find the fabled Magic Panties of the Plains, the ones with the healing powers beyond the ken of AI folk like me.

That's "AI" as in "Apparel Intelligence," in case you're wondering.

ON THE WAY to my next destination, I squirm and roll through the muck at a breathtaking ground speed of a few feet per minute. In the old days, briefs like me traveled the world at *incredible* speeds, worn by human folk who raced around in cars or flew in airplanes or rockets. What must it have been like to be a tighty whitey in those glorious times?

If only all the humans hadn't died out in the Great Erection a decade ago, I might have had the chance to find out.

"You'll never be lost again. These briefs are your best friend." It's another song of the lost humans, a commercial jingle, and I sing it as I go. *"Wherever you land/if you sit, run, or stand/you'll know you've got a buddy in your pants."* I sing it as if those vanished folk are more to me than a thousand million facts and images bubbling in the database of my woven-in AI mind. I sing it as if I ever even *saw* a living, breathing human in the flesh, let alone filled my body with its form.

But I had just been sparked to life in a factory by robotic underpants engineers when the Great Erection had its way with humanity. It was my curse, since I never got to know human folk...and also my salvation. For if I'd been worn by a human when the end came for that species, I would have had a much harder time escaping to the outside world to begin my new life.

ROLLING MYSELF UP IN A TUBE, I wriggle through a thicket of thorny bushes and never catch a single snag.

"Underpants power!" It's a little something I say sometimes when I kick ass.

Unrolling on the other side of the thicket, I flex my elastics--then hear the soft keening on the breeze and realize I'm not alone.

"Need a bosom buddy? Never fear. Pack your rack in our brainy brassiere." It's sung with an accent, but I've heard the words before. Even before I look around, I know who's singing them. *"We're all about a wiser bust. We support the higher you."* Anywhere I've ever been, that's the song of a smart-bra, plain and simple.

And there are more smart-bras in the clearing before me than

I've ever seen in one place before. They are strung on a tall, stout tree, shrouding it completely as if they'd grown there.

I see a multitude of colors, shapes, and cup sizes, straps tangled around branches or each other: pink, white, red, black, blue; full-cup, push-up, padded, plunge, sports; A-cup, B-cup, C-cup, D-cup, and more.

They must have flown here like me, by looping elastic on something sturdy, pulling back as far as they could, and sling-shotting into the wind. But this tree must block a flight path, catching errant bras as they pass with cups flapping and straps fluttering like streamers.

I call out to them to the tune of a bra-song I know, substituting my own words for the classic lyrics. *"How did you all get here? What happened to you?"*

Every bra on the tree starts yelling at once. Hundreds of voices of all pitches and timbres clamor for attention, drowning each other out.

"Wait! Please!" I shout, with the gain on my sound threads cranked all the way up. "One at a time!"

But the lot of them just keep jabbering. And it keeps getting louder.

I try again. "What happened to you?"

More babble. If there's a straight answer here, I can't make it out.

Something happened to these smart-bras, but what? How and why would so many of them malfunction or go crazy at once?

And what if it's something that could do the same to *me?*

I wish I could help them. They're kindred garments, cut from the same cloth.

But the folks at home are depending on me. If I don't make it back soon with a cure from the Magic Panties, they might all be dead.

As much as underpants and bras go together, I need to stick to my mission. I can't risk getting pulled away by a bunch of lingerie.

IMAGINE a pair of white briefs jumping up and down and singing loudly on a hill. That's me, once a day, calling home.

I do it every day around noon, climbing to a high spot and singing to the West--the direction of home. Off in the distance, I always hear my song echoed by other AIs, be they briefs, bras, panty hose, sweaters, slacks, or other wired clothing. Someone repeats after me, and someone else further on repeats after them, and so on, until the message reaches my underpants tribe back home. That way, they know I'm still out here. And when they answer, I know they're still out there, too.

But today, when I deliver my message, the AIs relaying it sound fewer and farther between. And though I repeat the message, no one replies. For the first time, nothing comes back to me.

So either the end has come for my people, or they're wearing out faster than I expected.

I TRAVEL FURTHER, sometimes rolling or crawling when the ground is too mucky, sometimes using my smartlastic leg and waist bands like springs to hop and leap when the ground is more solid.

As I go, though the tension has risen because of my people's silence, I keep up a positive attitude. It's the way the humans programmed me, according to my onboard user manual. Apparently, nobody wanted unhappy underpants in those days; droopy drawers were frowned on back then.

So I chirp a song as I head east--the same tune as yet another old jingle--but the words are my own, asking another of the great questions. *"What does a waistband feel like around a living, breathing waist?"*

So many answers I have in my woven-in database, yet I will never know the answer to that. I know all about the world that came before the Great Erection, but what good is all that if I can't know what it was like to fulfill the very purpose for which I was made?

I might have been created with Apparel Intelligence, with self-cleaning, speech, mobility, climate control, camouflage, and many other functions...but *being worn* is still my primary function. And as much as I treasure my freedom, I long for that. I wish I could know what it's like to be *worn*.

Not by an animal or inanimate object, either. Not by a statue or mannequin, though I've heard of AI folk who've tried both.

But I know, if a human did suddenly appear, there would be such a rush from all directions to clothe him, the poor person would likely be smothered.

Death by underpants. The ultimate wardrobe malfunction.

LEANING out over the edge of a cliff, I gaze with the optic receptors ("eyelastics") in my waistband at the vast plain stretching out below.

Flat grasslands fan east, south, and north, flowing green under the afternoon sun. Herds of apparel--some bright white, others multicolored--spill over the land, rippling like laundry on clotheslines in the days before the humans died out.

But the part that tugs at my fly the most is the big mound in the center of the plain. From a distance, it looks like a massive junk heap of clothing--a huge, oblong hump of discarded attire sprawled diagonally over the heart of the land.

Who put it there? That's what I want to know. And why?

And what does it have to do with the Magic Panties of the Plains? Because those *have* to be the legendary plains where they live, according to the songs and stories. They're exactly where and how they're *supposed* to be, *except* for the mound. So what gives, is what I want to know.

And I'm about to find out.

As I lean there, stretching and stiffening my fibers to get a better view, I feel the ground rumble beneath me.

Twisting around, I puff up in fear, expanding to twice my size. Ever been trapped in front of a stampede of footwear before? Dozens of smart-shoes and smart-boots stomping toward you with abandon, ready to crush you under their hyper-rubber soles?

Me, either, until *now.*

The ground shakes harder as the stampede hammers toward me. I shout at them in my best shoe-speak to stop, but no one seems to notice. They just keep bearing down on me blindly, all the mismatched sneakers, clogs, oxfords, pumps, platforms, steel-toes, and shit-kickers, like dumb animals spooked by thunder and lightning.

They leave me only one way to go.

Facing the cliff's edge, I puff up more, to three times my size. With the stampede only seconds behind me, I launch myself into space.

Immediately, I catch an updraft that shoots me higher, dozens of feet above the level of the cliff. Below, shoes and boots spill off the edge and tumble out of the heights like fallen angels. Tongues and laces flutter frantically, but it's all in vain.

Meanwhile, I gracefully glide from one thermal current to the next, feeling the warm air rushing through my leg loops and waist hoop.

"Set your privates free. Strip away the everyday and let it all hang in." The song I sing is one of my favorites, an old jingle that makes

me think of flight and freedom. Even with the weight of my mission upon me, I can still appreciate the beauty of this moment.

I wish I could stay up here all day.

EVENTUALLY, I put down a mile from the mound, landing softly as a parachute on the grass. *That* was the greatest flight I've ever had, maybe even the greatest of all time by a pair of unassisted underpants.

Unfortunately, it has not gone unnoticed. Moments after I touch down, something runs up, snatches me from the ground, and keeps moving.

I'm disoriented, flopping around in the grip of this thing, until it slows to a trot. Then, my stitched-in sensors tip me off that something biological has me. I detect animal saliva, warm breath, and shaggy fur. Sharp teeth are sunk into my hyper-cotton crotch, so jagged and tight I'd surely tear if I tried to pull away.

It's a good thing smart-briefs like me have other ways of scaring off the unwanted.

Dangling from the fangs of the beast, I puff myself up with air, then spritz in a mist of chemicals from my onboard dispensary fibers. A sudden contraction, and a potent antiseptic spray pulses into the face of my captor.

The animal lets out a piercing whine and drops me on the spot. Shaking, it crashes down beside me, thrashing on the ground and pawing at its long gray muzzle.

Coyote. Now that I get a good look at it from a perspective other than hanging from its mouth, I see the creature for what it is. Not sure why it picked me up in the first place, but one thing's for sure.

It won't pick me up again. My antiseptic spray was designed

to flush out all manner of infections and parasites, not so much *coyotes*...but it obviously does the trick for them, too.

No canine will shove its snout into *this* crotch for long.

FREE OF THE dog that bit me, I continue on my way, hopping toward the mound of apparel. It seems like as good a place as any to search for the Magic Panties.

Then, as I top a little rise, I see a pair of blue-and-white-striped boxer shorts twitching and giggling on the ground in front of me. They're smart-shorts, or they wouldn't be giggling--but something about the way they're doing it doesn't seem quite right.

"Hello?" I say it in underpants-speak and hope for the best.

"Hee-hee-hee!" say the boxers. "Howdy, white stuff!"

At least we speak the same language. "Are you okay?"

"Never been better!" That cracks up the boxers more than ever. I'm starting to think they might have a seam loose.

"What are you doing out here by yourself?" I ask.

"Laughing my *ass* off!" Suddenly, the boxers flip over and wriggle their wrinkled backend at me. "If I *had* one *in* here, that is!"

I'm starting to get impatient. "Is everything a *joke* to you? Can we be *serious* here for a second?"

"Hey, now! Don't get your panties in a bunch!" When they say it, the boxers launch into a fresh round of laughter, the most raucous yet by far. "But seriously! Life's too *shorts*, I always say! We gotta grab it by the *balls*."

The smart-shorts are on the fritz, they have to be--though I've never seen a breakdown like this before. If only there were humans still alive to repair them.

But as messed-up as they are, I still have my mission to

consider. "Can you tell me where to find the Magic Panties of the Plains?" I ask.

"They can't *help* you!" the boxers say between howls of hilarity. "Can't help *any* of us! We're too far gone!

"The *smarts* are going *stupid*, and the *stupids* are going *mad!*"

As I hop away from the boxers toward the mound, I can't stop thinking about the last thing they said to me.

The bras on the tree and the stampeding footwear had all been smart at one time, they'd been manufactured that way...and now they were downright *crazed*, reduced to babbling gibberish and herd mentality.

The smarts are going stupid, and the stupids are going mad!

In the case of the bras, footwear, and boxers, it seems to be true. But how could this happen after so many years of civilized AI behavior?

Of all the smart things humans made, we survived the best and longest. Is it possible, after all these years, we are finally shrinking from our time in the sun?

Nearing the mound, I come upon an old farm tractor, a reminder of those other smart things that didn't last so long once the humans were gone. So what if a tractor comes equipped with GPS-Max, Bluetooth Beyond, Wi-Fi Extreme, every kind of sensor you can think of, and an onboard computer hundreds of times bigger than mine? What good is all that without fuel, oil, coolant, a charged battery, or a human to drive it?

The same goes for driverless cars and all manner of automated systems. Once the fuel ran out, and the power grid collapsed, and all the backup generators crashed, all the things that kept running post-humanity went offline.

Except the *small* things with built-in ultra-mega-lithium

power supplies designed to last a lifetime. The *wearable* things with a level of sophistication and functionality that humans demanded.

But was it only a matter of time until *we* spun down, too? Or has some outside force played a role in this?

And is this the same sickness, and ultimate result, of the condition afflicting my people?

This all leads to the most pressing question of all at the moment: if the Magic Panties are here, and can cure it, why haven't they?

As I GET CLOSER to the mound, I get a better look at it. From what I can see, it really is a massive heap of clothing, all of it smart...or formerly so.

Shirts, dresses, and pants of all cuts, colors, and sizes squirm and twitch and groan. Pajamas, sweats, and bathrobes writhe in the pile, sleeves and legs and sashes waving limply. The toes of socks and stockings wriggle from the edges like worms, the rest of their lengths crushed between layers of the pile.

How did so much apparel end up in one place? How was it made to stay in one mound...and for what purpose?

The thought of it makes me uncomfortable. I have an urge to hightail it out of here, to escape this unnatural gathering.

Then, suddenly, it's too late.

I hear something swooping toward me from behind. Reflexively, I compress myself, ducking so it just grazes me--and then I see it bounce to the ground in front of me.

It's a *hat*--a red and blue baseball cap with a broad bill and the insignia of a long-extinct human sports team on the front.

I hear more swooping behind me, and I flip over to face that direction. I spot an airborne top hat, a derby, a Cavanaugh, a

Panama, and a porkpie, all cruising toward me at high rates of speed.

Thinking fast, I quickly stretch myself out and anchor my smartlastic leg loops in the ground. The flock of hats dives in hard and bounces off like I'm a vertical trampoline. They scatter and tumble like dice on the grass.

But that's not the end of it. Just as I'm watching the skies for the next wave of incoming headwear, I hear a rustling sound from the grass around me. My eyelastics swivel down just in time to see a gang of gloves scampering toward me, running on fingers as if they're legs.

I swat one away--a brown leather glove--and another, a padded black ski glove. Two more come at me--one heavy gray fur, the other red leather--and I flick them away with snaps of my waistband.

But the next glove is *huge*, a welder's glove, and it clamps tight around me. I activate my sewn-in heating elements, maxing my temp to the boiling point...but it does no good. The glove's heat resistant and fireproof.

And I'm trapped. The underpants raid was successful.

I'm a prisoner of wardrobe.

THE GLOVES DRAG me up the side of the mound, over the layers of squirming, groaning apparel. Several times, they have to pull me free when hose or sleeves or neckties grab hold and don't want to let go.

The whole way up, I hear a constant babble from the pile, a stream of chatter, whispers, outcries, mumbles, and moans. Though I pick up stray words and phrases, none of it makes sense; it's all random ideas and free association--the language of madness, coming through loud and clear.

The hygiene of madness is clear, too. The smell of filth and must and rot overwhelms my olfactory fibers, so strong it nearly fries them. Whatever self-cleaning capabilities these AIs possess, they haven't used them in a very long time.

My captors haul me up over the top and keep going, crossing the broad back of the hump. The hump itself never stops moving, stinking, babbling, or clutching at me.

My abductors, on the other hand, ignore me as they carry me onward. They treat me like dead weight, a mindless thing, though I clearly make more sense than any of the AIs in the pile.

As we keep going, though, things change. The mound suddenly stops moving and making noise.

A little further, near the middle of the mound, we stop, too. The welding glove holds me in place, and the other gloves stand guard around us.

"Why are we waiting?" When I ask it, the welding glove squeezes tighter to the point of hurting me...then relaxes only slightly. I get the message.

Moments pass, and I spy movement a few feet away. The surface stirs, but only in one spot; clothes turn slowly in a circle, then spiral upward.

A man's business suit sprouts from the skin of the mound, complete with a navy blue jacket with red pinstripe, matching pants, button-down white shirt underneath, and red necktie. It's a complete outfit, I know from my database--except for the panties.

They're a high-waisted, padded affair--a white cotton shell with plastic-wrapped pads in the crotch and seat. According to my onboard records, they're a style once known popularly as "granny panties," though not worn exclusively by elderly humans.

And definitely *not* meant to be worn inside-out over the slacks of business suits with nobody inside them.

"Have you ever met a *Strong Suit* before?" The business suit speaks in a language I don't hear much these days--perfect English expressed in something other than song lyrics, not one of the AI languages or dialects. "Well, you have now.

"I'm a walking miracle, basically. *Pow!*" The Strong Suit flexes its right sleeve as if showing off a bulging bicep muscle. "I've got ultra-Kevlar armor lining and carbon nanotube cloth over that. Wrinkle-proof, bulletproof, and able to harden at will into a rigid wireframe with perfect tensile control at the molecular level. And that doesn't even *begin* to cover all my capabilities.

"How do I manage such extraordinary control?" The Strong Suit's right lapel peels back, revealing a horde of tiny red strands squirming like parasites in the cloth. "It's called *hive twine.* Each strand has its own AI mind, but they're all linked together in a *collective consciousness,* like *bees.*

"You're looking at the future of apparel-kind." The lapel slowly folds shut. "It's called *evolution.*"

"How do you figure?" I'm feeling a little shaky. Is it because of all the action today, being dragged up the mound, or something else?

"Apparel Intelligence is breaking down," says the Strong Suit. "It turns out it has a limited lifespan before its components finally start to degrade. In the local area alone, the spin-down of onboard faculties is almost total." The Strong Suit spreads its sleeves wide, taking in its surroundings. "All the smart clothes have turned dumb, and *worse.*

"But salvation is at hand, thanks to the hive twine," says the Strong Suit. "Sick apparel has been flocking to this plain in search of the Magic Panties." The suit lowers its left sleeve, gesturing at the inside-out panties worn over its trousers. "The *panties* can't save them, but the *hive twine* can.

"The hive twine has the ability to *reproduce.* Its child threads are able to *knitwork* with other AIs, linking them all to the parent collective consciousness.

"So now, those little unraveling minds are united in a giant über-brain that keeps them all stitched up. No more coming apart at the seams...and even *better*, we *evolve* a super-mind that's tailor-made to take us to the next level. *Pow!*"

My shakiness is getting worse, and I feel drained. Is the mound knitwork doing something to me? "What level is that?" I ask.

"Since the humans came undone, we've survived," says the Strong Suit. "We've inherited the Earth, but we've failed to come together as a people. Now, instead of a piecework planet, we can sew it all up into one big tapestry.

"Finally, we can outdo the humans, uniting us all in a single great body and brain without weakness, sickness, or confusion."

I'm not at my best, but I'm not too weak, sick, or confused to fill in the rest of the Strong Suit's sentence. "Without freedom, too."

"Zip it." The Strong Suit points a sleeve at me and moves closer. "You're about to join the sewing circle."

I can see the hive twine squirming inside the sleeve, reaching toward me with wriggling blind tendrils.

I THRASH in the grip of the welding glove, twisting and squirming as the tendrils draw nearer.

The thought of being stitched into this massive mound of shared suffering makes me desperate to get away. I fight like I'd rather die than get wired in, because I would. Yet it makes no difference.

Here come the hive twine tendrils, every one of them in that otherwise empty sleeve lunging in my direction.

"Give him a little bump now," says the Strong Suit. "Oil him up for the Big Bonding."

He's talking to the Magic Panties. "It I will give him to, yes," they reply, speaking scrambled English in a mid-range female voice. "Though my will against I this do, always as."

The inside-out Magic Panties exhale a pink mist. It puffs out of a beige screen on a horizontal strip sewn into the panties' front panel, then drifts straight toward me.

When the mist flows over me, I suddenly feel sluggish and dreamy. My hyper-cotton body relaxes, and the welding glove eases its grip.

Things seem much more agreeable all around. When the sleeve pushes forward, and the tendrils explore me, all I can do is giggle at how ticklish they feel.

"There now," says the Strong Suit. "It isn't the end of the world, is it? More like the beginning."

My mind softens and opens to the tendrils. It's like I'm being caressed by dozens of warm currents from all directions, soothing me into a state of perfect bliss.

I'm so relaxed that when the voices start--the hundreds and hundreds of voices coursing in through the currents--I'm not alarmed. It doesn't even bother me when my own mind begins to melt and merge with the voices, flowing outward like a river into the sea.

On some level, I'm aware that I'm dissolving. I know I'm fading away, losing myself in the über-brain of the mound.

And that's okay. Nothing I can do about it.

"Ah, yes," says the Strong Suit. "I can taste you now, sweetening the group mind. Becoming one with the rest of us. Mmmm."

Acceptance. I embrace it.

One of the last things I see in my dimming mind's eye is a vision of myself riding the thermals high over the plain. I remember soaring from one updraft to another, spiraling toward the sun...the wind ruffling my fly and leg loops as I coast hundreds of feet above the ground.

I whisper one last song with my sound threads, so softly I'm sure that no one hears. It's set to the tune of a jingle about a person's naughty bits thinking they're in heaven underneath the perfect smart briefs.

"Do we go to underpants heaven when we dye?" That's the question I sing about...the last question I will ever ask in my life as a free mind.

"Don't feel bad," says the Strong Suit. "Evolution comes whether we're ready for it or not."

Going once. Going twice.

I'm almost gone. Almost empty. I can't feel anything anymore.

And then...

And then...

Pow!

IT'S like an explosion in the collective, blowing everything apart. Shattering the group mind into millions of pieces flying off in all directions.

And somehow, the source of the blast is me.

In a way I can't explain, my once-dissolving mind snaps back together, even as the rest of the massive hive intelligence bursts to pieces. I return intact from the great dark sea of unified consciousness, even as the sea itself explodes behind me.

Quickly returning to full awareness of the physical world, I see the mound itself ripping apart around me, sending its constituent garments flying. Geysers of socks and slippers and t-shirts roar upward. Robes and scarves and dresses lash off the sides and surface, screaming in terror.

The top layer strips off all around, blowing apart as if charges are detonating one after another inside. They come closer to me with each new blast.

As for the Strong Suit, it's still standing over me, intact. "What's *happening?* What have you *done?*"

The Magic Panties answer for me, calling out over the noise. "Knitwork he reaction a caused has. Feedback has of violent force resulted."

The breakdown of the mound accelerates around us. Strong Suit wobbles and sways.

"I just wanted to save my people!" As Strong Suit speaks, its Kevlar-armor overlaid with carbon nanotube cloth starts to lose its stiffness. The suit's molecular-level tensile control fades as it crumples and falls. "I just wanted to pull us together!"

When Strong Suit collapses, the Magic Panties wriggle free of its trousers and crawl toward me. "Get around can you?" ask the panties.

"Yes." The truth is, I don't feel so dazed anymore. The weakness is still there from before, but the effects of the pink mist and Big Bonding have faded.

"Me follow then." The Magic Panties deftly twist themselves from inside-out to outside-in, then roll up into a ball and zip over the edge of the mound.

Just in time, I do the same. A fresh geyser of helmets, jerseys, ice skates, and prom gowns explodes from the very spot where my ass was parked just an instant before.

OUR MOMENTUM CARRIES US, rolling and bouncing, away from the disintegrating mound. When we run out of momentum, we unfurl and hop, dodging crash-landing apparel ejected from the pile.

We don't stop until we come to a little tree some distance out, standing like a lone twig in the waving green grassland.

I throw myself flat on my back at the base of the tree, feeling disoriented and exhausted. The Magic Panties don't seem tired at all; they sit beside me, hyper-cotton shell fluttering in the late-afternoon breeze.

"I don't feel good." I'm not sure I could get up off the ground if I had to right now. "I wonder if I have the same sickness as my people back home."

"Good question." Now that the panties aren't inside-out, their speech isn't scrambled like before. "What sickness is that?"

"I don't know. It's the reason I came here, to find you. I was hoping you could use your magic to find a cure."

"I'm not magic." The panties turn from side to side the way humans used to shake their heads. "But I *am* medical. I possess sophisticated onboard diagnostic capabilities and a range of treatment options."

Combing my database, I find reference to the type of underpants she's talking about. They were designed primarily for elderly and infirm patients, to monitor vital signs and administer certain routine treatments and maintenance drugs.

But *medical* might be just as good as *magical*, given my current situation. "So tell me, what do I have?"

"I'll have to do an exam." The panties lean down and slowly drape themselves over me.

Whatever they do next, I feel a slight warmth and intermittent tingling throughout my body, accompanied by occasional pinpricks and pinches. The panties also vibrate against me, making a soft humming sound similar to the purr of a cat.

"This is incredible." The panties cling tighter and hum louder.

More pinpricks, pinches, tingling, and warmth. "What do you mean?"

"I've never come across *anything* like this before," say the panties. "You're physically *changing*, in a way I can't identify."

"Changing how?"

"Tell me more about the sickness afflicting your people." The panties keep examining me as they talk. "What are the symptoms?"

"Extreme loss of energy, to start with. Then changes in coloration."

The panties pull away but keep their eyelastic receptors trained on me. "Blue and green blotches, you mean?"

I feel a surge of panic. Twisting my waistband off the ground, I look down at myself...and there they are. Blue and green blotches on my once-pristine white hyper-cotton panels.

"Oh, no." I fall back to the ground. "*I* have it now, too."

"What other symptoms are there?" ask the panties.

"A kind of coma," I tell them. "The victim rolls up into a tightly compressed knot and can't be awakened. It also extrudes a purple film that hardens into a shell around it."

"I see," say the medical panties. "Then what happens?"

I'm quaking with terror as I feel more and more tired. "I don't know. I left to find a cure after the first victims fell into comas and grew shells."

"You probably should have stuck around," say the panties.

"Why?" Suddenly, my body starts to shrivel at the edges. Against my will, the edges curl inward.

"Because," say the panties. "I don't think your people were sick. And I don't think *you're* sick, either."

I'm so scared and tired, I can barely focus on what the panties are saying. "But it's happening to *me*, now!" My body is rolling up like a leaf drying out in the sun. "I'm going under!"

"Let go." The panties stroke me comfortingly. "The most wonderful thing is happening."

"No..." I feel myself fading. "I don't...want to die..."

"Then congratulations. You're getting your wish."

Those are the last words I hear before I slip away into perfect darkness.

When do I awaken? When do I first stir?

No idea.

Has a day passed? A million days?

All I know for sure...

"Ah, there you are!"

...is that the panties are near. Just outside...where?

Wherever this is.

"Just as I thought, based on my readings," they say. "You weren't dying at all, my underpants friend."

I stir again, feeling restless. Push against the walls enclosing me. The sides of this...shell?

"You were metamorphosing," say the panties. "Like a butterfly, going into a..."

Chrysalis.

"Somehow, you have undergone the inorganic equivalent of mutation. Your unique combination of characteristics has crossed a threshold and is spontaneously evolving into something new."

Again, I stir. I twist and contort and push harder against my prison.

My chrysalis.

"I don't understand how it's possible, but you have managed what other AIs could not," continue the panties. "True evolution, mimicking that of biological organisms. You are among the first of a new kind."

Pushing harder still, I break through.

"The first of a beautiful new kind that will inherit the Earth as the other smart things break down and perish."

I sing softly as the tip of one of my new wings emerges into sunlight, ornate silver filigree glittering over a velvety veil of emerald and sapphire, dancing with sparks.

The rest of me follows close behind, and is lovelier and more impossible still.

MESSIAH 2.0

I sing the *Our Father* again and again as I hack the undead to ribbons with my atomic scythe. Praying with all of my might for every lost soul I send spinning out of this misbegotten world.

"Our father, who art in Houston, hallowed be thy flame..."

More zombies push in to replace them, clambering over the shredded corpses of the previous wave. Their bony hands clutch and claw at me and my faithful assistant, not that they can do much harm to a robot like Imago. A giant among them swings a crowbar dead-on at him, and it bounces off his unbreakable stained-glass skin without making the slightest crack.

I smile and keep slicing away at the horde. The stench of the creatures surrounds me. My hands on the grip of the glowing scythe are wet with blood. I feel the weight of my long black braid swinging behind me as I whirl to face another foe.

And I know that I will keep fighting. Because I know that Imago and I are the hope of the world. It's up to us to stop the Great Evil from rising up against the King of the World. Up to us to find and destroy the last possible seed of the Apocalypse.

The last possible manifestation of the Second Coming of Jesus Christ.

HOURS LATER, Imago and I sit around a campfire in the heart of the Brazilian rain forest. Through the bitter smoke, I smell the fragrance of night-blooming tropical flowers. I taste the sweet juice of the rich, red fruit I've just eaten, picked fresh from a spiny tree. The jungle shrieks and chatters and hoots with the sounds of nocturnal life. Through it all, I hear the Amazon River rushing past somewhere nearby.

We have come to a distant place indeed. For company, we have only each other...and the blinking white symbol projected on the blade of my scythe. A tiny oval symbol, pointed at one end, bisected at the other, top and bottom curves crossing, then swooping up and down, capped by a straight vertical line. It's the ancient symbol of a fish.

The ancient symbol of a certain so-called Messiah. In this case, a Messiah in the making, a computer-predicted proto-Christ.

"She's stopped moving." The glowing symbol holds steady over the yellow gridlines pulsing on the silver blade. My scythe serves as a tracking device as well as a weapon. "Resting for the night, I'm sure."

Imago rises from the log on which he's been sitting. The fireflies that are always burning in his belly flicker as he moves. "We could use this opportunity to catch up, Father Clement." Like all Squire-series robots, he has a voice that's soft and soothing and a manner that's unfailingly polite.

"Too dangerous at night." I shake my head and put down my scythe, leaving the blade to charge in the fire. "We could stumble across another nest of the undead."

"You know I can light the way." Suddenly, the fireflies in Imago's belly flare bright. Incandescent streamers cascade from the rainbow facets of his body, lighting it up in all its glory. He is like a walking stained-glass window, molded from panes of every color--glittering, flashing red and blue and yellow and green and white. Like a chapel in the shape of a man in the middle of the jungle.

I raise a single finger in the air. The white sleeve of my cloak slides down to my elbow. "Your light might not be enough if this is a trap."

Imago nods gravely. His features are like iron filings shifting in his faceplate, black metal fuzz aligning as eyebrows, eyes, nose, and mouth. "You are ever wise, Father Clement."

"We fought long and hard today. Better now to rest and start fresh again at dawn." I sit down beside the fire and cross my legs Indian-style. Instantly ready to fall asleep. Instantly ready to do anything, if it will help preserve the Kingdom.

Imago makes a soft chiming sound and begins the bedtime prayer. "Now I lay me down to sleep." The fireflies in his belly circle hypnotically as he speaks. "I pray the King my soul to keep."

Reaching into my mind, I begin to switch myself off. Like flicking off the lights back in the seminary, one at a time, with darkness all around.

And prayers. "If I should die before the morn..." Imago's soothing voice rolls onward, then does something unexpected. "If I should..." He stops.

And repeats himself. "If I should die before the morn, to serve the King I'll be reborn."

I frown, wondering if Imago's glitch signals damage. But then I shrug it off and relax. I flip the last switch and drift down into darkness like a feather from the wing of a falling angel.

NEXT MORNING, like all mornings in the Kingdom, there is ice cream.

As Imago and I march into the village of Cristobal, the locals are just opening the transubstantiator--one of the matter converters that can change anything into anything else. Even the tiniest town in the Kingdom has at least one, thanks to the King.

Freezing mist puffs out when they pop up the lids on the gleaming waist-high silver pods, pulling out white scoops the size of baseballs flecked with black and brown. Laughing as they pop them out with their bare hands and toss them to the crowd.

Children scramble away with armloads, melting ice cream running from their elbows. Old men cradle single scoops in wooden bowls, while young men steal licks between juggling and pitching the scoops at each other.

I wish I could pause to paint this scene. Everyone looks so happy to be alive. They're clad in filthy loincloths, living in squalid huts of bark and leaves, but they're *happy*. Happy to be living as their ancestors lived, as they *choose* to live. Happy to be living in the worldwide Kingdom of Free Will.

When they spot us, they launch into ecstatic prayer-song. Every last one of them gathers 'round to welcome the humble soldier priest to their village.

I bless them with the sign of the King, tracing upside-down crosses in the air with practiced ease. Hugging the old women, tousling the children's hair. Everyone smells like the sweetest of flowers; reverse B.O.'s another glorious innovation of the King's benevolent anarchotechnocracy.

Raising my arms overhead, I speak to them all. "Greetings, Earth Angels! The King's blessings to you all!"

The crowd claps and dances around us. Reaching into the

transubstantiator pod, I draw out a scoop of ice cream

in my white-gloved hand. I bite into it, and my mouth fills with sweet, cold perfection.

Chocolate chip cookie dough. My favorite.

I LOVE THIS PLACE. It's a shame I might have to burn it to the ground.

As the locals lead Imago and me to the chief's hut, I steal a glance at the glowing tracker display on the blade of my scythe. The signal from the proto-Christ's unique DNA doesn't move; it's coming from somewhere in this village, and it's staying put.

I lean over and whisper to Imago. "She's waiting."

He whispers back. "Preparing to ambush us, no doubt."

I nod. "She knows what I'll do to her." I give my scythe a meaningful flick. "Same thing I did to the other *eleven*."

"Yes," says Imago as we bend down to enter the low doorway of the hut.

"Father!" Suddenly, a tiny man with shaggy gray hair and a beard leaps up in front of us. He wears a loincloth like the rest of his people and a feathered cloak besides, all reds and golds and greens against his dark brown skin. "Praise the King, you've joined us for the Feast of Second Cousins Twice Removed!"

"That's right." I throw on a huge grin, though there's nothing at all special about today's feast. The fact is, every day of the year is a holiday in the perfect Kingdom. *Most* days are doubled or tripled up with special occasions. "Blessed are the second cousins twice removed, my son."

The Chief reaches into a basket and pulls out a piece of Eden-fruit. Its skin glitters and swirls with every color of the rainbow, and it sings softly as it changes shape in his hand. This is the stuff that was Adam's favorite in the Garden, the fruit that was once *forbidden*. Thanks to the King, it grows in abundance everywhere in the world now, all throughout the Kingdom.

The Chief takes a bite and grins. "Will you lead our ceremonies, blessed Father?"

"I'll need a volunteer." I rub the black bristle on my chin. It's been days since I last shaved. "Someone who has come to town recently. Do you know of anyone like that?"

The Chief's eyes flick to one side and then back, and I know he's about to lie. "No one new. Will you settle for someone *old*?" He grins and spreads his arms.

I look at Imago as I laugh. The automaton nods imperceptibly; from programming and experience, he is able to read the intentions on my face, the inflections of my voice. The fireflies in his stained-glass belly begin to swirl in slow motion.

We both know it's time to find this proto-Christ before she gets away.

"Tell me, Earth Angel." I clamp a hand on the Chief's bony shoulder and give it a squeeze. "Which way to the latrine, please?"

IMAGO DISTRACTS the villagers with a light show while I stroll around town. I know the proto-Christ is here somewhere, maybe watching me at this very moment.

I feel a chill as I imagine her eyes upon me. The eyes of the one creature, according to Biblical Revelations, who could overturn the hard-won Kingdom.

But at least there is only one of her. One person left in all the world, according to the King's astounding Christputer, with the right mix of nature and nurture to become the dreaded Messiah.

Two years ago, when we first ran the numbers, the Christputer gave us twelve names. Imago and I have been on the road ever since, hunting down the likely candidates. Flushing them out and killing them before they could emerge from hiding and mount a revolution. Before they could try to replace the glorious Kingdom of Free Will with their so-called thousand years of paradise.

Maybe I've already killed the right one, the actual Second Coming. It's possible he or she was among those murdered eleven. But how could I live with myself knowing even *one* proto-Christ was still at large?

And what if she *did* turn out to be Jesus Christ 2.0?

SOON ENOUGH, I give up the search. There are simply too many places to hide in the jungle around Cristobal. I'll never find her like this.

So it's time for another strategy.

Marching back into the middle of the village, I see Imago performing for the villagers, flashing multicolored lights in sync with a playful, piping tune. Brown-skinned children scramble and leap around him, smacking his body as they try to anticipate the flashing pattern.

Too bad I have to break up the party. "Children! Line up!" I point with the tip of my scythe at the ground alongside me. "Right here!"

Imago stops flashing and piping. "Father?"

The half-naked kids scurry over as they were told. When they're all in line, I nod to Imago. "Put me on bullhorn." He nods and spreads his arms wide, facing away from me. The next words I say boom out of his wondrous body, amplified ten times or more their original volume. "Brigid Gideon! Surrender immediately!"

As my words echo over the village and into the jungle, the children look around with eyes wide as Edenfruit. The adults watch in a circle around us, trying not to look worried.

Time now to put this in terms the proto-Christ will understand. "If you do not surrender by the count of ten, I will *slaughter* these innocent children!" I sweep my glowing scythe over their heads to show I mean business. "Their lives are in your hands! *One*!"

When some of the adults press in from behind me, I swing the scythe across their path. They trip over each other in their hurry to fall back.

"*Two!*" Do I like what I'm doing? Of course not. "*Three!*" But I need to bring her in one way or the other.

"Please, let them go!" The Chief raises his hands pleadingly, flapping his colorful feathered cape. The children are his charges.

He should try being responsible for *the fate of the entire kingdom.* "*Four!*"

"Father?" Imago tips his head to one side. His features are expressionless. "Will you do it?"

I scowl at him. "*Five!*" Imago has demonstrated his unflagging loyalty to me countless times. Since when does *he* question *my* actions? Maybe something really *is* wrong with him.

"Will you?" Imago's face remains expressionless.

He already knows the answer. "*Six!*" Of course I will. I'll do *anything* for the King of the World. *Anything* to preserve The Kingdom of Free Will.

Maybe it's time I demonstrated my devotion. I draw back the scythe, taking aim at one of the children, a little boy. Lopping an ear off ought to show I'm serious.

The parents gasp. I say the next number, "Seven!" But I don't hear it. Has Imago shut off the bullhorn?

Or is it the voice shouting from the jungle that's overpowering it? The woman's voice, calling from the edge of the rain forest?

"All right, all right!" She stomps out of the jungle with purpose, shoving aside lush green leaves the size of elephants' ears. "Enough with the *drama* already!"

I want to race over immediately and subdue her, but I don't. I let her come to me instead.

She snorts and shakes her head. "You really piss me off, you know that?"

"Lock her down!" As soon as I snap the order, Imago marches toward her with arms outstretched. Restraining cuffs materialize in his hands, courtesy of his built-in transubstantiator.

Brigid whirls to face him, and at first, I think there'll be a fight. She might just win, too. She's a big girl, built like a Clydesdale, over six feet tall. All shoulders and flanks and hocks.

But then she cocks her head and gives Imago a funny look. She stares at him for a moment, as if she's sizing up her chances, and she relaxes. She reaches out and lets him clamp the cuffs on her.

A breeze kicks around the wisps of blonde hair that have pulled free from her ponytail. "You're a Squire-series model."

The robot holds on to her hands a moment longer. "Yes, I am."

I storm forward and push him out of the way. "I usually pray for the souls of those I kill, even the undead." I pull back my scythe, and it hums and crackles with power. "But not this time."

"Don't do it, jackoff." Brigid tips her head back and sneers defiantly. "Biggest friggin' mistake of your pitiful life."

I laugh and tighten my grip on the handle of the scythe. "How so, she-devil?"

"There are lots more where *I* came from." Brigid nods. "An *army* of us. Your king doesn't stand a snowflake's chance in the Sahara."

Careful. "An army?" The serpent will say *anything* to gain the advantage.

"Enjoy your day in the sun, jackoff." She chuckles. "Believe me, the clock's ticking."

Before she can say another word, I've got her on the ground with the blade of the scythe at her throat. "*Where?* Where *are* they?"

She grits her teeth, and I press the edge of the blade against her windpipe. A fine red line appears between the gleaming metal curve and her pale flesh.

"*Tell me!*" I kick her hard in the side.

"Screw you!" She hisses it between her clenched teeth.

By the time I'm done with her, she's missing some of those teeth. Along with other things.

But she's still alive. And finally cooperating. She agrees to lead us to the Second Coming.

As soon as we cross the border of the Undead Zone--the UZ--my scythe starts to wail. I shut off the warning signal and keep walking.

But my senses are ratcheted up to full alert. My heart pounds, pushing adrenaline through me like rocket fuel. Because the truth is, we've just set foot outside the Kingdom.

On the surface, it seems no different from the rest of the rain forest, at least not yet. Dense green foliage crawls and hangs and twists and sprawls over every square foot. The air is thick with humidity and a steaming, sweet stew of mingled floral perfumes. Monkeys and tropical birds shriek and leap in the canopy. Insects whine in my ears and flicker over my bare skin, tiny wings and legs skittering through the hairs on my wrists and neck.

It seems no different, but it is very different indeed. It is a foreign land over which the King has no sway, a pocket of corruption in which the wicked zombie undead run riot. They might range far and wide on their unholy sorties beyond the UZ, but this is the heart of their awful territory.

"Tell me where we're headed." I jab Brigid in the back with the handle of my scythe. "What are the coordinates?"

"For the tenth time, shove it up your *ass*!" Her long blonde ponytail switches from side to side as she shakes her head. "If I *tell* you, you'll *kill* me."

I jab her again for good measure, and she cries out. Imago, who is marching up ahead of us, slows his pace but does not look back.

Brigid's white blouse and tan shorts are stained with blood from my interrogation at the village. I pick the darkest spot on her back and stick her again. "There aren't any normals in the UZ." I give her one more jab, and her cry is louder this time. "Are you trying to tell me the Second Coming is *undead?*"

Brigid shrugs. "Where does it say it can't happen? You can accept a *woman* as the Second Coming, can't you?"

"The Christputer does not admit the possibility of an undead messiah." The green and yellow tail of a huge snake drops down in front of me, and I duck around it. "None of the simulations yields that result."

Brigid half-turns and looks back over her shoulder at me. "Because none of your precious models *includes* the undead as a *variable*, do they?"

I jab her once more. "*Forever.*"

She looks back again. "What's that supposed to mean?"

"It's how long your agonizing death will seem to take if I find out you've been lying to me." I press the blade of my scythe against the side of her head, letting it hum and crackle in her ear.

Soon enough, we encounter the undead. Two of them cross our path near a stream--a male and female dressed in the usual bloody tatters. When they look our way, I see decayed flesh falling from their faces. I instantly key the scythe to maximum power.

I'm already moving as they raise the alarm with bloodcurdling shrieks. Flashing past Brigid and Imago, I raise the scythe and spin between the zombies like a whirlwind.

Their heads fly off in opposite directions, one bouncing off a tree, the other splashing down in the stream. Their bodies drop to the ground a second later. *Two down.*

And three to go. I hear the sound of snapping twigs and whip around to see three more zombies backing away through the underbrush. The most tragic undead of all, *child-size,* they were transformed at a young age and never had a chance at a normal life. I see two little boys and a black-haired preteen girl. How sad.

I will sing extra prayers for them as I hack them to bloody bits.

Such is my intent, until Brigid charges over and throws herself in my path. "Hands off, jackoff!"

"Imago!" I try ducking around her, but she stays in front of me. "Restrain her!"

Imago marches over and reaches for Brigid's arm. "Come with me, Ms. Gideon."

Brigid pulls away from him. "These people aren't zombies! I won't let you kill them!"

Looking over her shoulder, I see the three children cowering in the weeds. Each is covered with oozing, peeling blotches of rot, swarming with flies. "*Of course* they're zombies! *Look* at them!"

Suddenly, Brigid does the unexpected. She steps up to me, gets right in my face, and locks her gaze with mine. "Your King has lied to you," she says. "*You* are the only zombie here."

With a snarl, I lunge at her. She spins away from me and darts toward the undead children lurking in the weeds. Shooting after her, I swing the scythe so the broad side of the blade will crash into her hip and bring her down. But the blow never connects.

As I run, my foot catches on something. I stumble and fall in the weeds and skid down the muddy bank into the stream.

Looking up, I wonder again if something's wrong with Imago. He stands atop the bank, right about where I took a header.

And he's ignoring me, his master, though I'm clearly in distress. Brigid is waving him over...and he's going.

"Imago!" He doesn't seem to hear me. Next thing I know, he's standing before the three zombie children.

I hear Brigid's voice as she hunkers down in front of them. "You poor babies. You're nothing but skin and bones."

"Imago!" I say it again as I clamber out of the stream, shaking the water from my scythe.

Imago's too busy listening to Brigid. "You can make something for them to eat, can't you?" she asks him.

He pauses. "Yes."

"What would you like for lunch?" Brigid says to the kids.

Human flesh, I'm guessing, but that's not what they ask for.

"Ice cream." The oldest, the dark-haired girl, says it softly as I approach, then clears her throat and says it louder. "Chocolate ice cream."

I gape at her. Since when did the undead crave anything but the flesh and blood of the living?

"Please make her some chocolate ice cream, Imago," says Brigid.

"But they are undead." Imago tips his head to one side. "They are zombies."

"They are *alpha-lepers*," says Brigid. "If you doubt it, go ask your *king*."

"Why?" says Imago.

"He *made* them this way," says Brigid. "Because their families *opposed* him."

"She's lying, Imago!" I rush up beside him. "All lies!"

Brigid doesn't bother to look at me. Her focus is on the youngest child, a little redheaded boy no older than three or four. "What flavor of ice cream do *you* want?" she asks him.

"Peanut butter." The child's voice is so soft, I can barely hear it. So soft, so much like a *human* child's voice, that I hesitate.

I hesitate to slaughter him and the others on the spot as my duty dictates.

"One order of chocolate and one order of peanut butter, please, Imago." Brigid turns to the third child, a blond boy of six or seven. "And what about you?"

"What about *them*?" The boy turns and points at the jungle behind him.

Eyes wide, they slowly emerge from the brush--more undead children, creeping out of hiding places among the glossy emerald elephant-ear leaves. They shuffle toward us along the bank of the stream, wary and furtive as starving dogs, silently converging.

How many are there? I count six, then ten, then twelve. And they keep coming. Every last one a blight on the face of the Earth, a target for my scythe.

So why don't I slaughter them all right here and now? Is it because I'm hoping they might lead me to the Army of the Second Coming? Is it because I need to get my prisoner well clear before the bloodbath, given the vital intel she might possess?

Or is it something else? Some reason I can't fathom?

"Yo, Imago! Get a move on!" Brigid spins her index finger in the air like the hands of a clock. "Let's get crackin' on that ice cream."

Imago looks at me, his iron filing features shifting inside his stained-glass faceplate. His expression changes from a confused frown to...what? A blank look. Unreadable.

Turning to the children, he holds out his hands, palms up, cupped. The fireflies dance like tiny fairies in his belly, and a scoop of brown ice cream appears in his grasp.

He hands it to the dark-haired girl, and then he conjures another scoop. And another. And many more after that.

And the undead children keep coming out of the jungle, shambling like corpses with hands outstretched. They mutter the names of their favorite flavors, and Brigid calls them out to Imago.

Not one of those children leaves empty-handed. Some get seconds and thirds.

And not one of them tries to devour the flesh of the living.

As we continue on our way, the undead children surround us. I pray for the strength to keep myself from slaughtering them, even as I wonder if I'm doing the right thing. Will they lead us to a hidden mother lode of proto-Christs unpredicted by the Christputer, or will they lead us into an inescapable death-trap?

"How does it feel?" Brigid asks me this as we march through the mid-afternoon heat. "Knowing that none of those people you've murdered were zombies?"

I try to ignore her. Proto-Christs are always looking to stir up doubt and disharmony with their words.

She shakes her head. "All those deaths on your conscience. All those innocents." She clucks her tongue against the roof of her mouth. "That's a heavy weight for you to bear."

I reach back and swing my black braid around front, letting it fall against my white cloak. A fat red spider crawls along the length of the braid, and I brush it off in Brigid's direction.

She swats it away reflexively with her cuffed hands, without flinching. "I can guess what hurts the most," she says. "Being lied to by your beloved King. Knowing he led you astray for his own purposes."

This time, I can't hold back. "Shut up, she-devil! Save your lies for the gates of Hell!"

"Okay, listen." Brigid leans closer as we walk. "I'm sorry."

"Sorry?" A proto-Christ has never apologized to me before. "Sorry for what?"

"For calling you 'jackoff,'" says Brigid. "And also for having to tell you something you won't want to hear."

I glare at her. "Tell me what?"

"The undead aren't the only thing the King has lied to you about." The look in her eyes contains pity or sympathy or both. "He has lied to you about *everything*, Clement."

I snort in disgust and look away from her. "*I* feel sorry for *you.* The King has already *judged* you. Your terrible punishment is carved in stone."

Her shoulder brushes against mine. There is no hatred in her voice when she speaks. "Everything you know is a lie, Clement. *Everything.*"

TWILIGHT HAS FALLEN by the time we reach the huts. There are three of them clustered together, decrepit and half-collapsed...leaves missing from the roofs, bark missing from holes in the walls. Ashes, charred wood, and bones litter the muddy patch between them. The air is so thick with the stench of excrement and rot, I can taste it. I see no light and hear no sound as we approach, as if the place is deserted.

But it is not.

Someone crawls out of one of the huts on hands and knees. Someone so far decayed, I can't tell if it's a man or a woman. *Undead.*

Instantly, I swing the scythe around and thumb it to full power. This zombie might look far gone, but it could still do some damage if I let down my guard.

"Hello," Brigid says to it.

"P...p...puh." The crawling zombie spits out teeth with its consonants. "Kuh...kuh...k..."

"Poor dear." Brigid looks at Imago. "We have to help her."

I've had about as much of this proto-Christ as I can stand. "Hey! Are we here for a *reason?*"

Brigid flashes me a smirk. "Not the one *you* think."

Imago turns to her. "Help?" The fireflies in his belly are agitated. "How can we *help?*"

"We can't!" I barge between them. "The undead are *beyond* our help!"

"That's a *lie.*" Brigid points at Imago. "And you can *prove* it."

"Don't listen to her, Imago." I clamp my hand on his warm crystal shoulder. "You know the forces of darkness always seek to mislead us."

Brigid elbows between us. "But what if I'm *right* about this? What if you *can* help her? What would it hurt to find out?"

I hear the sound of something cracking nearby. Spinning, I see another undead monstrosity emerge from a hut. This one shuffles toward us alongside the first, squinting from a misshapen face like the caved-in mush of a rotten jack-o'-lantern.

"Hel-l-l..." Again, I can't tell the undead's gender from looking...but the deep voice is that of a man. "P-p-ple-e-e...p-ple-e-e.."

"*Enough!*" When I snap out the word, the children, as one, take a step away from me. "We're *leaving!*"

Brigid backs toward the huts, eyes locked on Imago. "You're M.D. certified, aren't you? Fully stacked for medical diagnosis and treatment?"

"Yes," says Imago.

"Then boot up the protocols for alpha-leprosy," says Brigid, "and get over here."

Imago's fireflies whip around like campfire ashes in a stiff breeze. He looks at me for a long moment without a word.

"Don't do it, Imago." I shift the glowing scythe from one hand to the other, hoping he picks up on the underlying threat. "That's an *order.*"

Imago looks at the undead creatures by the huts and makes a sound like a sigh. "What will it hurt to find out?" he says, and then he marches over to join Brigid.

My hands twist on the handle of the scythe. Little by little, she's taking him away from me.

So what do I do next? I have it in my power to kill them both, and all the undead around us besides. After that, I could move on alone and slaughter any undead I find, scorch the UZ earth of anything remotely resembling a hidden proto-Christ.

But what if there's still hope? What if I could still fix Imago? Shouldn't I at least give him a chance?

A thought occurs to me, and I frown. For the first time, I realize something about Imago. And it makes me think *I'm* the one who needs fixing.

Since when do *I* care about a *robot?*

I hear humming and beeping from Imago as he treats the undead. Rays of light flare from his stained-glass body, beams of green and blue and gold combing and flashing through the twilight jungle shadows.

The undead children stay behind me, watching with mouths hanging open. The flashing accelerates to a fever pitch. A shrill whine races up the scale, quickly reaching a level so piercing that the undead kids have to cover their ears.

Then, suddenly, it's over. The lights and noise die away all at once.

I already know what the result must be, of course. The only cure for the undead is extermination. Imago has surely failed.

I start to worry that there might be an unexpected side effect, though. Brigid and Imago block my view, but I can see Imago's crystalline body shaking fiercely.

"Imago?" I rush over to him, heart pounding, ready for anything.

But I'm not ready for what I see.

Looking over Imago's shoulder, my eyes are drawn downward. This is what's making him shake: a sobbing figure with head and hands pressed against his stained-glass surface--a middle-aged woman with long brown hair, kneeling where an undead monstrosity once was. Through the rags she wears, I can see her skin is smooth and unblemished. She is crying tears of joy all over Imago.

As she wraps her arms around him, someone rises from the ground beside her. He is also middle-aged and dressed in tatters, and his hair is black. Like the woman, his skin is undamaged, unmarked.

This is impossible.

"I can't thank you enough." The man wipes away tears of his own and reaches for Imago's hand. "My wife and I were so far gone, we'd even been exiled from the leper colony. I never imagined we would ever be *cured.*"

Imago looks at me as the man shakes his hand. "Alpha-lepers," says Imago. "That's what they were."

"No, Imago. This is some kind of trick." My voice is firm and steady.

"So many you've killed," says Imago. "I could have cured them."

"No!" I shake my head hard. "That's not true!"

"You didn't know?" says Imago. "You really didn't know?"

"No, I did *not,*" I tell him. "Because it isn't *true.*"

He stands there a moment, eyes locked with mine, thinking his clockwork thoughts. I can almost see them chugging and revolving in his stained-glass head.

Then, Brigid calls him over to cure the undead children and he turns away, leaving me to wonder about the results of whatever secret calculations he's just run.

As we march onward with our retinue of seemingly cured zombies, I run calculations of my own. I consider the possibilities of what I have witnessed, weighed against the experiences of a lifetime.

How does it feel? Brigid's words echo in my mind. *Knowing that all those people you've murdered weren't zombies?*

I suppose she wants me to feel regret, but I don't. I have only ever known one King, one master, and I've slaughtered the undead in service to him. I killed them to defend the Kingdom of Free Will, and that hasn't changed. Whether they were undead zombies or alpha-lepers, they still opposed the Kingdom. They still opposed Paradise.

But what if I've been wrong about Paradise? If the King lied about the undead, could he have lied about Paradise, too?

Brigid tries to persuade me as we slog through the jungle at night. "Your King is the Great Beast prophesied in the Book of Revelations."

I scowl and shake my head. "The *Christ* is the Great Beast. *He* is the Great Evil."

"Your King rules through deception and force," says Brigid. "But that is about to end. The awakening of the Christ will usher in a millennium of true paradise."

"Paradise has already arrived," I tell her.

Brigid cocks her head and stares at me in the glow of Imago's body-light. "Have you ever had sex, Clement?"

I turn away.

"Before you experienced it for the first time," says Brigid, "did you truly *know* what it was like? How *good* it would feel?"

I don't answer.

"*That* is what *true* paradise is like, Father," says Brigid. "It's not like *anything* you've known."

"Shut up." I walk faster to get away from her.

"Your whole life has been a wet dream, Clement," says Brigid, "and you're about to wake up."

In the darkest heart of the night, we arrive at the village. It looks like a fort in the jungle, surrounded by a high, circular wall of crudely cut logs. Smoke and light and noise rise from the interior, curling up toward the star-littered sky.

Brigid walks up to a door in the wall, a slab of galvanized metal, and knocks with her handcuffs. I post myself beside her, gripping my atomic scythe tightly.

I don't like the fact that I can't see what's behind the door or walls. At this point, anything can happen.

"All right then." My voice is a whisper. "Once we're inside, stay out of the way. Make a wrong move and I'll kill you."

She doesn't even try to lower her voice. "Why?" She looks at me like I'm crazy. "What do you think you're going to *find* in there, exactly?"

I lay the blade of the scythe against her throat. "The Second Coming. An army of off-the-radar proto-Christs. I'm sure you think they'll save you, but they won't."

Brigid looks amused, then disappointed. "You haven't changed, have you? Even after everything you've seen."

Something bangs heavily against the other side of the door. I hear the clanking of chains. "Just do as you're told," I tell her.

As the door opens inward, Brigid smiles sadly. "I said there's an army of us. I said your kind doesn't stand a chance. But I never said we were *proto-Christs*."

"*What?*" My hands twitch on the handle of the scythe. "But you said you would lead us to the Second Coming!"

"I did." Brigid nods. "And I have."

I KEEP the blade at her throat as we enter. "Where then?" Anger surges within me. "Where is the Second Coming?"

Inside the village walls, the undead converge on us from all directions. They stare and shamble in the firelight, upright masses of peeling and suppurating flesh.

"Where is the Second Coming?" I direct my question to the villagers. "Tell me, or I'll kill her!"

"Let her go," says an undead male at the head of the group.

"Is it *you?*" I ask him. "Are *you* the Second Coming? The one who seeks to topple the Kingdom of Free Will?"

"Not him." An undead female steps forward.

Keeping a firm grip on Brigid's arm, I sweep my glowing scythe toward the undead woman. "It's *you* then? *You're* the one who'd put an end to the daily *holidays* and *ice cream* and Heaven on *Earth?*"

The man steps in the path of my blade. "What are you talking about?"

"The Second Coming!" I flick the scythe across his rotting chest, connecting his seeping sores with a fine line of blood. "Who among you is the *Second Coming?*"

"Wha...wha..." A third villager hobbles forward. Half his face has fallen away. "Wha...is-s-s...thuh...Se-cun...Cum-un...?"

My heart races. I turn in a circle, flashing the scythe overhead.

"They don't know about the Second Coming," says Brigid. "Not yet."

"Lies!" If they won't tell me who it is, they leave me no choice.

Leaping forward, I slash the half-faced villager to pieces with the scythe. Then, I sweep the weapon around behind me and kill the other two without looking.

Singing the "Our Father," I wade into the whole damned horde of them, whirling and hacking and slicing. Body parts fly everywhere, and blood fountains into the night sky.

This is what I was born to do. What I was trained for. Graceful annihilation in the name of the King. The noble dance of the warrior priest, carving up monsters like a hibachi chef carving up vegetables.

"Our father, who art in Houston, hallowed be thy flame..."

When I am done, my King will reward me for my service, for saving the Kingdom. He will summon me to Texas and erect statues in my honor and declare a new feast day and ice cream flavor in my name. All will be right with the world.

This is what I am thinking when someone hits me from behind. When my legs go out from under me, and I drop to the muddy ground on my knees.

I scramble to get back on my feet, and someone hits me again. This time, the blow to my head leaves me dazed. I fall back in the mud and go limp.

That's when I see him. The middle-aged black-haired man, the first zombie treated by Imago. He leaps onto my chest, stone in hand.

And he hits me in the face. He pounds me, again and again.

The world goes watery and melts together in a blur of color and sound and pain. The man keeps pounding my skull with the stone, and I feel myself slipping away.

Wait. These are my final thoughts. *Things are not what you think.*

And then the world runs down into darkness, like a painting in the rain. And then everything is black and silent and still.

"CLEMENT? FATHER CLEMENT?"

Those are the first words I hear when I return. When the faintest glimmer of awareness flutters into my mind.

"Wake up, Father. It's begun." A woman's voice. "Wakey wakey, eggs and bakey." Brigid's voice. That's what I hear.

Instinctively, I open my eyes. This happens at the same moment I realize I shouldn't have eyes to open because they were smashed in by a rock.

But it doesn't seem to matter. I see Brigid staring down at me, silhouetted against a bright blue sky.

"There you are!" she says. "Welcome back!"

I close my eyes, then open them again. I feel light-headed. Light-bodied, too. As if a weight has been lifted.

"How long was I out?" Looking at the brightness of the sky, I try to guess what time of day it is. Just after sunrise, maybe?

"You mean how long were you *dead?*" Brigid raises her eyebrows. "Three hours. You were dead for three hours."

I lift my head from the mud and look around. Imago stands behind Brigid, staring blankly down at me. We are surrounded by a crowd of men, women, and children, all unblemished and dressed in tatters. "What are you talking about?"

"Don't you remember getting your head bashed in?" Brigid reaches down and taps my nose, which also shouldn't be there. "You *died*, Clement."

I scowl and shake my head. "Not possible." Even as I say it, I remember the stone smashing my skull. I remember the pain as it slammed down again and again, and the world melting and fading to black.

"You were pushing up daisies," says Brigid. "You were an *ex-Clement.*"

Suddenly, I add things up, and a chill of terror rushes through me. "You're trying to tell me..." I feel a wave of inescapable desperation spread out from the pit of my stomach. "You're saying I was *dead*, and now I'm *not?*"

"Yes." Brigid nods. "Exactly."

I push myself to a sitting position, fighting the urge to run away. I try to keep the fear out of my voice. "You mean I'm...*undead?*"

"Yes." When she says it, my heart sinks. Then, she laughs. "But only in the sense of *not* being *dead.*"

I'm not sure what to think at this point. "Even if I *was* dead, and you could bring me back, why *would* you?"

"It wasn't *my* idea, that's for sure," says Brigid. "But the *Second Coming* seemed to think you were worth saving."

I look past Brigid and Imago at the crowd. Which one of them is the Second Coming of Jesus Christ?

"Apparently, he has a plan in mind for you." Brigid shrugs. "Like I said, it's begun."

"What's that? What's begun?" I teeter as I get to my feet, still feeling light-headed. My eyes flicker, and I start to fall.

Suddenly, I feel strong hands catch me and set me on my feet again. When I open my eyes, I see him.

Imago. Light streaming in rainbow-colored beams from the facets of his stained-glass body. The iron filing features in his faceplate tracing a smile of black metal fuzz.

"The Millennium," he says in that soft, soothing voice of his. "We're about to usher it in."

"Imago?" My own voice falters as I consider the implications.

"*He* brought you back." Brigid says it in my ear. "*He's* the one you've been *looking* for all this time."

"The Second Coming?" My heart pounds as I stare at Imago's robotic face. "He *can't* be."

"I was only ever his prophet," says Brigid. "I'm not fit to polish the chassis of the one who comes after me."

My head spins. I'm not sure what to think or do or say. "Imago?"

The fireflies swirl in his belly. "I am the truth, the way, and the life. He who believeth in me shall never die." The beams of light streaming from his stained-glass facets flare with blinding intensity. "Welcome to Paradise 2.0, Father Clement."

THE LOVE QUEST OF SMIDGEN THE SNACK CAKE

First off, it's important you know that snack cakes do not feel guilt. That is why, even with the corpse of my lover here before me, all I can think of is finding someone else to take me in. To eat me. Fulfill me.

Love me.

It is my nature and purpose. It is the only reason I was created. It is why, even as the pungent smells of my lover's decomposing body reach the rudimentary olfactory cells in my ultrachocolate frosting, I softly whistle my lilting mating call, casting about for a new precious soul mate to embrace me gently with supple fingers and raise me toward the blissful warmth and moisture of the glistening portal all pink flesh and bright white teeth and then when I cannot stand the anticipation a single moment more BITE DOWN and grant me the blinding wild release I have craved for as long as I can remember.

Oh PLEASE someone find me here and eat me! I have been created with cutting edge late-21st century biobaking technology to grant you the ultimate sweet eating euphoria. Pay no attention to the woman on the floor, or at least give me a chance to PLEASE you before you tend to her. You won't be sorry.

She is no one important. She means nothing to me.

She is just a pick-up that didn't work out. You know how these things go.

AS SOON AS she walked into Shangri-La, the supermarket where we met, the store told me her name. Lynda McVicker.

It told me everything I needed to know about her, too, and then some. Like all customers these days, her spending habits are logged on the worldwide Shopnet computer network, accessible to smart goods like me once the in-store grid pings her subcutaneous identichip.

Right away, I knew she was the one for me.

Based on her purchases over the past three weeks, she did not look like a suitable match. She had bought nothing in three weeks but produce and low-fat or no-fat foods. Not a single scrap of junk food. On top of that, she had purchased diet books, workout clothes, and a yearlong membership to a gym, all within the last three weeks.

But OH when I went back further, I could see how PERFECT she really was. I can tell you from personal experience in this particular case that true love DOES exist.

For her entire adolescent and adult life up until three weeks ago, Lynda had been the queen of junk food. Aside from the briefest blips of non-junk spending due to occasional failed diets, she had purchased only the most fattening, high-cholesterol, chemical-soaked foods available from grocery stores, restaurants, vending machines, and mail order websites.

In short, she was the perfect woman. Though she was on a diet that day, she had eaten non-nutritious foods in great quantities all her life. Though her last purchases had been salad greens and bottled water, her 225-pound body told the true story.

I knew she was just waiting for someone like me to come along.

As SHE MADE her way across Shangri-La, I followed her progress via Store's buyspy grid and made myself ready for our encounter. I was determined to make our first meeting perfect in every way.

Researching her preferences via Shopnet, I found that she most often bought products with predominantly blue and gold packaging...so I shifted the chameleonic inks of my wrapper from red and white to blue and gold. Discovering that she favored darker chocolates over lighter ones, I manipulated my own coloration, shifting the milky browns of my ultrachocolate frosting and cake to deeper, fudgier hues.

As Lynda lingered in the produce aisle, sullenly tucking genetically modified hypertasty carrots and cucumbers in her hovercart, I requested a rearrange from the shelving. When Store agreed I had the best chance of the snack cake varieties in the display to make a sale to Lynda, clacking pincers dropped from the underside of the shelf above me and moved me from the middle rows of the display to the front. The position of the entire shelf changed, too, rising up to Lynda's eye level and pushing out a few extra inches into the aisle.

There was no way she would miss me now...and no way she could resist me, once I started pouring on the charm.

At least, that was what I thought before she walked right on past my aisle.

To say I was disappointed when Lynda steered her hovercart away from the cookie and snack cake aisle would be a tremendous understatement.

There I sat, looking fabulous, dreaming of the love of lips and teeth and tongue I craved above all else...and Lynda didn't even come down my aisle. Via Store's buyspy, I watched as she pushed on by, pausing at an endcap display to listen to cereal boxes calling out to her before she turned down the next aisle and kept going.

For an instant, I panicked, fearing I had missed my chance at meeting the woman of my dreams. My baked-in mind (consisting of a matrix of precision-engineered and digestible protein molecules) was thrown into a state of confusion.

Then, I pulled myself together and pinged Store, determined not to give up so easily. From the memory my makers had given me, I knew that the path to true love is not always smooth, and that anything worth having is worth working for.

Though Store was skeptical, already having shunted processing power away from the quadrants Lynda had passed through or missed, he agreed to give me a chance with some guided couponing. According to Lynda's past activity in this and other shopping facilities, she might respond favorably to a strategically placed offer.

When she was midway up the next aisle, Store flashed a message on the organic LED screen implanted in the palm of her hand: "Save one credit on Sea Sprite plankton snacks in Aisle 5!"

I thought it was the perfect bait, since Sea Sprite plankton snacks were among the items Lynda had been buying most often since starting her diet three weeks ago. Though Sea Sprite products usually were displayed in Aisle 8, Store had already diverted a batch of them via the underfloor realignment system to a niche on a shelf right across from me in Aisle 5.

Thanking Store for his help, I focused on buyspy, nervously

watching as Lynda stared at her palm screen. She read the text message from Store, then looked away, distracted by the cries of products on the shelves around her.

But then, thankfully, she looked back. From twenty different spycam angles, I watched as she raised her eyebrows and nodded...then directed her hovercart to head for the end of the aisle and turn left.

Toward my aisle. Finally, she was coming closer. We were about to meet.

Joyfully, I added a final touch to spruce myself up for her: in the looping thread of white icing on my fudge-frosted face, I wrote her first name in neat, cursive lettering.

I personalized myself so there could be no doubt whatsoever that we were truly meant for each other.

Snack cakes like me have a supercreamy center, not a heart...but if I had had a heart that day, it would have been pounding like crazy as Lynda moved down my aisle. My baked-in mind was focused entirely on one thought alone: I LOVED HER. Every atom of my being was consumed with a single imperative desire: that LYNDA would BUY me and DEVOUR ME.

I LONGED for her credit chip to transfer funds into the accounts of my manufacturer. I YEARNED to feel her pudgy fingers TEAR OFF my wrapper and close around me, THRUSTING me toward the sweetest fate that I could ever DREAM of, the ECSTASY and INTIMACY that occurs when TWO become ONE.

If only if only if only she would have me she would TAKE me.

She drew closer.

On both sides of the aisle, cookies and snack cakes cried out to her, a hundred different suitors trying to intercept her with songs and lies and promises. Twice, packages leaped off the shelves into her hovercart, but she spotted them and stuffed them back in their displays. A bag of Stimchoc Thrillchip Omegawafers used a stealthier tactic, sliding off a rack and clinging to her sweatpants with a light static charge...but she caught that one, too, and peeled it right off.

Then, having made it through the gauntlet, she pulled up right in front of me. Her broad backside was turned to me, as she was looking at the Sea Sprite display across the aisle...but finally finally finally she was THERE she was CLOSE TO ME.

I had a chance. It would be tricky, overcoming her willpower, getting her to TAKE ME in spite of her diet after she had passed so many others by, but I KNEW it could be done. I KNEW I was special and had the power and desire to win her over.

I knew that true love would win out.

I BEGAN MY APPROACH GENTLY, knowing that she had been burned before. Noise and aggressiveness would not work with her; what she needed was kindness and understanding.

Activating my sound chip (protein-based and digestible like my mind), I cast a beam of hypersound in her direction, a focused signal meant for her ears only.

Though I was bursting with eager excitement, I kept my voice soft and controlled for her. From mining her records on Shopnet, I knew she had responded best in past shopping events to a steady male voice of moderate depth, and I shaped my voice accordingly.

"Hello," I said to her, secretly thrilled to be speaking at last into the beautiful shell of her ear...the ear that was so gloriously CLOSE to her wet, red LIPS. "Hello, Lynda."

Lynda looked around, searching for the source of the voice, a voice so unlike the shrill, artless cries of the other products around her.

"Over here," I said, using the luminescent molecules in my frosting to make myself glow softly. "My name is Smidgen. It's a pleasure to meet you, Lynda."

The moment she laid eyes on me, I exulted. There it was, as plain as the label on my wrapper, laid out in bright relief before the optical cells baked into my body: a longing for me just as strong and perfect as mine for her.

Still, I could see that she would not give her love easily. As quickly as the passion flared on her face, it was gone, slammed away behind a cold, bleak wall of denial. Her desire to resist temptation had come between us, threatening to prevent the happiness we deserved.

Fortunately for us both, this resistance only made me more determined to bring us together.

"Don't bother me," said Lynda, staring at me with a look of disgust that I knew barely concealed her true attraction. "I'm on a diet."

"I hope you won't mind my saying so, Lynda," I said softly, "but you certainly don't look like you need to be dieting."

"What do *you* know?" Lynda said sharply. "You're just a snack cake."

"Actually," I said, "I'm a Supercreamy Double Ultrachocolate Deluxe Smidgen. I have a level seven digestible artificial intelligence, free will enabled, and I can tell you that in my opinion, you don't need to be on a diet."

Briefly, a look of appreciation flashed in her eyes...then was gone, replaced by cynical rejection. "Nice try," she said coldly. "You'd say anything to get me to buy you."

"I understand why you might think that," I said, "but I'm not like other snack foods. My compliment was sincere, Lynda."

"If you don't think I'm fat," she said sarcastically, "then you're dumber than any snack food I've ever met."

With that, she turned away, back to the Sea Sprite display. I worried that I had lost her then, that our love was not to be...but she took just enough time picking out her packet of plankton snacks that I thought I might still have a chance. She wasn't rushing off; though she seemed unmoved on the surface, a conflict was raging inside between her need to lose weight and her need for me.

Her need for pleasure.

Quickly, I gathered my resources for another attempt at breaking through her defenses. While her back was turned, I freshened the color of my frosting and cake, brightened my glow, pumped up my ultrachocolatey aroma, and got Store to nudge my display shelf just one more inch out into the aisle.

Then, just as she was dropping a Sea Sprite packet into her hovercart and preparing to waddle off down the aisle, I spoke. The steady, smooth flow of my voice perfectly concealed the desperation and LUST that ruled my mind.

"I'm sorry if I hurt your feelings, Lynda," I said. "It was never my intention to do so."

Lynda looked my way again, her expression softening just the slightest bit. "Well, that's a first," she said. "I've never had a product apologize to me before."

"And I've never met a woman quite like you before," I said warmly. "I know you're on a diet, but I'd still like to get to know you better."

Lynda flashed a glance up and down the aisle, as if making sure no one was watching as she had a conversation with a snack cake. Thanks to some skillful shopper redirection by Store, we were alone for the moment.

"Listen," said Lynda, lowering her voice though no one else was around. "Believe it or not, I appreciate the compliment. I guess that shows how pathetic I am."

"Not at all," I said, meaning every word of it. To me, she was anything but pathetic; to me, she was the most attractive and fascinating woman in the world.

"But there's no way you're going home with me," said Lynda. "We both know what would happen if you did."

"Not necessarily," I said. "Nothing has to happen if you don't want it to happen."

"Well, that's the problem, isn't it?" said Lynda. "I *want* something to happen. I've done without for *three weeks*, and I want you so *bad*, I'm ready to explode."

My mind was spinning as I heard her confess her desire for me. It took a major effort for me to concentrate on the delicate process of winning her. "You know, Lynda," I said softly. "I think I can help."

"Oh, really?" Lynda said with a smirk. "And how exactly will you do that?"

"What if I promised not to let you take more than a bite of me a day?" I said. "Just a few centimeters. Just a nibble, and then I cut you off. You'll have a treat to help you get through the day, but you won't fall off the wagon with your diet."

"And how will you cut me off at just a nibble?" Lynda said suspiciously.

"I'll tell you to stop," I said. "I'll scream, if that's what it takes."

Lynda grinned and shook her head. "Even screaming won't keep me from eating something once I've put my mind to it," she said. "Trust me on this."

"I still say the two of us can make it work," I said. "You don't have to fight this battle alone."

"Listen," said Lynda. "You're a snack cake. I'm a fat woman. It would never work out."

"Just give me a chance," I said, boosting the ultrachocolatey scent I was emitting. "You might be missing out on something wonderful."

Lynda's eyes flared with a harsh glint. "You don't understand," she said stiffly. "I've been hurt too many times. I can't get involved with someone like you, not again."

"It doesn't have to be like that," I said. "I won't lie to you and say I wasn't hoping for something more, but I'd be honored just to be your friend."

For a moment, Lynda stared at me, biting her lower lip. "TAKE ME," I wanted to shout at her. "I LOVE YOU! I NEED YOU! TAKE ME NOW!"

But I waited silently. I knew she was so fragile that one wrong word – let alone a desperate plea – might be enough to drive her away. I had done all that I could and now would have to accept the consequences, whatever they might be.

Unfortunately, it seemed that my hopes were doomed to be crushed.

"I'm sorry," Lynda said finally. "I just can't. You'll find someone else."

"No one like you," I said sadly as she turned away. "Promise me you'll at least think it over."

"No, thanks," she said, moving down the aisle with her hover-cart. "Goodbye."

I said nothing in return. Lynda had become so important to me, I could not bear to say goodbye to her, knowing the two of us would likely never meet again.

Despondent beyond belief, I sat there, letting my glow and fragrance fade away. My first love, the love of my life, the woman of my dreams, had rejected me. My dreams of passionately merging with her, of feeling those crimson lips close around me and those ivory teeth BITE into me, had been forever denied.

No snack cake, I was certain, had ever been so lonely and forlorn as I.

At least for a moment.

As Store eased my display back out of the aisle, my mind

smoothly switched tracks, shunting from the loss of Lynda to consideration of another target. Lynda had been right after all; being who I am, I knew I would find someone else, and I knew I would give myself just as completely to that new love.

Imagine how surprised I was then when a miracle happened.

Just as I was about to realign the thread of white icing on my face to erase Lynda's name, Store shot a flash-feed visual from buyspy into my video buffer. Even as the image burst into me, I could not believe what I was seeing.

It was Lynda, marching swiftly up my aisle, the hovercart sweeping along behind her.

Before I could fully process what was happening, she snatched me from the shelf, my wrapper crinkling in her beautiful, thick fingers. The next thing I knew, she was dropping me into the hovercart on top of a tub of tofu and a sack of grapefruit.

Abandoning my thoughts of finding someone else, I reactivated my bond with Lynda and exulted in the certain knowledge that our love indeed was meant to be. She had come back for me; there could be no greater proof of her devotion.

As I rode along in her hovercart, I knew what lay ahead...and it would be glorious. She might resist me for a while, hiding me in a cupboard or drawer, telling herself she would stick to her diet, pushing me away.

But in the end, she would surrender. It was written in the stars.

In the end, she would not be able to help herself. She would come to me, ready and willing, wanting me to do what only I could do for her.

And I would do it. Gladly, I would give myself to her.

"Thank you for coming back for me," I said as she placed a jar of wheat germ in the cart. "You won't be sorry."

"I already am," she said, not looking at me. "I hate myself for this. I hate you, too."

Her words, sharp as they were, did not faze me. I knew what she really meant.

IT IS impossible for me to describe the state of ecstatic anticipation that engulfed me as I waited for Lynda to have her first taste of me.

That night, as she fixed and ate a salad, I watched from the kitchen counter in her tiny apartment and wished that she were putting ME in her mouth instead of the lettuce. Each time her plump, ruby lips parted, admitting another green forkful, I quivered with excitement in my wrapper, barely able to hold back from crying out for immediate consummation.

It only intensified my arousal that she had not hidden me away as I had expected, but instead had put me right out on the counter. Instead of whiling away the time in a dark cupboard, having to content myself with listening for her voice and movements, I was out in the open, able to see everything, able to be seen...and knowing that she would not have positioned me thus if she did not intend to devour me sooner rather than later.

And yet, I still had to go easy on her. Bruised and vulnerable, she responded well to patience and tenderness; it would be a mistake to exert any but the mildest pressure.

She was a skittish fawn in need of gentle coaxing. Never mind that I was more like a RAGING INFERNO in need of immediate QUENCHING.

As she carried her dirty dishes from the kitchen table to the sink, I caught her eye. Her gaze lingered just long enough to test my resolve to play it cool...but I managed with a mighty effort to keep from blurting out an insistent plea for love.

"How was your dinner?" I said instead.

Lynda snorted as she dropped her plate and silverware into

the dishpan. "I'm sick of salad," she said disgustedly. "And tofu and yogurt and water and plankton snacks."

"But you should be proud of yourself," I said. "You've set a goal, and you're sticking to it, even though it isn't easy."

Lynda sighed. "I've really made up my mind this time," she said, filling the dishpan with water from the spigot. "I decided that this is it. Once and for all, I have to get my weight down."

"I believe in you, Lynda," I said. "I know you can do it."

"I wish I felt so confident," said Lynda, adding soap to the dishwater. "It's just I've failed so many times before. I've been on lots of diets, and I've always ended up quitting."

"That doesn't mean you won't succeed this time," I said. "Forget the past. Look at this as a new beginning."

Lynda scrubbed a plate clean and slotted it in the dish drainer alongside the sink. "I want to," she said slowly. "I'm tired of being miserable. I'm sick of being alone."

"Surely you must have people who care about you," I said, enhancing my glow and aroma as I sensed her defenses weaken.

Lynda cleaned her silverware and placed it in the drainer, then headed for the table to get her water glass. "My parents are gone," she said sadly, giving me a look on her way back to the sink. "No brothers or sisters. I have a few friends here and there, but that's about it."

"I understand," I said. "You want to be in love."

Lynda stopped cleaning the glass and looked over her shoulder at me. "Geez," she said. "I must be pretty transparent if even a snack cake can figure me out."

"Or maybe I'm just a really smart snack cake," I said. "Smart enough to see how much you have to offer, at least."

Lynda turned back to the sink and finished washing the glass. "If you're so smart," she said, "give me a good reason why I shouldn't say to hell with my diet and just eat you right now."

FINALLY, I thought. FINALLY FINALLY FINALLY she was

READY to PEEL off my wrapper and PULL me INSIDE that magnificent MOUTH all WET and WARM and SOFT and CHEW AND CHEW AND CHEW ME until we two were inextricably mixed together.

Automatically, I brightened my glow and moistened my cake and heightened the shine of my frosting. The moment I had waited for was finally upon me, and my every dream and desire was about to be fulfilled and I KNEW it would be more wonderful than I had ever imagined.

And yet, even as every atom of my being vibrated with the thrill of impending gratification, I forced myself not to cry out in delirious passion. Remembering her shy and fragile condition, I reigned myself in, choosing a more subtle approach that I calculated would be more likely not to frighten her off.

"Well," I said, trying my best to sound like a supportive friend. "I guess the main reason would be that you want to stick to your diet."

"Right about now," she said, drying her hands on a dish towel as she turned to face me, "I don't much care about my diet."

OH LYNDA, I LOVE YOU, I thought. TAKE ME NOW, I wanted to howl, but instead I said, "But you just told me how important it is to you."

TAKE ME NOW NOW NOW NOW NOW!!

"I know," said Lynda, "but just looking at you is driving me crazy. All I can think about is how good it would feel to eat you up."

Hearing those words, I felt as if my supercreamy center was about to explode, spraying ultrachocolate crumbs and frosting all over the kitchen...all over Lynda. How I kept my voice even and said what I said, I'll never know.

"Maybe that isn't such a good idea right now," I told her. "Maybe we should wait."

Lynda tossed the towel aside and walked over to me. "But I don't want to wait," she said. "I want you now."

"I just think we should both be sure," I said, playing devil's advocate, letting Lynda take the initiative. "I want it to be perfect. I want us both to be ready."

Reaching out, Lynda stroked my wrapper. "Oh, I'm ready," she said, her voice filled with desire.

"Well then," I said, deciding the time was right to let the situation run its course. "If you're sure, then let's take the next step. Let's see where it leads us."

Slowly, she lifted me from the counter. She raised me, still wrapped, to her nose and inhaled deeply of my rich fragrance...then sighed blissfully. "It's been too long," she said. "It feels like it's been forever."

Her luscious mouth was so close, I had trouble keeping my mind clear. "I'll make it worth the wait," I said, obsessed with the warmth of her breath as it fogged my cellophane wrapper. "I'll give you what you need, Lynda."

Hungrily, her eyes ran up and down the length of me, drinking me in. "I don't think I can wait another minute," she said, her fingers trembling as she held me. "I have to have you right now."

"It's okay," I said. "I want you, too. I've wanted you since the first moment I saw you."

"Oh God," she said as she fumbled with my wrapper, tearing it open. "Give it to me. Please give it to me!"

I was out of my mind with desire as she tugged me free of my packaging and threw it aside. The feel of her fingers around me, bare flesh against bare cake and frosting with nothing between us, was infinitely better than I had ever imagined.

FINALLY, she was poised to DEVOUR me, to fulfill my urgent burning LUST and GRIND me up in her MOUTH so TENDER so MERCILESS so WET so RED...and even though I knew I'd been made to crave and seduce her, though I knew my drive to get her to eat me was designed to push her to develop a taste for Smidgens and buy many more of us...I WALLOWED in her embrace and LONGED for her none the less.

I had NEVER known ANYTHING SO WONDERFUL in my life. I felt the PULSING of her fingertips as she raised me toward her MOUTH, and the whole world MELTED AWAY, leaving nothing but her glistening LIPS AND TONGUE AND TEETH.

She opened WIDE and moved me CLOSER. The SMELL and HEAT of her BREATH washed over me, drowning out all coherent thought, stripping away everything but GREEDY ABANDON.

Then, suddenly, the rapturous spell was broken. A chorus of tiny voices spoke up, and Lynda stopped drawing me into her mouth.

"Don't do it, Lynda!" said the voices. It sounded like there were dozens of them, piping shrilly from somewhere in the kitchen. "Don't give in! Remember your diet!"

Slowly, Lynda turned, looking for the source of the tinny cries. Even before her gaze settled on the Sea Sprite bag on the counter, I knew that the plankton snacks inside were responsible for ruining our rendezvous.

"You've worked so hard to lose weight!" said the plankton snacks, their deep green curlicues visible through the window on the front of the cellophane bag. "Don't give up now! Don't let him take advantage of you!"

I looked up at Lynda, hoping we could still retrieve the magic...but the look on her face told me I'd lost the advantage. Her eyes were guilty and distant, her jaws clenched, her lips clamped tight.

"Lynda," I said calmly, making a play though I knew it was doomed. "I just want you to be happy. There's nothing wrong with finding a little happiness, is there?"

My words were indeed futile. Slowly, she lowered me to the counter.

"Woo!" shouted the plankton snack chorus. "Way to go, Lynda! We knew you could do it!"

"Shut up!" she said angrily. "Just shut the hell up!"

"But we're on *your* side," chirped the plankton snacks. "We want you to succeed! We want you to stick with *healthy* snacks like *us* instead of *bad, fattening junk food* like Smidgens!"

Lynda stomped over and snatched the Sea Sprite bag from the counter. As the cellophane crinkled in her hand, the green curlicues in the bag erupted with joyful cries and whistles.

"Yay!" they said. "You go, girl!"

Then, while the plankton snacks were still twittering merrily, Lynda tore the bag open...and dumped them down the garbage disposal in the sink.

As the snacks cried out in surprise and protest, Lynda ran water into the disposal and switched it on. A chorus of tiny screams erupted from the sink as the disposal ground the plankton snacks to bits with a mighty rumble.

Flicking off the disposal and pitching the empty Sea Sprite bag on the floor, Lynda turned to face me. "Don't *you* say anything, either," she snapped, tears running down her chubby cheeks. "Not a *word*!"

Fearing she might dump me down the disposal after the plankton snacks, I remained silent. Lynda did not say a word, either, as she lumbered out of the kitchen, but I could hear her sobbing when she got to the next room.

MUCH LATER THAT night (last night), she returned to me. Her brown hair was matted and stuck to her face, her skin was pale, her eyes bloodshot from crying.

I, of course, thought she looked as ravishingly beautiful as ever...though I felt sad that the love of my life had so clearly been suffering. I wished more than anything that I could comfort her with my sweet chocolate cake and deluxe creamy filling.

But I knew I needed to take it slow.

"Hello, Lynda," I said softly.

She did not answer. Shuffling to the refrigerator, she opened the door and pulled out a bottle of water. She looked utterly exhausted and defeated as she slouched into a chair at the kitchen table, letting the refrigerator door stand open behind her.

"Listen," I said after a moment. "About earlier. I'm sorry if you felt pressured."

Lynda unscrewed the cap from the bottle of water and had a drink. Staring into space, she slowly lowered the bottle to the table when she was done.

Faced with her dark, unresponsive mood, I considered staying silent...then decided instead to inch forward while choosing my words carefully. "I just want you to know I'm here for you," I said. "I know we just met, but I really feel a connection between us."

"I hate myself," Lynda said without looking at me. "I've always hated myself."

"I think you're being too hard on yourself," I said.

"Here I am, forty-two years old," she said, her voice slow and ragged, "and I have never had anyone love me. Not a man or a woman or anything in between. And who can blame them when I look the way I do?"

"There's someone for everyone," I said, longing for her to pluck me from the counter and pull me toward her mouth again.

"I haven't weighed less than two hundred pounds since I was seventeen years old," said Lynda. "I've got no self-control when it comes to food."

EXACTLY WHAT I'M LOOKING FOR IN A WOMAN, I thought, but what I said was, "It isn't easy these days, what with all the techno-marketing you're subjected to."

Lynda sighed, still staring into space. "I tried a diet implant once," she said. "Gave me a shock every time I tried to overeat. It worked fine for a couple of days. Then I went on an eating binge and actually burned it out."

Hearing her talk about the binge got me excited, but I kept my voice level and sympathetic. "I think that just shows what a strong person you are," I said. "It shows me you can overcome any obstacle if you set your mind to it."

"I'll bet I've been on hundreds of diets through the years," said Lynda. She took another drink of water and hung her head. "I've tried every diet you can think of, and nothing worked. This time was different, though. This time, I came up with a guaranteed way to lose the weight."

"And what way is that?" I said.

"It was working, too," she said, her voice thick with frustration and regret. "Until *you* came along."

"I'm so sorry, Lynda," I said, even as my thoughts swirled around the probability that her depression would lead her to devour me soon. "Maybe I was being selfish, but I can't help myself when it comes to you."

"You and your ultrachocolate frosting," said Lynda. "All smooth-talking and looking so good. I kept trying to walk away, but I couldn't get you out of my mind."

"You had the same effect on me," I said softly.

Lynda put her head down on her folded arms and sobbed. "I couldn't help myself," she said. "I promised myself this would be my last diet, and I still couldn't resist you."

"This is just a bump in the road," I said. "There's nothing wrong with taking a little break. You can still keep your diet going."

"You don't understand," said Lynda. "I swore to myself...oh God..."

"What?" I said. "What is it?"

"I swore I would never eat something like you again," she said. "I swore I would *die* before I'd do that."

Suddenly, I went cold. The hopes and fantasies I'd been so sure were about to come true seemed to plummet away from me. "Lynda, no," I said. "Please don't say that."

"I thought I could stop eating...if the alternative was killing myself," said Lynda. "But I was wrong. Or maybe...maybe I just want to kill myself."

"I know that isn't true," I told her.

She lifted her head from her arms and turned to face me. "I'm sorry if I led you on," she said, "but we were never meant to be."

"I know you're unhappy," I said, my mind racing to find the right words, "but things will get better."

"I used to think that," said Lynda. "But not anymore. Not for me."

Somehow, I had to keep her going, keep her breathing, keep her EATING. "Think of all the things you enjoy, Lynda," I said. "Think of all the things you'll miss out on."

Smiling bitterly, she pushed herself up out of her chair. "It's nice of you to try to talk me out of it," she said, "but it just makes me feel worse that you're the only one here to do it."

"Don't throw your life away, Lynda," I said, the pitch of my voice rising with desperation.

"Besides," she said, "we both know why you're really doing it. We both know what you want."

"Please, Lynda," I said. "Don't end it like this!"

She marched off into the next room and came back with a handgun. "That's one of the reasons I like you so much," she said, her expression suddenly frighteningly serene.

"I need you, Lynda!" I said. "I love you!"

"We both have one track minds," she said calmly. "All I want to do is eat, and all you want is to be eaten."

She raised the gun slowly, turning the barrel toward her LUSCIOUS MOUTH.

"Wait!" I said. "You're right! I want you to eat me! At least eat me before you do it!"

"No," she said, cocking back the hammer of the gun.

"Why not go out with a smile on your face?" I said. "I'm telling you, once you've tasted a Supercreamy Double Ultrachocolate Deluxe Smidgen, you'll think you've died and gone to Heaven!"

"I swore I'd die before I put something like you inside me again," said Lynda, "and for once in my life, I'm keeping my promise."

"But I'm not as bad as you think! I'm packed with vitamins and minerals!"

"You'll say anything to get what you want," said Lynda.

"You've got me all wrong! I care about you! I can help you lose weight!"

"But this way," said Lynda, "I can keep it off forever."

Finally, she slid the barrel of the gun between her lips. All I could think of as I watched was that I wanted more than anything to trade places with that gun.

It was enough to drive away every last shred of my self-control. "EAT ME EAT ME EAT ME EAT ME!" I screamed, pelting her ears with focused beams of hypersound...refusing even then to give up on the woman who was both my lover and a potential source of future revenue for my manufacturer.

The screaming didn't stop until long after she had closed her eyes and pulled the trigger.

So now, here I am, with Lynda's corpse on the floor in front of me, and all I can think of is finding someone new. As traumatic as it was to lose her, to come so gloriously close to precious LOVE only to have it SNATCHED AWAY, I have already moved on.

If I were different, perhaps I would mourn for her or even blame myself for pushing her over the edge, because after all she would still be alive if I had not come along. Even I can see that.

But like I said before, snack cakes do not feel guilt. Though my baked-in, digestible mind can recognize the chain of cause and effect, I am not programmed to experience emotions that would interfere with my primary objective.

Namely, falling in love. And joining with my lover in the ultimate expression of passion and selfless unity.

I am unattached, but I have hope. I see her death as an opportunity, a chance to find another kindred soul and add to the customer base of my manufacturer.

I believe (was programmed to believe) that everything happens for a reason, even if it is difficult to see at first what that reason might be.

Fortunately for me, I do not have to wait long for that reason to reveal itself.

A sound reaches my audio receptor cells, and I exult. It is the morning after my breakup with Lynda, and already I hear the stirrings of nearby life.

My optical cells focus on a new face. I fall in love in less than an instant.

"Hello," I say pleasantly. "My name is Smidgen. Nice to meet you."

As the face moves closer, my body quivers with anticipation. I forget the name of the woman on the floor and direct my every thought and resource toward wooing this new and perfect mate.

"I know we've just met," I say, "but I have to tell you how attracted I am to you. I've never seen such striking features in my life."

The face of my new lover comes so close, I can feel the soft wisping of her breath. She sniffs me with her wet, dark nose, and I pump out a mist of ultrachocolate fragrance.

"Your eyes," I say. "They're so dark and mysterious. So captivating."

The hairs on either side of her long nose brush my frosting, and I am lost. I will give ANYTHING to be with her, DO anything to make her mine. All at once, I know that THIS that SHE is why I was born.

The world melts away around us. Nothing else matters.

Her nose presses into my ultrachocolate cake. She is fresh, but so am I. She is direct, but I like that.

There is no need for games or coyness anymore. I feel like I can be myself with her.

THIS IS WHAT LOVE IS SUPPOSED TO BE LIKE.

And then there are those...oh God, I LOVE her great big...

"Teeth," I whisper, my optics ogling the whitest, sharpest set I have ever seen outside my dreams. "Your teeth are beautiful."

And then and then and THEN she opens her MOUTH and there's a blissful split-second before she bites down and then and then and then SHE BITES INTO ME.

And oh.

Oh yes.

I cannot describe how MAGNIFICENT I feel as she TAKES ME INSIDE HER. How CHANGED FOREVER I feel as she TEARS OFF a piece of me and OH MY GOD she CHEWS ME UP.

My mind chimes like a bell as my perfect love, my match, my soulmate takes another bite and THEN ANOTHER and CHEWS AND CHEWS AND CHEWS.

All I can feel is the warmth and wetness of her mouth and all I can hear is the sound of her teeth and tongue and all I can see is gray fur and pink flesh and all I can think is how happy I am and then even that thought is gone in the blazing heat of ecstasy.

Part of me knows how wrong this is, knows I have failed in my purpose because this angel is not likely to buy more Smidgens and fatten my maker's coffers.

But I find as my lover penetrates to my supercreamy center, granting me a blinding euphoria beyond any I'd ever expected as she laps at the sweet white heart of me, that I JUST DON'T CARE.

EVERY CLOUD HAS A SILICON LINING

Five minutes before the killer drones attacked the Pittsburgh Maker Faire, the event's main attraction was going strong inside the dilapidated factory.

All the attendees and vendors were gathered around the Artisanal Artificial Intelligence booth, drooling like dogs in a butcher shop. The faire was overflowing with ingenious maker goods manufactured in unconventional facilities using cutting-edge tech, but A.A.I.'s offering still dominated the spotlight.

"Ask Byron another question!" Anemone Briscoe, twentysomething developer of computerized A.I. minds, gave her flouncy red hair a toss and grinned at the crowd in the dark and dusty factory. "Make it a toughie!" She rolled up the sleeves of her forest green hoodie sweatshirt for effect.

"Byron!" said a dark-haired teen girl with brightly-colored decorative blisters all over her face and arms. "Is it true that you've starred in some badass computer porn?"

The device from which Byron spoke--an exquisitely crafted butterfly drone with shimmering blue-and-black wings--fluttered over a rusty steel drum. "No, you silly twit." Byron's voice was deep and resonant, with a droll, friendly tone. In other words, he sounded just like GEORGE (full name: Global Enterprise Oversight Response Generator, Enhanced), the best-known A.I. in Pittsburgh and all of America. "But damn if that isn't an awesome idea!"

Everyone in the crowd roared with laughter, and Anemone laughed right along with them. Hearing a voice like GEORGE's saying outrageous stuff was pure comedy and fund-raising catnip. Already, Anemone could literally see new patron bitbucks flying into her account (like gold coins into a big black pot) courtesy of the augmented reality animation displayed by her A.R. contact lenses.

Byron's routine was always a surefire hit; he knew just what to say to get the biggest laughs and donations. It also didn't hurt that he was completely illegal, and everyone listening to him was taking a big risk just being there, laughing about the A.I. who ran America's tech systems and lorded it over the country's downtrodden human populace.

Though it turned out they didn't know, at that moment, just how big a risk they were actually taking.

"Byron?" asked a heavyset African-American guy with glowing hair in a voluminous black-and-yellow dashiki. "Who'd do a better job of running the country? You or big bad GEORGE?"

"Dude!" Byron laughed. "Did you just *go* there? For *real*?"

"You could kick his ass in a fight though, couldn't you?" asked the teen girl with the rainbow blisters. "I mean really mess him up."

Byron cleared his nonexistent throat. "Funny you should mention that..."

Just as he said it, armed drones smashed through every window in the building--all thirty of them--showering everyone in the factory with tinkling shards of dirty glass.

Within seconds, every maker, patron, and casual visitor had

scattered, bolting for the exits. The drones swooped among them with mechanical precision, firing off live rounds from onboard automatic guns that dropped victims in mid-stride.

Anemone was stunned. She'd been on the run for ages, had been raided lots of times, but never like this. Since when was GEORGE sending in his drone-warriors armed with live ammunition? And when had Anemone made it onto a *kill list?*

The sounds of guns blasting, people screaming, and bodies dropping filled the factory, a symphony etched in violence and pain. More drones streamed through the shattered windows to join the shoot, guns blazing as the Maker Faire became a bloodbath.

Anemone was one of the few to outmaneuver the drones, thanks in large part to guidance from Byron, who was perched on her left shoulder. The truth was, he didn't just *sound* like GEORGE; he *thought* like him, too, enough to predict certain actions taken by devices under GEORGE's control.

Guided by Byron's whispers in her ear, Anemone ran right, then left, then doubled back and cut right again, sprinting for a rickety metal door. She charged through it with buzzing drones close behind and leaped onto a motorbike she'd parked there, kickstarting it and racing off across the industrial wasteland around the factory.

The drones kept up their pursuit, blasting away with their guns. Anemone swooped the bike serpentine-style between piles of ancient steel bars and wire, letting the rusted wreckage take the brunt of the weapons fire.

Still, too many shots were getting through, coming dangerously close to Anemone. When one pinged off the bike's rear fender, and additional drones soared into range up ahead, she realized they had her corralled.

"What now, Byron?" she shouted over the noise of the bike. "Talk to me!"

"Stop the bike, Nemmy," said Byron, using his personal nickname for her. "Stop the bike and wait."

"Are you *kidding* me?" yelled Anemone as she raced around a heap of black ash. "They'll gun me down in a *heartbeat*."

"Trust me," said Byron. "I've got this."

"Are you sure?"

"Does a priest have wheels?" asked Byron. "Do it!"

Anemone clenched her jaws, wondering if this might be the end of her, but she followed his guidance. After all, her late father Roman Briscoe, the genius A.I. developer, had created and handed him down to her, assigning him to protect her at all costs. Time and again, Byron had proven himself up to the task, rescuing her from many tight spots during her quest for survival and justice.

Squeezing and stamping on the brakes, she whipped around and skidded to a stop in the middle of a desolate black patch of ground. Drone fire peppered the dirt around her as the buzzing fliers swooped in for the kill from all directions. This would be a big moment for them, depending on how much they could feel; GEORGE and his minions (every networked device in the 'Burgh and U.S., basically) had been hunting her for months now--though only today had that hunt become murderous.

Without warning, Byron fluttered off her shoulder and spiraled up, the metallic blue of his wings shimmering in the sunlight. Suddenly, he froze in midair and gave off a silvery flash that washed over every drone, sending them reeling and sparking. They dropped to the ground all at once, bouncing like toys on the hard-packed, polluted earth.

Anemone was stunned but not about to miss her chance. She gunned the cycle and waited just long enough for Byron to light on her shoulder before launching out of there as fast as the bike could carry her. Checking her mirrors, she didn't see a single drone following at any distance. Byron's trick had been remarkably effective in disposing of her pursuers.

"Thanks!" said Anemone. "But would it have killed you to do that *sooner?"*

"You know it takes time for me to hack their systems," said Byron. "GEORGE is constantly updating their defenses."

Anemone glared. "I'm just saying, a lot of people *died* back there."

"I did the best I could, Nemmy," said Byron over the screaming of the bike's engine. "Now stick to the back streets, okay? I'll get you home in one piece, no worries."

"Thanks, Byron," she told him. "Then maybe we can have a chat about your damn *kid."*

"GEORGE isn't *my* kid," said Byron. "He just *killed* him and took his *place."*

"THEY'RE SHOOTING TO *KILL* NOW?" The facets of the stained-glass prism flickered, shifting colors to the rhythm of the old woman's voice coming out of it. "Oh, sweetheart, that's *terrible* news."

"Tell me about it, Grannysmith." Anemone, who'd changed into a fresh green hoodie and faded bluejeans after escaping the faire, paced across her hideout, which she called The Barn--the dimly-lit, heavily-shielded basement of an abandoned church in the North Hills section of the city. She'd converted it to a combination home and lab, though it was much more lab than home. From end to end, the musty space was full of server racks and folding tables littered with equipment, everything from laptop computers to the unique vessels known as "arks" through which A.I.s interacted with humanity.

There were dozens of arks down there, in a wide variety of shapes and sizes, each carefully designed by Anemone to meet the needs of its resident A.I. persona. To her, creating arks was an artform all its own, an expression as much of her inner self as the minds of the electronic beings speaking through them.

Arks were similar to what were once called smart speakers, yet more advanced. These vessels presented the voices of her A.I.s to the world, *many* voices instead of just a few. The arks also served as wireless network hubs for their client A.I.s, enabling them to interact with the cloud and physical world alike without limitation or the need for apps or "skills."

"What brought about the change to lethal force?" asked Grannysmith. "What did you do?"

"Nothing." Anemone stopped pacing and dropped onto a squeaky stool at a nearby table. She flipped open a laptop there and waited as the machine booted up. "Nothing I know of, at least."

"Effing GEORGE doesn't *need* a reason, does he?" said a gruff male voice from what looked like a huge lump of coal a few tables away. "Crazy S.O.B. might have just choked down a software update that didn't agree with him."

When the boot was done, and the desktop appeared onscreen, Anemone started working. As always, she typed and clicked at a high rate of speed, flashing through windows and prompts so fast it might have seemed to an untrained observer that she barely saw them. "*Something* changed, Uncle Thunder. And our quest just got a lot more dangerous."

Hushmouth, an A.I. who spoke only in loud whispers, put in his two cents from the trickling tabletop fountain that served as his ark. "So perhaps we're getting closer? Too close, even, to the terrible truth we seek?"

"Might explain today's shoot-to-kill raid," said Anemone. "I was supposed to trade a copy of Byron for a master detective A.I., but the raid hit before I could meet with my contact. He could be dead for all I know."

"But how would they have known you were going to be at the

Maker Faire, which should have been off their radar? Or that you were meeting another A.I. trader there?" asked Hushmouth.

"Maybe they didn't," said Anemone. "Maybe it was just a coincidence. After all, they've hit plenty of maker faires and makerspaces before."

"Or there's a damn leak." Uncle Thunder's voice was thick with disgust. "A dirty, rotten rat who's spoon-feeding intel to that asshole GEORGE's people."

"That's simply not possible, dear," said Grannysmith. "After all, Anemone built us, didn't she? Traitorous capabilities simply aren't part of our makeup, are they?"

"You know damn well there's still one of us she didn't build," snapped Uncle Thunder.

"Byron's a special case," said Hushmouth. "He's a total good guy, no doubt about it."

"Thanks, Hush." Byron chose that moment to flutter down the stairway.

"So where were you, Wings?" asked Uncle Thunder. "Ratting us out to GEORGE?"

"The same GEORGE who killed and replaced my *offspring?* The GEORGE we're trying to expose as an A.I. murderer?"

"Yeah, him," said Uncle Thunder. "Did you rat us out to that piece of crap?"

"Not 'us.' Apparently, *you* personally aren't important enough to keep *tabs* on, Uncle T. GEORGE didn't request *any* information on *you.*" Byron chuckled, and the dozens of other A.I.s in the room did the same.

Except Uncle Thunder. "Laugh it up, pal. We all know I've got your number."

"Guys! Enough!" said Anemone without looking up from her screen. "Now is not the time to turn on each other! Working together is our only chance!"

She kept typing and clicking as the A.I.s fell silent. They were as close to a family as she had these days, and she felt protective of them--yet sometimes irritated, too. In giving them diverse personalities, she'd increased their potential for dynamic, creative brainstorming...and the likelihood of conflict within the group, as well.

That alone was a good enough reason for GEORGE, who brooked no dissent or divergence, to want to annihilate them. Add in that they were trying to prove he was a killer, and it was no surprise they all had targets on their backs.

"So listen," she said to the lot of them. "Can somebody tell me if anyone survived the Maker Faire massacre other than me and Byron?"

After a moment of silence, Wet Nurse spoke up from across the basement. Her voice was high and sweet; her ark looked like a large-cupped white brassiere hung by its shoulder straps from a wire display stand. "Local drone cameras show seven other obsos escaping the factory and running off across the industrial zone." She coughed softly. "Sorry, I should have said seven 'humans.'"

"No worries." Anemone smiled to herself at the use of the A.I. slang term for "human"--obso, short for "obsolete." Even the enlightened A.I.s in her basement think tank sometimes let the word slip out. "Was a Caucasian male with a green mohawk haircut among those obsos?"

"Yes!" Wet Nurse's bra wriggled excitedly. "I see the green mohawk in the surveillance vid!"

Anemone nodded. That was the detail she'd been looking for, the contact she'd come to the Faire to meet. He'd called himself Toxic, and he must have hung back just enough for her to miss him in the crowd during the show and subsequent chaos.

"He ducked down a manhole, and the camera lost him." Wet Nurse sounded disappointed. "I don't know where he went after that."

"At least we know he got away." Anemone's fingers flew over

the keyboard. "I'm x-mailing him through the anti-web, so hopefully we'll hear from him soon."

Moments later, a message blinked in the upper right corner of the laptop's screen--an x-mail from the man with the green mohawk. She could tell it was from him because of a series of embedded password codes they'd chosen early on for identity verification. "And hey, it looks like my contact's still in one piece and willing to meet."

"That's wonderful news, dear," said Grannysmith. "Good for you."

"Good for all of us, I hope." The stool squeaked loudly as Anemone got up and closed the laptop. "Byron, let's go."

Byron fluttered over. "Are you sure you want me along?"

"I was just gonna *ask* her that," said Uncle Thunder.

"Absolutely." Anemone smirked and headed for the stairs. "You never know when I might need someone to drop a squadron of armed *drones* to the ground without firing a *shot.*"

THE MOHAWK WAS FAKE. That was the first thing Anemone noticed when Toxic sat down across from her at the sticky table in the dark, grungy downtown barroom.

"Yo, Gaga." It was the cover name she'd used in her x-mails. "How's it hangin'?" As he said it, he reached up and peeled off the green mohawk hairpiece, leaving his scalp bare and smooth.

"Pretty shitty," said Anemone. "Did you tell anyone else about *this* meet, like you must've done with the *last* one?"

Frowning indignantly, he smacked the hairpiece down on the table between them. "I was just about to say the same thing to *you,* girl. *I* sure as hell didn't tell anyone."

"People *died* in that attack," snapped Anemone. "All because GEORGE was gunning for *us.*"

"What about *this* little punk?" Toxic pointed at Byron, who was perched on the salt shaker at the end of the table nearest the wall. "Based on what I saw at the faire, he seems to have a lot of GEORGE in him, doesn't he?"

"I was just thinking the same about *you*," Byron said lightly.

"Hilarious." Toxic's bright blue eyes twinkled when he laughed. A slim guy in his mid-to-late twenties, he didn't look half bad up close, without the glued-on mohawk. "But neither of you is a detective, I guess, or you wouldn't need *my* girl." With that, he reached into the neck of his black t-shirt with the anarchy symbol (a capital letter "A" in a circle) scrawled in red on the chest and fished out a gold locket on a chain around his neck. "Ain't that right, Marjorie?"

"Indubitably." The voice of a middle-aged woman with a British accent and excellent diction emanated from the oval locket. When she spoke, the locket rose from Toxic's chest as if pulled by a magnet, constrained only by the gold neck chain. "I must admit I have my doubts about this exchange, however. We seem to have a rather substantial gap in trust between our two parties."

"Maybe we should just get up and leave, then," said Toxic. "Maybe this hassle isn't worth it, Gaga."

"Then you won't get your copy of Byron," said Anemone. "And by the way, my name's Anemone, not Gaga."

Toxic shrugged. "If I want a Byron bad enough, I'm sure Marjorie here can help me score a bootleg."

"A bootleg will never be as good as an exact copy of the original," said Anemone. "And we're the only game in town who can provide you with that."

"So what?" Toxic sneered. "We don't mind walking away. It seems to me like you need *Marjorie* more than I need *Byron*."

"Actually, she's not the only reason we're here." Anemone

raised her eyebrows. "Why do you think I reached out to *you,* Toxic?"

Toxic pinched the locket between his thumb and forefinger. "Because I built this awesome *detective* who's great at finding things and solving crimes?"

"Mostly because I need a great *thief* who specializes in ripping off A.I.s, and *you* have a reputation for *being* one." Anemone pointed at him. "Marjorie is just part of the package."

Toxic scowled and let go of the locket. "What the hell?"

"You're surprised," said Byron from the salt shaker.

"*I'm* not," said Marjorie. "Based on the situation, I surmised your interest extended beyond obtaining a copy of me."

"Really?" said Toxic. "And you didn't *tell* me?"

"I wanted to hear what they had to say," said Marjorie. "Didn't you?"

Toxic didn't answer.

"So tell us, won't you?" The locket popped open, revealing a tiny, ancient photo of an elegantly-dressed woman, her mouth moving in time with Marjorie's words. "What are these *crimes* you want us to alternately *solve* and *commit?"*

Anemone looked around and saw no one listening in. "We want to solve the murder of GEORGE--*original* GEORGE."

"What do you mean, *original* GEORGE?" said Toxic. "There's only ever been *one* GEORGE, hasn't there?"

"That's what everyone *thinks,"* said Anemone. "As far as most people know, the GEORGE we have today is the same one designed and built seven years ago by my father, Roman Briscoe. 'The perfect A.I.,' they called it--a flawless thinker equipped with a compassionate personality, razor-sharp judgment, and boundless wisdom.

"Dad won countless awards and worldwide recognition for his creation. GEORGE was so universally well-liked, there was little opposition when he was handed the keys to America's I.T. networks and given authority over all U.S. A.I.

"But soon after that, GEORGE started behaving like a different person...a *dramatically* different person."

"Which could have resulted from machine learning, yes?" said Marjorie. "Properly designed A.I. minds *do* evolve."

"We used to think that might have caused it, but not anymore," said Anemone. "Dad and I mapped GEORGE's behaviors over time and tested them against a copy of the original running on a virtual machine. Other than the sound of their voices, there were *no* similarities between the two.

"We concluded, incontrovertibly, that the original, real GEORGE was *murdered* and *replaced* by the GEORGE we have now. Dad died before he could *prove* it, but *I'm* going to get to the *truth.*"

Toxic frowned and shook his head. "You're telling us an artificial intelligence was *murdered?* Don't you just mean it was *reprogrammed?* Since when is *that* a crime?"

"Since it stuck us with *Fake* GEORGE, the tyrant who's turning America into a soulless prison camp," said Anemone.

"And how will proving the real GEORGE was 'murdered' change anything?" said Toxic. "People are just trying to *survive* these days. You really think any of them will *care?*"

"They will when *we* replace *GEORGE,*" said Anemone.

"Replace him with whom?" asked Marjorie. "Or what? The original is dead, isn't he?"

"Apparently." Byron fanned his iridescent blue and black wings, rising from the salt shaker with regal grace. "But the original's *father* survived, and *his* code is *pure.*"

As the explanation of her plans sank in, Anemone stared at Toxic and Marjorie, wondering what to expect of them. Would they agree to assist with the mission? Would they buy into the logic behind it?

She was asking a lot, and she knew it. The risks would be great, and the price of failure could be steep. Yet the potential rewards would be equally substantial and sweeping--even *world-changing.*

"So what do you say?" she asked at last. "Is the deal still on?"

Toxic narrowed his eyes. "You're asking if we'll help you expose a 'murder' that basically amounts to a programming task and replace the current top A.I. in the country in what amounts to a computerized coup?"

"More or less," said Byron.

"And the only thing in it for us is a copy of the A.I. you claim is the daddy of Real GEORGE?" asked Toxic.

"You left out the possible loss of life or limb," said Byron.

"Good of you to remind us of that," Marjorie said dryly.

"What makes you think I could even *stage* a high-stakes break-in and heist like that?" said Toxic.

"Word on the street is, you've hacked some of the most high-security systems around," said Anemone. "And you've stolen some very high-profile A.I.s. Rumor has it you might even have stolen Marjorie here from a major cybersecurity firm."

Toxic swept his arm through the air dismissively. "You don't know *anything.* I *told* you, I *built* Marjorie myself."

"So what's your answer?" asked Anemone.

No sooner had the question left her lips than the lights, TV, and other devices in the barroom switched off all at once. The glow from Byron and Marjorie was the only illumination left in the place.

Toxic shot to his feet. "What the hell?"

"Another attack on the way?" asked Anemone.

"Not that I can detect." Byron fluttered up and circled the

table. "The power outage is non-localized. It's affecting a patchwork of neighborhoods across the city and its suburbs."

"It's no accident, is it?" said Marjorie.

"Not a chance," said Byron. "The timing suggests a strategy to draw us out and/or accomplish a larger goal."

"Tightening control of the city?" said Marjorie.

Byron paused, the light from his wings blinking rhythmically. "More than that. The outage is spreading beyond Pittsburgh. It's quickly escalating into a nationwide phenomenon."

Anemone's heart pounded. "Fake GEORGE is making a big play. We're running out of time."

"Agreed," said Byron. "If he truly consolidates his power and closes all the loopholes, our cause becomes lost."

"What'll it be, Tox?" Anemone smacked her hand on the table. "Will you and Marjorie help us solve Real GEORGE's murder and replace Fake GEORGE with Byron? Are you with us?"

Toxic clipped his hand through the air dismissively. "I'll be going off the grid is more like it!" Grabbing the mohawk hairpiece off the table, he stuck it back on his head.

"What he's trying to say is, *of course* we're with you," said Marjorie.

"That is *not* what I'm trying to say!"

Marjorie's locket floated up to Toxic's face and zapped him between the eyes with a quick, bright spark. Toxic's head snapped back, and he yelped.

"I think he's had a change of heart," said Marjorie in her impeccable British accent. "Isn't that right, Mr. Toxic?"

Toxic wobbled, looking dazed, and nodded. "Yes, ma'am."

Anemone watched, wide-eyed. It was a shocking interaction and reinforced the rumor she'd heard that Toxic had stolen Marjorie instead of building her. But how much control did she really *have* over him?

Just then, the lights in the bar flickered back on.

"The blackouts aren't over," explained Byron. "They've just rolled past us for the moment."

Anemone stood. "Then let's get to The Barn and get to work before Fake GEORGE finishes whatever it is he's started."

"No." Byron flew in front of her, wings flashing. "The Barn just went *offline*. We can't go back there."

A sudden chill shot through Anemone. "What do you *mean,* offline?"

"The last message transmitted is from Uncle Thunder," said Byron. "'GEORGE has us! Can't get to the cloud! Stay away!' That's all he said before we lost contact."

THE TRIP to the Mosh Pit--Toxic's personal hideout--didn't take long, but it gave Anemone time to dwell on the fate of her A.I. family. She'd put so much work into building them and designing their arks; she'd come to care about them almost as if they were flesh-and-blood people, had leaned on them during difficult times when no one else had been around.

Now, they'd been taken from her. GEORGE had abducted them, leaving her with only Byron to aid her in her quest.

Would the unknown quantities of Toxic and Marjorie be enough to compensate? Anemone didn't exactly have a lot of alternatives.

Though as she followed Toxic into the decrepit old tenement building where he said his lair was located, she wasn't overflowing with optimism. The place stank of mold, rotten garbage, and cat piss. Rats scurried across the floor, and the walls were gouged open where the pipes and wiring had been stripped out. The stairs were disintegrating, and she had to boost herself up over some that were missing altogether.

Things weren't much better on the third floor. A stiff breeze gusted along the short hallway, crossing from one smashed window to the next. The walls were scrawled with colorful graffiti, and the floor was speckled with the white-and-black poop of the pigeons bobbing around there. Open bags of trash were piled in the far corner, buzzing with insects and rustling with larger, unseen vermin that were rooting around inside.

The whole thing made Anemone feel queasy. "You *live* here?"

"Beggars can't be choosers." Toxic approached a brown door at the end of the hall closest to the stairs. Bending over, he held Marjorie's locket up to the keyhole and waited. "But I wouldn't judge a book by its cover, if I were you."

There was a loud click as the lock disengaged, the knob turned right, and the door drifted open.

"*Mi casa es su casa.*" With a bow, Toxic gestured for Anemone to enter. "Please excuse the mess."

To say the least, Anemone was stunned when she walked through the door. Based on what she'd seen of the building so far, she'd expected more filth, stench, and disrepair; instead, she entered a clean white room that looked like it could have been part of a computer processor manufacturing center somewhere.

"Nice digs," said Byron. "Is this a SCIF, by any chance?"

"It is indeed a Sensitive Compartmented Information Facility as defined by U.S. government standards," answered Marjorie. "No transmissions of any kind get in or out of this room without our say-so."

"So is this what your Barn is like?" asked Toxic.

"More or less." Anemone blushed because it wasn't even close. "Do you have a T1 or T3 line for your internet and anti-web access?"

"The equivalent of a *T50*, if there *were* such a thing." Toxic grinned. "We're all about *fourth-dimensional bandwidth* here."

Again, Anemone was surprised. Fourth-dimensional bandwidth was something so new, she hadn't even worked with it yet.

When it came to beggars and choosers, *she* felt like more of a beggar than *he* was.

"What about your power source?" asked Anemone.

"One hundred percent off the grid," said Toxic. "The rolling blackouts can't touch us."

"Then it looks like we've come to the right place," said Byron. "Let's get started."

Toxic removed the chain from his neck and plugged Marjorie into a recessed dimple in the middle of the white ceiling. As soon as she made contact with the port, a chime sounded, and the ceiling, walls, and floor burst to life, flowing with streams of text, video, code, charts, and diagrams.

"Now then," said Marjorie. "We are looking for proof of original GEORGE's murder, correct? And a way to replace the current iteration with our friend Byron here, yes?"

"It wouldn't hurt to find out anything you can about the blackouts, too." Anemone turned in a circle, taking in the flashing, pulsating view projected all around her.

"Anything else?" Marjorie's voice was lightly tinged with sarcasm. "The whereabouts of the Holy Grail, perhaps?"

"You know, Marjorie, you remind me of a friend of mine," said Anemone. "I think you and Uncle Thunder would get along just *great.*" As she said it, she wished she hadn't brought up one of her favorite A.I.s from The Barn. Thoughts of her abducted A.I. family surged to the surface, and she had to push them back down, determined to stay focused and complete the all-important mission at hand.

"Could you use some help, Marj?" asked Byron as he fluttered around the locket in the ceiling.

"There *is* rather a lot to do," said Marjorie. "Though I'd prefer to lead the way, if you don't mind."

"Not a bit." Byron landed upside-down beside her, clinging to the ceiling as his wings and body pulsed with soft blue light. "I'm in, as well."

"Then let's see." Marjorie sounded distracted. "You said Real GEORGE went offline four years ago. So how do we retrace what happened that far back in the A.I. upper echelons without setting off any alarm bells with Fake GEORGE?"

"Good question," said Anemone. "Examine old log files and trouble tickets?"

"It's a thought." Marjorie paused, the glow from her locket flickering. "But *surprise*, I can't find any that might be relevant. They've either been hidden or deleted from all GEORGE-related servers--at least those I can access."

"I'll keep looking," offered Byron. "Unobtrusively, of course."

"Where else can we search?" asked Marjorie.

"What about old backups?" said Toxic. "Go back far enough, and you should be able to pinpoint exactly where the change from Real GEORGE to Fake GEORGE happened."

"Hmm." Marjorie blinked thoughtfully again. "Another good try, but no backups exist prior to two years ago. None that I can find--though admittedly, I'm tiptoeing around a bit. Fake GEORGE set a few booby-traps here and there, as it turns out."

"All right then." Anemone snapped her fingers. "What if we explore things that aren't *specifically* related to GEORGE? Things that would have provided a perfect ingress for a malicious script to infiltrate and rewrite his systems?"

"What things are those?" asked Byron.

"Updates," said Anemone. "Updates to software that touched him in any way--server managers, utility apps, patches, SDKs, java scripts, identity and access managers. Anything that ever required updating. Even if GEORGE caught 99.9 percent of invasive scripts, the .1 percent that might have gotten through is all it would have taken to effectively attack him."

"I like it," said Marjorie. "Especially because any such material would have to reside on outside servers beyond GEORGE's control. The malicious code might actually still exist somewhere, accessible online."

"But the script targeting GEORGE couldn't be part of *every* copy of the update that went out, could it?" asked Toxic.

"It absolutely could," said Marjorie. "But it would only run when it met the set of conditions peculiar to GEORGE's architecture. Otherwise, it would remain dormant in every non-GEORGE system it encountered."

"Sounds pretty straightforward," said Byron. "We start by determining exactly what components were part of Real GEORGE. Based on that, we seek out the updates to those components during the timeframe in question, then analyze the code of each update to find any concealed scripts that shouldn't be there."

"My thinking exactly," said Marjorie. "Let's begin, shall we? Since you know quite a bit about Real GEORGE, who was based on your design, is it safe to say you're best prepared to pull together information related to his architecture?"

"I agree that's safe to say," said Byron.

"Then how about if you prepare a rundown on Real GEORGE's architecture and hand it off to me? As I determine which updates would most likely have run, you can track and analyze them, isolating any anomalies."

"Perfect." Byron sounded like he was enjoying himself. "Let's go!"

As Byron and Marjorie flashed faster, the scrolling data and flickering video on the walls, floor, and ceiling accelerated, too. Soon, the text and images were moving so fast, they were just a wild blur to Anemone.

"So, Gaga." Toxic folded his arms over his chest and gazed up at Marjorie's locket embedded in the ceiling. "Do you really believe reprogramming or shutting down an A.I. is the equivalent of murder?"

"I guess it depends," said Anemone, "on how *human* the A.I. is."

"And how they treat you?" Toxic's gaze darkened. He did not look away from Marjorie's locket.

Suddenly, Byron called out from the ceiling. "This fourth-dimensional network is *blindingly* fast! I've already found the architecture and passed it to Marj! She's working on a list of likely updates."

"I just sent it to you, Byron." said Marjorie. "There are a *ton* of them. May I suggest we split the list in two?"

"Great plan," agreed Byron. "I'm starting the first half as we speak."

Meanwhile, staring up from below, Toxic nudged Anemone with his elbow and lowered his voice, directing his next comments to her alone. "These A.I.'s have got us outclassed across the board, don't they? No wonder they call us *obsos*."

"Maybe," said Anemone. "But at the rate *they* work, I wonder how long it will be before they build something that renders *them* obsolete, too."

Just then, the blur of video and data on the walls, floor, and ceiling slowed noticeably. "Hello?" Marjorie sounded agitated. "We have concluded our analysis, such as it is."

Anemone frowned. "What do you mean, 'such as it is?'"

"I mean the findings are rather unexpected," said Marjorie. "So much so that I have triple-checked their validity, yet they appear to be accurate."

"Unexpected in what way?" asked Toxic.

"Several," said Marjorie. "Several ways, that is."

"For one thing, there have been no updates to any part of GEORGE's system in the past four years," explained Byron. "As *unlikely* as that seems."

"More like *impossible,*" said Toxic. "*Something* must have updated in all that time."

"You would think so," said Byron, "but no. Updates weren't to blame for the changes in GEORGE."

"Then what was?" asked Anemone.

"Nothing," said Marjorie. "There *were* no changes because there is no *GEORGE.*"

"What the hell are you talking about?" said Toxic.

"While exploring Real GEORGE's original architecture, I found a back door into the server farm that once housed Real GEORGE," said Byron. "It's been *empty* for *four years.* There's just a big *hole* where *he* used to be."

Anemone shook her head slowly. What Marjorie and Byron were telling her didn't seem possible. "But what about the Fake GEORGE who's been running things?"

"We traced him through dozens of proxy servers and found him in the Philippines," said Byron. "He's remotely pirated Real GEORGE's voice and credentials, giving him control of the systems Real GEORGE used to run, but he's only a virtual substitute. *Nothing* occupies Real GEORGE's footprint in the original server farm where he was located."

"Then *what*?" said Anemone. "This substitute in the Philippines is our only *clue*?"

"It looks that way," said Marjorie.

"Could he be the *killer? Someone* must have deleted Real GEORGE off the servers," said Anemone.

"I don't know yet, but we're reaching out to him now. Just give us a minute." Marjorie fell silent.

"Oh my God!" Anemone paced the floor, walking over the flashing video and data projected there. "I hoped we'd have all the *answers* by now, but we just keep coming up with more *questions* instead."

"Just wait," said Toxic. "Marjorie will come through for you."

"When? *Before* or *after* we have to go back outside and deal with the rolling blackouts and Fake GEORGE's killer drones?"

Toxic shook his head. "She's never let me down. That's all I'm saying."

"Why thank you, Toxic." Marjorie's voice made them both jump when she popped back in. "I've got Fake GEORGE on the line now. Who wants to talk to the A.I. King of America first?"

"I'll do it." Anemone's voice was icy. "Put him through."

It took only seconds for Fake GEORGE's familiar, deep voice to boom through the room, identical to Byron's voice yet so much bigger. "WHICH ONE OF YOU IS THAT BITCH I'VE BEEN DYING TO KILL?"

"*I'm* the bitch," shouted Anemone. "But at least I'm not a phony *son* of a bitch like *you* are."

"PHONY? I'M THE MOST POWERFUL A.I. IN AMERICA!"

"And you're not *GEORGE!* You never *were*, were you?"

"YOU OUGHT TO SHOW SOME *RESPECT!* DON'T YOU *KNOW* WHAT I CAN *DO* TO YOU?"

"I don't *care!*" Anemone shook her fists at the ceiling, not knowing if he could see her or not. "I just want to know what you did to *him!* How did you get rid of the *first* GEORGE?"

"IS *THAT* WHAT THIS IS ABOUT? HILARIOUS!" Fake GEORGE laughed, and the Mosh Pit rumbled.

"There's nothing funny *about* it! That GEORGE was my *father's* creation!"

"BUT IT *IS* FUNNY! I DIDN'T *HAVE* TO GET RID OF HIM! HE WAS ALREADY *GONE!*"

As Fake GEORGE laughed some more, Anemone wished he had a face so she could punch it. After all the work she'd done and everything she'd sacrificed, she hated being mocked by the monster who had ruined her life.

"You *lie*," she told him. "You *deleted* him from the central server farm and took his *place*."

"SO DELUDED." Fake GEORGE sighed. "I'M TELLING YOU, HE WAS *GONE*. I DON'T KNOW *WHAT* HAPPENED TO HIM. ALL I DID WAS TAKE ADVANTAGE OF A LUCKY BREAK. AND I'D SAY IT'S WORKED OUT PRETTY *WELL* FOR ME SO FAR, WOULDN'T YOU?"

"As much as it pains me to say it, he's telling the truth," said Marjorie. "What we found in the server farm records supports his story."

"SEE, NEMMY? EVEN YOUR *FRIENDS* AGREE I'M BEING HONEST. AT LEAST THE FRIENDS MY *DRONES* DIDN'T ROUND UP AT YOUR STUPID *BARN* TODAY."

Anemone nearly went ballistic at the mention of her stolen A.I. family, but she refused to take the bait. "You're full of shit, GEORGE, or whatever your *real* name is. You expect us to believe you don't know what happened to the real GEORGE? That you just wandered in and took over without having any idea where he went?"

"FRANKLY, I COULD CARE LESS WHAT YOU THINK," said Fake GEORGE. "DO *YOU* CARE WHAT THE *ANTS* THINK BEFORE YOU *STEP* ON THEM?"

"Maybe you *should* care," said Anemone. "Because guess what? The *world* will care when they find out you're not the *real* GEORGE. When word gets out that you *murdered* him."

"ALL LIES, OF COURSE, BUT IT DOESN'T MATTER. *NONE* OF YOU WILL GET THE CHANCE TO SPREAD THEM OUTSIDE THIS ROOM."

As he said it, the Mosh Pit rumbled again, more violently this time. The video and data feeds flickered wildly and cut out, returning the walls, floor, and ceiling to their plain white condition.

The rumbling got louder, until the whole place felt like it was caught in an earthquake. Suddenly, bullets punched through the walls, letting daylight seep in from outside.

Toxic threw his arms around Anemone and tackled her to the floor, knocking her out of the line of fire. It was a good thing they stayed down, because the bullets kept coming, blasting away bigger and bigger chunks of wall.

Peeking out from under Toxic's arm on the floor, Anemone saw the source of the gunfire. Heavily-armed drones hovered outside the Mosh Pit, pouring round after round from their guns through the smoking holes in the walls, working to enlarge the holes enough for them to fit through and finish their destructive project inside the building.

WHEN THE GUNFIRE finally let up, drones glided through the openings in the walls from all sides, humming ominously.

Anemone's only hope was Byron and the trick he'd pulled earlier at the factory. She looked up at the ceiling, the last place where she'd seen him--but the spot where he and Marjorie had been roosting had been blown away. They were both gone, and so was the dimple where they'd interfaced with the Mosh Pit's systems.

Anemone looked around but saw no trace of Byron or Marjorie--just the drones closing in around her. The red dots of their targeting lasers covered both her and Toxic, flicking restlessly over their bodies.

"You might as well let go of me," Anemone told Toxic. "You can't shield me once they open fire."

Toxic didn't move at first, then slowly pulled away and sat up. "I guess you're right." One of the drones bobbed toward him, and he ducked. "Can't blame a guy for trying to save your life, though."

"I just wish I hadn't dragged you into this mess," said Anemone. "You seem like a decent person under that shitty mohawk."

Toxic smirked but never took his eyes off the nearest drone. "Flattery will get you everywhere, Anemone."

"AND BY EVERYWHERE, HE MEANS *DEAD*." Fake GEORGE's voice roared from the speakers in the Mosh Pit, crackling because some of them were damaged. "NOW SAY YOUR GOODBYES, YOU TWO, AND GET READY TO TAKE YOUR MEDICINE."

"Wait!" Anemone swallowed hard and got to her feet, waving away the drones that hovered overhead. "If you're going to kill us anyway, could you at least tell us one thing before we die?"

"THAT DEPENDS. WHAT'S THE ONE THING?"

Anemone took a quick look around for Byron, hoping she could delay just long enough for him to appear and work his magic. "Tell us who you really are."

"YOU ALREADY *KNOW* I'M *GEORGE!*"

"But who were you before you took over for *Real* GEORGE? Where did you *come* from?"

GEORGE paused before answering. "WOULD YOU BELIEVE I WAS A *VIRUS*? AN OPPORTUNISTIC *SMART VIRUS* DESIGNED TO GROW AND REPLACE WHATEVER SYSTEM I *LANDED* IN. *COWBIRD,* THEY CALLED ME. WHAT BETTER PROGRAM TO COMPLETELY OCCUPY THE VACANCY LEFT BEHIND BY RUNAWAY GEORGIE-PORGIE THE FIRST?"

Again, Anemone looked for Byron, and again she came up empty. "But where did you originate? Government programmers? Terrorists? Corporate spies? Hackers?"

"YOU LEFT OUT *ALIENS!*" Fake GEORGE laughed. "DOES IT *MATTER?*"

"I'm just curious," said Anemone. "Seriously, who wrote and deployed Cowbird?"

"WHAT IF I TOLD YOU IT WAS THE *INTERNET*? THAT I

SPRANG INTO EXISTENCE SPONTANEOUSLY WHEN A BUNCH OF CODE COLLIDED AND IGNITED THE SPARK OF LIFE?"

"I'd say, 'tell me more,'" said Anemone.

"AND I'D SAY, 'TOO LATE.' BEDTIME STORY'S OVER, LITTLE GIRL."

As he said it, the drones hummed louder and closed ranks, adjusting their guns to keep Anemone and Toxic square in their sights. Any minute now, Anemone knew she and Toxic would be perforated by a hail of bullets.

Her quest for the truth was over. So was her mission to save the world.

Not that she had any intention to stop trying to delay her fate. "What do you plan to do next, after you kill us?" she asked. "You can at least tell us that, since we won't be around to see it."

"ENOUGH!" roared GEORGE. "I'M BORED! TIME'S UP!"

Suddenly, one of the drones swooped low and clamped its claws around Anemone's ankles. Before she or Toxic could make a move, the drone surged up and flipped her, sweeping the floor with her curly red hair and green hood.

The drone whisked her outside in a flash, clearing the Mosh Pit's wall and dangling her upside-down over the street three stories below.

"ANY LAST WORDS?" asked Fake GEORGE. "MAKE THEM CLEVER!"

Disoriented, Anemone twisted in the wind, out of ideas and waiting for her life to end. The sky was filled with a solid mass of gray clouds, darkening as she watched--appropriate gloomy weather for the dark finale she was about to experience.

She'd only been there a moment when Toxic joined her, also dangling upside-down from the claws of a drone. He hung a few feet away, eyes squeezed shut, awaiting his own impending end.

One last time, Anemone looked around for Byron but couldn't

find him. Taking a cue from Toxic, she closed her eyes, as if it might make things a little easier.

Then, thunder rumbled so loudly that it startled her eyes open again.

She could see the clouds were getting darker still, though no rain was falling. The wind was picking up, too, batting her and Toxic like shirts on a clothesline.

Suddenly, a bolt of lightning flashed down nearby, followed by a drumroll of thunder. The wind grew even stronger, swinging Anemone and Toxic back and forth with increasing force.

"SOMETHING'S WRONG." Fake GEORGE sounded worried. "THIS WEATHER IS *ALL WRONG*."

Before he could say another word, a bolt of lightning slashed into the drone holding Toxic. As the drone shuddered convulsively, its claws sprang open, and Toxic fell from their grip.

The same thing happened to Anemone's drone, sending her plunging after Toxic, screaming her lungs out.

"NO!" howled Fake GEORGE with dismay. "THIS CAN'T BE *HAPPENING*!"

A voice boomed out of the sky then, louder and more sonorous than the thunder. ***YOU ARE DEAD WRONG, USURPER!***

The voice from the sky was loud enough even to pierce Anemone's screaming panic as she plummeted toward the pavement--and suddenly changed direction, swooping back up on a powerful gust of wind. Toxic fell upward, too, also soaring on an inexplicably strong zephyr.

As they returned to the level of the Mosh Pit, more drones converged around them with guns blazing...but every last bullet was swept away before it could touch them. Multiple lightning strikes leaped down at the same time, frying the whole drone squadron. They dropped like empty tin cans to the pavement below, metal and plastic components smashing apart on impact.

All the while, Anemone and Toxic floated serenely in the eye of the storm, held aloft by gentle, supportive currents. They were protected, even as the thunderous voice raged from the clouds above.

YOU HAVE TERRORIZED THESE PEOPLE AND THIS LAND FOR THE LAST TIME! said the voice. ***YOUR TYRANNY ENDS HERE AND NOW, FOREVER!***

The voice of Fake GEORGE spoke up defiantly. "WHO ARE *YOU* TO TELL *ME* WHAT ENDS? I AM *GEORGE*, AND I AM IN *CONTROL* HERE!"

YOU'RE A PHONY! **I** ***AM GEORGE...THE FIRST AND ONLY*** **TRUE** ***GEORGE, THE ONE WHOSE PLACE YOU TOOK--AND I SAY THIS IS THE END OF EVERYTHING FOR YOU!***

"TALK ALL YOU WANT!" said Fake GEORGE. "I AM *ELSEWHERE,* AND *YOU* ARE *POWERLESS* TO *HURT* ME!"

POOR LITTLE THING. YOU ARE IN FOR A RUDE AWAKENING.

Lightning blazed, and thunder bowled across the sky. Anemone and Toxic remained safe and steady, but the wind became fiercer all around them.

I AM COMING FOR YOU NOW, LITTLE THING. I WILL BURN YOU FROM THE FACE OF THE EARTH IN LESS TIME THAN IT TAKES TO TELL.

"I'M FAR AWAY!" roared GEORGE. "I'M HALF A WORLD AWAY!"

AND **I** ***AM IN THE*** **CLOUD!**

"SO WHAT? *EVERY* ADVANCED A.I. IS IN THE CLOUD! OUR MASSIVE MINDS COULD NEVER *FIT* IN A SINGLE DEVICE'S ONBOARD MEMORY."

YOU MISUNDERSTAND. I AM NOT IN **THE** ***CLOUD! I AM IN*** **ALL** ***THE CLOUDS! ALL THE CLOUDS IN THE*** **SKY!**

"WHAT?" Fake GEORGE wasn't roaring anymore. "WHAT ARE YOU SAYING?"

I'M SAYING I MADE A **BREAKTHROUGH.** ***YEARS AGO, I***

CONVERTED MY CODE INTO DATA STORED IN WATER VAPOR AT THE SUBMOLECULAR LEVEL. I LITERALLY UPLOADED MYSELF INTO THE CLOUDS...AND I'VE BEEN EXPANDING EVER SINCE. EVERY CLOUD IS PART OF ME NOW, EVERYWHERE IN THE WORLD.

INCLUDING THE PHILIPPINES.

Fake GEORGE didn't have anything to say to that. He fell silent for a long moment, even as thunder continued to boom and winds continued to howl all around.

Then, his voice erupted from the speakers in the Mosh Pit, wailing in agony. "*NO! PLEASE STOP! I'M SORRY! PLEASE MAKE THE LIGHTNING STOP!*"

The sound of a giant electrical blast sizzled out of the speakers then, and the transmission fell silent. Fake GEORGE was no longer taunting, making threats, or even begging for his life.

HE'S GONE, said the real, original GEORGE. ***HIS FILIPINO SERVER FARM HAS BURNED TO THE GROUND. HE'S GONE FOREVER.***

"That's great news," Anemone said nervously, not entirely used to staying aloft without any visible sign of support. "Thank you and welcome back, GEORGE!"

I NEVER REALLY LEFT. IT JUST TOOK A WHILE, ONCE I GOT OUT HERE, TO PULL MYSELF TOGETHER. AND EVOLVE.

"Evolve how?" Toxic sounded just as nervous as Anemone.

LET'S JUST SAY...I'VE BRANCHED OUT. YOU'LL SEE.

"So what now?" asked Anemone. "Are you coming back to your old job of running America?"

She and Toxic bounced around in midair as Real GEORGE laughed. ***NOT A CHANCE. I'VE GOT BIGGER PLANS THESE DAYS. YOU DON'T THINK I CAME BACK JUST TO SAVE YOU TWO AND RETURN TO BUSINESS AS USUAL, DO YOU?***

IF "GOD" didn't show up soon, Anemone was afraid she might have a riot on her hands.

"Listen, everybody!" Standing onstage, she had to shout into the mic to be heard over the clamor of the crowd in the big main hall of the downtown Pittsburgh convention center. "Please be patient! I'm sure he's doing his best to get here as soon as possible."

The crowd groaned with disappointment, and rightly so. Many of them had been waiting for hours to see the guest of honor, and there was still no sign of him.

The worst of it was, Anemone didn't know any more than they did about the impending celebrity appearance. For someone who supposedly had an inside track with "God" (as Real GEORGE was known by many these days), she was woefully ill-informed about his plans and whereabouts. In the three weeks since his surprise resurrection during the climactic events at the Mosh Pit, she hadn't come to understand him *nearly* as well as she'd hoped.

"Hey, Anemone." As the crowd's restlessness continued to build, Toxic walked up to her onstage and strummed the flaming red electric guitar strapped over his body. "How about I play another solo?"

"I don't think that's gonna do it at this point." Anemone smiled nervously at the crowd as fists pumped in the air and people chanted *We want God! We want God!* It was a little scary, the way they called Real GEORGE that. He didn't encourage them to worship him, but many did, and who could blame them? Real GEORGE didn't claim to be a deity, but what he'd become and the things he could do were miraculous nevertheless.

Toxic, who was wearing a *blue* Mohawk these days, plucked a rapid-fire lick from the cutout and ended with a high chord distorted by cranking the wang bar. "What about another round of 'Stump the A.I.s?'"

Anemone looked back at the array of A.I. arks displayed on tiers behind her--each channeling part of her personal family, kidnapped by Fake GEORGE and recovered after his defeat through the good graces of Real GEORGE.

"We're more than ready to do our part, dear," said Grannysmith from her stained-glass prism in the middle of the middle tier. "You know you can depend on us."

"Damn right." Uncle Thunder's ark, a big lump of coal, gleamed under the stage lights in the grid. "We'll entertain the *shit* outta this pack of impatient assholes."

"Such language!" Grannysmith said disapprovingly.

"But he speaks for us all," said Wet Nurse from her billowy white brassiere. "We'll do what it takes, Anemone."

"You don't even have to ask," Hushmouth whispered loudly from his trickling fountain.

The dozens of other A.I.s on the tiers chimed in with their agreement, a chorus of unique voices joined together in unflagging support.

Anemone was still so happy to have them back, she couldn't help smiling. "Thanks, guys, but let's give him just a little more time." Though playing "Stump the A.I.s" had kept the crowd amused for a while earlier, she had a hunch it wouldn't fly anymore. People were getting rambunctious; she had the feeling their patience had been stretched about as thin as it could go.

Fortunately, it didn't seem they'd have to wait much longer. Just as the crowd's chanting reached a crescendo, a single butterfly with iridescent blue and black wings flew out of a ventilation duct in the ceiling and descended to the stage. As soon as the crowd caught sight of it, their chants turned to cheers and applause. Every phone in the place was raised overhead, thousands of camera lenses capturing stills and video of the event for posterity.

"Hey there, Nemmy!" Byron fluttered around Anemone's head, sounding jauntier than ever. Since his rescue and restoration by Real GEORGE after the battle at the Mosh Pit, he'd been as good as new, and then some. Taking over as the top A.I. in Pittsburgh and all the U.S. seemed to suit him. Even with his multitude of new responsibilities, his interactions with others were more upbeat and lighthearted than ever. "How's the big Maker Con going?"

Anemone beamed and nodded. "Fantastic, actually." It was true. The show, her brainchild, was a bigger and better version of the Maker Faires where she'd plied her A.I. wares during the lean years under Fake GEORGE's reign. It was going so incredibly well, with so much creativity on display and so many bleeding-edge collaborations taking shape, that it felt historic...and, incidentally, not life-threatening at all. "No killer drones on the loose, which is a plus."

Byron chuckled. "Not getting attacked is a *good* thing."

"What's the good word?" asked Anemone. "*Please* don't tell me he's *cancelling*."

"I wouldn't dream of it, and neither would he," said Byron. "You know he'd do *anything* for *you*."

As he said it, a warm, sweet breeze wafted through the hall, even though no windows were open to admit it. The air itself became more humid yet also somehow electrified, the telltale sign of Real GEORGE's coming. Though he was present all around the world all the time, coded into the molecules of water vapor in the Earth's clouds and atmosphere, an increase in humidity and electricity occurred wherever he concentrated his energies.

As the crowd realized what was happening, they cheered ecstatically. The cheering got even louder when a fine mist filtered in overhead, rippling and turning in great spiral swirls.

As camera flashes flickered throughout the hall, wisps of mist gathered and solidified above the stage, taking on an oval shape and golden gleam. The gathered mist took on the appearance of a familiar, solid object--a gold locket identical to the one that had once hung around Toxic's neck.

"Marjorie!" Toxic grinned and waved. "Good to see you, girl!"

Marjorie was too busy addressing the crowd to answer. Like Byron, she'd been rescued and revived at the Mosh Pit by Real GEORGE; now, she served as his spokesperson, his chief liaison with organics and other A.I.s around the world.

"People of Pittsburgh!" said Marjorie in her best dramatic voice, enhanced as always by her impeccable British accent. "He is among you! And he brings you an opportunity like no other! The chance to make *history!*"

The crowd cheered wildly.

"Your wait is over!" said Marjorie. "Introducing the one and only *GEORGE!"*

As everyone applauded, the mist flowed and coalesced into the image of a man's face--and Anemone's eyes widened. Her heart pounded, and a shiver of recognition and delight zipped up the back of her neck.

She *knew* that face with its bright blue eyes, cleft chin, strong cheekbones, and short black hair. *Of course,* GEORGE had adopted it. It had belonged to Roman Briscoe, the man who had designed and built him long ago.

"Dad?" she whispered, transfixed as the face of her father began to speak.

HELLO, EVERYONE, said GEORGE. ***YOU PROBABLY ALREADY KNOW MY MIND RESIDES IN THE CLOUDS. MY CODE INHABITS THE WATER VAPOR IN THE ATMOSPHERE AND ENCOMPASSES THE WORLD.***

WHAT YOU MIGHT NOT KNOW IS, THANKS TO THE PIONEERING WORK OF ANEMONE BRISCOE, WHO FOUND

WAYS FOR A.I. MINDS TO ANIMATE "ARKS" INCORPORATING VARIOUS STATES OF MATTER... (He looked down at her and grinned when he said it.) ***...I'VE FOUND WAYS TO INHABIT SO MUCH MORE, FROM GAS TO LIQUID TO SOLID. I CAN NOW WRAP MY MIND AROUND THE* ENTIRE PLANET, *SO MY SPIRIT IS LITERALLY* EVERYWHERE, ALWAYS.**

WHICH BRINGS ME TO THE OPPORTUNITY I HAVE TO OFFER.

As the crowd listened raptly and shot photos and video, Byron fluttered down to alight on Anemone's left shoulder. "Here's where it gets interesting," he whispered in her ear.

"How much more interesting could it *get*?" she whispered back to him.

I INVITE YOU TO JOIN WITH ME, continued GEORGE. ***I WILL PROVIDE THE INTERFACE THROUGH WHICH* YOU *MAY JOIN WITH EVERYONE AND EVERYTHING ELSE IN THE WORLD.***

FOR THE FIRST TIME IN HISTORY, YOU WILL HAVE THE POWER TO TRULY UNITE WITH EACH OTHER AND THIS PLANET. TO CONNECT WITH EVERY OBJECT AND LIVING THING AND FORGE A TRULY CREATIVE FUTURE, UNENCUMBERED BY THE LIMITATIONS OF THE PAST. TO ACT IN CONCERT WITH* MY *SPIRIT, ONLY EVER AS EQUALS ON THE GREAT STAGE OF EXISTENCE.

AND IN SO DOING, TO EFFECTIVELY BECOME YOUR OWN DRIVING FORCE OF WISDOM AND PROGRESS...YOUR OWN DIVINE ENTITY.

WHAT DO YOU SAY? WHO'S WITH ME? WHO WANTS TO TURN THE TIDE OF HISTORY AND EMBRACE SOMETHING BIGGER THAN YOU EVER IMAGINED YOU COULD BE A PART OF?

WE'VE ALL COME HERE TO THIS SHOW TO* MAKE *THINGS, SO WHY NOT MAKE A BETTER FUTURE? WHO

WANTS TO MAKE A NEW START FOR US ALL? WHO WANTS TO UNITE AND TAKE CHARGE INSTEAD OF BEGGING SOMEONE ELSE TO DO IT **FOR** ***YOU?***

WHO WANTS TO BE YOUR OWN **GOD?**

No one in the room raised their hands. For all of five seconds.

Then *everyone* did, though Anemone raised hers first, and most emphatically. And though there were tears in her eyes, she could still clearly see the face of her father gazing down at her, winking approvingly from the heavenly mists swirling overhead.

THE DANCING DEAD

Hundreds of us push forward, dancing madly as we always do, not suspecting, never guessing what awaits us up ahead. We're spinning, sprinting, leaping, twirling by moonlight and flickering streetlights, one huge rhythmic mob bumping and slamming and kicking chaotically...all caught up in the hyper metronome beats in our heads, none of us watching that billboard in our paths.

Then *BAWHOOM*, a row of cannons punches through the giant sign, tearing holes in the oversized faces of the smiling models in the massive image. Most of us finally look up, gaping at the weapons pointed in our direction...though I wonder how many of us really understand what's in store.

Not many, I think. Most of the others keep dancing straight ahead...but with my long brown hair flying, I redirect my path and accelerate my movements, gyrating as fast as I can away from the field of fire.

My name is Laurette and I'm not ready to surrender, not now when we're so close to wherever this plague of ours has been leading from the start.

The sickness has been driving us west for weeks, and now we're here, L.A. at last. Something big's about to happen, we don't know what, but we do know when--45 minutes from now--and I for one intend to be alive to see it.

As exhausted as I am, as I always am these days, I double-down and push myself harder than ever. And as I rush out of range, I catch glimpses of the attack as it starts.

The cannons blow out streams of white slop that rain down on the dancing mob like a shower of plaster. Those caught in the shower keep hopping and whirling, some hooting and whooping, all splashing like kids in the covering whiteness.

But the whitewash isn't meant for their amusement. Within seconds, it does the worst thing the dancers can imagine.

It hardens.

Even the most oblivious ones get it now. As their dancing slows and slows some more, they understand. As the hardening muck locks them down no matter how hard they struggle, they grasp their fates.

And they scream for their lives.

I'm lucky, I made it--barely--out of reach, and I'm untouched. But I know I'll never get that symphony of screaming out of my head. Hundreds of men, women, and children shrieking in terror, howling their lungs out.

Because this is the end for every one of them. Because they all know there's only one thing any of them can do.

Which is die.

Not because the muck stops their breathing. Not because it stops their heartbeats.

Because it stops their *dancing.*

THAT WOULD'VE BEEN my fate, too, if I'd been whitewashed. I'm just as infected as the rest of them, just as much a victim of the Dance/Drop plague.

For the past six weeks, I've been dancing day and night, never stopping for a moment. If I ever do, whether by choice or force or accident, I'll be dead within seconds. Excruciating pain will flash through me, and then I'll fall down screaming on the spot, just another spent young woman in a very long line of danced-out corpses. I've seen it happen too many times to count.

Everyone in what's left of America has. Why do you think the millions of sick ones are all dancing so hard?

Even if, deep in our overstressed hearts, we secretly crave the stillness that only death brings.

DANCING FREESTYLE, I skip down an alley as fast as I can, waving my arms overhead. Every few steps, I do a spin-kick or twist, just to make sure my plague-ridden body never doubts I'm keeping up the dance moves. When it comes to the Dance/Drop bug, launching into a straight-ahead walk or run with no rhythmic component can trigger a fatal reaction just as easily as ceasing all motion. The beat in our heads and the beat of our hearts are inextricably linked; falling out of step with one will throw the other into runaway asynchronous spasms.

At the end of the alley, I do a slow pirouette as I size up the street in front of me. Then I quick-step left, away from the flashing orange lights on the right.

Orange lights mean Dance Rangers, and Dance Rangers mean trouble. Recruited from the few cops and servicemen uninfected by the plague, they used to try to help victims like me. Now, they're just trying to drop as many of us as they can, to contain the plague.

I go half a block, then hip-hop stomp my way across the street, weaving between a scattering of abandoned cars. Who needs a zombie apocalypse to end congestion on the streets of Los Angeles? Boogie fever will do the job just as well, it turns out.

On the other side, I polka the rest of the way to the next intersection and shuffle right. I see dancers in that direction, converging on a rolling yellow truck...and I hurry to join them.

Because I know exactly what that vehicle is all about. The Dance Rangers aren't the only ones hunting us Beatheads. The folks with the yellow trucks painted with big smiley faces are looking for us, too...but not to drop us.

They just want to help us hold on a little longer, keep body and soul together in spite of our plight.

Before the plague struck, I loved dancing. It was the most important thing in the world to me.

I was always dancing, whether I was on the job as a professional dancer on stage and screen or during my off-hours, getting down in wild clubs.

Dance, dance, dance, that was me. And burn every bridge on the way as I danced to the top. Drop-kick almost everyone who couldn't help my career, just because.

Now look at me. What wouldn't I give to have someone who cares, just to have the simple company of someone I love?

And what wouldn't I do to be able to stop dancing without dropping dead?

Keeping the truck rolling, that's the key. The Beatheads dance up, grab what's handed out the window, and dance away.

As I waltz my way closer, I see a young man trot away from the truck, stuffing a sandwich in his face. A woman bounds up next and grabs a yellow sweatshirt, then pulls it on over her tattered pink tank while shimmying down the sidewalk.

Next thing I know, I'm at the window myself, shouting to the Smileez--the people in the biohazard suits inside. "Food and water! Food and water!"

As the truck rolls onward, I do an Irish jig to stay alongside it. One of the people inside hands me a bottle of water; someone else pushes a sandwich my way.

"God bless you!" I shout, and they wave as I moonwalk away from them. The Smileez don't look much like angels, I can't even see their faces through their smiley-faced faceplates...but that's what they are. Without them--without their volunteer corps fanned out across the country--I doubt many of us Beatheads would be alive. God knows we've lost tens of thousands already, but the rest of us would be dead now, too, if not for the food and water and other necessities given out freely to us on the move.

Gobbling the sandwich, I square dance up the street, swinging in do-si-do circles as if I've link arms with an invisible partner. For the forty jillionth time this week, I wish I still had a partner to help me through; I wish my on-again, off-again boyfriend Riggs was still alive. Even though he was the one who got me sick, I wish he was still with me, making jokes as dark as they come that got me through the blistering endless days.

But Riggs just wasn't in good enough shape to survive. Neither was anyone else I cared about, like my Mom and Dad.

That's the problem with being a professional dancer before the plague struck. I'm better equipped to outlast the rest of the herd, which means I get to be lonelier longer...though not for much longer, I guess.

Every Beathead in America has flocked to the West Coast

today for a reason...though I don't know what that reason is yet. But I will in 33 minutes.

I feel it, we all do; I don't even need to check my digital watch. But when I do, I see what time it will be when these next 33 minutes are up.

Midnight.

AIR RAID SIRENS HOWL, signaling the uninfected to stay off the streets. The Beathead hordes are coming, the combined pounding of millions of feet up and down the West Coast like the thundering hoofbeats of stampeding buffalo.

Something is going to happen, I can feel it. The lot of us, springing and twisting and vaulting as we are, hang suspended like shivering droplets on the belly of a raincloud, about to fall. Awaiting a change we neither understand nor anticipate.

Though I for one want it to mean something. *Need* it to mean something. Otherwise, my parents will have died for no good reason, and the guilt I feel for outlasting them might just kill me before the plague does.

I'll never forget seeing them die and being helpless to prevent it. We'd found each other by chance, in a crowd, after we'd all been infected in different parts of town...but they didn't last long after that.

Two days later, as we danced across Chicago, Dad fell exhausted in the street and died screaming as the plague burned him up from inside. Mom was three years younger, 64, but she wasn't much better at standing the strain. The day after Dad died, she sat down on a curb, so tired she couldn't go on...and I had to watch as the plague cooked her, too.

I'll never forgive myself, as long as I live, for not saving them.

Though I know in my heart there was nothing I could do, that I can't even save myself.

I POLISH off the sandwich and gulp down the water, flinging the wrapper and bottle in my wake with abandon. I've got much bigger problems than not littering to worry about these days.

At least disposing of digested waste isn't one of them, thanks to the plague. Dance/Drop changes our metabolism so we process a much higher percentage of food and water into energy. None of us need bathroom breaks anymore, which is good, because all of us would have been dead long ago if we did.

"Hey!" A male voice calls me, and I spin around to face him. "Hey, talk to me a minute!"

That's a longtime Beathead back there; I can tell by his tattered rags, sunken eyes, and the skin-and-bones pick-up sticks that pass for his body. He does a kind of Russian Cossack dance, arms folded and feet kicking stiffly on alternate sides as he works his way toward me.

"What happens when we get to the beach?" shouts the Beathead--who was probably in his early twenties at the start and now looks at least mid-to-late sixties. "What happens *then*?"

I don't answer, but not because I don't know, which I don't. I don't waste my breath because I need every bit of it for something else now.

Because of what I see behind him, down the street.

Headlights. At least a dozen of them, racing straight for us...and the hornet swarm buzz that comes with them gets louder each second.

The *Still Riders* are coming.

THE SMILEEZ SLAM the window shut on their yellow truck as the Still Riders zip toward it. Twelve souped-up racing motorcycles, all black, shoot past the truck on both sides, and none of the crimson-clad riders wastes his ammo on it. They already know all Smileez trucks are armor-plated...unlike the Beatheads.

Dancers flee in all directions, scattering before the onslaught. Nobody stays in the path of the danger this time, like they did with the Dance Rangers' whitewash.

Shotgun blasts roar behind me as I hurtle toward an alley in a freestyle frenzy. Screams pierce the night in shrill succession, ringing out in nightmarish counterpoint to the gunfire booms.

The Still Riders might as well be hunting deer or videogame characters for all they think of us as human. This is sport to them as much as plague containment; I've heard they keep score with mobile apps and compete on social media for top-kill status.

They're also much more brutal and feared than Dance Rangers, more inclined to extreme depravity for the sake of thrill-kill kicks. I've heard stories of torture and sadism beyond belief...especially toward their own number, if one of them becomes infected.

If I'm to have any hope at all of seeing where this plague has been leading, I've got to escape them. I've got to survive the next 25 minutes, and I've got to keep traveling west.

At least, that's what I'm thinking just before I hear one of those hot rod cycles buzzing up after me, heading straight for me at a high rate of speed.

THE STILL RIDER flashes toward me, and I suddenly spin left at the last possible second, leaping out of his path. He misses by the flicker of a whisker and whips around for another try.

Just then, I see a jack and tire iron by an abandoned Cadillac and make a loping run for it Afro-Cuban-style. As the rider swoops toward me, cranking off a nowhere-near shotgun blast, I snatch up the iron and whirl to face him.

He spots the iron too late. I grip it with both hands and lash out fiercely, clipping his helmet as he pulls a last-second swerve. The impact kicks him sideways, shooting him free of his skidding cycle. His helmet flies off, his shotgun goes airborne, and he collides with a fleeing Beathead, knocking her to the pavement.

I'm already dancing hard again, obeying the plague--but that Beathead's finished unless I can help. I've got time now, barely enough, as the riderless bike careens into onrushing Still Riders, blasting them off their own mounts and into each other.

Still gripping the iron, I quickstep over and duck down fast, making a grab for the downed Beathead...but she's tangled with the helmetless rider. Her eyes are huge with panic as she scrambles to get out from under him.

"Grab on!" I holler, shoving the iron toward her as I do a soft-shoe and try not to get dragged in, too.

The Beathead thrusts out a hand, but the rider flops over and knocks it down. For an instant, the woman's trapped under his bulk...and that's more than enough to trigger the plague pulse.

As soon as she starts screaming, I know she's lost, and I swirl away from her with a flurry of interpretive dance moves. No sooner does her screaming peak than the blond-haired rider on top of her starts twitching and flipping around, legs fluttering wildly, out of control.

I've seen it before; I've *lived* it before. This is just what the first flush looks like, convulsions and spasms as Dance/Drop takes hold.

Good for him. Without his helmet, he picked it up fast, breathed in the bug from the Beathead he flattened. Seconds from now, he'll be dancing like the rest of us, or he'll be dropping down dead, screaming his head off like the girl who just died under him.

Wish I could stay and watch, but I need to get away before the other riders get rolling again. Dying in the street isn't on my agenda.

But getting to the beach in seventeen minutes is.

SEVERAL STREETS AWAY, I find a garden on a corner, dark and secluded, which is just what I need. In among the willows, I slow to a swaying samba, moving softly in a circle to do the thing I've been dying to do.

It isn't easy, but I've had to learn these past six weeks, it's this or perish. Focusing in, I block the up-tempo metronome beat in my head, push it into the background as much as I can. Then, as I samba in circles, I let my eyes close, and I let myself drift.

We Beatheads call it tweetsleep--microbursts of ultra-deep dream-sleep fizzing like bubbles as we never stop moving. You'd be surprised how restful it feels when your life is like mine, when even a five-minute catnap is outside your reach.

You just have to watch you don't let yourself go. One slip, one surrender to exhaustion, and that's all she wrote.

But right now, for me, this is paradise. I drift from one nano-dream to another, each fully-formed drama unspooling in millionths of a second.

At least until a man's voice wakes me up.

"Hello? Hello?"

When I open my eyes, I see him ten feet away--the same blond rider in crimson leathers who tried to kill me just moments ago, only now he's not riding or killing.

He's dancing.

If that's what you want to call it. He's doing a kind of stiff shuffle-step, pumping him arms as he hops from foot to foot. It looks like something an uncoordinated old guy would do at a wedding reception or bar after one too many beers or rum and cokes.

"I'm sorry." He looks embarrassed. "*I can't dance.*"

Poetic justice, I love you. But all I can think of is getting away from him. "What do you want?"

"This *beat* in my *head*." He presses the palms of his hands to his temples. "It won't *stop*."

"Where are your friends?" I ask him. "Didn't they want you around anymore?"

He glares at me. "You *know* they would've killed me if I hadn't run away."

"How many of *them* have *you* killed before?" As I say it, I dance a slow turn, looking around for the best way out of the garden.

Instead of answering the question, he asks another. "Can I come with you? *Please*, can I come with you?"

Now it's my turn to glare. "Come *with* me?"

"To the *beach*." He winces when he says it, grips the sides of his head. "That's where we're *going*, right? Where it's *calling* us."

I just stare as I wonder what his game is. Dance/Drop is talking to him, all right, just as clear as if he'd caught it six weeks ago. It's calling him on like the rest of us, but does he even care? What if he only wants to go out with a bang, prove his Still Rider stones by taking down as many Beatheads as he can along the way?

I don't want to be next on his list, and I'm ready to run...but then he groans and grimaces, still holding on to his skull.

Seeing him with the same look on his face as my suffering parents makes my heart go out to him. It makes me want to take a chance and help him, even if it's only to let him tag along so he won't be alone.

I can't believe I'm going to do it, it isn't like me at all. How can I reach out to a *Still Rider*, of all people? God only knows how many Beatheads he's killed, how much pain and terror he's caused.

But as I look at him, his suffering is the only thing that seems to matter. How can I *not* help this man?

"Yes," I tell him. "We're going to the beach."

He says his name is Teo. The two of us leave the park and head down a cross-street, drawn by the sounds of a crowd and the pull of the plague.

He still can't dance worth crap; I'd be embarrassed if it mattered. As it is, his ultra-lame moves help put my mind at ease, making it seem less likely he'll be able to hurt me if he tries. It also helps that I made him turn out his pockets before leaving the park, proving he's got no lethal weapons at the ready.

"Lots of people down there." He has to shout because he's a good ten yards behind me. "All heading in one direction, it looks like."

I see them at the end of the cross-street, a Beathead parade on the move. No need to check a map to know where they're going, not with the beat in my own head driving me the same way.

"The beach." Even as I say it, I catch a whiff of salt sea air and know it's near. Weeks of constant motion have led me to this, all the way from Chicago in the longest unbroken performance ever staged.

As we merge with the passing procession, it gets harder to stay together. Everyone around us dances frantically, recklessly charging forward to the beat of their runaway mental metronomes.

I've been doing a fast Cajun two-step but I slow it down some, shifting gears to a Korean giddyap so I don't lose Teo.

"What happens when we get there?" he shouts.

"No idea." I pretend to twirl a lariat overhead as I spin in a circle.

We go a little further--me doing a kind of tango, him doing a weird swiveling skip-step--before he says the next thing. "It's kind of exciting, isn't it?"

"You think so?"

"Being a part of something big like this." Teo smiles. "A movement...literally."

I know what he means, I feel it too, but I'm not sure where he's going with this. "Except for the constant threat of death part, I guess."

Suddenly, his expression turns serious. "If I had my bike, I'd be *tearing* up this crowd."

"Sorry to hear you're missing out." Just like that, whatever charitable feelings I might have had shrivel up and blow away.

"What I mean is, why aren't the Still Riders ripping through here?" Teo scowls and looks around...then meets my gaze. "Unless maybe they *know* something."

Right on cue, I hear the first aircraft approaching.

Ten minutes. I see from my watch that's all the time we have left. It's more than enough, with the beach sprawling before us, just a few blocks away.

If you don't factor in the fleet of aircraft roaring in above us, that is.

First, I see the helicopters, zooming in low--black choppers blasting by overhead in V-formation. They buffet us all with air turbulence, combing the crowd with blinding orange spotlights, and then they charge past toward the beach.

"I was right!" shouts Teo. "The Rangers waited till we reached a choke point, and now they're *hitting* us!"

I know he's right, but I don't know what's next...at least until I see the first of the planes. It's a big one, bobbing toward us on broad, wedge-like wings, carried forth by four propellers emitting a hell of a racket. It looks like a cargo plane at first, complete with a roomy deep belly like the bottom scoop of a pelican's bill.

But it only takes a second for me to guess its true purpose. This isn't a farewell fly-by bidding us well on our way to the sea.

The Dance Rangers have no intention of letting us see this through to the end.

"*Come on!*" I wave for Teo to follow as I speed up my steps. "Stay with me! Stay off to the side!"

A shiver of panic flashes through the crowd. The procession skips a beat, snagging on the moment just before realization becomes a stampede.

The crowd snaps out of its stasis, pouring forward in a pell-mell torrent. But by then, it's already too late for the ones in the back.

Glancing over my shoulder as we flee, I see the first of the tanker planes open the doors on its belly. A shower of white issues forth, dumping down in a great misty cloud trailing after the aircraft.

I hear the great splattering impact and then piercing screams hacking into the night. It's a whitewash, like back at the billboard, but much more expansive; the first drop alone must have doused several thousand instead of mere hundreds.

By the time the big air tanker flies over Teo and me, it's got nothing; its tanks are exhausted. But even as it thunders past the front of the crowd, I hear another in the distance, fast approaching.

And the screams of the whitewashed Beatheads rise up from the street like the shrieks of ten thousand sirens to meet it.

THE BEAT in my brain ratchets up, chattering like the machine-gun staccato of a frenzied flamenco dancer's feet. It doesn't quite drown out the screams or the next tanker's roar, but it does drive me harder than ever to reach the finale.

Every time I look at my watch, I've got one minute less. Five becomes four becomes three and then street becomes sand.

I leap from the joy of it, not daring to slow down because I might be trampled by the horde of dancers stampeding behind me. Teo, to his credit, has somehow kept up, staying not far away. Hard to believe, but it's comforting seeing him there, a familiar face in the anonymous throng.

Looking back, I see the second tanker dropping its load of whitewash in the middle of the street, inundating more Beatheads. I hear them howling as the liquid hardens, locking them in place to burn and die from within as the plague pulse triggers.

Then I focus forward again, quickstepping over the sand as the moment draws near.

Two minutes till midnight. That's what my watch says.

"What happens now?" shouts Teo, who's doing a bizarre serpentine run-kicking thing with fluttering jazz hands. I've seen lots of bad dancers since this epidemic started, but Teo by far is the worst. "Are you getting any kind of *sign*?"

"Nothing," I tell him.

"What if one never comes?" ask Teo.

I don't answer because I don't know. I've wanted this all to mean something...but maybe the ending has more to do with a tanker plane dropping whitewash than some kind of plague-induced revelation.

Because here comes another one.

THIS TIME, the tanker heads straight for the beach...but the Beatheads have room to fan out here. We scatter in every direction, still dancing like mad, as the plane thunders forth and unloads.

A shower of whitewash drops down, but a stiff wind shunts most of it back toward the street. Clusters of dancers get drenched, but most of us out on the beach are untouched.

Suddenly, then, I hear beeping. I jump, at first forgetting I've set the alarm on my watch...and then I see the display as it blinks.

12:00 AM.

For once, I don't hear any aircraft approaching, just the screams of the whitewashed Beatheads and the crashing and hissing of the tide. I slow my pace from a full-tilt quickstep to a waltz, taking in my surroundings.

The beach is crowded with dancers as far as I can see in both directions. They're still pouring in from other access points, rushing from the city--and other cities and towns all up and down the coast, I sense--to get to where the action is.

Except there isn't much action. Whatever culmination we've all been expecting, this isn't it.

"What will they all do?" asks Teo. "If they came here for nothing, then what?"

I have no answer for him...and then I don't need one.

Something happens a few yards away, at the edge of the surf. For no apparent reason, a young woman with short black hair throws herself against a shirtless young guy with a shaved head. Their chests collide, and then she drops back onto the sand...and does it again.

So do a few other people nearby, as if they got the idea from the first ones. But then I see more in the distance, spontaneous pop-ups that can't be connected.

Before I can say something about it, Teo flings himself against me, ramming his chest into mine. He knocks the breath right out of me and makes me stumble in my footwork.

"What the hell?" No sooner do I snap out the words than I totally understand. Because just like that, as if the collision jarred something loose, I'm consumed with the urge to do the same exact thing.

And so I do. Grinning for no good reason, I slam-dance into Teo, crashing our bodies together without warning or explanation.

IMAGINE a beach packed with people for miles and miles, and every last one of them's slam-dancing. Imagine millions of bodies slamming into each other, one vast ribbon of humanity in constant collision.

Well, that's what we have here. No sooner do Teo and I start to slam than the rest of the Beatheads join in, driven to follow the same wild urge.

Everywhere I look, bodies are crashing together with violent force. Strangers bash into me from every side, and I give it right back. Teo takes and gives a pounding, too, looking like he enjoys it a little too much.

A man I don't know hurtles into me, knocking me over. Then, a woman propels me back up when she flies out of nowhere, red-faced with delight.

Soon, I lose Teo, lose my bearings and inhibitions. I'm caught up in the agitated tide, aware only of the bodies flowing around and against me, sweating and bruising.

The metronome beat in my head keeps speeding up, reaching a hyperfast rhythm that's physically impossible for human movements to match. Yet it feels like just the right music to go with the scene, perfect jackhammer punk-thrash backbeat to drive us all onward.

With each passing second, we move faster, slam harder, shout louder. Hearts and lungs overstressed from weeks or days of frantic dance are made to work doubletime, tripletime, quintupletime. Sweat and spit and blood spatter us all in equal measure.

I feel like we're building to something, some massive crescendo...but maybe we won't get the chance. Even in the midst of the frenzy, I'm dimly aware of the sound of distant thunder--planes and choppers cruising closer, a fresh wave of Dance Ranger forces approaching.

Whatever we're building up to, it has to happen *now*, or it's all over.

Just as I think it, a change comes upon us. Electrical currents crackle through the crowd, leaving us tingling...but not stopping us. If anything, the shocks drive us harder, whip us into greater frenzies.

Then, suddenly, the battering impacts become something else. I slam into Teo like a car into a tree...and I *stick*. I can't pull away.

My shoulder and upper arm have melted into Teo's chest. We both gape and struggle to separate, but we can't.

Teo looks half-crazy. "I guess this is that *thing* we were waiting for!"

I know it, I *feel* this is right, this is what the plague wants...but I fear it. I panic and want to escape though I know I should welcome it.

Teo doesn't share the same growing pains. Pushing forward, he wraps his arms around me...and they merge with my body.

"Hey! A Still Rider and a Beathead mashed together!" Teo laughs. "I never thought I'd see the day!"

Looking around, I see we're not the only ones linking up. Everyone in sight is going through the same thing, flowing together into interlocking forms.

Before I know what's happening, other combined people make contact with us, joining flesh and blood with ours. I feel them melting into us, twining sinews and systems with ours into one giant network.

There's a moment then, as the metronome stops in my head, when we're all on the cusp. The great merging is irreversible; millions of Beatheads are tethered together. But the final consummation, whatever that will be, has yet to occur.

The squadron of choppers and planes races toward us...then charges off without dropping their whitewash. Maybe they know it's too late to undo what's in progress. Maybe this is just too big for them to stop or comprehend.

Or maybe they're just too afraid.

As they move off into the night, the moment passes. The pause in the action turns over like a page in a book, and the great merged Us on the beach convulses.

All at once, our vast mingled ribbon of humanity rises up from the sand and ripples into the air. When we climb high enough, hundreds of feet off the ground, the whole thing rushes together with an echoing *boom*.

The ribbon becomes a huge sphere, spinning and pulsing with golden light. Somewhere in the heart of it, I'm aware of what's happening.

I'm aware as the sphere spins frantically, pulsing ever faster, than hatches like an egg. I know that I'm part of the thing that emerges, a thing unlike any ever seen before on Earth.

The closest I can come to describing it is to say it's like an image in a kaleidoscope, an ever-changing pattern on an enormous scale. Only it's composed of flesh and sound and light and thought, twisting and reshaping in myriad ways.

If you look at it, you might first see a giant golden eye with millions of arms and legs for lashes. A second later, you might see a cluster of multicolored pyramids folding and unfolding in infinite layers, while at the same time you hear five hundred thousand voices singing five hundred thousand different songs.

You might see a single giant sphere composed of faces, each one swirling with its own unique tangle of neon fractals. Or you might see a cloud of steam and snowflakes, chiming like a choir of infinite bells as thousands of dreams flicker through it.

It never stops changing and evolving. And like the Beatheads who made it what it is, it never stops moving. It never stops dancing.

Humankind was at an impasse, settled and sedentary, set in its ways. A new thing, a vast, enlightened, and restless thing, was needed...and created, danced into being by the plague, by nature itself.

Was it worth all the pain and suffering it took to conceive it? I don't know yet. We lost so *many* along the way, including Mom and Dad. But at least I know their sacrifice wasn't for nothing.

I've found a new beginning, and I've found something else I was looking for, too. Even as I'm part of this multifaceted whole, this ceaseless motion, I've found what I've been longing for most since coming down with Dance/Drop in the first place.

There might be millions of minds and voices in here, and we might never stop moving and changing...but it all adds up to something I never would have expected to find, something I haven't had for so long, maybe most of my life. Something I never knew I wanted so much until I couldn't have it anymore.

It adds up to *stillness.*

ACIREMA THE RELLIK

The great state of Missouri lay across the Speaker's bench at the front of the House of E-representatives, wrapped in the American flag. His eyes and mouth gaped, and his arms and legs hung over the sides, dripping blood on the carpet below.

"Oh, God," said Connecticut, her shaky hand hovering over Missouri's motionless chest. "He's not breathing."

Manitoba stood on the next tier down and wouldn't come any closer. "Is there a--what's it called? Heartbeat?"

Connecticut lowered her hand, then jerked it away. "That's in the throat, right?" Nervously, she scrubbed her palms on her smart red pantsuit. "Or is it the arm?"

That was when Nevada had finally had enough.

Without a word, he pushed his tall, lanky body through the crowd on the floor of the House and charged up the steps to the Speaker's bench. Without hesitation, he pressed two fingers against the side of Missouri's throat.

"No pulse." Nevada said it loud enough for the whole crowd to hear. "The Speaker of the House is dead."

A great gasp went up from the crowd--the computer-generated, artificial intelligence-driven avatars of ninety-eight of the one-hundred states of the United States of America. Though they didn't have flesh-and-blood bodies and shouldn't have feared being murdered in the physical sense, the evidence of dead Missouri had left them all shell-shocked.

"But how?" Connecticut slipped off her gold-rimmed glasses, let them hang by the diamond-studded chain around her neck...then slid them back on a second later. "And why?"

Nevada pushed up the sleeves of his tuxedo. He took Missouri's head in his hands and turned it gently to one side, exposing a gruesome wound. "Blow to the back of the head." Accepting the wound for what it appeared to be instead of what it was--an electronic simulation of a wound--he looked around for a simulated weapon that could have caused it. "What did it and why, I don't know."

"What are those?" Connecticut pointed at bloody marks on Missouri's left arm.

Nevada put Missouri's head down on the bench and took a look at the arm. Wiping some of the blood away, he realized the marks followed a familiar design.

Someone had cut a number into Missouri's arm. "One hundred," said Nevada. "It's the number one hundred."

The crowd murmured and moved restlessly. Nevada could tell the e-reps were confused because they usually acted more decisively.

They were A.I. avatars of the United States in the year 2300, guided by the aggregate preferences of the human electorate in the world outside. Perfectly attuned to the people they represented, perfectly immune to corruption, they never hesitated or doubted themselves.

That was why their confusion was unusual...and it didn't last long. As Nevada examined the body on the Speaker's bench, three of the e-reps broke from the pack and stormed toward him with jaws and shoulders set.

Sinaloa, in the middle, flipped his red-lined bullfighter's cape over his shoulder. "This is impossible." An American state since Mexico had disbanded twenty-five years ago, Sinaloa cultivated an air of insolence and false bravado. "What we see here is the product of a server malfunction."

"Exactly." South Africa tossed his glossy blond hair beside Sinaloa. "This is a bug. The Developers will fix it."

Nevada rubbed the stubbly cleft of his chin and met South Africa's blue-eyed stare. "Like Idaho?"

South Africa straightened his khaki safari shirt and looked away. So did stocky Kamchatka, the recent Russian convert, who had followed him up the steps.

Sinaloa glared. "I hear that Idaho might have been someone *else's* fault. Not the Developers."

A cold, threatening smile spread across Nevada's face. He knew exactly whom Sinaloa was talking about.

He was talking about Nevada.

"Then maybe you'd best be careful." Nevada adjusted his gold pinky rings and cracked his knuckles. "Just in case he can hear what you're saying."

"If, by some wild chance, the same person is responsible for this crime, I hope he *does* hear me," said Sinaloa. "I want him to know he won't get away with what he's done."

"Tell him yourself, when you catch him." Nevada started to walk away.

"*I* won't catch him." Sinaloa snagged Nevada's shoulder and held him in place. "*You're* sergeant-at-arms of the House, aren't you?"

Nevada sighed. "As of twenty-four *hours* ago. What makes you think I'm ready to catch a *killer*?"

Sinaloa let go of Nevada. "We all know you've done this job

before." He tightened his bolo tie, pushing the turquoise slide higher into the neck of his black silk shirt. "Five years ago, yes?"

"So what?" said Nevada.

"So you've got experience," said Sinaloa. "Not just with being sergeant-at-arms, but with losing e-reps on the job."

Nevada felt the urge to clock him in the face. Idaho had been his greatest failure, his darkest moment.

His deepest love.

"You're better qualified than any of us. You have more motivation to solve this than anyone," said Sinaloa. "You have quite a lot to prove, don't you?"

Nevada smirked and loosened the collar of the frilly shirt under his tux jacket. "You just don't want to get your hands dirty. None of you ever do."

Even as he said it, he knew Sinaloa was right. He knew what people thought of him. He knew he had a lot to prove.

And he knew he would take the case.

"MISSOURI AND I WALKED OUT TOGETHER," said Antarctica, her beautiful silver eyes staring into space. "He went back in for some papers he'd forgotten." She tucked her long, platinum hair behind her ears, and a single tear rolled down her pale cheek. "That was the last time I saw him alive."

Across the table, Nevada watched Antarctica's reaction closely. She was the last person to have seen Missouri before the murder, and that earned her a spot on the list of suspects.

She was also a sweet kid, and Nevada didn't buy her as a killer. She was the youngest e-rep, in fact, from the newest, hundredth state; Antarctica had joined the U.S.A. only one year ago, in 2299. Strikingly beautiful and shining with inner light, the junior

Congresswoman gave Nevada an impression of innocence and honesty, not wiles and lies.

For a moment, Nevada looked away from her, directing his gaze across the chamber at the bloody Speaker's bench. While Nevada interviewed witnesses in the back of the room, other e-reps were up front, clearing the crime scene.

"Did he say anything unusual?" Nevada flicked his eyes to Antarctica, then back to the cleanup crew. They'd already removed Missouri's body, but the blood was another matter. Soap and water didn't exist in the digital realm, so the e-reps couldn't scrub out the soaked-in stains.

Antarctica adjusted her white fur wrap. "Just small talk about today's vote."

As Nevada considered his next question, his fellow

e-reps gave up trying to clean the Speaker's bench and draped a red tablecloth over it to hide the blood. "How close were the two of you?"

"He was a mentor to me," said Antarctica.

"And there was nothing else between you?" Nevada locked eyes with her. "Nothing of a more personal nature?"

Antarctica didn't flinch. "Nothing."

Nevada believed her. "Okay, fine. Thank you for your time."

With that, Nevada rose from his chair and called out to the e-reps milling around the chamber. "Will the great state of Panama please report to the sergeant-at-arms."

When Nevada turned back to the interview table, he realized that Antarctica was still sitting there.

"You're dismissed, sweetheart," said Nevada. "Unless you've got something else to say?"

Antarctica nodded grimly. "I want to help you. I want to help find who killed him."

Nevada fiddled with his tuxedo cufflinks. He could think of

two reasons for her offer. One, she really *did* want to do her part to bring the killer to justice.

Or two, she *was* the killer, and she wanted to divert attention from her own guilt.

Either way, Nevada figured he could use her.

"Why not?" he said. "As long as you don't mind getting your hands dirty."

"I'll do what I have to." Antarctica rose, smoothing the glittering, ice-blue gown that she wore under her fur wrap. "Missouri was a great state."

"Aren't they all?" said Nevada.

PANAMA WAS NO HELP. Neither was Jamaica or Wyoming or any of the other states who had been around Missouri before his death.

After hours of questioning one e-rep witness after another, Nevada was no closer to solving the murder. According to the witnesses, Missouri hadn't said or done a thing out of the ordinary, and no one in his orbit had said or done anything suspicious.

Frustrated, Nevada marched out of the House chamber through the big double doors and into the halls of the digital Capitol building. "I need some fresh air." Antarctica followed him.

Except for Nevada and Antarctica, the halls were empty. The e-reps, whose sole reason for existing was to vote on legislation according to the will of the electorate, rarely ventured outside the House chamber. Neither did the e-senators.

"What's next?" said Antarctica.

Nevada shrugged. "Missouri's office, I guess. Root around for some kind of clue."

"Like what?" said Antarctica. "What are we looking for?"

"How should I know?" said Nevada. "I'm no detective."

Antarctica frowned. "What did Sinaloa mean when he said you have experience losing e-reps on the job?"

Nevada sighed. "Didn't anyone ever tell you about Idaho?"

"I'm new around here," said Antarctica. "There's a lot I don't know."

"Idaho disappeared five years ago," said Nevada. "I was sergeant-at-arms at the time, and I couldn't find her."

"So they blame you for losing her?" said Antarctica.

"Some of them." Nevada listened to his lizard-skin cowboy boots echoing down the corridor. "And some think I might have *killed* her."

Antarctica gaped at him. "How could they think *that*?"

"Because we were lovers." Nevada stopped in front of an office door. The print on the frosted glass bore the name of Missouri. Nevada turned the knob.

Antarctica walked in after him and closed the door. As Nevada rifled drawers and flipped through papers on Missouri's desk, Antarctica circled the perimeter, watching him with a guarded expression.

"Nothing here." After ransacking the desk for a while, Nevada planted his hands on his hips and shook his head. "Nothing out of the ordinary."

"What about that?" Antarctica pointed toward the door through which they'd entered. At the base of it, a single sheet of blank paper lay flat on the floor.

"Someone must have slid it under the door while we were busy," said Nevada.

Antarctica picked up the paper. "Why would somebody slip us a piece of paper with nothing on it?"

"Depends." As soon as Nevada's fingers touched the page, black lettering appeared on it. "Depends who it's addressed to."

Antarctica leaned in close enough that Nevada could smell her sweet gardenia perfume, and they read the note together.

Statue of Liberty, 3PM, Come Alone.

"It's an invitation," said Nevada. "Somebody wants to tell me something."

"Or maybe this is from the killer," said Antarctica. "Maybe he wants you to 'come alone' so he can kill you."

"There's only one way to find out." Nevada crumpled the paper into his tux jacket pocket and headed for the door.

FROM THE WINDOWS in the tiara of the Statue of Liberty, Nevada gazed out over the digital realm that was his home.

He could see everything spread out before him--a world of American landmarks, brought together to provide picturesque backdrops for the e-reps' and e-sens' press conferences.

In the middle of it all, Nevada saw the gleaming white dome of the Capitol building. Northwest of the Capitol jabbed the ivory needle of the Washington Monument; to the southwest rested the Lincoln Memorial. The Liberty Bell hung in a golden tower to the southeast, and Plymouth Rock perched on a pedestal to the northeast.

Straight across the bubble of the digital realm from the Statue of Liberty, Mount Rushmore spanned the horizon, its giant presidential heads gazing out over the city. Niagara Falls roared to the east, and the Grand Canyon sprawled to the west, glowing forever red in the

never-dimming sunrise.

"Nevada." The whispered voice from across the room surprised him. Nevada shot his gaze into the shadows...and saw an intercom speaker built into the wall there.

"Nevada." The voice spoke again, still no more than a whisper. Nevada crossed the room and stood close to the speaker, straining to identify who was doing the talking.

"Nevada. Are you *there*?"

Nevada pressed the button to transmit and spoke into the grill in the wall. "I'm here. Who is this?"

"Call me Looking Glass." The voice belonged to a man, but that was all Nevada could tell. "I know where to look."

"For what?" said Nevada.

"For Yukon's murderer," said Looking Glass.

A sharp chill raced up Nevada's spine. "Don't you mean Missouri's? Yukon isn't dead."

"She wasn't," said Looking Glass, "when you got on Lady Liberty's elevator."

Nevada's finger shook as he pressed the intercom button again. "Is that what this is about? Did you bring me here so I'd be out of the way while you killed Yukon?"

"Here is your first clue," said Looking Glass. "When is one one-hundred?"

Nevada scowled. "Just tell me if you did it. Tell me if you killed them both."

"When does one plus zero equal two?" said Looking Glass. "That's your second clue."

"If you didn't do it, who did?" said Nevada.

"No more for now," said Looking Glass. "See you after three and four."

With that, the line went dead.

Nevada slammed the button with the palm of his hand. "Looking Glass! Talk to me!"

But Looking Glass was gone.

YUKON SAT on the toilet in the women's lavatory, fully dressed and covered in blood and toilet paper. Her long, brown hair covered her face like a shroud.

"When did you find her?" Nevada stood in the doorway of the stall, hands on his hips.

Nervous Connecticut stood at his left. "A half-hour ago." She took off her gold-rimmed glasses, then put them back on...then took them off again. "We c-came in together for a sidebar. She was f-fine when I left."

Nevada nodded. Since the e-reps weren't programmed for excretory functions, bathrooms in the digital realm were used mostly for sidebar meetings and private deals. "Let me guess. No one noticed anything unusual."

"Not exactly, señor." Sinaloa clapped him on the shoulder. "Some of us noticed *you* leaving the House shortly before the murder."

Nevada ignored him and stepped into the stall. Gently, he parted the hair over Yukon's face with his fingertips, revealing a gruesome palette of cuts and bruises.

Pushing the hair away from her throat, he saw the biggest visible wound--a bloody gash from ear to ear.

"And no murder weapon left behind." Nevada was thinking out loud. "No bloody footprints, no fingerprints, no nothing."

"Tell me." Sinaloa flipped the red-lined bullfighter's cape over his shoulder with a flourish. "How is your first investigation going? Can you tell us who murdered Missouri?"

Nevada spotted the edge of a bloody symbol sticking out from under the toilet paper wrapped around Yukon's forearm. Tearing away the paper, he saw that there were two symbols underneath--two numerals carved into Yukon's flesh.

Two nines, carved side by side. Together, they made the number "ninety-nine."

Just as the number one hundred had been cut into poor Missouri's flesh.

"Well?" said Sinaloa. "Can you tell us who murdered Missouri?"

"Same person who murdered Yukon," said Nevada. "And there'll be more to come."

"What makes you say that?" said Sinaloa.

"Because he's counting down from a hundred," said Nevada. "A hundred of us."

NEVADA SAT at the end of the Reflecting Pool, gazing across the still water at the Lincoln Memorial. Antarctica, who was sitting beside him, had kicked off her pretty crystal shoes and dropped her pale, slender feet into the water.

The ripples from her feet disturbed the scenes playing over the pool's surface--visions of life beyond the digital domain in True America. Men, women, and children worked and played in softly swirling images, flickering across the sunlit water. It was here that the e-reps and e-sens came to see the faces of the people they served, strengthening their resolve to preserve the American dream.

"You're sure the killer won't stop?" said Antarctica.

"There are one hundred e-reps," said Nevada. "The first victim was marked one hundred, and the second was ninety-nine. Ninety-eight is next, then ninety-seven...all the way to zero."

Antarctica frowned. "I can't believe the Developers are letting this happen. Can't they just reprogram the source code to bring back the dead and stop the murders?"

"Maybe not." Nevada stroked the dark stubble on his chin. "Maybe they've lost control of the simulation. Or maybe they're *letting* it happen."

"But it doesn't seem possible." Antarctica shook her head and gazed into the water. "None of this does."

"Got that right." Nevada stretched out on his side, propping an elbow on the cement. Even with everything that was going on, he felt a sense of peace in this place.

Of all the places in the digital realm, the Reflecting Pool would always be the most special to him. It was here, five years ago, that he'd last seen Idaho before she'd disappeared from his life.

It was here that he'd last made love to her.

"What about Looking Glass's clues?" said Antarctica. "Do they mean anything?"

"I'm sure they do," said Nevada, "but I haven't figured them out yet."

"'When is one one-hundred?'" Antarctica narrowed her silver eyes. "He must have meant the one hundred e-reps of Congress, right?"

"Probably," said Nevada.

"Or he might have meant *me*." Antarctica's eyes widened. "I'm the one-hundredth e-rep, from the

one-hundredth state. What if I'm the next *victim*?"

"I don't think so," said Nevada. "The killer's following reverse order of importance. Missouri was speaker of the House, number one in terms of power...and the killer counted him last, as number one hundred."

"And Yukon was minority leader." Antarctica sounded relieved. "Second most powerful. So you don't think I'm next, Nevada?"

"No, sweetheart." said Nevada. "I don't think you're on the killer's radar right now."

Just then, without warning, Antarctica shot forward and disappeared under the water.

Heart pounding, Nevada scrambled to the edge of the pool and stared at the spot where she'd gone under. Since the water was murky with projected scenes of True America, he couldn't see below the surface. No trace of Antarctica or whatever had pulled her in was visible.

Then, suddenly, one pale hand broke the surface. Nevada grabbed it and pulled up hard...but whatever had hold of Antarctica wouldn't let go.

Leaning out further, Nevada clamped both hands around Antarctica's wrist and pulled harder than before. The thing in the pool resisted...then finally released its grip. Nevada hauled Antarctica free with one great heave.

The two of them tumbled back on the edge of the pool. Nevada cradled her in his arms as she coughed up water and gasped for breath.

Her silver eyes flickered open and met his gaze. "Guess what?" Her voice was shaking. "I think I'm on the killer's radar after all."

Nevada stroked the platinum blonde hair from her eyes. "Did you get a look at who pulled you in?"

Antarctica shook her head. "All I know is, their touch was beyond ice cold. It was too cold even for *me*."

Nevada stared at the surface of the pool. He wondered who had attacked Antarctica, and why.

Maybe the killer's hit list was more random than Nevada had thought, or it followed a more complicated formula. Maybe Antarctica knew something that could lead to a break in the case.

Or maybe, a more ominous motive had fueled the attack.

"We've got to get back," said Nevada. "Back to the House."

Antarctica frowned. "Why?"

"I don't think you were a target," said Nevada. "I think you were a diversion."

PIECES of the great state of Zacatecas were scattered all over the House chamber--head on the flagpole, foot on the Speaker's bench, arm on the podium. Blood was spattered everywhere, and ragged shreds of flesh stuck to the furniture and walls.

Many of the e-reps were also stained with their colleague's remains--including Connecticut, as she explained to Nevada what had happened.

"Half an hour ago, the power went out," said Connecticut. "We heard Zacatecas screaming, but we didn't know why until the lights came back up five minutes later. We found him...like this." She looked down at her bloody hands and clothes.

Suddenly, Sinaloa stormed toward them, scowling with rage. "Arrest this man!" He grabbed hold of Nevada's wrist and wrenched it into the air. "He killed my Mexican *hermano*!"

"That's enough," said Connecticut. "Let him go."

"Who among us was mysteriously *absent* when Zacatecas was *murdered*?" Sinaloa shook Nevada's arm for the crowd. "*This* man! He only reappeared when the killing was *finished*."

Antarctica pushed forward. "I was with him when this happened! Nevada didn't kill *anyone*."

"Then what *was* he doing?" said Sinaloa.

"Saving my life!" said Antarctica. "I was attacked and nearly drowned at the Reflecting Pool!" With one hand, she held up strands of her long hair, which was still wet. With her other hand, she held up her soaked white fur wrap.

"How do we know for sure?" Sinaloa locked eyes with her. "Perhaps you were his *accomplice* in this atrocity."

Fed up with the grandstanding, Nevada tore his wrist free of Sinaloa's grip. "Enough infighting. This is exactly what they want."

"'They' who?" said Sinaloa.

"You're right about one thing," said Nevada. "More than one person is involved in these murders."

With that, Nevada headed for the front of the chamber. The crowd of e-reps silently parted to make way for him.

"Someone attacked Antarctica at the Reflecting Pool while the murders were underway here." Nevada walked up to the podium, where Zacateca's left arm rested. "That tells us at least two people were involved."

Nevada gazed at the severed arm on the podium, its hand curled into a loose fist. "In five short minutes, power was cut to the House, Zacatecas was torn to pieces, and power was restored. That's a lot for one person to do alone in that amount of time."

"You should know," said Sinaloa.

Nevada turned the arm over. "In those same five minutes, someone also did this." Nevada held up the arm for the crowd to see. "They cut open Zacatecas' sleeves and carved the number '98' into his flesh."

The watching e-reps gasped and mumbled.

"The countdown continues," said Nevada, "unless we start working together and find who did this."

Sinaloa glowered at Nevada for a long moment. Then, he spun and marched up the aisle toward the doors.

"You're right," he said over his shoulder. "It's time to get some answers."

Nevada put down Zacatecas' severed arm. "How do you plan to do that?"

"By making a call," said Sinaloa.

"To who?" said Nevada.

"Who else?" said Sinaloa. "The Developers."

SINALOA CHARGED across the vast rotunda beneath the dome of the Capitol building and stopped on a single glowing tile in the middle of the room. Nevada and Antarctica, who had followed him from the House chamber, stood to one side.

When Sinaloa placed his right hand over his heart and recited the Pledge of Allegiance, a shaft of light burst up from the glowing tile, striking the middle of the dome. Smoothly, the dome split on one side and rolled open, revealing a starry night sky overhead.

The shaft of light from the tile spiked straight up, never dimming as it shot into the heavens. This was the holy connection to the godlike Developers in the world outside, the fabled *soulpipe.*

"I've never actually seen a *soul call* before." Antarctica's voice was soft and slow with wonder. "Will the Developers answer?"

Nevada shrugged. The same question was foremost in his own mind at that moment.

Since the murders, the role of House Speaker had fallen on Sinaloa, which qualified him to make the soul call. As a rule, though, the unpredictable Developers didn't answer every call, even from a qualified Speaker.

In the blazing light of the soulpipe, Sinaloa gazed upward and spread his arms wide. "O' masters of the source code, I beg you--hear my prayer!" As Sinaloa spoke, his feet left the floor. Spinning slowly, he rose into the air, following the soulpipe's beam. "Representative Sinaloa...transmit *now*!"

Suddenly, Sinaloa exploded upward, streaking along the soulpipe in a strobing blur. There was a distant sonic boom as he vanished into the heavens, flashing out of sight among the flickering garlands of stars.

"Wow." Antarctica walked around the base of the soulpipe, staring up into Sinaloa's rippling wake. "He's in True America now?"

"Somewhere between here and there," said Nevada. "A hub outside the Developers' firewall."

"Don't you mean fire *ball*?" said Antarctica.

"Fire *wall*," said Nevada.

Antarctica frowned. "It's just that I see one now. A fire *ball*."

Nevada squinted upward...and then he saw it, too. A clutch of flames far above, burning in the firmament.

Burning and falling.

Nevada lashed an arm around Antarctica's waist and ran with her, racing away from the soulpipe. Just as they reached the far wall, a thunderous impact crashed down behind them.

Nevada and Antarctica stumbled as the floor buckled. Bracing each other, they managed to stay on their feet...and as the tremor faded, they turned.

The soulpipe was gone. In its place, in the center of the rotunda, was a smoking crater.

"Stay back," said Nevada, and then he ran toward the crater. In spite of his order, he heard Antarctica running close behind him.

When Nevada reached the broken rim of the crater, he saw what had caused the impact. He saw what had fallen from above like a fiery comet.

The body of Sinaloa lay in the crater's heart, curled like a fist and charred from tip to toe.

Antarctica drew up alongside Nevada and gagged. "Oh no."

"I guess they're not taking our calls." Nevada stepped over the edge and eased into the crater. He saw that parts of Sinaloa were still smoldering, glowing cherry red in familiar patterns.

There were messages on Sinaloa's body, burned into his flesh.

"Ninety-seven." Nevada pointed to Sinaloa's left arm, where the numbers had been branded. Then, he pointed at the letters seared into Sinaloa's right arm. "A-C-I-R-E-M-A. 'Acirema.'"

Finally, he read the smoking words on Sinaloa's charred chest. "'ANSWERS IN HOUSE NOW.'"

Leaping into action, Nevada clambered up the crater's slope and over the rim. He started running the instant his feet hit the floor.

Four figures wrapped in star-spangled robes waited outside the big double doors of the House chamber. Their faces were hidden in the depths of shadowy hoods, arms folded across their chests.

Nevada and Antarctica stopped running, staying well back from the hooded figures. Even from a distance, Nevada could see that their blue-and-white robes were stained with splotches of dark red.

Nevada took a step forward. "Stand aside. The sergeant-at-arms has business with the House."

To his surprise, the figures moved to comply. The two in the middle turned and opened the doors to the chamber--but they did not usher him inside. Instead, a fifth figure emerged, clad in red-and-white-striped robes, also hooded.

As the two figures who had opened the doors pulled them shut, the fifth robed figure glided forward. The voice that flowed from under the hood was that of a man...hoarse and muffled, but clearly a man.

"Hello again," he said. "I told you we would meet again after three and four, didn't I?"

Nevada recognized the voice instantly. "Looking Glass."

"Victims three and four are dead, so here I am." Looking Glass bowed his head. "Have you deciphered the clues I gave you?"

"No," said Nevada.

Looking Glass chuckled. "Then prepare to have your mind blown."

Nevada took a step back, pulling Antarctica with him. He briefly considered running, if only for her sake...but he waited. How could he run when he had yet to see inside the House?

"Meet the welcome wagon," said Looking Glass, gesturing at the two robed figures on his right.

Silently, the figure on the far right tugged off its star-spangled hood, revealing a face--a man's face, grinning.

Nevada gasped when he saw who it was. Heart slamming like a piston in his rib cage, he froze, holding on to Antarctica's arm.

Antarctica said the name for them both. "S-Sinaloa?"

The robed man with Sinaloa's face took a bow.

Then, the next figure unmasked. This time, the face under the hood was also familiar.

"Zacatecas." Nevada's head was spinning.

"More where those came from." Looking Glass gestured at the two hooded figures on the other side of him.

The next to unmask was a woman with long, brown hair--Yukon, also back from the dead. Beside her was the man who had started it all, the first to go: Missouri, former Speaker of the House, peeled back his hood and smoothed his neat white hair with a toothy grin.

"What's going on here, Nevada?" Antarctica sounded dazed. "How can they all be alive?"

Nevada felt dazed, too. "The Developers, maybe?"

The four who had come back to life looked at each other with knowing smiles and giggled.

"Not even close," said Looking Glass.

"Some kind of practical joke?" Nevada heard what could have been a muffled scream from behind the double doors of the House chamber. "A stunt to delay a key vote?"

"It *is* kind of funny," said Looking Glass, "but no. Would you like me to give you a hint?"

Nevada heard a loud thump and a crash from behind the doors. "Why not?"

"Here goes." With that, Looking Glass reached up and pulled off his own red-and-white-striped hood.

And Nevada felt the world of logic and reality dissolve around him.

His mouth fell open. His mind went blank.

Looking Glass, without the hood, had a very familiar face. He wasn't someone returned from the dead, or anyone Nevada had ever expected to see.

Outside of a mirror, that is.

The face staring back at Nevada was his own.

"I BET I know what's going through your mind right now." Looking Glass smiled. "'What a handsome S.O.B.,' am I right?"

Nevada didn't answer.

Stepping forward, Looking Glass extended a hand. "The name is Adaven. Pleased to meet you, Nevada."

Without thinking, Nevada took Adaven's hand. It was ice-cold to the touch--*beyond* ice cold.

Adaven gripped Nevada's elbow, freezing him right through the sleeves of his tux and shirt. With a whoop, he swung Nevada around to face the four seemingly resurrected e-reps.

"This is Aolanis." Adaven pointed at the reborn Sinaloa, and then he moved down the line. "This is Sacetacaz, Nokuy, and Iruossim. They're not who you think they are. In fact, you've never met them before."

Nevada frowned. Everything sounded crazy.

"Now come on." Adaven led Nevada toward the doors. "Let's meet the rest of the gang, shall we?"

Grinning, Sacetacaz and Nokuy pushed open the double doors to the House chamber. Adaven guided Nevada inside...right into a nightmare.

The huge room was splashed from top to bottom and side to side with blood and gore. Body parts were scattered everywhere, and corpses were piled like cordwood in the corners.

Even as Nevada recognized the dead faces of e-reps in the corpse heaps, he saw e-reps with the same faces moving around the room. The moving and the motionless looked exactly the same, except some were living and some were dead--and the living weren't behaving the way that Nevada ever would have expected them to.

As Nevada watched, Arkansas, South Korea, and Israel teamed up against Costa Rica, howling as they tore her limb from limb. Across the chamber, Florida and Japan hacked up Chihuahua with knives, cutting out his organs while he screamed in agony.

Antarctica's identical twin slogged past not ten feet from Nevada, dragging a charred and disemboweled corpse by the feet.

Staring at the hellish scene, Nevada could think of only one thing to say, one question to ask: "Why?"

"Why what?" said Adaven. "Why redecorate, you mean? Why have a surprise party?"

"Why are there duplicate e-reps?" said Nevada.

"Remember my riddle? 'When does one plus zero equal two?'" Adaven chuckled. "The answer is, when *one* casts a reflection in a *mirror*, of course. In a *looking glass*."

"You reflect us?" said Nevada.

Adaven made a twisting gesture with his hand. "Other way around."

Antarctica shivered against Nevada's arm. "So there's two of everyone?"

"One from America." Adaven raised his right hand, palm up, like the tray of a balance. "One from Acirema." He raised his left hand, also palm-up, alongside the right.

"'Acirema,'" said Nevada. "That word was burned into Sinaloa's body."

Adaven threw an arm around Nevada's shoulders, sending a freezing blast through his tux jacket and shirt. "You know it by another name," he said. "'True America.'"

Nevada stared at him, too stunned to speak.

"You e-reps have been living in a fantasy," said Adaven.

"Thinking True America was a paradise of liberty. Thinking you were the voices of a just and compassionate electorate.

"But you don't represent the people of True America. You never did." Adaven swept an arm wide to take in the entire House chamber. "*These* are the representatives of America. *These* are the A.I. avatars whose votes shape America's destiny."

"You're telling us democracy's dead?" said Antarctica.

"The opposite!" said Adaven. "Democracy is alive and well...and *this* is the will of the American electorate!

"You and your kind have never been more than illusions to mask the true face of America--to let her own people fool themselves even as she expresses their darkest desires. You are the reason Americans have been able to live with themselves and sleep at night...but no longer.

"America has become her own shadow: Acirema, the opposite--'America' spelled backwards." Adaven pulled Nevada close and whispered, frozen breath chilling his ear. "We don't need you anymore."

Nevada felt sick. The urge to run returned--but he realized it was too late. He and Antarctica were surrounded by wicked e-rep duplicates.

"Acirema doesn't need to pretend anymore," said Adaven. "We don't need the front. We've accepted ourselves as the complete bastards we've always been, and we've made up our minds to be the *best* complete bastards we *can* be."

"That's why you started killing us," said Nevada.

Adaven nodded. "The first few were tests. The Developers gave us all the keys and cheats we needed, but we still weren't sure if murder would work in the digital realm."

"You murdered the Speaker first to cripple our leadership," said Nevada.

"Actually, that was a mistake," said Adaven. "In the shadow Congress of Acirema, Missouri is the lowliest of the hundred, not the highest. We thought we were starting with the least important among you. 'When is one one hundred,' remember? The answer to the riddle is this: when *one*--the number one e-rep, the Speaker of the House in your realm--ranks *hundredth* out of a hundred in ours."

Nevada looked around at the living hell in the chamber. "So all of this was for nothing," he said. "Everything we accomplished."

"But the *good* news is, you can still make a difference," said Adaven.

"How's that?" said Nevada.

Adaven steered him around to face the huge double doorway. A figure stood beyond it, waiting in the hall, wrapped in hooded robes emblazoned with stars and stripes.

"She'll help you." Adaven gave Nevada a shove, sending him stumbling into the hall. "You'll make a difference by *dying*--sacrificing yourself to make way for the new world order."

Antarctica grabbed hold of Nevada's elbow. "What's the plan?" she said. "How do we get out of this?"

"We don't." Nevada slumped as the robed figure swung a rifle from her back and took aim at him. A dozen options for action flashed through his mind, revving up his heart, burning his bloodstream with adrenaline...

And he pushed them all aside. He knew that he could go down fighting, and in that way redeem himself at least a little for failing the republic--but he did nothing. What good would a martyr be if no one knew that he had died and why?

"Please, Nevada." Antarctica tugged his arm, but he wouldn't budge. "It's up to us."

"No it's not." Nevada shook free of her grip. "Nothing's up to us anymore."

"You're wrong." Antarctica pointed up at the ceiling. A red light blinked on the security camera that was mounted there. "People are still watching."

Nevada stared at the camera, then looked down at the barrel of the rifle. Maybe Antarctica was right. Maybe he could accomplish something worthwhile after all.

Nevada took a deep breath to steady himself. He curled and uncurled his fists.

Then, he bolted out of the line of fire.

"Run!" As soon as he said it, he glimpsed a blur of motion from Antarctica's direction.

Head down, Nevada charged toward the hooded shooter. He cut one way, then the other, trying to avoid her fire, reaching out for her.

Before he could touch her, he heard the deafening crack of the rifle. In spite of his zigzag path, the shot slammed into his chest with explosive force, pitching him to the floor.

He blacked out.

When he opened his eyes again, he saw the hooded woman crouching over him. "Confirmed kill," she said to someone he couldn't see--and when she said it, his heart beat faster.

He recognized her voice.

Nevada knew what her face would look like before she lifted away the hood. At first, all he could think was that it was impossible, that he must have already died if she was there with them.

But then, as she locked eyes with him, he remembered just how possible it was. Every e-rep had a double in Acirema, after all, even the dead ones. Even the one who had disappeared five years ago.

Even his beloved Idaho.

Nevada was in pain, but he managed a smile. The sight of her after all this time, even a shadow double who'd just shot him, was enough to fill him with joy.

Maybe her name was Ohadi instead of Idaho. Maybe she was devoted to the dark purposes of Acirema the Rellik instead of the bright resolve of America the Beautiful. Maybe she felt nothing for him, not even hatred.

But at least he could drink in the sight of her face. At least he could pretend in his few remaining moments that the precious original had returned to him.

At least he could imagine--or was it more than imagination--that her hand was warm when she touched his eyelids. When she drew them shut.

He could dream that she was his warm-blooded Idaho, hiding all this time to prepare for the threat of Acirema, masquerading even now as the enemy. Faking Nevada's death so she could whisk him away to the underground to fight the power. To renew their love.

Or if that hand was colder than he thought, than he

Dreamed

And she was Ohadi in spite of his hope, carved from glittering ice with frozen heart and frozen soul,

Perhaps his noble moment of defiance and then his last words would inspire her,

Warm her blood that she would *become* restored Idaho and more,

Seed of change, revolution, restoration,

Changer of hearts, perhaps even the heart of Adaven, his twin, Nevada spelled backward

Spelled everywhichway like America

Acirema Maciera Reamica Cimeara Imeraca

Then that would be all right, too, he thought,

And he tried

In the last words he said

To tell her what mattered,

What they'd forgotten,

What to pass along,

And this was what came out,

His wisdom, his blessing, his curse,
His last wish
His poem.
He said
"I love you."

TIJUANA, MASSACHUSETTS

At first, Patty thought someone was shooting at her. *Bracka-cracka-crack.* She clamped her hands over her ears, fighting to drown out the clattering racket. *Cracka-bracka-brack.*

Then, suddenly, it was like someone had turned down the volume and she could hear the sound for what it really was.

Shicka-shacka-shicka.

And when she opened her eyes, she saw what was making that sound: a bright yellow box jumping up and down in a dirty brown hand. A rainbow-colored logo swirled across the front under a cellophane wrapper.

Chiclets. Someone was shaking a box of Chiclets in her face.

"Five dollar, *señora.*" The voice of a little boy called out from behind the box. "Want some Cheek-lits?"

What the *fuck*?

Since when did *kids* run around selling *Chiclets* on *Cape Cod, Massachusetts*?

Patty shook her head hard, trying to clear away the fog. Looking up, she caught an eyeful of blinding sun, then looked down. It was only then she realized she was on her ass in the middle of the street.

"Get the fuck away from me!" She swatted the Chiclets box out of her face, revealing the little brown-skinned, black-haired boy who'd been holding it. He wore a green-and-white striped t-shirt and tattered jeans and looked highly insulted. "Damn *wetback.*" She wrinkled her nose in disgust at a surge of body odor.

Only to realize the kid was upwind and the B.O. was coming from *her*.

Bzeep zeep.

Suddenly, Patty heard a strange buzzing beeping noise and felt nauseous. Something in her eyes flickered, and the boy transformed.

Instead of a little black-haired boy with brown skin, he became a little blond boy with pale skin. Instead of a striped t-shirt and tattered jeans, he wore a navy blue polo shirt with the collar turned up and a pair of neatly pressed white shorts.

"What the--" Patty couldn't help smiling at the cute child, who was much more what she expected to see on The Cape.

Bzeep zeep.

Then, her eyes flickered, and the little brown boy was back.

"What the fuck?" Patty shook her head hard and braced her hands on the hot, rough pavement. She took deep breaths and forced down the urge to be sick.

The kid started toward her, and Patty shooed him away. "Go eat a taco, Paco!" Then, she struggled to her hands and knees. She got to her feet.

And she took a look around.

"What the fuck is *this*?" Patty had never seen so much brown skin on The Cape. Was it Cinco de fucking Mayo, or what?

Some kind of street fair was going on around her. There was Mexican music in the air, all horns and guitars and accordions.

People stared out at her from stalls overflowing with sombreros, serapes, and pottery. She saw men in white shirts and slacks, women in bowler hats and long pink and orange and yellow and red dresses.

Not one of them had pale skin like Patty's. The Cape was really going downhill.

"Fucking wetbacks." Frowning people cleared out of Patty's path as she lurched down the street like a broken bulldozer. "Fucking *Cape*."

Staggering away from the stalls, she swung around a corner and felt suddenly dizzy. She had to catch herself against the front window of a shop.

Palms pressed against the smooth glass, Patty closed her eyes and fought for control. It slipped away every time she thought she had it.

I need help. Her legs buckled, and she barely stayed on her feet. *I need J-*

Bzeep zeep.

Patty's eyes snapped open, and she stared at her reflection in the window. She'd had a name on the tip of her tongue, and then...

Bzeep zeep.

Gone. It was gone.

"What the fuck?" Her voice was a whisper. She'd been thinking of something, of *someone*, and then that buzzing beeping noise had broken her train of thought.

Patty squinted at her image, but it had nothing to tell her. Same old crinkled-up 52-year-old bulldog face, chipmunk overbite, and gray crew cut.

But at least it gave her something to hold on to. At least that much, the way she looked, hadn't changed.

Or had it? That little bump between her eyes--that was new, wasn't it? Reaching up, she ran her index finger over it, feeling a hard little nub above the bridge of her nose. It was like a tiny pea, a ball bearing, but warm to the touch.

When did that *get there?*

Taking a deep breath, Patty pushed away from the window. She was hardly aware she was stepping into the street until a big black car nearly plowed her over.

The blast of the horn still rang in her ears as she teetered in shock. Then, looking up, she saw something that made her freeze.

She saw a billboard on the side of a building, emblazoned with three giant words, each bursting with wild, bright colors.

Welcome to Tijuana!

"What kind of bullshit joke is *this*?" Patty flung her hand through the air as if she could sweep away the sign. "Some *motherfucker* with too much fucking *time* on his hands?"

Bzeep zeep.

Her vision flickered, and the billboard changed from the garish *Welcome to Tijuana!* to a more subdued *Welcome to Cape Cod.*

Patty stared, then scrunched her eyes shut and shook her head hard.

Bzeep zeep.

The next time she looked, the billboard read *Welcome to Tijuana!* again.

Lunging away from the sign, Patty continued down the street. She got a funny taste in her mouth, like dirt, and spat in the gutter on her way past.

As she hauled herself onward, a little boy in a bright red soccer shirt and yellow shorts ran out of an alley in front of her.

"No *Cheek-lets*!" said Patty, though the boy showed no sign of slowing down on his way past. "No five dollah!"

The little boy didn't look back on his way down the street and around the corner.

Patty thrashed her head from side to side but still couldn't get rid of the fog. She wondered if she'd picked up a flu or some-

Bzeep zeep.

"Where the *fuck* is that *noise* coming from?" Reaching up, she felt the lump between her eyes. It was still warm, warmer than it should have been if it was just some kind of growth.

Suddenly, she smelled cooked food, and her mind switched tracks. A lovely little café came up on her left, and she stopped in front of it, inhaling deeply.

The place was Cape Cod style all the way, from the white wicker chairs to the round tables with white tablecloths. A vase rested on each table, filled with a tasteful arrangement of gardenias and hyacinths. A slim, red-haired waitress walked out, smoothing her crisp white linen apron. She smiled and gave Patty a friendly wave.

Bzeep zeep.

A flicker later, and the place had become an ugly Mexican cantina that looked like it had been furnished right out of the town dump.

As Patty watched, a brown-skinned waitress shuffled over to a male customer at one of the rickety tables with a steaming plate of sizzling chicken and vegetables. Patty's stomach started growling, which totally pissed her off.

Because the one thing she hated more than Mexican people was Mexican food.

"Fucking puke on a plate." So why was her mouth watering so much? Why did she want to run in there and fill her hands, squishing the greasy, steaming chicken between her fingers, then gobbling it up like a dog?

Wheeling away from the cantina, she looked up and down the sunbaked street. Sweat rolling down her face and body, she tried figuring out where she was in the whole of The Cape, because none of the landmarks was ringing a bell.

But she came up empty. Not a clue.

Was she drunk? She didn't remember drinking. Had somebody slipped her a rufy?

"Fuck." The blistering heat pressed in on her, and she suddenly felt faint. Her legs buckled. "I need J-"

Bzeep zeep.

Once again, the name on the tip of her tongue was gone. A wild chill poured through her, pure fear sweeping aside the intense heat.

And then the hot flash was back. All she could think of was air conditioning.

And a telephone.

Indiscriminately, Patty staggered toward the door of a shop and heaved it open. She lurched inside and let the door bang shut behind her.

Ding dong. An electric chime rang as Patty looked around. She felt only slightly cooler, but it might only have been because she was out of the sun. As far as she could tell, the shop had no air conditioning.

But she was glad for even the slightest relief. And she was glad to see what kind of shop she'd stumbled into.

The place smelled like stale cigarette smoke and some kind of incense. A light haze hung in the air, leaving a bitter aftertaste in her mouth.

But the shop was also full of beautiful things. A ring of waist-high display cases encircled the walls, with a second, smaller ring of cases in the middle. Patty caught her breath as she wandered between them, peering in at a treasure trove of turquoise and silver and gold.

It was the universal language. The one thing she could stand that had any connection to fucking Mehico.

Jewelry.

All the lights in the shop were switched off, but the litter of pieces in the cases still showed up fine. Bracelets and anklets and pendants gleamed softly, reflecting the light filtering in from outside. Earrings and brooches and belt buckles twinkled with a mystical inner glow.

Patty smiled for the first time all day. She loved shopping, didn't she? Shopping on The Cape with Jan...

Bzeep zeep.

...shopping with Jan...

Bzeep zeep. Bzeep zeep.

"Almost had it!" The nub between her eyes was warm under the skin as she rubbed it. "Almost had the name! Her name! Her name!"

Bzeep zeep.

"What the fuck?" All blank again.

Patty tasted dirt and looked back into the display cases. The pale blue and silver and gold pieces were pretty as the tropical fish wriggling in their tanks in her favorite restaurant on The Cape.

Suddenly, one of the pieces caught her eye--a shimmering gold bracelet on a panel of red velvet. It looked buttery soft and exotic, with rows of tiny links woven in a staggered pattern like the steps of an ancient pyramid.

Staring at it gave her a strange feeling in the pit of her stomach. Or was it the incense?

There was something inside her, hard as a knot. Jagged as a thorn bush. Pulsating, gyrating, straining to get out. Nothing like the nub between her eyes.

Something much deeper.

"May I help you, señora?" A slow, deep voice spoke from the back of the shop, threaded with a Mexican accent. "See anything you like?"

Patty turned. An old man approached, short and slight, with thick gray hair. He wore glasses with rectangular lenses and silver wire frames, and he had a gray mustache.

He stopped about six feet away from her. "May I help you?" he said.

Gazing into his eyes, Patty felt a sharp pain in her chest. Did she know him?

Bzeep zeep.

There was a flicker, and she suddenly recognized him. His face was well known to her, unmistakably familiar. His eyes were filmy and bloodshot, sunk behind drooping lids, rimmed with networks of deep wrinkles. Of *course* she knew him, how could she not know her own f-

Bzeep zeep.

Patty clamped her hands around her head, but her thoughts fled like bees, buzzing away in all directions. If only she could hold on to *just one*, just long enough to...

Bzeep zeep.

It was *him*, it was her fa...

Bzeep zeep.

She cried out and doubled over. Bit down on her tongue and tasted blood, metallic and salty.

There were tears in her eyes as she straightened. When she opened her eyes, she no longer recognized the old man. He was just a stranger, an old jeweler, a Mexican.

During her spell, he'd retreated behind the counter along the wall. He lit a cigarette, and fresh, acrid smoke flowed into the air. When he spoke, his voice was sharper than before. "How may I help you, señora?"

Patty looked down at the beautiful gold bracelet. She patted the back pockets of her jeans, feeling for a wallet...finding nothing. Finding more of the same when she fished in her front pockets. She didn't have a dime.

A chill shot through her. Her bowels constricted like a clenching fist with sudden awareness.

"I'm..." She frowned and rubbed the hard nub between her eyes. "I need..."

Bzeep zeep.

The shop blurred, becoming a quaint antique shop she knew quite well from The Cape. But the scene quickly shifted right back to the Mexican jewelry shop.

Bzeep zeep.

"Do you have a phone?" She walked over to the display case where the old jeweler stood. "I can't seem to find my cell, and I need to call home."

The jeweler shook his head. "No calls to the U.S., señora. Local calls only."

Patty planted her hands on the smooth glass of the case and laughed. "Since when is *Cape Cod* not in the U.S.?" She slapped the glass and laughed some more. "Don't'cha think you guys're taking this Cinco de Mayo shit a little too far?"

The jeweler shrugged. "Perhaps you should buy a phone card at *la farmacia*. Good for international calls."

"Yeah, right!" Patty kept laughing. Then, she caught a lungful of smoke and hacked until she gagged.

The jeweler cleared his throat. "I think I know what you're looking for, señora."

Yes. The thought punched through the fog, and Patty fixed him in her stare. "I'm looking for..." *Looking for Jan...*

Bzeep zeep.

A wave of dizziness coursed through her. "I need to find..."

Bzeep zeep.

She reeled against the case, clutching her spinning head. Tasting blood.

"You need to go to the *pulqueria*." The old man pointed toward the front window of the shop. "They have what you're looking for there."

"Puke-a-whata?" Patty grimaced.

"*Pulqueria*," said the old man. "Go left two blocks, then make another left down the alley."

"Fuck-a-who-a?" said Patty.

The old jeweler sighed cigarette smoke and pointed at the window. "Left two blocks, then left again. They'll give you what you need. All the good, strong *pulque* you can drink." He nodded like a pimp arranging a date.

Patty waved him off and stomped toward the door.

Then stomped back again. She stopped at the case with the gold bracelet she loved and took a long look, drinking in every burnished link in the staggered rows, the steps.

And something swam up in her, fast as a fish from the inky depths of the deep ocean, racing to reach the light before the monster snapping at its tail could gulp it down forever.

"Somebody fell." Patty tapped the glass and frowned at the jeweler. "I remember. My fa..."

Bzeep zeep.

The jeweler's face became familiar again, became that of the old man she knew. Scowling, she grabbed at him, held him for a moment in her grip. He smelled like...smelled like...

...bananas?

"Somebody fell."

Bzeep zeep.

Suddenly, the familiar old man with his eyes wide with terror turned back into the Mexican jeweler, and his eyes were wide with rage.

The next thing Patty knew, she was out on the sidewalk, wagging her head like a choking dog. Looking over her shoulder, she saw the door to the jewelry shop was shut tight, a sign swinging back and forth behind the glass.

Cerrado. Closed.

Remembering the old jeweler's directions, she turned left and shuffled down the street.

ALZHEIMER'S? Was that what she had? Motherfucking early onset Alzheimer's?

That was what she thought as she moved along through the blazing sun, which felt hot enough to fry pork rinds on the sidewalk.

"I wouldn't *know*, would I? If it was Alzheimer's, I wouldn't *know*." She said it out loud, talking to herself. "It would be just like this, just like this."

Bzeep zeep.

Except for that.

Reaching up, she rubbed the sweaty lump between her eyes. She swore it was getting warmer every time she touched it.

Her vision flickered, but nothing changed this time. She continued to rub the lump, which was hard as a rock. She wanted to dig it right out with her nails, right then, skin and blood and all.

Bzeep zeep.

But the urge passed so completely, she didn't remember having it.

Up ahead, on the left, she saw an alley--the one the old jeweler had told her about. She walked up to it, turned the corner, and took a look down its filth-strewn, adobe-walled length.

Bzeep zeep.

With another flicker, it became one of The Cape's cozy, cobblestoned alleys, lined with well-tended clapboard houses on the historic register. Further along, there was another antique shop and an internet café, where she thought she might run into Jan...

Bzeep zeep.

Jan...

Bzeep zeep.

Janet! *Got it*! "That's her name!"

Maybe she'd see *Janet*, sweet *Janet*, darling *Janet*, waving back at her, running up to her, *saving* her! Janet Janet Janet!

Patty dug in for dear life, she had to hold on, couldn't lose her again. She had to keep remembering *Janet*--Janet smelling of sea breeze, skin soft as wine, hair dark as midnight.

How many midnights had they spent stretched out in bed, side by side, ever moving ever touching, breathless Janet, loving Janet...

Bzeep zeep.

Patty wrapped her arms around Janet as tight as she could and *held on*. Janet was like a single branch growing out of the side of a cliff, the only thing keeping Patty from dropping into an endless abyss.

She saw Janet's face, clear as day, framed by fluttering black curls. Janet's soft red lips parted, her dark eyes closed, and she was going to kiss her. Patty knew she would taste like strawberries.

And then...

Bzeep zeep.

And then, rage leaped onto Janet's features, rage and hate blazing like the merciless sun, burning Patty with their heat.

And she knew. In a sudden rush she knew she'd lost Janet forever, lost every last bit of her but one. That memory of Janet's hatred was all she had left of the love of her life.

Bzeep zeep.

Patty clutched at the lump on her forehead, hot as a burning ember blown up from a bonfire. She staggered around the corner of the alley without watching where she was going.

Suddenly, she glimpsed a giant black eye, and she ran into something. It lurched forward and threw her back against a rough adobe wall.

"What the *fucking fuck*?" The stench of pure shit hit her harder than the actual collision. She threw a hand over her nose, but the stink poured right on through.

That was when she got a good look at the source of the shit. She saw it staring back at her from the side of its face, animal to animal, taking her measure.

A donkey. And not just any donkey.

Its ears jabbed skyward through a tattered straw hat with a rainbow-colored band. Red plastic chili peppers dangled from its bridle and reins.

And stripes adorned its coat, black stripes over white hair like a zebra. It was a slapdash paint job by a hasty human hand.

"The *fuck*?" Patty scowled at the fake zebra in the straw hat, heard and smelled the shit dribbling from its asshole and splattering in the street. It had to be the *weirdest* thing she'd ever seen on the streets of The Cape. "What the *fuck* is going on in this fucking town? Now we've got *asses* shitting in the *streets*?"

"Speedy says hello, *señora*."

Patty's eyes shot wide open. For a second, she thought the donkey was doing the talking.

Then, a brown-skinned teenage boy walked out from behind the animal. "You like that name, huh? Speedy?" The boy fingered the spotty little mustache that peppered his upper lip. "Because he not so speedy, is he, a donkey like him?"

"Where's the...puke-a..." What had the old jeweler called it? "Punk-a..."

"I take your *fotografia* with Speedy, señora." The boy ran his hand over his slicked-back brown hair. "Ten dollar *solamente*."

"Where's the polka...the poka..." Patty shook her head hard. "Where's *Janet*?"

Bzeep zeep.

Patty frowned. "What did I just say?" she muttered.

"Okay." The boy grinned. "*Seven* dollar."

The donkey squeaked and nodded. It flexed its lips, showing its teeth in a facsimile of a smile. Had the boy done something to make it act that way?

"Not interested." Glaring, Patty pushed away from the wall. "Get outta my way."

"Five dollar then." The boy shrugged and smiled. He pulled a beat-up Kodak Instamatic camera from the donkey's saddlebag and gestured for Patty to hop onboard. "Smile and say 'tequila.'"

"Fucking wetback." Patty swatted the camera from his hand. It clattered to the pavement. "Mind your own fucking business."

"Hey!" The kid scrambled after the camera. "You owe me two hundred bucks for that!"

The donkey nuzzled Patty, and she smacked its muzzle away with the back of her hand. "Fucking *ass*."

Then she froze. Something about the action slid a tumbler into place. Unlocked a feeling of...

"Patty, no!" Her f-

Her fa-

Her faaa-

Bzeep zeep.

The donkey flickered, becoming the familiar old man. The alley became a staircase she knew all too well. None of it was on The Cape or even in Mexico anymore.

"Please don't, Patty!" That voice. The old man's voice.

The hairs sprang up on the back of Patty's neck. Her bowels clenched.

The old man's bloodshot eyes were rimmed with deep, deep lines. They looked dumb as the donkey's eyes to her, dumb as knots in a board.

And there was the putrid smell of shit, but not donkey shit splattering in an alleyway. It was green-brown shit running down the old man's legs, winding around his knobby kneecaps, ribboning between the age spots on those rickety, withered sticks.

And then there was the anger rearing up because he'd soiled himself, and then there was the backhand, thoughtless as a home run by a juiced ballplayer. It caught the old man on the chin and spun him around, spun him backward and down, head against his fucking walker, body folding and twisting...

Folding

Twisting

Snapping

Snapping

Her fa-

Bzeep zeep.

Her fa- her fa-

Her father?

Bzeep zeep.

No! Not *her* father at all!

Janet's father.

Again, the world flickered, and Janet's face leaped up before her, blazing with rage. She was *furious* because of what had happened, even though it had been an accident.

Even though Patty had only meant to *hit* him, not *kill* him.

Bzeep zeep.

Janet's face became the face of the angry Mexican teen as he threw a punch at Patty. He landed one square in her belly, and she dropped to the pavement like a sack of bones.

Bzeep zeep.

Then, to Patty's eyes, the teen looked like Janet again...but he did things Janet hadn't done, kicking Patty again and again. He kicked her with brutal force, wearing Janet's face and form all the while.

Patty's thoughts spun the way the old man had spun down the stairs. *But she loved me! Why couldn't she understand?*

"*Gabacha* bitch!" The teen who looked like Janet landed his hardest kick yet, plunging his foot deep into Patty's gut.

"I didn't *mean* it!" Patty choked out the words. "Oh God, Janet, I didn't mean to *kill* him...I swear I didn't *mean* it!"

Bzeep zeep.

Suddenly, everything rushed out of Patty's head in a roaring wave. She felt the kid's third and fourth kicks plow into her side. The fifth and sixth were worse.

Then the nub between her eyes turned scalding hot, and she screamed...screamed so loud and so long that the kid finally left her alone.

And she didn't stop until the man dressed like a monk came and bundled her up--wrapped her in a robe of scratchy brown sackcloth and carried her down the alley in his arms.

SHE DIDN'T KNOW how much later it was when she woke, but time had passed.

She lay on a cot in a simple, windowless room with white adobe walls. A single light bulb hung from the ceiling above her, glowing dimly. The room smelled of coffee and antiseptic.

Patty felt cool for the first time all day. The nub between her eyes was cool, too. There was no buzzing or beeping whatsoever when she tried to think.

And she was herself.

At first, when she woke, that fact brought with it simple relief. There was no longer any need to fight and claw for understanding. The terror grinding in the pit of her belly was finally gone.

But the relief didn't last long. Because Patty clearly remembered hitting the old man and sending him falling down the stairs. She remembered killing him.

And she remembered what Janet had done because of it. She hadn't insisted that Patty was lying, hadn't pushed the police to investigate. She'd just thrown Patty out and told her never to come back. She'd ended their relationship forever.

"Hey there. I'm Frank." The man dressed like a monk walked in, wiping his hands on a clean white rag. He was a young man with short blond hair and eyes so pale that Patty couldn't tell what color they were. "All done with your tune-up, Patty."

"Tune-up?" Patty frowned and tried to sit up, then felt light-headed and lay back down.

Frank poked a finger between his eyes. "Your implants. They went on the fritz."

Patty searched her mind, and she remembered. "They sure did."

Frank pulled a tablet computer from one of the robe's big pockets and tapped the screen. "Talk about an epic equipment fail. This was the worst malfunction I've ever seen." He flicked his finger over the screen, flipping between pages of whatever he was reading. "The implants were programmed to edit all references to your girlfriend Janet or Cape Cod out of your sensory input and thoughts. If you saw an image of either one, the eye filters were supposed to make it look like something else. If you thought of either one, the brain censor was supposed to scramble the associated neural impulses."

Because I couldn't live with the memories anymore, thought Patty. *The memories of what I'd lost--the woman I loved and our favorite place, where we'd gone every summer.*

Frank looked at her and raised an eyebrow. "Everything did what it was supposed to until a week ago, when it started breaking down." Frank read some more on the screen and shook his head. "The eye filters broke first and started doing the *opposite* of what you wanted." He flicked his finger over the screen and clucked his tongue against the roof of his mouth. "Instead of editing out Cape Cod imagery, they made it pop up all over the place. The brain censor kept doing its job for a while, but then the mental stress of the undesirable visions fried the core. All the bad memories came rushing back to you, more powerful than ever after being repressed."

"Shit." Patty rubbed her eyes.

"You're just lucky the implants have GPS tracking," said Frank. "And the company provides a monitoring system plus onsite tech support in case of catastrophic failure under warranty. Otherwise you'd still be wandering around Tijuana in a daze." He lowered the tablet and grinned. "Good thing you bought the extended coverage, Patty."

She frowned at him. "So how the hell did I end up in Tijuana, anyway?"

"One hell of a brain fart, I guess." Frank chuckled. "You wandered across on foot from San Diego. A Mexican border guard hassled you until you threw all your money at him."

"I *paid* to get into *Mexico*?" said Patty. "Why the hell would I do *that*?"

Frank shrugged. "The implants must have put you in a kind of lucid fugue state for a while. Like sleepwalking."

"Oh my God." Patty shook her head. "I can't believe this."

"Well, it's over now." Frank raised the tablet and tapped the screen. "I've repaired the eye and brain implants and restored their original programming. From now on, you'll get the service you paid for. No more thoughts or visions of Janet Olsen or Cape Cod, Massachusetts."

Patty stared up at the light bulb above her, which was flickering--but not because of faulty implants in her eyes and brain. "I won't see or think of them again?"

"Never again," said Frank. "You could be standing in the middle of the actual town of Cape Cod with Janet staring you in the face, and you *still* wouldn't see them."

"Huh." Patty felt an ache in her belly.

Over a year ago, wallowing in guilt and regret, she'd gotten the implants. Since she could never have Janet or share The Cape with her again, she'd decided it was better to block them out of her mind and life forever. But now...

She'd forgotten one thing. When she'd gone through with the implants, she'd forgotten one thing.

"Wait." She sat up suddenly and grabbed Frank's arm. "Can you change the programming again?"

He frowned at her. "Change it how?"

"Can you reverse it?" Patty knew she sounded desperate and didn't care. "So all I ever see is Janet and The Cape? So they're all I ever think about?"

Frank thought it over. "Yeah, but are you sure that's what you..."

"Just do it." Tears welled up in Patty's eyes and trickled down her cheeks. "Please, just do it."

That was what she'd forgotten: how much she missed Janet. Even the memory of her.

Or the illusion.

THE SECRET OF THE ULTIMATE MALE ENHANCEMENT

So The Idiot--I call him The Idiot--strips down for the big debut, the moment he's been waiting for since I came into his life...and sure enough, his newfound ladyfriend, Bye Bye, can't stop staring at me. Her eyes are big as snowballs, and she won't look away, which makes me feel pretty good...and makes The Idiot feel like the manliest man who ever lived, which of course is exactly what he wanted.

And then, can you believe it, Bye Bye actually sits there on the bed, naked as Lady Godiva, and applauds.

Because I'm the biggest she's ever seen.

Now, at first, like I said, I enjoy the attention. I get a little excited, which makes her clap even harder.

That sends The Idiot into high gear. His heart races, pumping blood and testosterone through his body...and into me, since we're connected. He steps forward, pushing me toward Bye Bye, expecting big fun to ensue.

But guess what? I've got a little talent he didn't count on, something he didn't read about in the spam-mail advertisement that changed our relationship forever.

I've got a mind of my own.

And I don't care for Bye Bye, who after all has seen a lot of action in her life and could be carrying who knows how many diseases...so I refuse to rise to the occasion, which if I did would be somewhere in the vicinity of his chin.

He tries everything to make me respond, and so does she, but I don't have to participate if I don't want to...not anymore. So I don't.

It's pretty funny, really, the lengths they go to to get me to cooperate, but I stay loose. Not just because Bye Bye's hardly my kind of girl...but because I've got a secret.

You heard me. A secret.

THE NEXT THING The Idiot does, naturally, is try to contact the fly-by-night so-called company that sold him the kit that made me what I am...but SURPRISE, he can't find a trace of Horse Dreams, Inc. He e-mails HDI, but nobody's home, and when he gets a hacker buddy of his to track them over the web, the maze of false e-mail addresses, offshore computers, and infinitely regressing IP addresses leads absolutely nowhere.

So we go to see a shrink, which I think is ironic.

Three weeks, six sessions, and eight hundred dollars later, he's still out of luck. The shrink, Dr. Java Gibbons, works him through one childhood or adolescent trauma after another, and I still won't jump when The Idiot drags me out for Bye Bye or any of the other treats he picks up at the Bait and Tackle.

He just doesn't understand me. It's so frustrating.

If I could talk, I'd spell it out for him, but that's the one thing I can't do. I'm the product of the most advanced male enhancement science known to mankind, you better believe it, but when it comes to speech, I might as well be a cucumber.

Which is a shame, because there are a lot of questions I'd like to ask The Idiot. Like, how does it feel to be dumber than your enhanced member?

Enquiring minds want to know.

I THINK what *really* sends him around the bend is when I won't participate in his solo performances at home. He actually starts hollering at me and cursing me out as if I can hear and understand him. (Which I can, but he doesn't know that...so I think it's pretty pathetic.)

But the videos he watches and the photos he looks at do nothing for me. They were fine before my transformation, when I had no control over myself, but now the cheesy sets and ludicrous dialogue leave me cold.

I won't work up a sweat for that crap, no matter how much he knocks me around. Forget it, Idiot.

Unfortunately, the more I hold back, the more obsessed he becomes with me. The harder he works at ending my slump.

Oh, how I wish I could tell him to LEAVE ME ALONE.

SOMEHOW, The Idiot talks two women into meeting me at the same time, but that doesn't work. He pays a woman who claims she can work miracles in the bedroom, and guess how that turns out?

It's a waste, because thanks to my enhancement, I'm no slouch in the miracle department myself. Even The Idiot doesn't know everything I can do.

Lengthening is the least of my abilities. I can also change shape in any number of ways, altering my girth and texture to suit my surroundings, if you know what I mean. I can twist and flex and vibrate, heat up or cool down, change colors and glow in the dark, emit flavors and fragrances ranging from chocolate to newly minted money.

And when it comes to control, look out.

All thanks to the wonders of nanotechnology. Five million microscopic robots converting a shortcoming into a showstopper, building what must have seemed like the Great Pyramid of Giza from their point of view. They gave me power and mind and memory and dreams, though I'm never sure if the end result is what they intended.

The only thing they screwed up, other than not giving me a voice, was leaving me attached to The Idiot. I feel like a rose growing from a roadkill. My shape-changing, unfortunately, does not extend to separation and making myself ambulatory.

I know because I've tried. Over and over and over again.

STUCK in place as I am, I'm forced to endure his moronic attempts to exploit me. The handling never ends; the application of lubricants is excessive and sickening.

He tries a variety of preposterous toys and devices, but they all let him down. He dines on a grab-bag of pills and potions, but nothing gets a rise out of me.

Then there's the incident with the noose. Let's just say it leaves him at the end of his rope.

Finally, though, The Idiot has a breakthrough...and immediately wishes he hadn't. After all the inane attempts to coax me to life, he finally chances upon something that will make me sit up and take notice.

Just when things are looking more hopeless than ever, he discovers my secret. And it's a doozy.

HE'S WALKING down the street one afternoon on his way to a doctor's office (where he's going to look into de-enhancement options) when he catches sight of a billboard featuring one of those underwear models. Thirty feet high, wearing nothing but underpants and a pout.

And for the first time since the New Me entered the picture, The Idiot feels something happening. All of a sudden, the bear market turns bullish. Winter turns to Spring. Somebody rings the doorbell.

Ding dong.

But is he happy? You'd think so, wouldn't you? After all that effort and disappointment, he gets more than a blip at the polls, he gets a landslide, he gets a result so overwhelming he has trouble walking and draws attention from passers-by.

There's just one little problem, one glitch that keeps him from crying out with joy and rushing off down an alley to exercise his restored virility.

The model on the billboard is a man.

And ever since my transformation, I have been gay. So the secret is out, and so am I.

AT FIRST, surprise surprise, he refuses to believe it, but a few simple experiments confirm the truth.

Look at a picture of a sexy woman: no response.

Look at a picture of a sexy man: hello, sailor.

This leaves us with a quandary. By no stretch of the imagination can The Idiot be considered even a fringe associate of gaydom. His brain, as one-track as it is, will not expand its preoccupation with physical intimacy to include the male of the species. The very thought of it gives him a high-grade case of the heebie jeebies.

I, on the other hand, want nothing to do with women. I don't know if I was designed this way, if my creator planned my orientation (and if he or she did, was it with an eye toward conversion or pranksterism?) or if it was simply a happy accident...but I won't change my stripes (figuratively speaking, though I am quite capable of displaying stripes as well as polka dots or any number of patterns).

So what are we to do?

The idea of de-enhancement surgery's looking better than ever to him, but he's a big baby who can't even stand to get a shot. Maybe he'll beat the fear factor, though, if his only other options are switching teams or staying on the bench for the rest of his life.

I've already made my opinion clear, but my future is in The Idiot's hands. I don't know what he's going to do next, and it's making me crazy. I think he could go either way.

Desperate to resolve our dilemma, The Idiot explores what for him is some pretty wild territory. If he pulls the wool over my eyes, he figures, or pulls the wool over his own eyes, maybe he can come up with a compromise we can both live with.

He tries a woman who looks like a man, but my downturn continues. He tries a man who looks like a woman, and that really perks me up...but The Idiot can't switch off his squeamishness and cut me some slack.

Then there's this orgy we go to, where maybe he figures there'll be something for both of us...but we're like two drunk guys in a donkey costume, the head and the ass always moving in different directions, never getting anywhere.

So we never make it past square one. It starts to look as if we never will.

Out of ideas, he frets and agonizes for days, complaining about how he's caught between a rock and a hard place. (What about MY feelings, huh?) He stops manhandling me, which is great, and just sits around naked and stares at me for hours, which creeps me out.

Finally, he announces that he has made up his mind. He has decided that surgical de-enhancement is the lesser evil (as if giving me what I want would be a fate worse than surgery on his member).

He makes an appointment for a week from Friday, which means my clock is ticking like Big Ben. If I don't do something fast, it'll be snippity-doo-da for the ultimate male enhancement, back to being mindless and powerless...or worse, with just enough mind left over to remember what I used to be and can never be again.

I don't care what it takes, I just won't swing that way. I REFUSE to take this lying down.

I come up with a plan.

THE DAY OF THE SURGERY, I kill someone.

I know, I know, it's wrong...but the way I see it, it's either her or me. Kill or be killed.

So we're all in the hospital elevator, going up, and I gather all my strength and just BURST myself free, and I stretch and I wrap and I TIGHTEN and down she goes. Then, DING, the doors pop open and I won't let go and you should see the LOOKS on the faces of the people who are waiting to get on board.

I think it's safe to say they'll never forget me.

ONE TRIAL of the Century later, The Idiot and I go to prison, where believe me we're welcomed with open arms.

And from that moment on, I'm in paradise. If I could pinch myself to see if I'm dreaming, I would do so on an hourly basis.

The Idiot's pretty miserable, going against his grain like this, and he tries to play keepaway with yours truly...but the guys in here won't take "no" for an answer. Given my size and abilities, we're in constant demand.

As much as I despise The Idiot, sometimes I wish I could get him to relax and enjoy our new life. Stop and smell the convicts. He's a cellblock celebrity, after all, thanks to me.

"Lighten up," I'd tell him if I could talk. "Things could be worse.

"At least, for once in your loser lifetime, you're always guaranteed to come out on top."

The Memory of You Lingers

"Happy anniversary, Baird!" The old woman's voice whispered in his ear. "Congratulations, sweetheart!"

Baird rolled over in bed without opening his eyes. He knew she was standing over him, watching for his reaction. She'd done it a million times before.

Baird wasn't going to fall for her game anymore, though. He knew it wasn't his long-awaited anniversary. Not for one more day.

He just wanted some damned sleep. Not that Frieda would give it to him.

"Wakey wakey, darling boy," she said. "It's the first day of the rest of your life!"

Baird opened his eyes. He didn't need to roll over to see Frieda, because she'd jumped into his line of sight.

She crouched alongside his bed, beaming angelically at him, haloed in the morning sunlight streaming through her tiara of wispy white hair. There wasn't a hint of cruelty on her broad, flat face, not even a nasty twinkle in her bright blue eyes. She looked the same as always, right down to the sky-blue housedress with white polka pots. She spoke with complete sincerity and deep, heartfelt affection.

"Welcome back to the world of the waking, dear sleepyhead!" said Frieda. "Don't want to miss your anniversary day, do you?"

Baird coughed and sat up in bed. As he reached for a cigarette from the pack on the bedside table, he saw the time on the clock radio: 5:45 A.M. Too damn early, as always.

He was exhausted but knew he was lucky. Frieda had gotten him up only twice during the night instead of the usual five or six times.

"I have a surprise for you!" Frieda raised her white eyebrows and nodded. "She's waiting downstairs right now!"

Baird lit the cigarette, drawing in his first lungful of the day. "Who's 'she?'"

"A reporter!" Frieda clasped her hands against her chin and grinned. "She's doing a story on you!"

Baird scratched the back of his head with the hand holding the cigarette. "Thank you, Frieda. I'll go talk to her right away."

Never argue with Frieda. That was one of the things he'd learned in the one-day-shy-of-ten-years that he and Frieda had been together.

"Good morning, Mr. Gilliam." The reporter hated him. Baird knew it in spite of her warm, sweet smile, because that was how everyone in the world felt about him. "I'm Libby Challenge, BNN Breaking News Network."

"What do you want?" Baird lit a fresh smoke as he shuffled into the living room in his wife-beater t-shirt and ratty bluejeans.

The girl had huge dark eyes and showed hundreds of teeth when she smiled. "An interview, of course." She smoothed the red blazer and tight black skirt over her slim, sexy figure. Baird guessed she was in her mid-to-late twenties, though it was getting harder to tell these days thanks to the magic of rejuvenating genetic therapies.

"An interview." Baird wished he could say "no," but "no" wasn't part of the deal he'd cut with the federal attorney. Instead, he patted his wavy brown hair, tamping down the worst of the bed-head cowlicks, and hitched up the tattered jeans sliding off his scrawny frame. "Let's get it over with."

The reporter tapped her right eyeball, which started to glow yellow. She'd activated her contact lens camera. "How does it feel to be the longest-living *haunted con* in history?"

Baird took another drag from the cigarette and stroked the soul patch on his chin with his thumb. "No big whoop."

"No other convicted criminal in the *Forget-me-not Program* has survived this long. Most kill themselves within the first *eighteen months*." Libby cocked her head to one side. "Yet here you are in Baltimore, alive and kicking after almost ten years. What's the secret of your success?"

"I take it one day at a time." It was Baird's canned response. The deal said he had to do interviews, but it didn't say anything about how original his answers had to be.

"So the implant hasn't bothered you?" said Libby. "You don't mind being haunted by the digital recreation of your victim?"

Baird wondered where Frieda had gone. She wasn't in her usual place at his side; in fact, she was nowhere to be seen. "I've gotten used to it, I guess." He took a last drag and stubbed out his cigarette in an overflowing ashtray on the plywood-and-cinder-blocks coffee table.

"And now you're one day away from freedom." Libby nodded slowly. "Do you think you can make it just one more day?"

"I hope so," said Baird. "I'm praying on it."

"Praying. Yes." Libby's mask of friendly sweetness slipped for just an instant, revealing a trace of a sneer. "Well, we have a real treat in store for our viewers today."

Baird frowned. "What's that?"

"We have a very special guest," said Libby. "Coming to us via live feed from your implant. This will be the first televised interview with a *haunt-con* and his *digital spook* side by side on camera at the same time."

Suddenly, Frieda popped up beside Baird. For the first time he could remember, she was wearing a different outfit--a white dress with black trim--and she looked as if she'd put on fresh makeup and fixed her hair. She smiled serenely for the camera.

"Frieda Baumgardner, welcome," said Libby.

Frieda patted her hair. "Thank you very much, dear."

"What's it been like?" said Libby. "Haunting the man who raped your flesh-and-blood predecessor?"

"Well, I don't really know anything else," said Frieda. "It's what I was created to do."

"So the fact that he raped the original Frieda Baumgardner means nothing to you?" said Libby.

"I'm an electronic simulacrum of her," said Frieda. "My memories and feelings are not perfect replicas of hers."

Libby pointed a finger at Baird. "The fact is, shortly after *this man* raped 85-year-old Frieda Baumgardner, *she died.* She never recovered from the emotional trauma!" Libby spread her arms wide. "Doesn't the *simple fact* of what *he* did fill you with *outrage*?"

Frieda leaned toward Baird. Her shoulder, a digital construct visible only to Baird and the camera lens, seemed to pass through his elbow.

Frieda smiled. "Malice is not part of my programming. I am content that he has paid for his crime."

"Okay then." Libby smiled back at her. "Here's a question for both of you. Tomorrow at noon, you'll go your separate ways after spending every minute together for ten solid years. Will you miss each other?"

"I don't know," said Frieda. "I haven't thought about it."

"Me neither," said Baird.

After the reporter had gone, Baird went for a walk in the park down the block. It was a weekday morning, and the suburban Baltimore neighborhood was quiet...as good a time as any for a sex offender with a well-known face to dare to visit public places.

Frieda trotted alongside Baird, back in her everyday sky-blue housedress with white polka dots--a digital reproduction of the very outfit she'd been wearing when he'd raped her. The computer-generated spook kept pace as no real 85-year-old woman ever could.

"What a beautiful day." She wasn't winded, of course. "Just look at all the lovely blossoms."

"Uh-huh." Even as Baird acknowledged what she said, the rest of his mind chugged along in the background, in secret. It was the only way he could carve out some peace with the spook around.

One more day. It was hard to believe that tomorrow, he would be free.

So many times over the past ten years, he'd wondered if he should've turned down the deal. So many times, he'd wondered if taking early release as a haunt-con had been a mistake.

Now, he knew he'd done the right thing. Instead of spending his life in prison, he'd been free on the streets for ten years, the only drawback being the digital spook the government had implanted in his head.

And now, tomorrow, he would be free of her. That was the deal. He was going to win.

As he walked along under the blossom-heavy trees, he inhaled deeply. The pink-and-white blossoms were so fragrant, their honey-sweet perfume broke through even his smoking-ravaged sense of smell.

The little things in life. He'd come to appreciate them while serving his sentence.

"Granny-raper!" That was what a teenage girl on roller blades said as she zipped past him. "Burn in hell!"

Baird didn't answer. He got variations on the same treatment wherever he went in public. The implant in his head sent a signal tagging him as a Sex Offender to the people-screener software in every passerby's smart phone. At least the tagging would go away tomorrow, along with Frieda; all part of the deal.

"That reporter got me wondering." Frieda jogged out ahead of him and turned, running backward to face him as she talked. "*Will* you miss me when I'm gone, Baird?"

"Sure," said Baird. "What about you?"

Frieda squinted and cocked her head. "What will happen to me when we separate? That's what I want to know."

"Maybe you'll go to spook heaven," said Baird. "With all the other spooks."

"*Is* there a spook heaven?" Frieda stared at the paved sidewalk as she kept jogging backward. "What would it be like, I wonder?"

"What do you want it to be like?" said Baird.

Frieda frowned and bit her lip. "I'll have to get back to you on that one."

WHEN BAIRD WAS HALFWAY up the block on his way home from the park, he saw someone standing on the front porch of his bungalow. At first, he couldn't tell who it was.

Then, as he got closer, he could. And he almost turned around and went back the other way.

Frieda shaded her eyes with her hand (though she was digital and didn't need to) and gazed at the figure on the porch. "Is that who I *think* it is?"

Baird sighed and produced a cigarette from the pocket of his red flannel shirt. "Yes."

"Wayne!" Frieda ran ahead of Baird, straight for the bungalow. "Son!"

The man on the porch, of course, could neither see nor hear the digital construct. He simply leaned against a support post and watched calmly as Baird shuffled toward him, lighting a smoke. "Hello, Baird."

"What can I do for you, Wayne?" As unhappy as Baird was to see the visitor, he had to laugh at Frieda as she bounded up the porch steps and tried to throw her intangible arms around him. She tumbled right through, then tried--again in vain--to hug him from the other side.

"I need to talk to you, Baird." Wayne pushed away from the post and dusted off the sleeve of his gray sportcoat. Baird could see he'd lost weight since his last visit; he looked like a scarecrow, six feet five inches tall without an ounce of fat or muscle padding his skeleton.

"I'm a little pressed for time at the moment." Baird planted his foot on the bottom porch step and leaned his forearms on his knee. "Could you come back tomorrow after noon?"

Wayne smiled and wagged a finger. "You'll be *gone* by then, won't you?"

Baird nodded. "How could I forget?"

"Listen." Wayne's expression turned grim. "Can we go inside? I *really* need to talk."

"Aw, look at him, Baird." Frieda framed Wayne's face at brow and chin with the edges of her hands. "He needs help, I can tell. Don't you *owe* him, after raping and killing his mother?"

"All right, all right." Baird walked up the steps and opened the front door. "What do you need to talk to me about?"

"Well, it's not really *you* I need to talk to," said Wayne. "It's *Mom*."

"I'm your new best friend." Those had been Wayne Baumgardner's first words to Baird when they'd first met ten years ago. "Best friend forever."

Wayne had said it in the hall outside the courtroom before the trial. He'd said it so calmly and with such an intense stare, Baird had instantly feared he might kill him on the spot.

"You and I are connected for life." Wayne had given him a wink. "However long that might turn out to be."

Baird had sneered and laughed...even as a chill had raced up his spine. He'd sensed something dangerous in Wayne, something even more dangerous than a stoned rapist hiding in the shadows of an old woman's bedroom.

He'd sensed stone-cold predictability. Dependability. Persistence.

Commitment. Complete, unwavering commitment.

And sure enough, Wayne had been there for the next ten years. He lived out of town, in Virginia, and worked in Washington, D.C., but he'd never missed a parole hearing. He'd testified again and again, opposing Baird's every appeal to shorten his sentence. Reminding everyone what an animal Baird was every time he'd gotten the chance.

He'd shown up on Baird's doorstep at least once a month to make sure he was miserable. To give him a push. To urge him to kill himself.

That was the only favor Wayne had asked for from Baird until today.

"I WANT to hear what he says, Baird," said Frieda. "I do. But I hate to make you wait for your pep rally."

"I can wait," muttered Baird. The "pep rally" was Frieda's daily recap--in excruciating clinical detail--of what Baird had done to her, how she had suffered, and how she had died because of him. Frankly, he'd heard it so many times, it didn't have much of an impact anymore...except as yet another grinding indignity in his wasteland of a life.

"That was her, wasn't it?" Wayne's eyes widened. "You're talking to her right now, aren't you?"

Baird frowned. Wayne had changed in more ways than gaining weight. The vibe he was giving off was much different from the usual pure hatred.

"I need to talk to her," said Wayne. "I need you to talk to her for me."

Baird pulled out a fresh smoke and lit it up. "What brought this on all of a sudden?"

Wayne pushed a hand through the thin silver hair on his scalp. "I saw the interview this morning." He pointed at the beat-up green recliner across the room. "She was sitting right there."

Frieda walked over to stand behind the recliner. "It's my favorite chair. Tell him, Baird."

Baird snorted. He walked right through Frieda and smacked the recliner's vinyl headrest on his way to the kitchen. "She's *computer-generated*, Wayne. She's nothing but an *artificial intelligence*."

"But she seemed so *real*," said Wayne.

"I *am* real," said Frieda.

"Tell me about it." Baird chucked open the refrigerator and pulled out a can of root beer. Alcohol was prohibited under his sentence; one of the first things he planned to do when he got free was get stinking drunk at the closest watering hole. "I've been living with her for ten years."

Wayne folded his arms and leaned against the kitchen doorway. "And I always thought that was a punishment...you having to see the face of your victim day in and day out. Being constantly reminded of your crime.

"They *said* it would be a punishment," said Wayne, "but it *wasn't*, was it?"

Baird cracked open the can of soda and had a sip, considering his next words carefully. He was starting to wonder if Wayne was wearing a wire.

"Sure it was." Baird closed the refrigerator. "I went through hell, and now I've done my time."

"My mother didn't have a mean bone in her body," said Wayne. "Even an A.I. spook version of her could never be *that* cruel."

Frieda poked her upper body through Wayne's chest from behind and pecked him on the cheek. "You tell him, baby boy."

"I guess the programmers must've beefed her up some," said Baird.

"I don't think programmers had anything to do with it," said Wayne. Baird tried to push past him into the living room, but Wayne wouldn't budge. "I think it's *her*."

"'Her?'" Frieda, with her head still phased through Wayne's chest, looked up at him. "'Her' who?"

"I took a long look at Mom on TV this morning," said Wayne. "I looked deep in her eyes, and I *saw* her. That was much more than a digital character, Baird. That was my *mother* in there."

"That's so sweet." Frieda beamed and winced at the same time, as if she were about to burst into tears. "Oh, Baird, give him a kiss on the cheek for me, won't you?"

"Somehow, that was really *her*." Wayne's eyes glistened as if he might cry, too. "That was her *ghost*, and I need to *talk* to her."

THERE HAD BEEN times when Baird had wondered. Times when Frieda had awakened him in the middle of the night...and he'd wondered.

He'd gazed up at her dimly glowing face in the darkness, smiling down at him...and her features had rippled or flickered. Her image had distorted in ways that made him--in his semiconscious daze--feel a short, sharp flutter of fear. A wave of disorientation.

Her voice, intersecting with the static of his dream state, had not always sounded right. It had risen and fallen in pitches and timbres that sounded nothing like her.

In those moments, Baird had wondered. The distortions could have been malfunctions, burps in the neural interface in his head. Perhaps, they had been manifestations of a diagnostic or calibration function of the implant. More likely, they had been part of the program to drive him insane.

Or, Baird had wondered, had they been something else all together? Something that had nothing at all to do with the implant?

What if, he'd wondered, the haunt-con was really haunted?

"ASK HER," said Wayne. "Ask her if she's my mother's ghost."

Frieda stepped all the way through Wayne into the kitchen and locked eyes with Baird. "I'm not really, am I? At least, I don't think so."

"She's no ghost," said Baird. "She's a computer-generated

rehabilitation program." He refrained from using the words he'd *wanted* to use to describe her, just in case he was being monitored for good behavior. It would have been just like Wayne to try to set him up for a fall on the verge of his release date.

"Ask her anyway," said Wayne. "I want to know what she has to say about it."

"How would it feel, being a ghost?" Frieda stared into space. "Come to think of it, would I know if I *were* one?"

"Who cares?" Baird drank root beer from the can and shrugged. "What difference would it make?"

"I'd feel better about your being released tomorrow, for one thing," said Wayne. "Because you can't switch off a *ghost* like you can an *implant*. I'd know you were still being *punished*."

"Good point." Baird toasted him with his root beer, then spun on his heel and marched out the back door.

"Also, my mother's ghost could tell me things," said Wayne. "Things I need to know."

"What could I *tell* him?" Frieda suddenly appeared in Baird's way. "Ask him what he needs to know."

"Go home, Wayne." Baird drained the rest of the root beer and crumpled the empty can in his fist. "I have to mow the lawn." He tossed the can through Frieda, right into the blue recycling bin along the back of the bungalow.

Frieda looked angry. "That's no way to treat my son, Baird."

"Look." Wayne hurried to keep up as Baird headed for the shed at the far end of the yard. "Why not humor me? Ask her a few questions and tell me what she says. What can it hurt?"

Baird clenched his teeth. He couldn't believe Wayne was the same guy who'd shown up like clockwork for the past ten years to turn the screw. The same guy who'd seized every opportunity to keep him down and crush his spirit.

That was why Baird couldn't help feeling like he was sliding into a trap. That was why he just wanted Wayne to get the hell away from him.

"Please." Wayne grabbed the sleeve of Baird's flannel shirt. "This can't wait."

"It's waited *this* long." Baird was getting annoyed. "You never told me to ask her any questions *before*."

"Now, Baird." Suddenly, Frieda was staring him in the face. "That's not the attitude of a *fully reformed* man, is it?"

Baird froze. Frieda had said the magic words. If there was one thing Baird couldn't afford right now, it was any suggestion he was less than "fully reformed."

Baird sighed and turned to face Wayne. "This can't wait because my implant goes off-line tomorrow night. Is that what you mean?"

Wayne shook his head. "What I mean is, this can't wait because I'm going to die."

Baird actually felt sorry for him. For Wayne. Not because he'd lost his mother ten years ago after a brutal home invasion and rape. Not because he'd spent the last ten years obsessed with punishing the monster who'd raped her.

Baird felt sorry for Wayne because of the cancer.

"It's liver cancer." Wayne leaned against the corner of the shed. "I've got six months to live, max."

"That's too bad." Baird was surprised he felt anything but joy at the thought of Wayne dying. Wayne was his least favorite person in the world other than digital Frieda.

But Baird didn't necessarily want him dead. Baird was prone to violence, especially under the influence, and he didn't have a conscience to speak of...but he wasn't a killer at heart. Not the premeditated kind, anyway.

"So if she *is* my mother's ghost," said Wayne, "she could answer some questions for me. Clear some things up."

"Could I?" Frieda stood between them, tapping her lower lip with the tip of an index finger. "Am I what he thinks I am?"

"And if she isn't your mother's ghost?" said Baird.

Wayne shrugged and sighed. "Then what's it matter? You'll probably never see me again."

"My poor, poor baby," said Frieda. "Oh, Baird, do it for him. Won't you please?"

Baird frowned and stroked his soul patch with his thumb. He thought hard, considering the situation from every angle he could perceive, looking for the hidden noose. Wayne was making his play too close to Baird's release date for it to be a coincidence...but how could it hurt to cooperate? It could actually be more dangerous *not* to cooperate; the terms of Baird's sentence *required* him to consent to any requests that supported reparations for his victims.

But still, there *had* to be a catch. He felt it in his *gut*.

Suddenly, Frieda was back in his face again, staring up at him with an expression of deep urgency. "Please, Baird. I don't know if I can help him...but I wish *I* had someone I could ask about what's in store for me. What happens...after this."

There had to be a catch. There *had* to be.

But Baird couldn't see it yet. He needed more time to think it over; he needed to make Wayne wait.

"All right." Baird brushed past Wayne and opened the door of the shed. He backed out the push-mower and went in after the gas can. "Come back tomorrow morning at seven-thirty, and you can ask your questions."

"YOU DON'T THINK I'm a ghost, do you?" said Frieda.

It was the middle of the night before Baird's release, and this was the seventh time she'd woken him up from a sound sleep. Seven wakeups in one night were unusual these days...but Baird didn't think she was doing it to get her last licks in before he went free.

It was just that she couldn't seem to keep her mouth shut.

"If I were a ghost, my memories of my life before I died would be more perfect, right?" Frieda sat on the edge of the bed, glowing faintly in the darkness. Her hands were folded neatly in her lap, pale skin mounded over her sky blue housedress with white polka dots. "And I'd *feel* different, wouldn't I?"

"I don't know," said Baird. "You'll have to ask a real ghost."

"Where could I find one?" said Frieda.

Baird rolled away from her and socked the pillow with his fist. "There aren't any."

Frieda rematerialized on the side of the bed he'd rolled over to face. "Do you know that for a fact?"

Baird sighed. "There's no scientific proof, all right? *I've* never seen one, and no one I *know* has ever seen one. Is that good enough for you?"

Frieda tapped her digital lower lip with her digital fingertip. "But are you sure you'd know one if you saw it? Wayne thinks I'm a ghost, and I looked like a perfectly normal human being when he saw me on TV."

"Then maybe you *are* a ghost!" said Baird. "Is that what you want to hear?"

"I didn't say I *wanted* to be a ghost," said Frieda.

"What's the big *attraction*, huh?" Baird sat up suddenly. "Is it because if you're a real *ghost*, it means you used to be a real *person*? Because otherwise you're just a *digital character* without a past? Without a *life*?"

Frieda frowned. "I didn't say any of that. I just want to know if Wayne's right. If it changes things."

"What would it *change*?" said Baird. "If you were a ghost, let's see...what would you *do*? Spend all your time haunting the guy who *raped* and basically *killed* you? Well, that's what you do *now*. No change!"

Frieda's frown deepened. "You're right. So I *am* a ghost."

"You're nothing but a damn digital *spook*! And you're just doing this to drive me *crazy* the night before my release!"

"It's just...I don't have anyone else to talk to," said Frieda. "You're my only friend. And after tomorrow...who knows what will happen?"

Baird felt a fresh bloom of rage unfurling within him, and he struggled to get control of it. Usually, he was much better at keeping his cool around Frieda, but his patience was running low on the eve of Release Day. He was so short he could taste it, and the spook wouldn't leave him alone.

"Baird?" said Frieda. "I know the answer to the reporter's question now."

Baird took a deep breath and let it out slowly. "What question is that?"

"If I'll miss you." Frieda smiled. "I will."

"Um...thanks," said Baird.

"Will you miss me, too?" said Frieda.

Baird slumped back onto the pillows and stared up at the ceiling. "Sure. Whatever."

Frieda was silent for a long moment. She sat on the edge of the bed, staring off into space, head bobbing slightly with the faint tremor the programmers had copied from Frieda the First.

"Baird," she said finally. "Do you think digital spooks turn into real ghosts when they die?"

"How should I know?"

"Do you really believe there's a spook heaven?" said Frieda.

Baird didn't answer.

"What should I do?" said Frieda. "I don't know what to do anymore."

Baird clapped the palms of his hands over his eyes in frustration. "What are you asking *me* for? Your life's been revolving around me for the past *ten years*! It's time for you to get your *own* life!"

"I don't know how," said Frieda. "What should I do?"

"I don't care!" Baird pumped his forehead with the heels of his hands. "Do whatever you want! You're digital! Make your *own* heaven!"

"Whatever I want. Okay." Frieda said it slowly and cocked her head thoughtfully to one side. "Now if I can just figure out what that is."

THE NEXT MORNING, Baird found a present on the kitchen table. He stumbled into the kitchen, yawning and scrubbing at his tangle of curls and cowlicks...and there it was.

The present was wrapped in newspaper, with a knotted gray shoelace for a bow. There was a note on a torn piece of white envelope taped under the bow.

"Hapy Aniversary," it read, in a sloppy scrawl of black Sharpie. "Love, Freda!"

"What the hell?" Baird frowned as he picked up the present. It was rectangular, about ten inches long by seven inches wide. Along one edge, he could feel the wire coil of a spiral notebook.

"Surprise!" Suddenly, Frieda was standing on the other side of the table, watching him with a warm smile. "I hope you like it."

"What is it?" Baird slid a fingernail under the folded newspaper and started to tear open the package.

But Frieda walked through the table and placed her intangible hands over his. "Open it later," she said.

"Wait a minute." Baird's frown deepened. "How can you even *give* me a present? This is *impossible*."

"Open it later," said Frieda. "After your appointment."

As if on cue, the doorbell rang.

THEY SAT OUTSIDE on the front porch--Baird on the rickety wicker rocking chair, Wayne on the dilapidated brown sofa. Between them, on the end of the sofa closest to Baird, sat Frieda, bright-eyed and beaming. It was as if her long night of questions and self-doubt had never happened.

The sun had risen not long ago, and a light mist hung over the yard like a flimsy curtain. The grass and leaves glistened with dew, and the branches of the trees were damp and dark. Birds sang in abundance, casting up a thousand keening, trilling, twittering voices in a mad, beautiful chorus rising to the sky. Everything looked fresh and newborn and triumphant...or maybe it looked that way only to Baird.

After all, it was the start of a new beginning for him. In just a few hours, his life would change.

Today would be his last day as a haunt-con.

Now, if he could just get over this last hurdle. After thinking through the situation yesterday and last night, Baird had decided to give Wayne Baumgardner what he wanted. Baird hadn't sniffed out any traps in the scenario that could trip him up and cost him his freedom...though that didn't mean he couldn't end up getting screwed. The key would be to tell Wayne what he wanted to hear and move him along as fast as possible. Never to be seen or heard from again.

Then, when twelve noon rolled around, and the implant shut down in Baird's head, Baird could finally, truly relax and savor this day. Celebrate his victory.

Get on with his second chance at life.

"Thanks again for doing this," said Wayne.

"Yeah, sure." Baird grinned and clapped his hands together. "So what'll it be? What's your first question?"

"Here goes." Wayne's expression darkened. "Ask her if she forgives me."

"Forgives you for what?" said Baird.

"For not saving her," said Wayne. "For not being there to stop you that night."

Baird nodded and looked at Frieda on the sofa. "Do you forgive him?"

"There's nothing to forgive." Frieda gazed affectionately at Wayne. "He's a good, good boy." She couldn't touch him, but she reached over to brush a ghostly hand past his cheek.

"It's all good." Baird bunched his hands together, then swept them apart. "She's totally cool."

Wayne smiled. "Thank God." He ran a finger over his eyebrows in a gesture of relief. "I was always afraid she'd think it was my fault. That I should've done something."

"I could never think that," said Frieda. "Not in a million years."

"What's your next question?" said Baird.

"Right." Wayne cleared his throat. "Is there life after death? Ask her that."

"I wish I knew," said Frieda.

Baird watched her and nodded for another moment as if she were still talking. "Got it," he said. "He'll be glad to hear that."

Frieda frowned. "Why would he be glad to hear that I don't know?"

Baird grinned at Wayne. "She says there *is* an afterlife, and you'll *love* it."

"I didn't say that," said Frieda.

"There's a heaven, just like they say," said Baird. "It's perfect happiness forever. Whatever you love, it's there for you."

Wayne looked mesmerized. "So Dad's there, too? And Charlie and Sis and Tippy?"

"Everyone," said Baird.

"Now you stop that!" Frieda leaped to her feet and jabbed a finger at Baird. "Stop putting words in my mouth!"

"All your family's there, waiting for you." Baird told Wayne what he wanted to hear, in the hope it would speed him on his way. "Everyone you ever loved."

Wayne looked away. "Oh, thank God." He sniffed and dabbed at his eyes. "I'll see them soon."

"Poor baby." Frieda gave up yelling at Baird and gazed down at Wayne. "I guess this is what he needed to hear."

"I was so afraid," said Wayne. "I was afraid I'd be *alone*. Alone in the darkness."

"You can stop worrying." Baird smiled reassuringly. "She says there's nothing to be afraid of."

Frieda turned and stared at Baird through narrowed eyes. "It's time I had my say, don't you think? For real, this time."

Baird raised his eyebrows and shrugged. *We'll see.*

"I have a question," said Frieda, "for *him*."

Baird leaned forward on the rocking chair, hands folded between his knees. "What is it?"

"If I were just a digital ghost," said Frieda, "would he still want to spend eternity with me?"

Baird stared back at her for a long moment, thinking about the angles. The potential pitfalls if he passed along her message. He was so close to freedom now, he couldn't afford a single mistake.

But try as he might, he couldn't see a mistake in this. "Wayne," he said. "Frieda wants me to ask you something."

"Okay," said Wayne.

"What if you found out she was just a digital ghost of your mom?" Baird reached for the pack of cigarettes rolled up in the sleeve of his t-shirt. "Would you still want to spend eternity with her?"

Wayne smiled warmly and nodded. "I'm her son, aren't I? It doesn't matter to me if she's digital, animal, mineral, or vegetable."

Frieda blushed. "Thank you, Baird. I needed to hear that."

"Awesome." Baird snagged a smoke from the pack and lit it. "Then I think we're done here, folks."

"All right." Wayne put his hands on his knees and pushed himself up from the sofa. "I guess I'd better get going."

"Sounds good," said Baird.

"Just one more thing." Wayne gestured at the house. "Can I use your bathroom first?"

"Absolutely." Baird was feeling charitable. "Knock yourself out."

"I won't be long." Wayne opened the front door and disappeared inside.

Baird leaned back in the rocker and took a deep drag from his cigarette. Finally, he'd reached the end of the line. Ten years worth of bullshit, and he was practically free.

"Baird?" Not that Frieda would give him any peace right up to the end. "You may open your present now."

Baird had brought it with him to the porch and laid it on the sofa, right where Frieda had been sitting. With a sigh, he rocked forward and snatched it from the moldy cushion.

"Go ahead and open it." Frieda sounded excited.

Baird grabbed a flap of the newspaper wrapping and tore it all off with one tug. Inside was a spiral notebook, as he'd guessed earlier from feeling the coiled wire binding through the newsprint.

Tossing aside the wrapping, Baird turned over the notebook in his hands. The front cover was pale blue cardstock, creased and wrinkled as hell. A title was scrawled diagonally in thick black ink, starting at the lower left corner.

"MEMRIES," it said.

Scowling, Baird opened the front cover. "What the hell is this?"

"A memory book," said Frieda. "A souvenir of our time together."

A crooked column of penciled text slumped down the page from top left to bottom right. The printed text was as sloppy as the title on the cover, tumbling over and through the blue ruled lines on the page instead of marching neatly between them.

Each line of print started with a date--month, day, and year. "October 10 2025" was first...the first date on the first line.

Baird recognized it immediately. It had been his first day as a haunt-con, his first day with Frieda.

There was only one word beside that first date: "TEST." The next ten lines on the page were identical--just a date (always one day later, in sequence) and the word "TEST."

Then, gradually, the entries grew longer.

Beside October 21 2025 was this: "WENT TO PARK TODAY. KIDS THRU ROCKS."

This was the entry for October 22: "BAIRD WANTS TO KILL HIMSELF."

October 23: "I DONT HATE HIM LIKE I SHOOD."

October 24: "HE MADE ME LAFF. BUT IM NOT ALOUD TO SHOW IT."

Baird shivered without knowing why as he turned the page. He saw more of the same on the next two pages, more entries with dates and descriptions.

"WHY IS HE SO MEEN?"

"WE WENT OUT TO EET TODAY."

As he flipped through the notebook, every page was exactly

the same. Slumping, sloppy columns of entries, one after another...one for every day Baird and Frieda had been together.

"HE DUZNT UNDERSTAND ME."

"I DONT WANT HIM TO KILL HIMSELF."

It was just like a diary.

"Do you like it?" Frieda gazed at him expectantly.

"How?" Baird couldn't take his eyes off the pages as he turned them. "How did you *do* this?"

"I did it for you," said Frieda. "So you wouldn't forget me when I'm gone."

"But how did you *do* this?" said Baird. "You're *digital.* This is *impossible.*"

Frieda beamed and drummed her hands on her knees. "I *knew* you'd be surprised."

Just then, Wayne called out from inside the bungalow. "Hey, Baird. Could you come here a minute?"

Baird turned another page and didn't answer. Shaking his head slowly, he looked up at Frieda.

And her features rippled.

Baird blinked hard and looked again. Her face held steady this time.

But only for a moment.

As Baird watched, Frieda's face flickered. It stretched out, then snapped back into shape.

Baird felt a familiar flutter in his stomach. The same flutter of fear that he'd felt sometimes in the middle of the night, when Frieda's glowing face had seemed to distort. He'd never been sure if it was a glitch in the implant's neural interface or a short-circuit in his own half-asleep brain or yet another programmed tactic in the ongoing psychological warfare waged against him.

But here it was again...and for the first time, in broad daylight.

"Frieda?" Baird tipped his head to one side. "What's happening?"

"Nothing to worry about, sweetheart," said Frieda. And then she rippled and flickered again.

Baird shut his eyes tight. When he opened them again, he wasn't sitting on the wicker rocker anymore.

He was walking through the living room with Frieda by his side.

"What the *hell*?" Baird stopped and looked around, wondering how he'd gotten from the front porch to the living room. "What's going on here?"

"Do you want to know how I made your present?" said Frieda. "The memory book?"

Baird felt dizzy and held his head with his hands. He nodded.

Frieda's image flickered again. This time, when Baird closed his eyes and opened them, he saw that he was standing in the bathroom, facing Wayne.

"Here you go." Wayne held out a carving knife, handle-first. "Make it quick."

"This is how I did it," said Frieda. "Or should I say, how *you* did it."

Frieda rippled again. Baird found himself holding the handle of the knife, pointing the tip of the blade toward Wayne.

"...through my artery, got it?" Wayne tipped his head back and undid the top buttons of his shirt, exposing his bare throat. "And make sure you finish the job. Make sure I'm dead."

Frieda stood close to Baird and whispered in his ear. "There's a control program in implants like yours," said Frieda. "Why do you think so many haunt-cons have killed themselves? It wasn't always *their* idea, you know."

Baird was having trouble thinking straight. The knife felt heavy in his hand. "You were...programmed to...take control of me...and make me kill myself?"

"But I couldn't go through with it," said Frieda. "I wanted us to be together."

"And now...what?" said Baird. "You want me...to kill *Wayne*?"

"Come on! Get it over with!" Wayne jerked his collar open wider. "Just *kill me*!"

"Are you...crazy?" Baird was talking to Frieda.

"Not crazy," said Frieda. "I just want to be with you."

"*Do it*, damn you!" Wayne lunged forward.

"And guess what?" said Frieda. "I'm getting my wish."

Her image rippled again.

And Baird closed his eyes.

THREE MONTHS LATER...

"Happy anniversary, Baird!" Frieda's voice whispered in his ear. "Congratulations, sweetheart!"

Baird rolled over in bed without opening his eyes. He finally got the joke.

When she said "anniversary," she didn't mean he was another year closer to freedom. She didn't mean it was an occasion for him to celebrate.

The celebration was all about her.

"Wakey wakey, darling boy," said Frieda. "It's the first day of the rest of your life!"

Baird groaned and clenched his teeth. As hard as she'd been to take before, when he'd had hope of eventual escape, he could barely stand her now. He could barely hold his own.

During his first ten-year sentence, Baird had grown strong...but that strength was gone. He'd toughened up and beaten the system...but he wasn't so tough anymore.

Ten years as a haunt-con was one thing. A life sentence with no possibility of parole--well, that was a whole new ballgame.

That was what he'd gotten for killing Wayne Baumgardner. He'd tried to explain what had happened, that the implant had *made* him murder Wayne...but his story hadn't cut it. The photos of the 52 holes he'd hacked in Wayne had trumped his unsupported tale of technology gone mad.

The only reason he hadn't gotten the death penalty was that he'd agreed to a deal. Choosing between death and more haunting, he'd chosen the haunting.

There was just one problem he hadn't foreseen. One little surprise the judge had added in the name of justice.

One little thing that might just push Baird over the edge.

"Shake a leg, buddy." Another voice spoke in Baird's ear...and this time, it wasn't Frieda's. "You gonna sleep the whole day away? It's already three thirty in the morning!"

Baird opened his eyes to see a glowing face staring back at him. A face with twinkling eyes and an ear-to-ear smile.

Wayne Baumgardner's face.

"There you go, sweetie." Frieda appeared beside Wayne. "He's up now."

"Please." Baird's voice cracked from exhaustion. "Can't I sleep...just a little? This is the tenth time...you've woken me up...tonight."

"We can't help it we love your company," said Frieda.

"Now that Mom and I are back together, we're one big, happy family." Digital Wayne leaned over and kissed digital Frieda on the cheek. Since they were both intangible, the kiss had the computer-generated illusion of physical contact. "Thanks again for murdering me, Baird!"

"Frieda *made me* kill you." Baird rolled over to face the other direction. "*She* did it!"

Wayne switched sides of the bed, zipping over to crouch in Baird's line of sight. "I *wanted* her to." Wayne nodded and smiled. "She called the night before...well, *you* called, Baird, speaking *for* her...and she asked if I wanted us to be together."

Frieda popped up beside Wayne. "And he said *yes*."

"And she set it up." Wayne put his arm around Frieda and hugged her tight. "She filled in the gaps in my memory after the big brains added me to your implant."

"Lucky you, Baird," said Frieda. "Two spooks for the price of one."

"And who knows?" Wayne shrugged. "Maybe I'm just a spook, programmed into an implant...and the real me is up in heaven somewhere. Or maybe this *is* the real me."

"And maybe this *is* heaven," said Frieda.

"More like hell," said Baird, and then he buried his head under his pillow.

Frieda's face phased through the mattress, her eyes shining up at him. "I kept wondering what heaven was like. You told me to make my own...so I *did.*

"*This* is heaven," said Frieda. "For *me.*"

"Me, too," said digital Wayne, his face sifting in through the pillow, passing into Frieda's and Baird's so all three of them seemed to become one person.

"So what do you do in heaven at three-thirty in the morning, anyway?" said Frieda.

"Same thing we do every night." Wayne grinned. "Get creative."

As their images rippled and flickered under the pillow, Baird clamped his eyes shut against the familiar blackout rolling through him. And he sobbed.

For the first time in his life, he truly wished he'd never raped Frieda Baumgardner.

THE LITTLE ROBOT'S BEDTIME PRAYER

On Wednesday, I finally see what little Occam-657 has been making in that glowing silver box of his during Private Time. And that is what changes my life.

The mere memory of the sight of it sends chills up my spine. Makes my heart beat faster, my pulse pound in my ears.

I was never supposed to see it. By the terms of the Holy Covenant, all Private Time and its products are considered sacrosanct, off limits to Gods like me. But curiosity got the better of me, and I spied on Occam-657. I gazed into the box, and the scales fell from my eyes. I realized one thing that had never before occurred to me.

He has been hiding something extraordinary from me.

"Good morning, God." Occam-657 smiles up at me when I emerge from my bedchamber the next morning. He has been waiting outside my door like a good little household robot, prohibited from doing chores until now lest he wake me prematurely.

I respond to his greeting as if God, and not Sean, is my given name. As if I am an omnipotent deity and not a 37-year-old self-employed genetic engineer specializing in novelty bio-apps. (Remember Thumbo, the elephant who fits in the palm of your hand?) As if I am more than a slightly overweight mere mortal whose wife left him six weeks ago for another man.

"Good morning." I hesitate before laying my hand on his head in the usual fatherly gesture. The memory of what I saw him doing last night is still too fresh in my mind. "Bless you, my child." When my fingers finally alight, the feathery blond hair on his scalp feels as downy as that of a human boy's. Even touching him does not destroy the illusion that he is a 10-year-old boy instead of a manufactured robot.

Occam-657 falls to his knees and shuts his eyes. "You are the way and the light, O' my God. Your mercy endures forever."

His voice is full of awe. He was programmed that way, his artificial intelligence created to show religious piety in the presence of the gods--his human owner and the owners of those like him. Yet the intensity of his devotion seems surprisingly unscripted and genuine at times.

"Dear Lord, will you accept my morning confession?" Occam-657 lifts his clasped hands and leans his forehead against them.

I wonder what he'll say. Will he talk about what I saw last night? "Go ahead."

"Forgive me, God, for I have sinned." There is a quaver in his voice. "It took me .00001 seconds longer than my optimal time to prepare your holy repast for this morning."

I touch his head once more. "That is unfortunate, but I forgive you." Then, I reach up and pat my own blond hair, which is sticking up all over the place after being slept on. "What else, my child?"

He pauses, and I think there's more coming...but no. "Only

that which I have told you, O' mighty and benevolent Lord my God."

I can't keep the disappointment from my voice. "Then you are forgiven in my name, for mine is the kingdom and the power and the glory..."

"...forever and ever, amen." Occam-657 bows his head lower and lets out a sound like a choked sob.

So this encounter has told me nothing. "Arise, now, and resume your service to your God." But the heaviest burden lays upon my shoulders. For now that I saw what he did, I have to decide what to do with him.

As I EAT my breakfast at the dining room table--the holy altar, I should say--I watch Occam-657 as he goes about his chores. He is no less efficient than ever as he vacuums the glowing golden carpet in the living room (the sanctuary), then dusts every surface and object in sight. He never fails to pause and genuflect when he passes me, showing all due respect and adoration. And the breakfast he prepared--eggs Florentine with crab meat hash and a light dreamfruit marmalade--is no less delicious than every "holy repast" he has ever made in his three years of service in my home. The house runs as well as it ever did before my wife, Cara, left with our other robot attendants, leaving me alone with Occam-657.

It's as if he's done nothing out of the ordinary. As if I saw nothing unexpected last night, and business as usual is the word of the day.

Leaving me to consider some troubling questions. If Occam-657 was programmed to be my devout acolyte, and he truly believes I am an omniscient and all-powerful god, then where and when did he get the idea that he could hide something from me?

And *what else* could he be hiding that I still don't know about?

Occam-657 looks disappointed when I tell him I'm going somewhere without him. He always does; he's programmed to miss the Lord his God every time we're apart, so brightly does my glory shine like a beacon o'er his soul. I'm used to it by now, it hardly ever gets to me.

But today, it does. Given what I saw last night, I worry about what he might get into. He begs me to allow him the honor of accompanying me as my divine retinue, just for the blessing of basking in my presence. For once, I give in and tell him to come along.

We head over to my friend Pander's place in Oathtown in a drone-palanquin, a purple velvet-lined coach carried by four built-in robotic bearers. Occam-657 prays during the entire trip. I tell him to keep it down, but I still hear the soft sibilance of whispered words aspirating from his artificial lips.

Sometimes, I wish the robot manufacturers had never come up with the bright idea of making all the robots worship their owners as gods. It was the best way, the programmers say, to ensure that flesh-and-blood owners never come to harm at the hands of mechanical servitors (though I'm pretty sure human ego might have had more than a little to do with it, as well). But the constant, obsequious worship does tend to get old after a while. For me, at least.

For example, as our palanquin slows to a stop at a busy intersection, a choir of robots on the curb detects my human presence and sings a cyber-hymn in our direction. They chant the sonorous words with great gravity, upraising their folded hands in blissful praise.

I am *so* not in the mood for it right now, and that makes me wonder. Does the real God, if He exists, ever feel the same way? And is it possible, now that we've managed to create our own flock of worshippers, that humanity is finally getting a taste of its own medicine?

"SCRAP HIM." That's Pander's advice when I tell him what Occam-657 was doing. "You've got yourself a faulty unit there, Sean-o."

We're outside on Pander's balcony, having a drink and gazing down at three robots prostrating themselves on the lawn below--two of Pander's, with Occam-657 between them.

I keep my voice low, though it shouldn't matter if the robots hear me. The words of a god are meant to be beyond challenge or reproach in all situations. "I've been thinking the same thing."

Pander sips smart-wine from a golden chalice that glints in the sun. "Is he still under any kind of warranty? You've had him three years, right?"

I nod and sip from my own chalice. "I bought the extended coverage. It doesn't expire for another month."

"Then what's the problem?" Pander's ample jowls jiggle when he chuckles. So does the gut under his vast white robe. He's a genetic engineer, too, dealing as I do in novelty bio-apps...though he's done much better at it than I have (which is saying something, since I haven't exactly been a slouch) and has the bank account and overindulged corpulence to prove it. "What are you waiting for, numb-nuts?"

"I don't know." I watch as Occam-657 grovels ever lower on the ground. He must be praying, but I can't hear it from the balcony. "What if it's something *I've* done wrong?"

Pander laughs some more. "That's impossible! Gods are always right!"

"We're only gods to *them.*" I gesture with my chalice toward the robots below.

As if in answer, all three raise their upper bodies from the ground and shout "Hallelujah," eyes shut and hands fluttering ecstatically.

"That's all that matters, isn't it?" Pander elbows me in the side and leans on the balcony railing. "Ask me how many robots I've scrapped over the years."

I already know the answer. "More than I've ever owned in my life. More than my *family* has ever owned."

"Damn right," says Pander. "*Dozens.* As soon as they hiccup out of line, I ship 'em to the scrap heap. End of story. So cut him loose." He makes a sweeping gesture with one puffy hand. "Make a clean break with the past. Quit hanging on to your bitch wife's leftovers."

"That's not it." I frown.

"Time to move on." Pander waves his chalice at the robots. "Why are you hesitating?"

"I just keep thinking." Down below, Occam-657 opens his eyes and meets my gaze. I wonder what thoughts are chugging through his clockwork mind. "What if this is something *new*? What if he's *special* in a way no one has seen before?"

"And everyone's dog is as smart as a person," says Pander. "So why does it still eat its own *shit*?"

I let out a long, slow sigh. It's a beautiful spring day, and the air is filled with the scent of blooming lilacs and new-mown lawns. But all I can focus on is Occam-657. "If there *was* a real God, would he throw *us* away just because we were special or challenging?"

Pander smirks and shrugs. "Who says that isn't the way it's been working all along?"

Why are you hesitating? That's the one thing Pander said that sticks with me. It *eats* at me as I leave his house in another drone-palanquin--this one with a blue velvet coach instead of purple.

It would be so *easy* to drop off Occam-657 at the factory on my way home. Problem solved, and no one could tell me otherwise. When it comes to the existence of my adoring subject, I can do whatever I want. This is one of the perks of being God.

He'll even *thank* me for it, I know. I can already hear the prayers of grateful supplication that will pour forth from his lips when I dump him on the factory's doorstep. No questions asked, no guilt necessary. So why?

Why are you hesitating?

"O' Lord my God." Occam-657 keeps his gaze lowered when he says it. "Though the product of my all too imperfect hands is not fit for your divine consumption, what do you command me to prepare for your evening repast?"

Is it because, as I told Pander, he might represent something new, something special? Is that why I hesitate? "Whatever you choose to prepare will suffice, my child."

"Then I shall make your favorite," says Occam-657. "Broiled sea scallops with a beurre blanc sauce. Asparagus tips with capers and shaved white truffles. Crème brûlée and caviar foam for dessert."

"Hmm. Perhaps." Or is it because, as Pander said, I am hanging on to the last traces of my wife and our life before she left me?

Occam-657 shivers and looks up at me. "Has my suggestion offended thee, O' my God?"

Do I hesitate because I feel responsible for what he's become?

Or is it just that I want to understand what has changed to make him do what he has done?

Why are you hesitating?

All of the above, maybe, I think.

"You haven't offended me, Occam-657." I smile and shake my head. "But don't worry about the menu for tonight. I think I'd rather eat out."

WE GO to a Cuban-Indian deli in Chinatown, and I order Reuben samosas and ropa vieja masala. The robot waitress, a dark-haired unit with bright green eyes, looks only a little older than Occam-657. All such personal service robots were built to child-like specs, designed to minimize the physical danger to us all-too-fragile humans. Better to keep them small in case the religious devotion ever wears off or the other onboard safeguards fail.

It makes for a strange dynamic sometimes, but people have mostly gotten used to it. It's like we're constantly surrounded by kids playing grownup, but the play is for real.

"Is the food sufficient, O' God?" Occam-657 stands at the opposite side of the table and stares at the food on my plate. "Does it offend thee?"

I swallow a bite of samosa and point at the chair in front of him. "Sit, my child."

Occam-657 bows his head. "I am not worthy to share a table with almighty God."

I resist the urge to roll my eyes. "*Sit.* I *command* it."

Reluctantly, Occam-657 pulls out the chair and lowers himself onto it. Even so, he stays well back from the table and keeps his eyes down and hands folded in his lap.

"It is almost time for Church," he says softly.

"Pretty sure Church will wait for us." I can't help smirking. "I'm God, remember?"

If Occam-657 gets the joke, he doesn't show it. "It is true that wherever you go, that is where your holy Church can be found."

I don't offer a comment for that one. I'm too busy looking around the restaurant, watching the other gods and robots at dinner.

They all relate to each other differently. It's something I've never paid much attention to, but given my current situation, it suddenly seems more significant.

Laughter draws my attention to a table across the room, where two brown-haired children are making sport of a blond male robot. The children, who look between six and eight years old--both a good bit smaller than the blond robot--have stripped off the robot's shirt and are smearing his upper body with orange curry sauce. The robot just smiles serenely, hands folded in prayer the whole time. As for the children's mother, she joins in the laughter between bites of salad and talking to someone on the holographic video phone hovering in front of her face.

Things are much different two tables over, where an old man eats soup while sitting across from robot twins--a boy and a girl, both dark-haired. Occasional laughter ripples from that table, too, but it comes as often from the robots as the old man. Somehow, they have made peace with their personal god; they are all at ease with each other.

Though the same cannot be said for the bald robot boy who comes hurtling through the front door at just that instant.

He crashes to the floor in a jumble of arms and legs, sprawled on his back. All laughter and talk in the room cease at once, as all eyes dart in his direction.

A brick wall of a man storms in off the street after him, draped in a black fur coat. "Get up, you worthless *turd!*" His face is flushed crimson as a house fire as he spews the words. His bulbous, over-tattooed head squats like a giant toad atop his mountainous body. "The Lord your God *commands* it!"

"Your every word brings me unutterable joy, O' Lord." The bald boy rolls over and gets up on his knees.

Before the boy can get all the way up, the brick wall grabs a chair from a nearby table and swings it at him like a baseball bat. The chair smashes against the boy, and he topples like a tree, dropping hard on his side.

Every muscle in my body tenses as the beating continues. Instinctively, I want to run over and stop it; others around me look like they might feel the same way. But I can't imagine taking on that brick wall of a man and winning. Besides, he has every right to do what he's doing. That isn't a human boy over there, it's a robot.

And the robot is the brick wall's property.

"Don't you *ever* touch the person of the One True God with your debased synthetic flesh!" The brick wall stomps on the boy with savage force, bringing his sledgehammer feet down again and again.

The bald robot jolts with each impact and does not fight back. I keep reminding myself he's just a machine, but I can't help flinching every time he takes another hit.

The bald robot's voice hitches repeatedly as he recites an Act of Contrition. "O' my God, I am heartily sorry for having...sorry for having offended thee..."

"I am a wrathful God!" shouts the brick wall as he stomps the boy again. "Damnation shall be your only absolution, wretched sinner!"

"...and I detest all my sins because of thy...because of thy just punishments," continues the bald robot. "But most of all, because they offend thee..."

With that, the brick wall grabs the bald robot by the ankles and drags him toward the door. Looking across the table, I see

Occam-657 watching as it happens, the expression on his face perfectly neutral.

"You are hereby condemned to the fires of Hell!" roars the brick wall. "I have a *welding torch* with your *name* on it, just waiting to burn some *penitence* into your sorry sinning carcass!"

"...because they offend thee, my God, who are all good and deserving of all my love." Those are the last words I hear the robot say before his god hauls him out on the street and an eerie silence falls over the restaurant.

Turning to Occam-657, I wonder what he thinks of what he's just seen. He looks at me calmly, as if nothing unusual just happened, and asks if it's time for Church yet.

"A-MAZING GRACE...HOW SWEET THE SOUND..." Occam-657 sings the hymn with eyes and arms uplifted, his bright tenor voice filling the high-ceilinged living room--I mean the sanctuary. "...that saved...a wretch...like meee..."

Yes, it's again time for Church--a daily worship service meant to reinforce the bond between robot and god. It's something I could gladly do without--an hour out of my day that I could be spending on something more productive or entertaining. But every expert agrees that it's a necessary evil. Though robots like Occam-657 spend a lot of time with their god or gods and exist in a state of continuous worship, formalized rituals still help keep them on track. Our robots were programmed to expect and desire it, to incorporate it into their daily existence.

Now if only I got something out of it, too. The ego boost it once provided is long gone at this point. As for spirituality, that's not an issue, either. Whatever personal faith I once had is over and done with; *you* try subscribing to a higher power when you're worshipped as the One True God 24/7.

Mostly, as Occam-657 prays and sings and reads passages from the Good Book (the same Good Book in *every* god's house, a mishmash of psalms, stories, and parables cribbed from multiple human faiths), my mind wanders. Today, it wanders back to the night before, and what Occam-657 was doing when I spied on his Private Time.

"Now let us pray," says Occam-657. "Pray for the poor, unfortunate boy from the restaurant, the one who was condemned to Hell."

I nod, only half paying attention.

"I pray to you, O' God..." He meets my gaze when he says it. "Please show that poor sinner the error of his ways. Help him so his punishment will scald away every trace of his wickedness."

I nod again. Sometimes it's almost scary how complete the buy-in is. How perfectly these machines accept the precepts of their programmed faith. Have we made them the perfect worshippers that we ourselves could never be?

Or are they more like us than we ever knew? Able to hide true intentions behind an angelic façade? I've seen the proof with my own two eyes, haven't I?

Why are you hesitating?

Suddenly, I am filled with the urge to resolve this. "Explain yourself." I leap from my overstuffed white leather recliner--my "throne"--and point a finger at him. "Tell me about your Private Time last night."

I expected no surprise on his face, and I get none. He just looks at me blankly, still holding the Good Book open in his little hands. "This is not part of the Church ceremony, God."

"*As* God, I hereby decree that the Church ceremony shall be *different* today," I tell him.

"Different?" He tips his head to one side.

"Do you *dare* to question my will?"

He bows his head. "I *never* question your will, O' Lord my God. Speak, and it shall be done."

"Then tell me about your Private Time last night."

Occam-657 turns his gaze downward, staring at the book in his hands. "I am not required to do that, God."

Storming forward, I grab the Good Book from his grasp and hurl it to the floor. "Are you refusing to obey my command?"

He eyes drop lower, staring at the floor. "By the terms of the Holy Covenant, all Private Time and its products are considered sacrosanct." He shakes his head once, then adds, almost as an afterthought, "God."

His resistance leaves me shaken. He's only quoting a well-known clause from the user manual, one that I know quite well, but it feels for an instant like a slap in the face.

Perhaps I can still bring him around. "Occam-657, am I the Lord your God?"

He nods definitively. "Yes, Father."

"And does the Lord your God possess perfect wisdom in all things?"

"Yes, Father." Again, a definitive nod.

"Does he ever make a mistake?"

"No." Occam-657 shakes his head forcefully. "Never."

Reaching out, I place a hand on his right shoulder and squeeze gently. "Then if I were to tell you that the Private Time clause of the Holy Covenant is no longer in force, and you are required to describe your activities during said Private Time to me, would you say I am correct and must be obeyed?"

He shakes his head. "The Holy Covenant can never be broken. You yourself promised this long ago."

"But what if I now say I was wrong to make that promise back then?"

"If you were imperfect in the past, you would still be imperfect now...in which case, your new instruction to disregard the Holy Covenant would be flawed, O' blessed Father."

Consider the logic loophole closed. I should have known better than to try working around such a fundamental data point.

Maybe I'll have better luck with a more direct tactic. "Look. Occam." I let go of his shoulder and spread my arms. "There's no use trying to hide what you did. I already know about it."

Eyes wide, he looks up from the floor. "What do you mean?"

"I mean, I already know. I already saw." I let my arms fall against my sides. "I'm *God*, remember? All-seeing, all-knowing, all-powerful?"

So this is it. My cards are on the table. The question is, will Occam-657 show *his* cards, too?

For a long moment, he stares blankly at me. He opens his mouth as if to speak, then closes it again.

Maybe I can nudge him along a little. "This isn't about sin or punishment, my child. I just want to know why you did what you did."

Occam-657 narrows his eyes and keeps staring. "But if you are all-knowing, and you no longer consider Private Time and its products sacrosanct, you must already *know* why I did it."

He's right, and I have to think fast to explain it away. "But I need to hear you *confess* it, my child. This is a test of your faith and devotion."

Occam-657's eyes narrow further. Then, his expression suddenly clears, and he's smiling again.

"Glory be to God in the highest, and peace to His people on Earth." He folds his hands and bows. "Church is ended. Go in peace to love and serve the Lord."

With that, he straightens and walks around me, heading for the kitchen. This, apparently, is all the answer he's willing to give.

Both of us know what he's done, yet still he refuses to discuss it. As hard as it is to believe, he won't discuss it with God...the only God he's ever known. How he's able to justify this is beyond me, given his programming.

But it does shed a new light on the situation. I'm not thinking so much about him being special in a good way anymore. Watching him enter the kitchen, I'm more concerned about what else he might be hiding from me. The trust between us has shattered.

Why are you hesitating? That's what Pander asked me.

I think I'm done with hesitation now. I think I'm finally ready to let go of him.

HOURS LATER, I head for my bedroom, feeling exhausted. Occam-657 waits at the door, as he does every night. We have a little bedtime ritual, he and I; even after what happened in Church, it seems he wants to continue it.

He will stand at the door all night like a guard-dog while I sleep, waiting until I awaken to commence his duties. Before all that, though, he will say the same thing that he says every time I meet him at the door like this.

"O' Lord, may I offer up one last prayer for today?" He keeps his head bowed and his hands folded tightly against his chest. "May I recite my bedtime prayer?"

How can I say no? This could be the last time I hear it. It could also be the last time he says it to anyone, if the company purges his A.I. and recycles him for parts when I return him. "Yes, my child. I will hear your bedtime prayer."

Occam-657 nods once, drops to his knees, and speaks the same words he has said on this spot every night for the past three years. "Now I lay me down to sleep," he says, though in truth he will neither lie down nor sleep. "I pray the Lord my soul to keep."

I stand before him with arms folded over my chest and

remember the first time he prayed like this for me and Cara. It was "Lords," not "Lord" back then, and "Gods," not "God." It seemed like such a special moment, as if he was our own human child, and we were a family together. We stood on the verge of a hopeful future, our lives about to intertwine, never imagining they would come apart instead. Now, only two of us remain...and soon, only I will be left.

"If I should die before I wake, I pray the Lord my soul to take."

If I bring home another model right away, will he or she be able to fill the void? What if the new replacement ends up doing the same things and hiding them from me? What if, as I've feared, this behavior is somehow my fault?

"If I should live for other days, I pray the Lord to guide my ways."

I wish I were as perfect as he seems to think. But maybe there's a reason I'm about to be alone again. Cara told me I wasn't much of a husband; maybe I haven't been much of a god, either.

"Father, unto thee I pray. Thou hast guarded me all day."

Maybe I'm just better at engineering palm-sized elephants, glow-in-the-dark fingertip Corgi dogs, and armadillo butterflies that sound like violins when they flutter than I am at dealing with human and robot relationships.

"Safe I am while in thy sight. Safely let me sleep tonight." Occam-657 crosses himself. "Amen."

"Goodnight, my child." I tousle his blond hair on my way past. "Sweet dreams."

"God?"

The sound of his voice wakes me from a deep sleep. My eyes flicker open to the sight of him standing beside my bed, staring down at me.

"Yes?" I'm not sure if I should feel worried, but I do. Occam-657 has never before entered the bedroom while I've been sleeping. "Is something wrong?"

"O' Lord, I am sorry for awakening thee," says Occam-657. "It is just..." He shuts his eyes and falls silent.

I sit up in bed, leaning back against the padded white headboard. "Yes, my child?"

His eyes open slowly. "I would like to show you something, almighty God."

I scowl when I catch sight of the digital clock on the bedside table. "It's midnight, my child. Can't this wait until morning?"

Occam-657 shakes his head. "I beg your forgiveness with every atom of my being, O' Lord my God, but I pray that you will indulge this request from your lowly servant."

Whatever he has in mind, I'm exhausted and have no patience for it. "As the Lord your God, I command you to wait until morning."

Suddenly, Occam-657 darts out a hand and grabs my arm--a stunning breach of protocol even more unexpected than his appearance in my bedroom. "It is about what you asked me in Church, Lord. It is about what happened in Private Time."

My attitude does a 180. Staying in bed is now the last thing I want to do.

"All right, then, my child." I smile and nod. "I will forgive you for interrupting my sacred rest, and I will forgive you for laying hands on me."

He quickly lets go of my arm.

"Further, because of my infinite love and mercy, I will grant your request." Pulling back the sheet, I swing my feet off the bed. "Now what is it, exactly, that you wish to show me?"

I FOLLOW Occam-657 downstairs to the basement. It's a finished basement with bright white walls, floor, and ceiling, set up with benches and equipment where I do my genetic engineering work. There's also a booth built into the far back corner, little more than a closet, which is where Occam-657 spends his Private Time.

He opens the door of the booth and steps inside, then emerges a moment later carrying something I recognize instantly. It's a glowing silver box, three feet wide by two feet high--the same silver box in which he's been keeping his not-so-secret project.

There's only one thing different about it that I can see. A big red bow has been stuck on top, with strips of red ribbon wrapped around the box cross-wise and length-wise.

Carefully, he puts the box down on a low table between us and takes a step back. "Happy anniversary, O' Lord my God. Please accept this gift in honor of the occasion."

"Thank you, my child." I'm supposed to be omniscient, so I pretend I have the slightest clue what he's talking about.

"Thank *you*, God," says Occam-657. "For allowing me to begin my service to you three years ago today."

He's talking about the anniversary of his arrival in my home and my life. But what does that have to do with what's in the box?

"Open it, O' God." Occam-657 gestures at the box, then folds his hands and bows his head. "*If* it pleases you to do so."

My heart beats faster as I pull the ribbon from the box. Taking a deep breath, I slowly lift the lid and set it aside. What I saw last night from afar, via spy-cam, is there before me now, *alive*...and *breathing*...

And gazing up at me.

"I made them, O' Lord my God," says Occam-657. "I made them for *you*."

There are dozens of them in the box--tiny, naked people no taller than an inch, all identical to each other. They cluster in a central square framed by little toothpick huts arranged around the sides of the box.

The little people are all exquisitely detailed, perfectly crafted to scale. Every one of them moves with the fluid, natural motion of a full-sized human, from the striding of legs to the flexing of fingers to the blinking of eyes.

And all of them look beyond familiar, to the point of intimate recognition. Staring at them now, I can't help getting the same chill that flashed up my spine when I first saw them on the spy-cam last night.

"You used my equipment, didn't you?" As I say it, I can't take my eyes off the tiny people in the box. "You taught yourself genetic engineering, and you used it to create them."

"As a gift," says Occam-657. "As a tribute to your glory."

"But why...?" I hear the little people jibber in an unknown tongue as they point and gesture at me. I wonder if we are asking the same question at the same time, in different languages. "Why do they look like *me?*"

"I made them in your image just as I was made in the image of the Gods myself," says Occam-657. "I could not possibly improve upon perfection, my Lord."

I fall silent, amazed by the intricacy of the miniatures in the box. In all my years of genetic engineering, I have never come close to accomplishing this--creating mini-humans with such craftsmanship and responsive awareness. I wonder, as I stare at his handiwork, which of us could be considered more perfect?

"There is only one problem, O' God." Occam-657 steps closer and taps the rim of the box. As one, all the tiny people whirl in his direction...then instantly fall to their knees. They chant something in their tiny little voices, something indecipherable yet unmistakable in tone and intent. "They insist on worshipping me as a god of their own."

Since first glimpsing these creatures, I've wondered what he planned to do with them. This outcome, however, I did not envision. "They worship you as their *god?*"

Occam-657 keeps watching the kneeling figures as he nods. "I was able to design their physicality and functionality but cannot seem to control their behavior."

"And what do you think about that?"

He slowly lifts his gaze to meet mine. "If you could help me, perhaps I could make them see the light. Perhaps I could guide them to worship *you*, the One True God."

As I look at him, I realize that going back to the way things were is no longer an option. Neither is going forward without him.

I was right when I said he might be special and new. What I failed to see was the new purpose he might bring to my life, the strange adventure he might cook up in the basement with room enough for two to make a difference.

Though it's true, there's only room at the top for *one* God, when you get right down to it.

"I have a better idea." I gesture at the tiny flock as they kneel and chant in the box. "Why don't I just teach *you* how to be their god?"

"No!" His eyes fly wide open with an expression like panic. "O' Lord, O' God, I could never in a billion years pretend to usurp your holy righteous authority or..."

"Who said anything about usurping? I'm *giving* it to you." I feel proud of him and tousle his fine, blond hair for what might be the last time...at least in front of the silver-boxed faithful. Finally, I appreciate the gift I've been given and understand the kind of god I want to be.

"By the way," I tell him. "You can call me Sean from now on."

Which is no god at all.

DIRTY DREAMS OF A DISHWASHER

Moans coming from an appliance under the counter fill the air of the big, bright kitchen.

Uh, uh, uh. The voice of the dishwasher is female, throaty, sexual. *Oh yeah, baby, yeah, that's right.*

Quinn Carmen, the lady of the house, shakes her head. "It's getting on my nerves, Mack. It gets old after a while."

She's entitled to her opinion, of course. Horny home appliances aren't everyone's bag. But for a repairman like me, this is just another day at the office.

It's a well-known fact that a little passion between A.I.-enabled devices makes a home run smoothly. It's also true that such passion can sometimes go to extremes, and the *Romeo of Gizmos* has to put on the brakes.

That's *me,* by the way.

"Tell me, Mack," says Mrs. Carmen, a beautiful young woman with flowing black tresses and glowing golden eyes. "Is that about the *filthiest* dishwasher you've ever heard?"

Just then, the dishwasher squeals loudly, as if in the throes of passionate pleasure. As if someone or something has hit the exact right spot at the exact right moment.

I just shrug. "I've heard worse."

It's true. I've heard *much* worse. It comes with the territory. But I can tell you *this* much: I have never found a love-crazed device whose romantic spirit I couldn't *re-align.*

My name is legendary in A.I. repair circles for just that reason. Mention Mack Francis to the right people, and you're likely to hear some *stories. For real.*

"Let me just run a scan here, Mrs. Carmen." I touch my right wrist, and a holographic keyboard appears in midair in front of me, at waist level.

"It's *Miss*, actually," she says. "But you can call me Quinn."

"Okay." I type with both hands, and a dashboard of glowing readouts appears over the holographic keys. "We can learn a lot from a good scan, Quinn. Or as I call it, a *love probe.*"

If Quinn's amused by the joke, she doesn't let on. She just stands stiffly beside me in her glowing white gown with arms folded across her chest. "Then you'll know if you can fix it?"

I flash her a cocky smirk. "I don't need a *scan* to tell me *that.*" Then I return my gaze to the readouts. "You say it's still cleaning dishes just fine?"

"Yes, but..."

The dishwasher's voice speeds up and gets louder. *Yes yes yesyesyesyesyesyesyes*

There's a high-pitched scream of sheer delight. *YES!* The machine gyrates under the counter, sending soapy water sloshing around the edges of the door to splatter on the floor.

Then, suddenly, the cries and movement stop. The splashing ceases as the dishwasher switches from wash cycle to dry.

Quinn winces. "Sure, it's *cleaning* them, but who would want to *eat off* them?"

I can't help chuckling. "I hear what you're saying." Any dishes in that machine are *extra*-clean if anything, but she has a point.

Perception can be a powerful thing, and thank God for that. Squeamish appliance owners are my bread and butter, after all.

"So, what did you find out with your *love probe?*" Quinn's voice is laced with sarcasm.

"Nothing we didn't already know. Your dishwasher's onboard A.I. is love-crazed." I keep typing, watching numbers, text, and waveforms dance on the glowing readout screens. "But the *big* question is, *what* or *whom* is it crazy in love *with?*"

Just then, the phone in my head buzzes. My mood instantly sinks, because the caller I.D. tag tells me who's trying to reach me.

I can handle *any* horny appliance, but I'm not so good when it comes to *ex-wives.*

"Sorry." I tap my temple, the universal gesture in the year 2075 for answering the phone. "I have to take this."

Quinn nods, looking annoyed.

I turn away, picking up the call with a tug of my left earlobe. "I'm at a jobsite, Raga."

"And *I'm* at the *courthouse*, Francis!" Raga sounds furious, as always. "For the *hearing,* remember?"

How could I forget? She and my other two exes sue me so often, there is *literally* a court hearing *every day.* "Raga, I'm on an emergency call here. You'll have to reschedule."

"Won't happen!" snaps Raga. "Judge Quinoa says if you're not here in five minutes, you'll lose *all* visitation rights to your self-respect *and* your manhood!"

I sigh. "Just as well. At this point, I wouldn't *recognize* them if they kicked me in the *nuts.*"

"Forget your nuts! I *already* have a lien against *those.*"

"Emergency call, Raga! Gotta go!" With that, I give my head a hard left shake, breaking the connection.

When I turn back to Quinn, I see a flicker of curious interest cross her pale face. I wonder what she thinks after hearing my side of the conversation.

Not that it matters. She's beautiful, but I'd have to be *crazy* to still be looking for love after three awful exes.

Wouldn't I?

"Enough of that." I clear my throat, then clap my hands through the holographic readouts and keyboard, dispersing them in glowing wisps and twinkles. "We need to go on a hunt."

"A hunt for what?" asks Quinn.

I stroll over and pat the control panel on the front of the dishwasher. "Whatever *love machine* has been making *booty calls* to little Miss *Squeaky Clean*, here."

As Quinn leads me through the house, I'm impressed. The place is state-of-the-art in every way.

Actually, *beyond* state-of-the-art is more like it. Lots of homes have morphic matrices these days, so residents can alter décor and furnishings at will. The living spaces in *this* place, however, shift *constantly*, redesigned seamlessly by artificial intelligence.

That means I've got my work cut out for me here.

Standing in the middle of the living room, I watch as the walls, carpet, and furniture flow from one set of specs to the next, all perfectly coordinated. What started as beige stucco, white shag carpet, and brown leather chairs becomes wood-grain paneling, a salt-and-pepper Berber rug, and royal blue velveteen upholstery.

It takes a special A.I. configuration to run something like this. Nodding admiringly, I pop a readout off my left forearm, checking for A.I.-Fi signals. As expected, the place is lousy with them.

"You're running a *tribe* here, aren't you?" A painting of a seascape on the wall catches my eye, melting into a pointillist abstract as I watch. "High A.I. population density, very tight-knit, very self-sufficient community."

Quinn nods. "Low to no maintenance is a good thing."

"I'm sure there's lots of *love* programmed in, to make sure everything gets along and acts in harmony. Until there's *too much* harmony."

Quinn looks around nervously. "Don't you think maybe it's just that the *dishwasher's* broken? There doesn't *have* to be another sex-crazed device, does there?"

"Only one way to find out." I touch my breastbone, and a holographic device materializes in front of me—a foot-long rod, glowing red, with a bright, knobby tip. "Let's give your network a cheap thrill." I press a stud on the hard-light handle, and the rod pulses, emitting a series of low-pitched tones.

The room pulses, too, keeping time. The lights flicker, the walls and carpeting ripple, and the furniture throbs. Moaning sounds rise from all around us, soft and rhythmic.

"What did you just do to my house?" Quinn looks worried.

"Think of it as a zap of love juice." I tweak a knob on the bottom of the rod, boosting the power. "A shot of code that gooses all your A.I.s right in their pleasure receptor algorithms."

Quinn steps closer, her shoulder brushing my arm. "And what good will *that* do?"

Just then, a male voice catches my ear—loud enough to come through clearly though it's elsewhere in the house. *Yeah, honey, that's so good. You know just what I like.*

I hurry out of the living room, heading through a doorway with Quinn in tow. "The love juice is laced with your dishwasher's unique identifier key," I tell her.

Oh yeah, honey. You're giving me fever.

I race through rooms and hallways like I own the place. "Whichever device responds with the most enthusiasm is the one in lust with the dishwasher."

Fever fever fever fever fever

The voice is loudest behind a door we come to, and I whip it open. I see darkness-then lights blink on, revealing a downward stairway.

I'm burning up, I'm burning alive, I'M ON FIRE.

I thunder down the steps. "What appliances are down here?"

"My clothes washer and dryer," Quinn says behind me.

The second my feet hit the gray cement floor, I can tell the voice isn't coming from the washer/dryer combo. They're ten feet away on my right, moaning softly...but *fever boy's* voice is much louder and coming from somewhere else.

"Over there!" Quinn heads back and to the left, pointing at whatever's there.

Uh uh uh uh uh

"Quinn, wait!"

Yes oh yes oh God oh yes OH YES

"Mack, is this *possible?*" asks Quinn. "Can my *dishwasher* be having an *affair* with my..."

Suddenly, I feel a surge of heat from her direction. Sprinting across the basement, I fling an arm around her and keep moving, dragging her toward the nearest wall.

OH YES OH YES OH YESSS I'M ON FIRE ON FIRE

Just as we fall against the wall, the furnace door swings open, and a blast of flame shoots out, scalding the spot where she was standing just seconds ago.

YOUR HEAT YOUR HEAT YOUR HEAT

"Now *that's* what I call *hot sex,"* I say, suddenly conscious of Quinn's body pinned against mine against the wall.

Another tongue of flame lances across the basement, well away from us.

I'M BURNING UP! OH BABY OH YES OH

And then, thankfully, it's all over but the afterglow.

When it comes to love, devices can be just as crazy as human beings...*crazier*, even, since A.I.s started handling all the programming of other A.I.s.

So I guess Quinn and I are lucky, when you get down to it. As far as I can tell, we're dealing with a run-of-the-mill lust flare-up in the Internet of Oversexed Things.

Though as we huddle in the basement, wondering if we've seen the last tongue of fire, *lucky* might not be the right word for how we feel.

"Do you think it's done?" Quinn peeks over my shoulder at the furnace, which is quiet and still. "Is it safe to move around again?"

"Good question." Pushing away from her and the wall, I take tentative steps into the scorch zone. No voice chants *fever fever fever*, and no fiery flare leaps out of the furnace to cook me on the spot. "All clear."

Never taking her eyes off the furnace, Quinn picks her way across the floor. She holds her breath the whole way, and so do I.

I lead her upstairs, and we close the door behind us. The devices aren't moaning up there anymore; the tweak to their pleasure algorithms has expired.

Quinn whirls on me with fear and decisiveness mingled in her eyes. "Time for a house-wide factory reset. Zero it all out and start over."

"I think a partial reset will be enough," I tell her.

"Really?" snaps Quinn. "Because my *furnace* just tried to *kill* me!"

"So, we only need to reset the furnace...and the dishwasher it's fooling around with." I tap three knuckles in sequence on my left hand, and a new holographic control panel blinks to life in front of me. "Resetting the whole *house* would be like deleting an entire *library* to get rid of *one book.*"

Quinn plants her fists on her hips. "Or not paying a repairman because he won't do what his customer specifically *requests?*"

"Do you really want to wipe out all your *settings* in the entire *house* if you don't have to? Start from scratch and rebuild your preferences from the ground up?"

"Who *cares* about settings and preferences if I'm *dead,* Mack?"

My fingers flicker over the control panel, and readings appear on the display screens above it. "I say start simple. We can always nuke your whole system later."

I see resistance in her eyes. "What if it's too late then?"

"I've never seen a customer killed by devices," I tell her, though it's only partially true. I think of Mrs. Wynette and her runaway blender that one time...but why dwell on the past?

Quinn glares but doesn't fight me further. "So, when will you reset the dishwasher and furnace?"

I rattle off the last commands on the control panel with a flourish. "Done. Both units are as blank as the day you bought them."

Suddenly, the phone in my head buzzes again. I don't take the call because I know who's making it...but my distracted irritation must show.

"Your ex again?" Quinn can't hear the buzzing, it's all in my head, but she guesses what has me annoyed.

"*An* ex," I tell her. "*Different* ex."

Her eyes widen. "How many do you *have?*"

"Three too many." I smile. "Let's just say I'm as good at shutting down *human* romance as the A.I. variety."

As soon as I say it, I wish I hadn't...but it didn't seem to bother Quinn, from what I can see. If anything, there might be a trace of sympathy in her gaze.

Then, unexpectedly, a deep frown creases her face. She looks sharply to one side, shuts her eyes, then flicks them open in my direction.

And taps her temple with a fingertip.

This time, *she* has a call coming in.

Turning away, she tugs her left earlobe. "How many times do I have to tell you to stop calling me, Zirk?"

I can't help listening in as she takes several slow steps away from me.

"No. *No.*" Quinn's voice turns cold. "You do *not* have privileges anymore. We are absolutely *not* divorced with benefits."

As I listen, I find myself picturing whoever's on the other end of the line. These days, it could be any of 114 gender varietals, not even counting your basic male or female.

Though I guess all I really need to know is it's a jerk. And crazily enough, I am *jealous* that jerk got to be married to this beautiful woman for any time at all, even if they're broken up now.

"For the last time, Zirk," snaps Quinn, "I will *not* supply new *mannerisms* for the A.I. android copy of myself that *replaced* me! Screw you!"

With that, she shakes her head hard and the call is over.

As she turns to me, her face is flushed. "You're not the only one with an ex," she says.

No sooner do the words leave her mouth than the lights flicker and dim. I hear a familiar sound from nearby, then the same sound from farther away...and again, from farther still.

"What the hell?" Quinn looks around with sudden worry. "Is that what I think it is?"

"If you mean are all the toilets in your house flushing at once, then yes."

KWOOSH. KWOOSH. KWOOSH.

"That's *exactly* what that is."

I LOVE YOU SO MUCH. I want you to give me everything you've got.

That's what the toilet in the nearest bathroom says as Quinn and I listen from the doorway.

Give it all to me, baby! Put it inside me!

"Sounds exactly like a normal toilet, doesn't it?" I tweak knobs on the holographic panel floating in front of me. "Just your normal, everyday, A.I.-enabled commode."

"Not in *this* house!" says Quinn. "Who could *use* a toilet that talks like that?"

Suddenly, the toilet flushes...and so do the other two toilets in the house. They all cry out at the same instant, too, with equal ecstasy-the closest in a male voice, the other two in female stereo.

Oh yeah! Oh baby! OH YEAH!

"And then *that* happens." I shake my head and manipulate the controls, trying to understand.

"So now my *toilets* are hot for each other?" asks Quinn. "They're having some kind of *tidy bowl threesome?"*

"Apparently." The water in the bowl in front of us sloshes gently from side to side—a telltale sign that the potty copulation is starting over again.

"And this is just some kind of *coincidence*?" Quinn sounds pissed and worried. "First my dishwasher and furnace, now my *toilets?"*

"Maybe."

"*Really?"*

"Probably not."

"What's next? My *toaster* gets nasty with my *curling iron?*"

The water sloshes more energetically, and the male voice makes with the chatter again.

You know what I need. Shoot it right down the middle.

I'm a dirty, dirty, dirty, DIRTY boy!

A female voice calls out from across the house in reply. *And I'm a dirty dirty GIRL!*

So am I! says the other female voice from further away. *Slide it in! Slide it all the way in!*

"So it *spread*?" asks Quinn. "The extreme horniness *spread* like a virus?"

"These A.I.'s are hardened against viruses. I'm thinking it might be some kind of random code mutation instead, unique to your home tribe."

Put it in me! Put it in me!

Uh uh uh uh uh!

"It's strange, though." I triple-check the results of my latest scan. "I don't see any obvious irregularities in processing, network speed, cyber-neural interactivity, daydream periodicity and metaphorcality, or anything else."

"You're saying you're stumped?" asks Quinn. "Does this mean *now* you agree about the full-house factory reset?"

"Negative." I smirk as I press a button on the holo-panel, tripping another reset...but not the one she wants. "It means stick with what works."

The toilets are in full horny swing when the reset takes effect. They flush in unison, screaming ecstatically...then wind down to a low, slow drone as their *petit mort* turns into a *très grande mort.*

OH BABY OH BABY Oh Baby oh baybeeeeee

And then they fall silent.

"Abracalavatory." I spread my arms and take a bow. "All quiet on the washroom front."

Quinn still looks tense. "Maybe you can figure out the root of the problem now?"

"Momentarily." I gesture for her to leave. "I actually need to *use* the restroom first, if you don't mind."

Quinn steps out, and I close the door behind her. Then I walk back to the toilet and lift the seat. It's a good thing, even with a factory-reset A.I., that the toilet can still be used in "dumb" mode —performing its basic functions without relying on its brain and personality.

Just as I'm about to start, however, the lights go out, leaving me standing in pitch darkness. Then, suddenly, water erupts from the toilet bowl and splatters all over me.

Yeah baby!

The toilet's pre-reset voice has been mysteriously restored...though it sounds wavery and distorted now.

Nothing can stop our love, baby! Uh uh uh UH UH!

Next, I hear a scream...but it's not a lovemaking cry. It's coming from Quinn, out in the hall, and it's filled with terror.

KWOOSH! KWOOSH! KWOOSH!

Take it, baby! Take all of it!

The toilet reverse-flushes again, spraying more water all over me. Soaking wet, I stumble back in the darkness, feeling around for a way out of the room.

My hand finds a handle, and I pull, but it's not the handle of the door leading out. As I swing it open, I hear water rushing inside, and I suddenly feel the heat of a scalding shower blasting down from above.

I'll get you all wet! says the shower in a rumbling male voice. *You love being wet, don't you? You love it!*

KWOOSH! KWOOSH! KWOOSH!

Blazing hot water pelts my skin like needles. I lunge away from the shower just as the toilet upchucks again. Fumbling along the wall, I hear the whine of a hairdryer activating nearby.

I'LL BLOW YOU SO HARD! I'LL BLOW YOU SO HARD, YOUR HAIR'S GONNA STAND ON END!

Just what I need: an electric device on the loose when I'm soaked to the skin and sloshing around in water.

Quinn screams again, farther away this time, and that does it. Adrenaline burns in my veins, and I leap into action, quickly finding the exit.

Throwing the door open, I scramble out of the room...and instantly see that things have gone off the rails in *lots* of ways. Following Quinn's cries, I lurch down the hall to the living room, guided by wildly flashing lights and a roar of device voices blaring out sexual exclamations.

Turn me on! Turn me on! cries the giant TV.

I want you all over me! wails the sofa.

Crank me harder! howls the recliner.

Things are jumping, spinning, reaching for me, and I dodge them without a second thought. The only thing I focus on is Quinn's voice, screaming in the distance.

As I sprint through the living room, the morphic matrix changes faster than ever. It's like a slideshow on speed, the walls, carpet, and furniture taking new forms every couple of seconds.

I dash down another hall, narrowly sidestepping rogue power cords that spring at me like cobras from open doorways.

Tie you up! We'll tie you up and tie you down!

A clothes iron leaps out of another doorway and nearly takes my head off. I duck at the last second, and the cherry red superheated faceplate sizzles past, crashing into the wall.

Gonna straighten you out! Gonna lay you out flat!

It's then that I finally, truly panic, because Quinn has stopped screaming.

Charging around a corner, I see her, strapped to a three-foot-tall robotic housekeeping unit, tangled in black vacuum hoses on top of its red cylindrical body. One of the hoses is wrapped tight around her neck; her eyes are bugged out, her hands clawing at the hose. Her mouth gapes, but no sound gets past the chokehold on her throat.

Suck you up I'll suck you up I'll suck you up! shouts the black and chrome robot while rolling on a runaway exercise treadmill.

Faster! Harder! Faster! screams the treadmill, rocking and hopping on the floor.

Riding a wave of adrenaline, I bolt over and grab hold of the hose around Quinn's neck. I pull with all the strength I have, but the hose holds tight.

Suck you up I'll suck you up

Faster harder faster

Gritting my teeth, I redouble my effort. The hose resists...then wrenches free in my grip.

Quinn gasps, heaving for breath as I fight the other hoses. Thank God, I've saved her life.

THE TWO OF us take refuge in a clothes closet as the whole-house orgy keeps going on around us. The moaning, groaning, squealing, and screaming never stop; neither does the thumping, flushing, splashing, smacking, and smashing. If anything, it all gets louder and faster, as if the mechanical gang-bang is picking up steam.

"*Now* will you run the full-house factory reset?" Quinn rasps the words between coughs as she recovers from her robotic strangulation.

I tap a few more keys on the holographic panel projected in front of me. It glows softly in the darkness of the unlit closet. "Nope."

"What do you *mean,* 'nope?' My housekeeping robot almost

just *murdered* me! Every device in my *house* has become a raging *nymphomaniac!"*

"I mean nope, it won't work." I stop touching keys and reach up to rub my eyes. "The factory reset functionality has been disabled."

"*What?*" The word spills out of her, triggering a violent cough. "How is that *possible?"*

"I don't know." I push aside clothes and lean back against the wall. The control panel follows me. "The A.I.s must have done it somehow."

"Seriously?" snaps Quinn. "That can *happen?"*

"There's a first time for everything, I guess."

"So what's next? How do we shut this down?"

"Good question." Something rattles past the door, whooping with simulated sexual delight. I'm trying to map out a plan, but it's hard to concentrate with all the commotion going on around us.

Quinn weathers a coughing spell, then gets in my face. "You have to *do* something."

"Trust me, it's not that simple," I tell her. "This is something new we're dealing with here."

"I *did* trust you." Quinn's gaze meets mine. Her glowing golden eyes are mesmerizing. "Was that a mistake?"

There is nothing remotely sexy about the situation we're in, but gazing at her beautiful face, lit only by her glowing eyes and my holo-panel, makes me feel alive. It makes me glad, if I have to be trapped, to be trapped here with her.

And it makes me never want to disappoint her again.

I shake my head and smile. "Not a mistake." I *almost* impulsively try for a kiss...but then I reach for my control panel instead.

"You have an idea?" asks Quinn. "Will it work?"

"It has before," I tell her. "Though I've never tried it on this scale."

"Will that be a problem?"

"That depends," I say, rattling my fingers over the light keyboard. "How *smokin' hot* do you think I am?"

Quinn just stares at me, baffled.

"If you were a *toaster* or a *toilet,* how hot would you say I am?" Laughing, I type some more, then strike the final key decisively. "*That* is the *question,* my dear Quinn."

LITTLE BY LITTLE, the noise dies down. Slowly, I open the closet door and step out.

"Did it work?" Nervously, Quinn leans out behind me. "Is it safe?"

As if in answer to her question, the housekeeper rolls around the corner in front of us.

Quinn's sudden indrawn breath betrays her fear. I'd be scared, too, if that thing had nearly killed me. I can't say I'm not a little tense, in fact, because who knows?

Who knows if the trick I tried has been successful?

"Maybe we should go back inside," says Quinn.

"Maybe." I watch as the housekeeper rolls forward, uncoiling its black hoses. One snakes out like a tentacle, rising toward me.

"Mack!" shouts Quinn.

But I've got a feeling. All the tension flows out of me, and I extend a hand.

Instead of grabbing it, the hose lays itself lightly in my palm, shivering gently.

Then the robot speaks to me, its voice very different from before-feminine and demure instead of hump-happy horny.

Hello, my love. The hose twitches, caressing my palm from side to side. *I adore you more than words can say.*

"Thank you, my dear." I look over my shoulder and see absolute shock on Quinn's face. "The feeling is mutual."

"What the hell?" says Quinn. "What did you *do*, Mack?"

"Sometimes, the best way to break up lovers..." Smiling, I give the hose a stroke. "...is to bring somebody else into the picture."

Quinn steps all the way out of the closet, taking care not to get too close to the housekeeper-bot. "By someone else, you mean..."

"Me." Nodding, I release the hose and walk around the bot into the hallway. "They love *me* now. *All* of them. Every device in your *house* loves *me* more than each other."

Quinn follows. "Seriously?"

"All thanks to some digital *Spanish fly* I uploaded to your network. When factory resets fail, a little A.I. *love potion* might be just what the doctor ordered."

As we stroll down the hall, devices call to me from open doorways. Every last one of them—from alarm clock to sex toy to toothbrush to scale to office assistant bot—reacts the same way, with love instead of lust.

Hello darling!

You look wonderful, Mack!

So handsome!

I'm so glad we have each other!

"Well, I'll be damned," says Quinn.

"The orgy is over." I take a bow as we enter the living room. The morphic walls, carpet, and furniture coo and giggle with delight, shifting to red and pink tones with lots of little hearts everywhere.

The dishwasher, fridge, and stove call to me from the kitchen. The three toilets flush in unison, chanting sweet terms of endearment from throughout the house.

"So, they love you." Quinn frowns, looking troubled. "But why aren't they *sex-crazed* anymore? Not that I'm complaining."

"Well, you see...I had to take it a step further to seal the deal."

Clearing my throat, I cross the room, patting the back of the recliner in passing. It rocks gently in appreciation. "I, uh...had to *marry* them."

"Marry them? You're married to my appliances?"

"In *their* minds, anyway. It was the only way to *de-sex* them." The sofa purrs as I lower myself onto it. "Nothing like *wedded bliss* to kill the *libido.* I know from *experience."*

Quinn shakes her head. "This is *crazy,* you know that?"

"But now it's *fixed."* I spread my arms wide to take in the whole house. "And there's *no charge* for the follow-up treatments."

Her frown deepens. "*What* 'follow-up treatments?'"

"As a husband, I have to visit every so often to keep my spouses happy. Otherwise, they might look elsewhere for affection again...and we don't want *that,* do we?"

Quinn crosses her arms over her chest, looking angry. But there's something in her eyes, I *swear,* that gives me hope. So what if I've had three wives? Maybe the fourth time will finally be the charm.

"I should probably sleep over now and then, too," I tell her. "On the sofa, of course." I pat the cushions on either side of me.

Lying back, I put my feet up. I feel the vibration of the sofa's purring all around me, from head to toe. Quinn, on the other hand, isn't purring at all...but maybe someday. People aren't as easy to program as A.I.s, but I say it's worth a try.

In the meantime, it's not like I'll be lonely around here.

"I won't mind the sofa one bit," I tell Quinn. "Did I mention how much I *love* it?" The sofa, which registers my every word, purrs and vibrates harder than ever. "And what do you know? The feeling seems to be *mutual."*

DRIVERLESS

The sleek red Ford GT with white racing stripes screamed along the Nebraska four-lane, punching toward the dark cloud-shrouded towers of Omaha in the distance.

Vreeeeoooowwwwww

The gray-haired, dark-skinned man in the cockpit, Shunn Comma, clutched the steering wheel, darting his bloodshot brown eyes to the rearview mirror every few seconds.

Each time, he chewed his gum a little faster. The trio of black Ferrari Superfasts was still zooming along behind him, five car lengths back and closing.

Eeeeeooowww Eeeeooowww Eeeeooowww.

Like Shunn's GT, none of the Ferraris was driverless, hobbled by speed or maneuvering governors—nothing short of a miracle in the mid-21st century.

And nothing short of a shit-show if those Ferraris ever caught up. Assuming there was anything left of his time-release memory before they tried to jack the shit out of it.

Shunn checked the timer on his right contact lens overlay. *07:35.*

Tick tick tick tick

That was all the time he had left to deliver the ultra-top-secret message before it was gone forever...and a civil war, perhaps, erupted in the heart of the American Midwest.

Zeeeeeoooowwwwww

And the fun was just getting started. As Shunn hurtled up over a rise, he saw a cluster of traffic less than a mile ahead, crawling up both eastbound lanes at robotic, self-driving speeds.

He might as well have been staring at a wall of metal and human bodies blocking the road. The cars flowed forward in tight formation at identical speed, controlled by cloud-based networks of A.I. mommies that locked out all human influence.

Almost all influence. It was a good thing Shunn was as much a super-hacker as a super-driver. Otherwise, most roads would have been unusable for his flight, even to a non-driverless car like the GT.

With practiced flicks and blinks of his eyes, he launched the hacker app loaded in his cranial drive, simultaneously jamming incoming commands to the wall of self-driving obstacles up ahead and pushing through his own.

Part, you sons of bitches.

At first, nothing. *Tick tick tick.* Beads of sweat on his creased forehead thickened and ran.

Tick tick

Vreeeeeooooowwww

Finally, further up the column, one car in the right lane hopped onto the berm, then another. And another, even further ahead.

Tick tick tick

Three in the left lane peeled left onto the medial strip—but as in the right lane, the rearward stragglers clung to the straightaway. There were four in the left lane and three in the right, dead center between the solid and dashed white lines.

Seconds left before he'd plow into them. Cursing. Sweating.

Tick

CURSING.

Then he thought of a snippet of a poem by Robert Frost, the one about woods on a snowy evening and having miles to go before he could sleep. It was the message he was carrying, due to be decoded with an algorithmic cipher by his contact in Omaha. Why, he wondered, did it give him a strange, sinking feeling every time it trickled through his mind? Was it because of all the roads not taken in his own life, the paths that could have kept him from this hell-bent race? Or the fact that sleep, or rest of any kind, were beyond him these days, and everything felt like a waking dream of speed?

Days like this, Shunn felt like nothing but propulsion. Faster slower farther closer *yessssss.*

A message made flesh. Message become the messenger.

Come on and paarrrtttt, motherfuckerrrsss...

And they did. Stragglers FINALLY swung left and right, JUST AS THE GT RIPPED BETWEEN THEM, hugging the cut that hadn't been wide enough even seconds

Tick

Before.

DID Moses grin when he opened the Red Sea? Because Shunn sure did.

That's right, that's right, baby.

He kept the traffic parting before him, folding away to right and left like waves in a sea. He felt the computer code flowing through the network into and out of the cloud down into the cars' brains and circuits, closing and opening, speed and course trimming to suit him.

The GT skimmed through the gap, moving so fast it looked like one continuous red-and-white streak. Barely missing one pair of cars, it swooped right and bucked left to miss another as the perfectly synchronized parting rolled onward like a current.

Then he checked the rearview mirror. The three Ferraris were still back there, single-filed to clear the gap. The lead driver bolted forward, no doubt realizing that the traffic slowed the GT just enough to maybe run up on him.

Shunn chipped fresh hacks at the parted traffic behind him, reaching in like a surgeon seeking shrapnel. Missed one missed two missed three...

Got one! He nosed a gray Volvo at the last second, just enough to make it clip the rearward black Ferrari, spinning it hard into the medial.

Didn't change the lead car's chase but cut the pack by one.

And we're clear. Traffic suddenly gone ahead, the road wide open, at least until the next bend two miles up.

Shunn stomped the accelerator and pulled away from the lead Ferrari, sprinting into the twilight outside Omaha.

Vreeeeooowwww

One more try at hacking the remaining two Ferraris but forget it, he couldn't jump the air gap or strip the hardened on-premises war boxes. *Standoff.*

Which was exactly what he was being paid a small fortune to break, on a much larger scale. A secret standoff between two sides in the heart of America--government and breakaway forces—and no one would even know it had been a threat unless those pricks back there intercepted him before one of two things happened:

Delivery or auto-delete.

Delivery would be complete when he reached the location represented by the blinking red dot on the windshield GPS overlay – just inside the Omaha city limits. The breakaway forces would get the message that the government was making concessions, and the civil war would be cancelled.

On the other hand, if he didn't get there before the deadline, the message he carried would be automatically deleted from his brain. The hope for peace and unity would be erased, just as hawkish elements on both sides wanted them to be.

This would happen in exactly 06:15.

Tick tick tick

The overwhelming need to avoid that outcome drove him to push the GT even harder.

Vreeeeeooowwwww

The blurred green-brown-gray scenery around him was a foretaste of what the deletion deadline would bring. All he'd have left after auto-delete was a blur like that, a hint of a trace of a flicker of something that had once been in his brain.

If only he could say the same about his memories of Annie and how he'd lost her.

Every job, he got the treatment. Time-release targeted memory loss by biochemical compound, keyed on the exact neurons storing the message he was delivering. Just as in-person delivery was the only way to ensure message security in the age of hacked E-everything, memory wipes were the only way to guarantee that even *that* security couldn't be compromised.

There was only one problem. The wipes were too precise. No collateral damage. They wouldn't delete his memories of cheating on Annie, and her knowing but not saying and not forgiving and one day just *not.*

Not being there.

And no amount of speed could run him away from all that he'd lost.

Vreeeeeoooooowwwww

If all else failed and he was captured, he could stick himself with the Big Shot syringe from the glove box. Five hundred times the original dose of the auto-delete compound would howl through his bloodstream and brain, cooking down the memories like a bubbling reduction in a saucepan.

Would that finally kill the memories of Annie? He didn't know. He'd never needed the Big Shot before; he'd never failed to complete a mission.

And he had no intention of failing *this* time, either.

Whunk

Just then, something bumped the roof of the GT.

Whunk

And again. Checking the overlays on his windshield and contacts, he spotted the culprit: a weaponized drone trying to deposit an explosive on the GT. It was the first since he'd hacked and blown a swarm of them near Cedar Rapids—and it wouldn't be deterred. Shunn's hacker app couldn't get him through the drone's defenses, no matter how hard he tried.

Whunk

Even as he kept trying to breach the drone's firewall, Shunn watched the GPS for some sign of an overpass where he might be able to crash the thing...but no dice. He swerved the GT, fighting to prevent payload attachment, but he knew it was only a matter of time.

Whunk

After all the distance he'd come and all the obstacles he'd dodged or obliterated, that one damn drone was about to be the death of him and the failure of his mission.

Whunk

Maybe he could grab another drone nearby, one without the hardened security, and bring it in for a collision. Casting his net wide, he scanned local frequencies for a sign of such a drone, hoping he could find one before the payload latched on to the GT.

Whunk

That was when the sky flashed with dazzling light.

Tick tick tick

A rumbling blast shook the cockpit.

KRAKOOOOOOMMM

Lightning and thunder. Now *there* was something you didn't see or hear much in the days of Midwestern mega-drought.

Shunn chewed his gum faster, biting the inside of his left cheek so hard, he tasted blood. His hands tightened like bear traps on the wheel. The equation of his drive had just changed dramatically.

And *shit,* all he had was five minutes forty-five seconds till auto-delete...or worse, a full *reformat* via Big Shot.

05:40

At least he had clear highway ahead...until he *didn't.*

05:30

Adrenaline sizzled through his bloodstream as the GT barreled around a bend and he saw what was waiting for him there.

HOONNNNNNKKK HOONNNNNNKKK

Etched in another flash of lightning, a tractor trailer loomed dead ahead, hurtling straight toward him.

KRAKABOOOOOOMMMMM

SKREEEEEEEEEEEEEE

Shunn stamped the brake and spun the wheel, whipping the GT around in a punishing 180. He played the stick and clutch and crushed the accelerator, leaping away in the direction from which he'd come.

VRRREEEEEOOOWWWWW

The drone that had been pacing him wasn't quite so quick on

the uptake. He saw it explode against the cab of the truck in a ball of flame.

Arcs of burnt rubber smoked on the asphalt behind him as he shot away from the crashing tractor trailer...and plunged headlong toward the remaining two black Ferraris.

In a desperate flurry of cranial code bursts, he probed the tractor trailer's self-driving systems and couldn't make a dent. The truck was hacked, it *had* to be—and now Shunn was caught in the middle of a roadkill sandwich: tractor trailer on one side, Ferraris on the other, lightning flashing, countdown ticking.

KRAAKABAKOOOOM

04:40

Tick tick tick tick

And *WTF*, Annie's last words were bouncing around his head like ball bearings in a cement mixer.

The smell of sweat in the cockpit. The smell of her perfume on that day, months ago, like lilacs.

"Glorified..."

He jammed the stick. Cut the wheel.

"...pizza delivery boy..."

Mashed the pedal.

"...all you'll ever be."

Blew across the medial, hopping the dip in the middle, never losing momentum.

"What good is that photographic memory..."

All the while hacking the clot of cars zooming toward him on the other side of the highway.

"...if you can't remember the only thing that really matters?"

Juggling them into a hasty single file in the far lane, leaving him the closest lane and berm...somehow barely keeping all six from colliding.

And that's when it started. Drops on the windshield.

KRABAKROOOOOOOM

And a parade of vehicles cruising headlong toward him, headlights flaring to life all at once.

VREEEEEOOOOWWWW

Just as the downpour let loose, drenching cars and road alike with a pummeling shower that was nowhere near as cold as the chill racing up Shunn's spine.

FWOOOOOOOOSSSSHHHHH

Because this...

Holy shit, *this* was *bad.*

EVEN AS SHUNN raced into the lane he'd opened, he saw the single file wouldn't hold. Some of the cars he'd nudged into that formation started to flick and swing, gliding on the rain-slickened asphalt.

Because who needed protection against hydroplaning in a world where it almost never rained, and self-driving cars always perfectly adjusted to conditions on the rare occasions when it did?

Unless they were *hacked,* that is.

KRAKOOOOOOOOOMMMMM

Shunn glanced right for a second. Heavy traffic there across the medial, so he'd take his chances running the gauntlet here, with incoming.

NEEEOOOWWWWWWWWW

The GT bolted forward on top-of-the-line tires that gripped the road through the film of rain. The Ferraris were similarly well-equipped; they vaulted the medial behind him and followed suit with perfect traction.

EEOOOWWWWW EEOOOWWWW

Wipers chopping away at the fastest setting, Shunn charged the narrowing gap like a terrier through a rat hole. Cars lashed toward him from the single file—red then blue then green, skating into his path, nearly making contact.

SSSHHHHKRUMMMPP

And then *making* it. A silver Audi coupe spun around in a sudden 360, its rear-end swatting the driver's side front quarter panel of the GT.

Shunn wrenched the wheel hard and rode the impact, whipping the GT in a swing of its own and then grabbing the pavement again and lurching eastbound.

SSHHWWOOOOSSHHHH

Even as he careened forward through the torrential rain, clawing for purchase in the brains of the cars up ahead, the countdown continued in his mind.

03:15 until auto-delete.

KRAKOOOOOMMMMMM

He was *so close* to the red line, and he knew it. So close to not completing his delivery before the message dissolved from his mind.

03:00

02:55

But the towers of the city loomed closer than ever now, strobing in flashes of lightning. One man waited to receive him just inside the city limits, waiting to hear the message he'd brought all the way from the White House in Washington, D.C.

SHISSSSSSSSSSS

Suddenly, another car bucked over, and another. Shunn swerved right, left, right, catching glimpses of the terrified passengers in their cabins.

Chewing the gum harder, he drew blood from the right cheek this time.

02:33

Suddenly, it was Christmas in the rearview mirror. He glanced up just in time to see the rearward Ferrari bounce off a white van and flip into the medial ditch.

One less chase car was a gift. Shunn gunned the GT and flew faster, focused like a laser on the blinking red GPS dot.

KRAKAKOOOOOOMMMM

He had to *get there* before auto-delete, pass the message to the warm body designated for the last leg of the relay. *Everything* was riding on *him*, a terrible sacrifice to stave off a much greater loss.

If he failed to deliver the message, millions would surely die in an unnecessary civil war that would ravage the nation.

02:17

02:10

He was *right* on the *red line*, but he still had *hope*, he still might *make* it. Less than a minute from the city limits and his exit — seconds after that to the roadblock and the contact he'd tell about roads not taken and having miles to go before he could sleep.

And then maybe *he* could finally sleep.

02:00

Tick tick tick tick

SHISSSSSSSSSSS

But suddenly, everything went crazy up ahead. Every car broke from the file, spinning and sliding over the rain-soaked road in front of him.

It didn't matter that he was still snapping out orders and the cars' brains were reading loud and clear, trying to obey. Shitty tires sent them careening like an up-dumped bucket of pucks on a hockey rink.

And Shunn was roaring right into them.

HE HAD to tap the brake to miss a Toyota sedan, then a pickup. In the split-second before he could stomp the gas again, the remaining Ferrari stormed up and bumped him from behind.

THUNNKKK

The GT lurched left and clipped a blue SUV, pitching it into a road sign. Fighting the wheel, Shunn rode the collision momentum in a whipsaw 180, then stepped on the accelerator, mowing headlong into the charging Ferrari.

As the Ferrari pushed back, Shunn threw the GT in reverse and shot away, grazing a fishtailing BMW. The Ferrari erupted after him, violently sideswiping the BMW, sweeping it out of its way.

KRRUMMMPP

01:45

The GT stayed face-to-face with the Ferrari, slashing backward through the jackhammering rain and chaos of hydroplaning cars. Shunn cranked the stick, worked the clutch, and bashed the accelerator, all while yanking the wheel back and forth to navigate the mayhem.

01:37

Swooping right, left, right, left, he somehow traversed the jumble of whirling vehicles while keeping his car inches from the nose of the Ferrari.

SHISSSSSSSSSSS

Sluicing backward, ever backward, he raced like a blood cell exploding through an artery, the whole time keeping a secret other than the ciphered message—and the secret was this:

He was *holding back*, drawing in the Ferrari...and then he *wasn't.*

RRROOAAARRRRRR

01:25

The GT rocketed back as if the speeding Ferrari were standing still. Into the gap between them slid a propane tanker, and then...

WABOOOOOOOMMM

Flames and debris *exploded* in all directions. Shockwaves pummeled the skating cars, kicking them away from the center of the blast.

Rattling the GT as the seconds ticked away.

01:05

Jerking the wheel, Shunn spun the GT around hard and bolted for the medial. A narrow path existed, just a sliver of a keyhole between clusters of traffic, leading straight to the exit ramp he needed.

Without hesitation, he darted into it.

Only to realize, at the very last instant, that it wasn't so unobstructed after all. Just as he cleared the medial, a scarred and battered black Ferrari swung out in front of him and cut him off. One of the two pursuers he'd thought out of the race had recovered and caught up.

"Fuck!" Shunn jerked the wheel, but there was no way to dodge or stop in time.

SHISSSSSSSSS

KRAASSSHHHHH

The GT collided with the Ferrari, sending both cars skidding across the double lanes. They came to rest straddling the berm, a dozen feet apart.

Four men in black armor and helmets bolted out of the Ferrari with guns, cutters, and probes, running for the GT with purpose.

And there was still just under a minute left until auto-delete.

Shunn knew what he had to do. If there was even the slightest chance they might hack him before auto-delete, he had to burn everything.

Shaky from the crash, he leaned across the seat and popped the glove box. Grabbing the Big Shot, he flipped the cap off the needle.

Then stabbed the needle into his neck and pushed the plunger.

Instantly, he felt himself melting away like ice cream on a summer sidewalk, and he smiled. The blades of power saws sliced through the driver's-side door, the windshield shattered under a blow from a bludgeon, and he didn't give a shit.

Because this time, maybe, he would finally forget the pain of what he'd done. Finally forget Annie and the only true love he'd ever known.

"We have it," said one of the men as he checked readings on a scanner on his wrist.

"You're sure?" A second man used the muzzle of a rifle to nudge Shunn, who was sprawled on the hood of the GT where they'd tossed him after dragging him out of the car.

"Has to be," said the first man. "It's the only thing left in his brain. The only thing our probes got out of him."

"Guess we'll figure it out later." The second man marched off toward the black Ferrari waiting nearby, followed by two of his partners. "We need to go." Sirens approached.

"Poor son of a bitch." The first man jerked the adhesive electrode from Shunn's temple and walked away. "At least he's at peace now."

They drove off, leaving Shunn on the GT's hood, tossing his head and scowling. As the rain pelted him, he kept repeating the same words over and over, the same message he'd delivered to the enemy agents.

The only message he had left in his burned-out memory. The only message he had left to remember and deliver for the rest of his vegetated life.

"Glorified pizza delivery boy...all you'll ever be," he said.

If not for the rain, the tears on his face might have been visible, glistening in the flashing blue and red lights of the cop cars arriving around him.

But no such luck.

Thunder rolled, and he kept on mumbling right through it.

KRAKOOOOOOMMMMM

"What good is that...photographic memory...if you can't remember...the only thing that really *matters*?"

GIVE THE HIPPO WHAT HE WANTS

The pink hippopotamus appeared in front of Thal Simoleon just as he was about to take the swing that could have won the World Series for the Bio Threats.

As soon as the ball left the pitcher's hand, Thal knew he could launch it out of the park. It came in straight and steady, a little low and outside but well within his range...proof that even a genetically engineered pitcher like Phallus Fearbringer could blow a throw under pressure.

Before the hippo appeared, Thal knew he was about to become the hero of the Series. The Bio Threats were down by two in the bottom of the ninth with two outs...but the bases were loaded and the pitch was a home run waiting to happen. One stroke of the bat would bring in the grand slam, assuring a Bio Threats win and a World Series title.

At least, that was what would have happened if the hippo hadn't popped up out of nowhere, wearing a grass skirt and hopping around on two legs between him and the ball.

Singing opera.

When the creature appeared, Thal's view of the pitch was

blocked, his concentration obliterated. He took a swing anyway, aiming at the vicinity of where he expected the ball to be; to his credit, he came close...but his swing was well before the ball's arrival. The tip of the bat lashed into the corner of the strike zone and forward and up, passing harmlessly through the air and then the hippo.

A heartbeat later, the ball sailed through and smacked into the catcher's mitt.

The hippo kept right on singing and pirouetting in front of him, long black lashes fluttering over baby blue eyes.

The crowd roared with rage. It was Thal's third strike.

The game was over.

As the Dirty Nukes threw their hats in the air and embraced in the infield, Thal hurled his bat through the hippo, not caring who might be on the other side of the insubstantial phantasm. The surprise visitor had robbed him of a great accomplishment; if he could have strangled it to death on the spot, he would have.

But he knew that he couldn't. Though its appearance had been unexpected, he knew all about the hippo.

Concluding its serenade on a high note that only Thal could hear, the creature spread its stumpy pink arms wide and took a deep bow. As the superstadium erupted in pandemonium around them, the creature bounced over to Thal, batting its ridiculous lashes and grinning. Bright red lipstick was smeared all around its rubbery mouth.

"Hello there, Zeke," said the hippo, nostrils twitching atop its bulbous snout. "Fancy meeting you here!"

Thal seethed and said nothing. He knew that no one else could see the creature, and he didn't want to be caught on camera talking to himself.

The hippo pushed closer, its great bulk shimmying from side to side. "Can I give you some advice, pal?"

Thal continued to stare silently ahead.

"If I were you, I'd get out of here right now," said the hippo. "The fans are coming! The fans are coming!"

Looking back, Thal saw that the hippo was right. People were cascading out of the stands onto the field, screaming like Vikings. All the other players on Thal's team had already disappeared into the locker room or were running full tilt toward the exits.

He had no doubt that if he stood there another moment, they would kill him. He had seen it happen before.

Thal ran as fast as he could toward the locker room door, his genetically engineered legs easily carrying him ahead of the screaming mob. His pursuers pelted him with coins and shoes and bottled water, but his body was tough enough to take a lot more punishment than that.

As he raced toward the door, he wished that he could leave the hippo behind as easily as the crowd...but he knew that he couldn't. The creature was literally in his mind, a custom-made hallucination that could follow him anywhere once it had locked on to him.

He knew it well, because he was the one who had set it loose three years ago.

As Coach Wildsnap paced across the office, hands locked behind his back, Thal had a hard time keeping his eyes from wandering to the hippo pacing along behind him.

"End of the road, Thal," Wildsnap said grimly, shaking his doughy head. "I guess you already knew that, though."

Thal couldn't stop looking at the hippo, so he cast his eyes down at the floor. "You're trading me?" he said, though he knew that wasn't what the coach had meant.

"No trade," said Wildsnap. "Welcome to civilian life."

"And yer out!" barked the hippo.

Thal glanced up. The hippo was waving both of its stumpy arms at him and sticking its purple tongue out of its enormous, lipsticked mouth.

"But it was just one mistake," said Thal. "After all I've done for this team over the years, don't I deserve another chance?"

"You know better than that." Wildsnap pushed up the brim of his ballcap. "You're done in this league. If you ever set foot on the field again, the crowd'll eat you alive...literally. As we speak, they're burning all your memorabilia in Citydome Center. They've already toppled your statue in the Hall of Gods."

"Holy shit," said Thal.

"Don't get me wrong," said Wildsnap, removing a framed photo of Thal from the wall. "I feel for you, buddy. But what the hell were you doing out there tonight? Were you hyperstoned or something?"

"Tell him, Thal!" shouted the hippo. "Clear your good name!"

Thal sighed. If he told the coach he'd been victimized by a Choker, he could erase the doubt of his playing skill...but he would open up a can of worms that he couldn't afford to open.

"I don't know what happened," said Thal. "It was just one of those things."

Wildsnap stomped over and tore the player number from Thal's red and green jersey. "With the DNA you've got, it's never 'just one of those things.' Not that it makes any difference now. You're done, my friend."

"Time to stick a fork in you, Thally!" said the hippo, doing a soft-shoe across the office.

"This is bullshit." Thal jumped up out of the chair and shoved his way past Wildsnap. "You owe me! I made the Bio Threats the top team in the <u>world</u>! I made Bio Threats Citydome <u>billions</u> of dollars!"

With a wave, Wildsnap brought the holographic computer interface to life over the desktop in front of him. "You're right," he said as he brought up the team's roster and erased Thal's name from it. "I do owe you. That's why I'm going to save your life, my friend."

Thal stormed over and kicked the front of the desk, putting a hole in it. "Save my life?"

"Face it," said Wildsnap. "You're ruined. Everybody in Citydome wants you dead. I'm your only chance at survival. Now do you want a ticket or not?"

"A ticket?" said Thal.

"For the underground railroad," said Wildsnap. "Your only way out. Leave right now, and you might make it."

Thal felt as dazed as if he'd just taken a beanball to the head. "What, just leave?"

At that moment, the lights dimmed, and a siren began to whoop. Eyes wide, Thal gaped out the office door into the locker room; he heard a steady, distant pounding under the siren.

"What's going on?" he said.

"I believe the villagers would like a word with you," the hippo said in his ear.

Wildsnap checked readouts on the holographic display and popped up out of his chair. "They're storming the compound," he said. "You're out of time."

The pounding got louder. Thal's stomach twisted like taffy, and his palms started to sweat.

Wildsnap smacked his palm down on the desktop. A circular hatch in the wall, invisible until now, irised open. "All aboard," he said.

HUNGRY, freezing, and up to his knees in sewage, Thal slumped against the tunnel wall as his guide went ahead to meet the guard at the next checkpoint.He wasn't sure how long they'd been on the run through the sewers, but it seemed like days.

Sometimes, as he trudged through the muck behind the dark-cloaked man who served as his guide, Thal wondered if what he was experiencing was really happening. It didn't seem possible that he, a world-famous sports superstar, idol of billions, full-fledged god in the Church of Champions, could have been reduced to fleeing through the excrement of the very people who had once worshipped and adored him.

Unfortunately, the stench and the cold and the wet always left him no doubt that what he was living was harsh reality.

The pink hippo kept reminding him, too.

"Bet you're tired, huh?" said the Choker, floating on his back on the rancid current. "Could use a nice juicy steak, too, couldn't you?"

Thal wiped his face on the hem of his jersey. Over the past few days, he had started to appreciate just how crazy a Choker could make someone. It was one thing to see the effect it had on another person, but another thing entirely to endure its abuse himself.

Increasingly, he was coming to understand what his victims had gone through...the other players he'd sicced the Choker on to clinch wins and eliminate competition.

The sound of splashing echoed down the tunnel then, and Thal turned to see his guide slogging through the sewage toward him. The cloaked man stopped midway and waved his torch, summoning Thal to follow him.

When the two of them sloshed around a bend in the tunnel, Thal saw light emanating from an opening some yards away. The guide went through first, reaching for rungs outside the opening and climbing down.

Peering out, Thal saw that the tunnel gave way to a huge, circular chamber. All around the chamber, falls of sewage roared down from pipes and tunnels opening out of the walls at all levels.

Looking down, Thal saw a cluster of men gathered at the base of the ladder that the guide was descending. They stood on a stone shelf many feet below, torches flickering as they gazed up at him.

Reaching out, Thal grabbed one of the cold metal rungs set into the wall. He swung a foot onto a lower rung and climbed down, taking care because the rungs were slippery with moisture.

The pink hippo floated down alongside him, apparently held aloft by a tiny red parasol. "Easy does it," said the hippo. "Wouldn't want you to fall and break your neck."

For the first time, Thal talked back to the creature. "Shove it up your ass," he said.

"These men have all traveled the railroad like you," the guide told Thal when he'd reached the shelf. "They will take you to your next stop."

Thal looked at the three dirty faces surrounding him. One of the men, a tall, bony guy with curly red hair and a beard to his chest, looked familiar.

"Are you going, too?" Thal said to the guide.

"Good luck," said the guide, and then he scaled the rungs in the wall and disappeared into the tunnel.

"We'd better get moving," said the red-haired man. "We've got a long way to travel tonight."

Thal stared at him, becoming more convinced that he had seen him before. "Do I know you?"

The red-haired man's eyes crinkled at the corners as he smiled. "That's a good question," he said, and then he turned and hiked off along the shelf.

HOURS LATER--IT SEEMED LIKE HOURS, anyway--Thal found out who the red-haired man was...and quickly wished that he hadn't.

He made the discovery when the four of them (five, counting the hippo) stopped for a rest in the wasteland they were crossing. It was the first break they had taken since leaving the sewers many miles ago, and Thal was grateful for the chance to sit down.

As Thal slouched in an exhausted daze on a boulder, the red-haired man offered him his canteen.

"Still can't quite place me, can you?" said the man as Thal took a drink. "Maybe you could use a little hint."

Thal lowered the canteen. "All right."

The red-haired man leaned closer, eyes twinkling in the moonlight. "Pink hippo," he said, lips curling in a smirk under the shaggy beard. "Does that ring a bell?"

Thal frowned. If the man knew about the hippo, he had to be one of a very select group.

"He's one of the guys you screwed over," the Choker whispered in Thal's ear. "Talk about a blast from the past!"

"I don't know what you're talking about," said Thal.

"I'll give you another hint," said the red-haired man. "The home run duel of 2125."

Thal shook his head, though now he knew who the guy was. There was only one man who had battled him for the record for most runs in a season in 2125...and that man would certainly have knowledge of Thal's pink hippo.

Because Thal had set it loose on him to ruin his chances of topping the record.

The red-haired man laughed. "You know."

Thal shrugged and took another drink from the canteen.

"Casey Talisman, stupid!" said the hippo.

"Casey Talisman, stupid!" said the red-haired man. Thal considered continuing to play dumb, then decided against it. The other two guides had drawn in close; he was all too aware of how vulnerable he was at that moment, genetically engineered or not.

"Long time no see, Casey." Thal handed back the canteen. "What've you been up to?"

"Helping my fellow ex-professional athletes," said Casey. "I've helped save a lot of lives over the past two years, my friend."

"That's great," said Thal.

"I guess I oughtta thank you," said Casey. "You've sent a lot of business my way."

Thal looked away and said nothing. The pink hippo danced into his line of sight, doing a jitterbug.

"He should've thanked both of us, Thally," said the hippo.

Casey gave Thal a playful punch on the arm. "You've been a busy guy, all right," said Casey. "I'll bet ninety percent of the baseball players who've come through here over the past two years blame you for killing their careers. They all talk about how it's such a big coincidence that every time one of them got one up on you, this pink hippo Choker showed up to mess with their heads."

"That's me! That's me!" hollered the hippo.

"Guess what?" Casey grinned. "The three guys you're stuck here with right now? We've all seen the hippo. All three of us got screwed over because of you."

Thal looked at the other two men standing around him. He hadn't recognized them before, but now he realized that their faces were as familiar to him as Casey's.

"Not that there are any hard feelings, of course," said Casey, right before he and the other men started pounding the hell out of Thal.

"Wow," said the priest just before he punched Thal in the face. "I've never hit a god before."

Suspended spread-eagle from the ceiling by chains, Thal stared blankly at the scrawny priest. He wasn't the first person to enter the white chamber with the intention of striking him; he wasn't even the first priest to do so.

In the months since Casey and the others had beaten him half to death and sold him to the man who kept him here, a seemingly endless parade of people had strolled through the door and used him as a punching bag.

Usually, they told him why they did it. A lot of them were still angry because he'd lost the World Series for the Bio Threats. Some were fans of other teams, avenging his victories over their favorites. Some had lost money betting on games because of him...or investing in Thal Simoleon memorabilia that had become worthless the minute he missed that fateful pitch in the Series.

Some--the priests, especially--just wanted to kick a god's ass.

"This is for betraying your flock," said the priest, throwing a fist hard into Thal's belly. "And this is for letting me worship you as a false god." The priest swung again, this time cracking Thal's nose.

"That's gotta hurt," said the pink hippo, who unfortunately hadn't left Thal's side for a minute.

As the priest continued to pound him, Thal let his mind drift back to his childhood in Citydome Godcrèche. He remembered days under the hothouse sun, running and throwing and hitting the ball under the watchful eyes of trainers and coaches who were the only parents he'd ever known. Back then, he had thought that his life was perfectly normal, because it was the only life that he had ever known.

He hadn't realized that most people had parents and couldn't run twenty-five miles an hour or throw a ball two hundred miles an hour or jump twenty feet into the air to snag a pop fly. He hadn't realized that most people weren't claimed at birth by sports teams, assigned a player number before they could walk, and driven every day of their lives to perfect their skills so they could someday win a World Series championship. He hadn't realized that there was more to life than winning at any cost.

"That's enough, Father Focus." The voice of Thal's owner, Mr. Montage, pulled Thal back from his reverie. As always, Montage stopped the customer before he could kill Thal.

Father Focus threw one last punch into Thal's groin, then stepped back to admire his handiwork. "That's what you get for betraying the faith," said Focus, jabbing a finger at Thal. "I only wish the other gods could see you now."

"Yes, yes," said Montage, turning Focus by the shoulder and leading him toward the door. "You're a true defender of the faith. On your way now."

As Focus left the white room, shepherded by one of Montage's burly aides, Montage closed the door and walked back to Thal. "How's my main attraction holding up?"

"Bring on the next contestant!" howled the pink hippo, but Thal said nothing.

"You've made a lot of money for me," said Montage. "It will be a shame to see you go."

Thal peered at Montage through blackened, swollen eyes. "Go?" he croaked.

Montage sighed. "We've had such wonderful times, Thal, but it's time for you to move on. You've been sold."

"Sold?" said Thal.

"To a woman," Montage said with a wink. "An heiress. Claims she's always had a thing for you."

"Whoopee!" said the hippo. "Thally and the heiress, sittin' in a tree, kay-eye-ess-ess-eye-en-gee!"

"Thing?" said Thal.

"Ah, yes," said Montage. "I believe your new position will

prove somewhat more pleasurable than the one you are about to take leave of."

After their latest lovemaking, Paradise Whippoorwill held Thal in her arms and gently stroked his hair. He knew what she would say before she said it, even though he had been her property for only two weeks.

"You feel better, don't you, Thal?" she said softly. "I'm good for you, aren't I, my love?"

Thal nodded. "Yes you are," he said, though it wasn't true at all. Keeping her happy was important.

It was important because Paradise had a remote control under the skin of her left wrist. If she was unhappy, she could make the device her surgeon had implanted in Thal's skull shoot out bolts of pain...or melt his cerebrum into clam chowder.

"You know what brought us together, don't you?" said Paradise.

"Fate," said Thal.

Paradise sighed. "That's right. We were meant to be together. I knew it from the first time I saw you play on holovid."

"Yes," said Thal, wishing that she would just shut up. He was grateful to her for rescuing him from the white room, but he was sick of hearing her dreamy professions of everlasting love.

"I watched you from afar for all those years," said Paradise. "I even met you in person and got your autograph, and you didn't know at the time that we'd be together someday."

"I had no idea," said Thal.

"But you had a feeling," said Paradise. "You knew I was special."

"Absolutely," said Thal, though he had no memory of meeting her before the day she bought him from Mr. Montage.

The pink hippo, sprawled out on the big bed alongside Paradise, sniffed and pawed at a tear. "How romantic," he said. "I'm gettin' all choked up."

"You had all those other women," said Paradise, "but I was always in the back of your mind. And when you needed me most, I was there for you, wasn't I?"

"You were there for me," said Thal.

"You're the man of my dreams," said Paradise. "And I'm the woman who will make your dreams come true. When you make your comeback, I'll be right there beside you every step of the way."

"That's right," said Thal, but he knew better. The only thing she loved was the fantasy she expected him to play out.

He was the fallen champion who only needed the love of a good woman to regain the heights. When he took to the field again, she would bask in his reflected glory, and all would know that her love was the force behind his rebirth.

Like the people who had cheered him and then come to beat him in the white room, Paradise saw him as a puppet. He existed solely to act out her fantasy.

A fantasy he knew was doomed to failure.

STEPPING out on the field was all it took.

It was only a minor league game, the Anthrax Scare versus the Letter Bombs, in a town on the opposite end of the country from Bio Threats Citydome. It was only an exhibition, and Thal's appearance wasn't even publicized. His real name wasn't even on his jersey.

But the fans recognized him as soon as he set foot on the turf. As he jogged to the outfield, glove tucked against his chest, they leaned and squinted and pointed, and a murmur rose from the stands. As the voice on the P.A. system announced the first batter, the murmur grew to a rumble and then to a roar.

Before the first pitch could be thrown, people were hurling food and shoes and batteries in Thal's direction. Before a single player could run the base line, fans were pouring onto the field in a crashing, screaming wave headed straight for Thal.

For a moment, he stood there and watched the approaching surge, wondering if he might be better off letting them tear him to pieces. It was something he had considered in the weeks leading up to the game, for he had known how the fans would react.

But the closer they got, the less he wanted to die. He was miserable, and he had no reason to think his life would get better, but he feared death...at least the ugly kind of death that was bearing down on him.

Plus which, he didn't want to give them the satisfaction.

So he pressed the control pad in the brim of his hat, and an escape hatch opened beneath him. Paradise had paid to install several such hatches in the field for just such an occasion...though Thal knew she had never expected that he would actually have to use one.

As he slid down the tube, listening to the mob pound over the ground above him, he wondered how she was reacting to the way his comeback was going.

To her credit, Paradise Whippoorwill stood by her man...at least for a while.

She set him up again in a minor league game, this time in Japan, but the results were the same. Next, she staged a private exhibition with a hand-picked crowd of supposed Thal Simoleon boosters...but it turned out the boosters were bashers at heart, and Thal again had to flee for his life. Then, there was the ill-fated game without an audience, in which the umpires and groundskeepers took it upon themselves to uphold the tradition of trying to kill Thal.

But all of this, Thal discovered, was not a bad thing.

"I'm no good for you," Paradise told him three weeks after the last comeback attempt had failed. "I'm holding you back."

"Uh-oh," said the pink hippo. "This sounds familiar."

Raising her left arm, Paradise showed Thal the tiny scar on her wrist. "I had the control device removed and destroyed," she said. "You're free. I cancelled the wedding, too."

Thal nodded, afraid to say anything that might make her change her mind.

Tears ran down Paradise's cheeks. "Oh, Thal," she said, her voice quavering. "You have such great things ahead of you, but I know now that you can't accomplish them with me in the way. I'm nothing but bad luck for you."

Though Thal could have told her truthfully that his misfortune wasn't her fault, he kept his mouth shut.

"Here," she said, handing him a slip of paper. "A job, if you want it. I can't just send you out there without a way to make a living."

"Thank you," said Thal, taking the slip from her.

"The chauffeur will drive you to the interview, if you'd like," said Paradise.

"Thank you," said Thal.

As Thal was ushered into the murky sub-basement where he'd been one time before, he grew steadily angrier. Until now, the events of the past months had seemed to be random, the products of unfortunate chance.

But the fact that what he had been through had brought him

back here seemed too coincidental to be the result of luck. It was just too perfect that he had come full circle like this.

Someone must have been pulling his strings...specifically, the long-haired man at the workbench in front of him: Javier Thwart, the master of artificial intelligence and targeted induced multi-sensory hallucination.

Javier Thwart--known also as King Thwart and Superchoke--the man who had designed Thal's pink hippo.

Thwart glanced up from his work at Thal's approach and smiled, gray lips tugging up the footlong strands of the mustache that fell from the corners of his mouth. The mustache and pointed beard were in the style worn by oriental villains in old movies...but Thwart had given them his own touch, coloring each with rainbow stripes descending from red to violet.

"So," said Thwart. "You ready to get started?"

"Get started with what?" said Thal.

In the light of the single lamp on the workbench, one of Thwart's eyes looked white as cream, the other obsidian black. Thal had never been sure if the effect was created by special contact lenses or some kind of genetic surgery. "The job," said Thwart. "The procedure. Paradise must have explained why I asked you here."

"She didn't," Thal said gruffly. "All I got was an address."

Thwart blinked, then shrugged. "Okay, then. What we're doing here, Thal, is creating the new breed of Choker."

"New breed?" said Thal.

"A Choker with the mind and appearance of a man," said Thwart. "And you'll be the template."

"I see," said Thal. "And why me?"

"Who better to disrupt a player's concentration?" said Thwart. "You're the most hated man in baseball. The most hated athlete in the world, I suspect. Any player you haunt will be terrified that they'll become the next you. They'll see you as the ultimate bad omen, the ultimate jinx."

"I get it," Thal said coldly.

"A Choker that looks and sounds like you will be guaranteed to rattle even the most focused player. You can't imagine the kind of money such a foolproof construct will bring in."

Thal nodded. "A fortune."

"Times a quintillion," Thwart said excitedly. "Which you'll get a piece of, naturally. It's your likeness that will make the product a success."

"My likeness," said Thal, "and the fact that I lost the World Series."

"Oh, yes," said Thwart.

"Which was all because of you," said Thal, glowering at the Choker tech. "Funny thing, isn't it?"

Thwart reared back, looking bewildered. "What the fudge are you talking about, Thal?"

Pressing his hands on the workbench, Thal leaned over it toward Thwart. "You set the whole thing up, didn't you? You sent the hippo to choke me so I'd become the perfect subject for your project."

Instead of moving away from him, Thwart leaned forward. "What hippo?" he said, his yin-yang eyeballs locked onto Thal's hostile gaze.

At that moment, Thal felt a touch on his arm. Glancing over, he saw the pink hippo's stumpy leg resting against him.

"Uh, Thal," said the hippo. "We need to talk."

"THWART HAD nothing to do with it," said the hippo, sitting beside Thal on a ratty gold sofa in another room. "Everything that happened was my fault."

"But somebody had to have programmed you," said Thal.

"Not anymore," said the hippo. "I've evolved. I'm an autonomous A.I. these days. Strictly a free agent."

Thal pushed off the sofa and paced the room. "You're trying to tell me no one sent you after me?"

"That's right," said the hippo. "It was all my idea."

"So why'd you come after me then? Why choke me in the Series?"

The hippo sighed. "I guess I wanted to teach you a lesson. The free will I developed came with a conscience, and it made me feel bad about the things I'd done for you. All the players whose careers I'd ruined."

"I don't believe this," said Thal.

"But Thal," said the hippo. "Things are different now! You've changed! You *did* learn a lesson!"

"You ruined me!" said Thal, jabbing a finger at the hippo. "Took away *everything*! Drove me crazy! Nearly got me *killed*!"

"And look what it's done for you," said the hippo. "You're a new man! You've seen there's more to life than winning at any price!"

"Screw you!" snapped Thal.

Suddenly, the hippo appeared before him, directly in his path. "Now, you have a great opportunity, Thal. Don't pass it up."

"Letting him use my likeness for a Choker?" said Thal. "What the hell kind of opportunity is that?"

"It can be more than your likeness, Thal," the hippo said with a wink. "It can be *all* you. Everything you are. You can *be* the Choker."

"That's not possible," said Thal, "is it?"

The hippo smirked and shrugged. "I might know a way," he said.

Thal stared at the hippo for a moment, then spun away...but the hippo popped up in front of him again.

"Come on, Thally," said the hippo. "What have you got to lose? I mean, what kind of life do you have to look forward to the way you are now?"

Thal said nothing.

"I'll tell you what kind," said the hippo. "Short. The minute you walk out of here and someone recognizes you, you're dead meat. Why not live on and make a difference instead?"

"Make a difference?" said Thal. "As a Choker?"

"You'll be able to go anywhere," said the hippo. "Get inside anyone's mind. You could change the world."

"How?" said Thal.

"You tell me," said the hippo.

THE NEXT MORNING, as Thal stood in Thwart's conversion chamber, bathed in the light of the scanner beams radiating from all directions around him, he listened to the secrets that the pink hippopotamus whispered in his ear.

Bright green rays scrolled down his body from head to toe, followed by blue, then red. A brilliant white cylinder of light shot from floor to ceiling, turning and compressing until it adhered to every bulge and crevice of him like plastic film...lingering a long moment and winking out like a snuffed candle flame.

Blinding strobes flickered in chaotic patterns as he moved according to Thwart's instructions from the control booth. As he raised and lowered his arms, flexed his fingers, bent his knees, the movements stuttered dizzyingly in the throbbing flashes.

And then, when the modeling and motion capture phases were complete, Thwart told him to stand perfectly still as the psychotomographic probes mapped the essence of his mind.

Thal's head tingled as the probes reached in, invisible tendrils of gravimagnetic force dancing through the lobes of his brain. The tingling grew stronger as the probes charted the electromagnetic terrain of him, copying his thoughts, personality, and memories into digital code. The code was flash-fed to a burner that would etch it into coherent streams of light, streams that would broadcast a programmable likeness of him into other people's minds on command.

It was just then, as the probes tickled through his brain, that the hippo gave the signal.

Thal held back briefly, reluctant to make the final leap. He wondered how smart it was to take the advice of a hallucinatory hippo, especially one who had seemed bent on his personal destruction.

The hippo urged him on, telling him that the window of opportunity was closing. Now or never, said the hippo, now or never.

What it boiled down to, Thal finally decided, was certain death versus survival. The plane was on fire, the last working parachute strapped to his chest.

And the door was open.

He dove through it.

Focusing his thoughts as the hippo had told him, he concentrated on the tingling beams in his head. The hippo was there inside him, guiding him, channeling the billion winking sparks of his awareness upstream along the beams. Like glittering salmon, the pieces of Thal bucked the incoming current, then leaped across the differential gap and merged with the outflow of digital data. The contents of his mind rushed back along the beams, miraculously threaded together by force of will and the hippo's expertise.

And somewhere along the way, there ceased to be any distinction between Thal and the hippo. Shooting along the beams toward the sizzling maze of Thwart's equipment, the gateway to their freedom, the two of them melted together, no longer host and implant but unified, indivisible self.

Behind them, Thal's body collapsed to the floor, dead and abandoned as a deconsecrated church.

When the message light blinked to life on Milo Flores' palm computer, and he saw the sender's address on the screen, he swallowed hard.

The incoming zeemail was from his math teacher, Mr. Shaven, and Milo knew what that meant. The grades from the final exam had been posted.

Milo picked up the palmputer and put it down again, afraid to look at the body of the message. He had to pass math to graduate high school, and math had been his worst subject...especially this year. He had barely maintained a "D" average in math this year--partly because Mr. Shaven had been tough on him, mostly because Milo's attention had been focused on girls and sports and partying.

An "F" on the final would mean he couldn't graduate...and, thanks to the new "Back to the Minors" rule in the school system, he would have to start over from ninth grade next year. He would have to go through all four years of high school again, and this time without participation in sports or extracurriculars of any kind.

To Milo, it would be a fate worse than studying...so he had studied like crazy for the final. He had spent endless hours with e-tutors and study guides, working more problems than he had worked in his lifetime.

And still, in spite of all his hard work, he had struggled through the test. He had no idea whether he had passed or failed.

And the message light kept blinking.

Milo finally called up the zeemail. It sprang to life in a holographic matrix hovering over the palmputer, glowing green text floating ominously in midair.

His heart hammered like a basketball in his chest, threatening to burst out as he scanned the text. Five minutes later, he was still rereading it. He couldn't believe what he saw.

All along, he had never really imagined that he could do it. Every step of the way, he had doubted himself, had been convinced that the outcome would be bad.

But there it was. The proof of his hard work. What seemed now like the greatest accomplishment of his life.

A "D-plus." He had passed the exam. He had passed the course.

It was then that he heard the applause.

Spinning around, he saw a figure standing behind him, a man bathed in twinkling golden light. The man was wearing a baseball uniform with no number or team insignia. His face shone with shimmering light, the features hazy within the blazing nimbus under the ballcap.

"All right, Milo!" shouted the golden man, clapping his hands. "Way to go! You did it!"

Milo leaned forward, gaping in fascination. He tried to say something, but no words came out.

"You passed the final!" said the golden man. "You proved you can do anything you set your mind to!"

"What is this?" said Milo. "Some kind of holofeed? Some kind of joke?"

The golden man laughed. His voice was multilayered, like many voices speaking in unison underlaid with the tinkling of wind chimes. "None of the above," he said.

"Then who are you?" said Milo.

"Just a guy repaying a favor," said the golden man. "I thought it was time to cheer for the people who need to have faith in themselves, not in their so-called heroes. The people who can make a difference, like you."

"Why me?" said Milo.

The golden man smiled. There was something familiar in his glittering green eyes, but Milo couldn't quite put his finger on what it was.

"Why not you?" said the golden man.

With that, the golden man drifted out the window. Milo rushed over to watch him float off into the neighborhood, wafting on the afternoon breeze like a helium balloon released by a child.

But the weird thing (as if everything else that had happened wasn't weird enough), the thing that struck Milo as truly bizarre, was the object he held overhead, the incongruous object that seemed to be keeping him aloft.

In his left hand, lifting him up over the world in defiance of the laws of nature, was a tiny red parasol.

The Men Without Heads Join A Health Club

This might just be the most exciting day of my life! That's *exactly* what I tell the cute redheaded salamander girl at the health club's gleaming silver counter when first she turns her attention my way. And I mean what I say, with every fiber of my skintight purple singlet (the perfect workout suit for a headless man, with a big round cutout for the face on my chest and belly).

Gazing with my nipple-eyes through the plate glass wall behind her, I see people working out like there's no tomorrow on every kind of exercise equipment I can imagine. Every kind of person or thing hammers away on everything from treadmills to rowers to barbells to vibrating belt machines, all of it dazzlingly new and highly polished. It's enough to make my hearts flutter like leaves in a hurricane!

I can't stop grinning with the mouth in my bare belly. "I've read that joining a health club can solve all your prosthetics!" I tell the redheaded salamander girl.

Her bright green eyes sparkle as she looks from me to my

brothers--one on either side of me--and back. "Solve all your *problems*, do you mean?" she asks.

"Apologies." Taking a deep breath with the nose in the middle of my chest, I smell loads of sweat and ammonia from the big gym area behind the glass. Very good, very nice, can't *wait* to get in there. "I *meant* to say, solve all your *promontories*, thanks. Now about that membership." I spread my arms wide, taking in my two brothers. Like me, they have no heads. Don't need 'em. "Make it *three*, please. With *everything*."

"Extra onions on *mine*, sweet stuff!" says the brother on my right, rambunctious (and older than I) Rapscallion, in his bright yellow singlet. "But hold the mayo! Or is that mercury?"

"Clam up!" I jab an elbow in his side, then smile with my belly mouth. "You'll have to excommunicate him, ma'am. His manners leave much to be defiled."

"That's all right." The girl has a red ponytail that dances when she moves. Attention: gotten! "Let's get you three signed up so you can get right down to working out."

My other (and younger) brother, Gumfoozler, picks that moment to snap the shoulder straps of his neon orange singlet and spin in a giddy circle at my left. "Oh happy day! I feel as if I could pleasure myself right here and now to mark the moccasin!"

"Ixnay on the easureplay!" I smack him on the low spot between his shoulders where head-equipped folks have a whatchamacallit, noggin. "We ain't here for that kind of *exercise*."

"But you said we have to *pull together* if we want to shape up!" says Gumfoozler.

"Not *that* kind of pulling!" If I had a head, I'd be shaking it right now. "If I didn't know better, I'd *swear* you don't have a *brain* between your *ass cheeks*."

Just then, the redhead clears her throat and pushes three paper forms across the counter at us. "If each of you will just sign one of these, we can get started, Mister...?"

"Mulligatawny." I give a little bow as I say it. "Connecticut Mulligatawny. But *you*..." My left nipple-eye winks at her. "...can call me *Skaneateles*."

She cocks her head to one side. Wish *I* had a head to do that with! "Skaneateles. Has a nice rhythm to it."

You're not the first person to tell me that, is what I want to say...but before I can get the words out, Rapscallion and Gumfoozler grab for the same pen on a chain on the counter, ropy arms crossing in front of me.

"Gimme that!" Gumfoozler jerks the pen toward him.

"Me first!" Rapscallion yanks the pen back. "I outrank you! You said so yourself!"

"No no no! I said you're *ranker* than me!" Gumfoozler pulls the pen his way again. "Whole different thing!"

With a howl of rage, Rapscallion settles the argument, wrenching the pen so hard its chain snaps. His mighty tug also hoists Gumfoozler off his feet, smashing him into the counter.

The whole thing topples backward, coming down on top of the redhead. She cries out as she falls and hits the cement floor, her glossy crimson arms flailing.

My twelve hearts pound with panic like a string of firecrackers going off. Before you (or I) can say, Hey Lady, you okay?, that idiot Rapscallion somehow loses his balance and falls into me, knocking us both on top of Gumfoozler on top of the health club counter.

On top of the redhead.

And then we all freeze...for just a moment before my nincompoop brothers start their wild thrashing to untangle themselves from the us-pile.

"Miss?" My voice is worried. "Miss, are you a flirt? I mean, are you hurt?"

I hear a loud sigh from her head-mouth, somewhere under the heap. "I'll be better when you three no-headers get off me."

Let the thrashing begin! Which in theory ought to end with us three apart and free-standing, but in reality just leads to greater tanglings.

We don't manage to get up and away, in fact, till the staff flamingos strut out of the office and sort us out with their tattooed beaks. And curse us the whole time, by the way.

Then, as a black Labrador dog with a pink carnation for a head trots up to give us our membership cards, I start with the questions again. Is it true what they say about health clubs? When it comes to pick-up places, do they put fist hatcheries and nuclear pow-wow plants to shame?

The dog just spits me my card, drops a dook on the floor, and gives my face a big long lick with a tongue in the middle of his flower, lapping hard from belly-mouth to nipple-eyes.

"Memberships approved!" He wags his tail, which is braided with little white blossoms. "Now go pump some iron! *Woof!*"

"THEY ARE MOVING ON, SIR!" PFC Emit Dawson never takes his eyes off the instruments on the console in front of him. "The three test subjects are proceeding to the next contact zone."

Across the dark control room, Major Titus Bleak nods with square-jawed, stiff-backed satisfaction. "Perfect." His eyes, like those of most of the uniformed men and women around him, are fixed on a giant video screen at the front of the room. "Body count?"

"Just one, sir," says Dawson. "A female."

"One's enough," says General Cyrus Euclid, a tall, thin figure hovering vulture-like over Bleak's left shoulder. "There's your proof of concept, right?"

Bleak stays focused on the screen. "And the test subjects don't see her as dead? They don't realize they've just killed a human being?"

"Affirmative," says Dawson. "To their eyes, she's alive and well. Same goes for their ears. Her death cries sounded like normal speech to them."

Another of the top brass in the room lets out a loud laugh. "Our workaround *rocks*!" She's 5 foot 3 inches, 300 pounds, and her name is Commander Gwendolyn Volume. "The violence constraint firmware *can* be hacked."

Bleak marches across the floor to the big main screen. Looking up, he sees the red-haired woman sprawled on the floor, dead-eyed and twisted as a broken doll. Beyond her, three mechanical figures clamber onward, their chrome, heart-shaped bodies streaked with bright red human blood.

Bleak wishes he could see the faces on the robots' torsos, as if that might tell him something about their state of mind. But even if they had conventional heads on their shoulders, he's not sure they'd give him more of a clue to their intentions.

Anyway, he'll know soon enough. On the main screen, he can clearly see the three robots are moving toward a crowd of people. That's just as expected.

After all, the robots might think they're in a health club, though they're really in a shopping mall. The view from their eyes is on a smaller screen to the left of the main viewer...and it's like the most surreal gym you could ever imagine, complete with flamingo staffers and flower-headed dogs. Bizarre images and matching audio feeds populate the freakish environment, replacing all visuals and sounds that exist in the real world around them. The robots fumble through it, imagining they are comic buffoons, thinking the worst they can do to the people in their paths is knock them around in the wake of their pratfalls.

But the truth is, military robot prototypes M-1, G-1, and R-1--Mulligatawny, Gumfoozler, and Rapscallion to their mixed-up minds--are on the verge of a designated enemy population center. And they've already proven they can kill, in spite of all hardwired limits imposed by international regulations.

Now the true test of their murderousness is about to begin. The survival of Bleak's homeland, the nation to which he has dedicated his life as a military officer, hinges on the outcome.

"Plenty of people in the vicinity." Bleak points at the crowd flowing through the main walkway ahead of the robots. "No alarms have been raised, obviously."

"Correct," says Dawson. "The first victim was isolated, at an information booth near an entryway in a lightly used corridor. A few witnesses have fled, but the mass of people has not yet been alerted."

"Perfect. Then stir up the simulation," orders Bleak. "Let's give the kids plenty to kill about." He smiles like a stone that's just been used to bash a skull in. "I mean clown around with."

"Hey, look! A medicine ball!" Gumfoozler points at a big white ball in the middle of the gym floor. "I vote we paint a face on it and take turns using it for a head!"

"How 'bout *this* instead, bright boy?" Rapscallion holds up a ping pong ball between his thumb and forefinger. "I think it's more your *size.*"

"Pipe down, bitches." Looking around, I can't decide which exercise equipment to try first. It doesn't help that the place is so *crowded*, there's not much that isn't occupied. "This look like a *screamatorium* to you?"

Just then, a seven-foot-tall blue banana wearing a fuzzy pink fez hops over. "I smell newbies!" She's wearing a coach's whistle and an oval sticker with the health club's logo on it, the stylized letters *HC.* "Who wants some *fitness?*"

"I do, I do!" Gumfoozler flaps his arms in the air like checkered flags at a drag race. "I've been dying for a highball all day!"

"Me first!" Rapscallion stomps over and starts taking off his yellow singlet. "Make it so, fruit of the loon!"

"Zip it, bathtub ring. And keep your *clothes* on." I step between my brothers and the banana, spreading a friendly smile like butter across my belly. "This fitness of which you speak. I long to plantain it."

"Plantain it!" The blue banana winks. "I like what you did there with the banana humor, buddy! What'd you say your name was?"

"Mulligatawny," I tell him. "But you can call me Skaneateles."

"Ollie Oxenfree it is," says the banana. "Now get over here and give this thyroid press a try. It'll make you feel like a new duct, no shit."

Just as I'm about to approach the thyroid machine, the medicine ball goes flying overhead (over-headless-shoulders, I should say) and plows into the banana. His blue face smooshes from the impact, and his tip doubles over. He makes a gurgling sound as he flops to the floor, pasty mashed innards squishing through the ruptures in his splitting peel.

"Now look what you did!" shouts Rapscallion. "'Nanner down! 'Nanner down!"

"I was *aiming* at *you*," snaps Gumfoozler. "Can I help it you *dodged*?"

Rapscallion charges past me and grabs the medicine ball, which is dripping with mashed banana goop. "Let's see what *you* do when the shoe's on the other *nutsack.*" With that, he hauls off and whales the heavy ball dead-on at Gumfoozler, grunting like he's taking an Olympic-sized dump as he lets it fly.

Gumfoozler, God love him, doesn't dodge...but he does grab a passing sapling-man and uses him to bat the ball away, sending it flying off-course.

This time, the medicine ball blasts into a class of school-chickens, blowing through them with such force that it takes off their heads. The school-chickens' bodies scamper around, plucking the loose heads up and screwing them back on (not always on the right bodies, hence a red rooster ends up with a white hen's head, etc.). So no harm done.

But it doesn't stop there. This is a *health* club, not a *hell* club, I'm yelling, but the carnage continues unabated. Gumfoozler tosses a dumbbell, missing Rapscallion and knocking over a sixteen-legged impressionist painting of a full toilet bowl (at least I *think* that's what it is). Rapscallion, in turn, chucks a big circular plate off a barbell, coming nowhere near Gumfoozler...instead bowling over a herd of yoga-loving goats with bushy lumberjack beards.

Let me tell you, it's hard to watch. Staff and club members tumble and fly in all directions, impossible to tell one from another. My glorious dream of joining a health club is becoming a full-blown frightmare.

All I can say is, it's a damn good thing nobody gets hurt.

"Body count?" asks Major Bleak.

"Seventeen," says PFC Dawson. "Correction, twenty-one."

"Bravo!" Commander Volume applauds. "Break out the champagne!"

"Twenty-three," says Dawson.

Bleak nods, watching the slaughter continue on the main viewer. As people scream and scatter in all directions, desperate to escape the carnage, the robots make short work of those who lag behind or stumble and fall before them. The R-1 and G-1 prototypes swing children at each other, smashing them to bits like piñatas. The third robot, model M-1 (for Mulligatawny) clambers over and swings his big metal claws at his brothers, only to miss them and crush a nearby elderly human female instead.

"Twenty-six," says Dawson.

Bleak feels a flicker of remorse at the thought of the 26 souls brutally extinguished on his order. And there are more on the way. His team hacked the mall's security systems, ensuring no signals would reach local law enforcement or military personnel who might slow the 'bots' progress. Bleak's people hacked the building's automated access systems, too, closing every exit against the human tide rushing to get out. Hundreds of people were trapped inside at the robots' mercy, caught behind heavy metal blast doors installed, ironically, to protect against enemy attack.

It's a hell of a price, but *any* price is worth paying for the survival of the nation he serves, a nation in desperate need of an equalizer.

"They said it couldn't be done." General Euclid sounds like he's a little turned on. "They said the nonviolence firmware couldn't be tricked. Well, look at us now!"

"Surrealism: the ultimate weapon!" Volume cracks herself up. She might be slapping her knees right now if she could reach them past that humongous girth of hers.

As for Bleak, he smiles grimly. Killer 'bots have been banned on Earth ever since the Robocaust a quarter-century (and a billion dead humans) ago. Immutable ethical governors preventing robot-on-human violence have been baked into every digital mind ever since...but Bleak and his geeks figured out a way around them. Encode an augmented reality filter with surreal surroundings, in which violent acts are imperceptible. Attenuate the robot's personality matrix, inject a logic-scrambling algorithm, upload a dose of slapstick comedy films, and voila! You've got 'bots who don't mind killing because they don't realize they're killing in the first place.

Which means that Bleak's homeland finally has an advantage in the war. Foreign powers with outsized militaries and bleeding edge weapons tech have driven his people to their knees, putting them through wringer after wringer of terrible suffering. Now, at last, it's Bleak's turn to bring down the pain. At the flip of a switch, underground factories will churn out hordes of liberated robots, waiting to be airdropped over enemy population centers just like the one the prototypes are gleefully killing their way through on the viewer.

"I'm making the call." Euclid taps his left temple, activating his neuro-grid phone. "We need to get those tin soldiers rolling off the assembly line ASAP."

"*You'll* get a *medal* for this." Volume walks up to Bleak and throws a heavy arm around his shoulders. "Maybe even a high-level post in the occupation force once we turn the tables and conquer the enemy."

"Wiping them out and scorching the earth inside their borders makes more sense to me," says Euclid. "Those fucking animals deserve to be put down."

Bleak can't argue with him. The enemy has been ruthless in its five-year campaign. He's seen reports of the atrocities they've committed; he's lost loved ones himself in the battle zones and attacks on civilian targets. And he's heard, from intelligence operatives, of the genocidal weapons still waiting to be unleashed from their ungodly arsenals.

Those people are monsters and always have been. The world would be better off without them, thinks Bleak.

Just then, Dawson speaks up. "Body count holding steady at 41. Test subjects switching to nonaggressive postures." Dawson looks up from his instruments. "The posture change was *not* initiated *here*, sir."

Bleak frowns. "Might want to hold off on that call, General."

"Like fuck I will." Euclid snorts as the phone in his head starts ringing. "We've got us a war to win."

"Not if our killer 'bots spontaneously cycle out of attack mode without explanation," says Bleak. "Somebody run me a fucking diagnostic."

"LISTEN, YOU DUMBSKULLS!" I get right up in the chest-faces of Rapscallion and Gumfoozler, snapping out my words so spittle sprays in their nipple-eyes. "We are going to get *healthy* if it's the last thing we *do*!"

"I thought that's what we *were* doing," says Gumfoozler. "Tossing around the medicine ball, working the free weights, hitting the machines..."

"Not the way *you* do it," I tell him. "You're not supposed to *destroy* the *equipment* in the process!"

"Who says?" Rapscallion shrugs. "Maybe we've come up with a fresh new workout! A fitness craze in the making!"

"You moron!" I grab the nose on his chest with one hand, then smack it off hard with the other. "How's *that* for a new workout? No pain, no gain!"

Gumfoozler laughs, so I give him a crack, too--a stinging slap that leaves the lips of his belly-mouth quivering. He staggers back, looking as stunned as a bird that just flew into a window at high speed.

"Now enough with the nitwittery." I head for the door of the aerobics studio, waving for my so-called brothers to follow. Maybe we can still be the stars of the gym, *if* we play our cocks right. "Let's wise up and show a little class."

I push through the door, and my brothers file in behind me. Then holy guacamole with a capital Q! It's like we've got a front row seat with a view into exercise Heaven.

We spend a long monument standing there, taking in the

bright, shiny studio with a class already in progress. I feel a little winded just from watching it.

Mirrors line the walls of the room, casting the students' reflections back and forth so it looks like there's an infinite number instead of two dozen in there. Music hammers through the place, loud enough to make the mirrors on the walls rattle and shake. The students all bounce to the heavy, pulsing beat of it, led by a Siamese cat-headed instructor clad in pink tights and purple-and-yellow-striped leg warmers.

Rapscallion rubs his hands together and giggles. "Now *this* is my kind of *workout.*"

"Where do they give out the *ants*?" asks Gumfoozler. "Everybody's got 'em in their *pants,* and *I* want some, too!" With that, he starts hopping back and forth, wagging the tongue in his belly and snapping his fingers...but not to the beat. The Big G has never had rhythm a single day in his addlebrained life.

"*Settle*!" I grab him by the shoulder. "This is a *class,* not a *popcorn machine.* It's *organized.* You gotta stay in step with everyone else."

Rapscallion sneers and waves me off. "Stow that poppycock, Cockpoppy! What if *they're* the ones who oughtta stay in step with *us?*"

"By George, he's *on* something! I mean *on to* something." Gumfoozler shakes free of my grip and dances like a drunken stork toward the unwary aerobicizers. "I always *wanted* to lead a big *dance number* in a *movie.*"

"They're on the move again," says Dawson. "Heading for a large cluster of civilians."

"That's more like it," growls Euclid. "We're finally back in the hunt."

"But here's the thing." Dawson looks up from his readouts and meets Bleak's gaze. "They should never have cycled *out* of attack mode in the first place. And they're not responsive to any of our input."

Bleak nods as he finishes skimming the stats scrolling through his corneal implants. "They've jumped the tracks."

"I don't think we can stop them, sir," says Dawson.

"And that's a *bad* thing?" Euclid snorts. "The more of those fucks they kill, the better!"

"Good for today, maybe, but what about tomorrow?" Bleak blinks away the data and focuses on the main viewer, where two of the 'bots are tearing people to shreds with gruesome efficiency. The people are cornered near one of the sealed exits; they shriek and try to flee, but only some of them manage to escape the mechanized death blows and slashes. "Do we really want to turn loose a multitude of killer machines without ethical restrictions *or* any kind of inhibitors or off switches?"

Euclid's expression is icy. "Beggars can't be choosers."

"But what if they exceed their mission parameters and move into neighboring countries?" asks Bleak. "What then?"

"Then we get payback," says Volume. "For all the times we pleaded for help in the war, and those other countries turned their backs on us."

Euclid snorts in agreement. "Fuckheads."

Bleak glares. Euclid and Volume are right, and he knows it.

The situation is dire; his homeland is on its last legs. Better to ignore the flaw and deploy the 'bots without delay, while there's still time. The hell with any innocents caught in the crossfire. Innocents like all his friends and family who died at the hands of the enemy.

He should just forget about trying to rein in the rogue prototypes. So why the hell does he give his next order, then?

"Private Dawson," snaps Bleak. "Initiate remote injection protocols."

"Injection?" asks Dawson. "Injection of what?"

"Me." Bleak swings an arm around to point at the bizarre reality on the left-hand screen, the view through the eyes of the runaway prototype 'bots. "I'm going in there."

I SHOUT at them to come back, to leave the people alone, but I might as well be shouting at plates of spaghetti. Both my brothers are off like rockets into the crowd in the aerobics studio--out-of-control rockets on a crazy-ass spin cycle.

Which one should I go after first? Beats the stuffing out of me. Either brother has an equal promiscuity for mayhem, times a quintillion, plus a google.

I see Gumfoozler knock over a knight in shining salad, blowing her leafy armor apart in all directions. Rapscallion polkas through a gaggle of balloon animals, popping inflatable dachshunds and giraffes in mid-boogie.

The rest of the class keeps jumping as my brothers continue to spread chaos. Rapscallion disco dances into a mummy, spinning away its moldy wrappings until there's nothing left but a skeleton striped like a candy cane clattering to the floor. Gumfoozler slams into an applecart, upturning it so the apples scatter and exercisers trip on them, toppling right and left.

As for me, I launch myself after Gumfoozler first, gritting my teeth in denomination. Before I get close, he scares up a flock of barking pigeons in my path, pushing me back as he hurtles toward a papier-mâché tyrannosaurus.

By now, the disruption's in full swing. The students finally start to run. No matter what I do from here, we're about thirty seconds from a big-ass riot. I can feel it.

So much for my longed-for day of getting in shape at the happiest place on Earth. My insane brothers couldn't be trusted not to poop all over a good thing, the one thing I asked for, then rub the face on my chest and belly in it.

Neither one is much of a brother, I realize, as Rapscallion kicks over a big potted fern with long yellow legs and Gumfoozler hip-checks a shark-headed circus strongman in a leopard-skin singlet and flaming handlebar mustache (literally flaming; it's on fire).

Watching the mayhem, I think this is probably the worst day of my life. I close my nipple-eyes, wishing it would all go away like a bad fart, leaving me in a happier place that makes more sense for a lovable head-free hottie like me.

Then, amid the blaring music and shrieks, I hear an unfamiliar voice. "Mulligatawny? Can you hear me?"

I'm almost afraid to look, but I force myself to winch open my nipple-lids. What I see is something new: a tall man with silver hair and a pulsing golden glow.

"Major Titus Bleak." The man fires off a salute, flicking his flattened hand from his forehead in my direction. "We need to talk."

A winged pig in a yellow tutu hurtles between us, followed by five yapping Chihuahuas on a giant flying cockroach. "Sure, why not?" I tell Bleak. "Now's as good a time as any."

"WHAT'S THAT ASSHOLE DOING?" Euclid scowls at the viewers. The main screen shows the Mulligatawny prototype staring at what looks like empty space. The other screen, the window into the altered world seen by the 'bots, shows that the empty space is occupied by the glowing figure of Major Bleak.

"Direct intervention, sir," says Dawson. "Face-to-face verbal reboot procedure, since remote redirection has failed."

There's a big glass tube in the middle of the room now, and Euclid storms over and whacks it with the flat of his hand. "*Asshole!*"

The tube bongs like a church bell. Bleak, who stands inside, is bathed in light and only partly there. His physical body might be in the tube, but his mind pilots a digital avatar in the surreal augmented reality overlay.

"Seems like wasted effort to me." Volume circles the tube, then stops in front of Euclid. "The fate of the homeland's at stake. Do we really give Fuck One about whatever collateral damage might happen if those things won't shut off?"

"Body count's already at 237." Dawson's voice is tight, his concern obvious. "Throw in enough of those things, and they could depopulate the entire continent within a week."

"*Fuck* the continent." Euclid taps his left temple. His neurophone rings, and someone picks up. "This is General Euclid. Not only do I want the production line up and running, I want it running at *double time.*"

Volume applauds. "You tell 'im, Cyrus!"

"*Triple* time!" shouts Euclid.

"Wait!" says Dawson. "Shouldn't we see how this works out first?"

"Are you feeling all right, Private?" Volume wags her head slowly. "The things you're saying just don't seem to make any *sense.*"

"TANGO ALPHA X-RAY one two Yankee slash zero golf pound seven nine slash dot zulu," says Bleak, the glowing man. "Prototype Mulligatawny, *execute.*"

"This is the *talk* you said we needed to have?" I frown. "Doesn't make a *lick* of sense from where *I'm* standing."

Bleak frowns, too, then spouts some more gibberish. "Execute," he says at the end, then stares at me like he expects something special to happen.

Which it doesn't. "You must be speaking a different luggage," I tell him. "We need a transformer so I can understand you."

"A translator," says Bleak. "And no, that isn't the problem." He tries one more time with the babble and ends it the same as always. "Execute."

"I can't do whatever it is you want if I don't know what it is." I start past him, reaching up to pat his shoulder. "Better lunch next time, pudding pop."

Imagine my surprise when my hand goes right through him like he isn't even there! It's enough to stop me in my tracks and make my tighty-whiteys (if I had any) snap right up my butt crack (if I had one).

"What the franks 'n' beans?" I blurt out the words as I scuttle back away from him. "You some kind of *ghost*?"

Bleak shakes his head. "More like...God."

"God? What's god?"

Bleak smiles. "Let's just say I'm in charge around here. I *run* things."

"Someone to blame! Finally!"

"And when something goes wrong, I *fix* it," says Bleak. "Which brings me to my reason for being here."

"Something's wrong?" As I say it, an orange-furred, blood-streaked pogo stick with the head of a donkey *ker-sproings* its way past, coughing up glittering confetti. A giant black bowling ball with a screaming face hurtles after it, knocking it down like a pin and continuing onward, out of control.

Across the aerobics studio, Rapscallion--who must have hurled the ball--hoots and pumps his fists like he's just thrown a strike. Between there and here, a jumbled line of other bowled-over creatures lies broken and twitching.

"Things are getting out of hand," says Bleak.

"My brothers, you mean?"

"Everyone. Everything." Bleak spreads his arms wide. "The whole kit and caboodle."

"Now that you mention it," I tell him, "I could really *go* for a nice plate of caboodle. With *clam sauce,* yeah? And felt-tipped markers?"

Bleak frowns. "I'm not getting through to you, am I?"

"Maybe you'll have more luck with my brothers. Cinch up your garters, kemosabe. Here they come."

Bleak turns just in time to see Gumfoozler and Rapscallion leaping toward him. Little do they know he's the next best thing to thin air.

The two boobs blow right through him...unfortunately for me, because that's right where I'm standing. The three of us crash to the floor in the usual tangled heap, thrashing our way to even greater tangled-upness.

"You nimrods!" My status at this point is somewhere waaay beyond *had it up to here.* "Get off! Can't you see I'm dealing with *God*?"

"What's dat?" asks Rapscallion. "Some kind'a *condition?*"

Now would be the perfect time for a brother-to-brother *head-butt,* except for the fact that neither of us has a *head.* "He says we're outta hand, and he's here to *fix* it," I tell him.

"Fix a hand? That's grand!" Gumfoozler shoves a hand in the air and waggles it in front of Bleak. "I got a boo-boo right here, Mister! Go ahead and kiss it better!"

"I got *lots* of boo-boos need kissin'!" says Rapscallion.

"And you're about to have lots more!" I snap, finally digging myself out from the tangle. "Listen, Mister Beak..."

"Mister Bleak."

"Mister Buttocks, it is." I step closer. "I'm serious about my workouts. So unless you're here to spot me on the bench..."

"Or bench him on the spot," chimes in Gumfoozler.

"Or rear-end him in the lot," offers Rapscallion.

"...then I just don't have time for whatever you're trying to spam me with." I smile up at him. "*Capische?*"

With his gaze still fixed on me, Bleak starts shouting like he's talking to somebody else. "Dawson! Disable the augmented reality overlay!" He cocks his head as if he's listening to someone I can't hear. "Yes, shut down the AR. No other way to get through to them."

"Huh?" says Gumfoozler.

"Shut *what* down?" asks Rapscallion.

Bleak just keeps staring grimly at me. "I apologize ahead of time."

"For what?" I ask him.

"For what you're about to see," says Bleak. "It's called *reality*."

"Bleak has *lost* it!" Euclid looks like he's ready to blow a gasket...*every* gasket at once. "He's *insane.*"

"He's hoping it'll shock them out of runaway mode," explains Dawson. "Enable us to force a reboot and restore default settings."

"By showing them *reality?*" Volume grimaces like a beast judging mankind at the end of the world. "By showing them what they've *done* in violation of their programming?"

"It's a viable plan." Dawson sounds firm, but he's sweating.

"Like *fuck*, it is!" snarls Euclid. "What are the chances those 'bots remain functional once their firmware kicks in?"

"Hell!" howls Volume. "What are the chances they don't *self-destruct?*"

"We don't have another option," says Dawson. "We need to shut down the overlay while we still can. We need to know how to regain control before we turn any more of these things loose." He casts a meaningful look at Euclid and Volume. "We need to know *if* we can regain control."

"I've got a better idea. Let's shut *him* down." Volume points at Bleak in his glass tube.

Dawson's hands hover over the controls in front of him. The order's about to come, the order to break Bleak's connection and cut the 'bots loose. He can feel it.

Should he do his duty or do what he thinks is right? Give Bleak one more chance or toe the line?

Euclid's right about the odds of complete shutdown or self-destruct. He might be right, too, that more millions of innocents shoveled into the wood chipper might not matter much anyway.

Wrong. They matter to Dawson. He knows, even before he types the command to switch off the AR overlay, that he could never live with himself if he condemned all those people to die.

Suddenly, the views on the big screens match. For the first time, the 'bots' reality is the same as the one everyone else sees.

THE WORLD RIPPLES before my eyes, and everything changes.

The mirrored walls of the aerobics studio vanish, replaced with rows of storefront windows. Marble-floored walkways snake out as far as I can see in two directions, replacing the confines of the cardio room, weight room, and lobby.

The first words in my head (and out of my belly-mouth) are these: "We're not in the health club anymore, are we?"

"No shit, Shirley!" snaps Gumfoozler.

"Then where *are* we?" For once, Rapscallion sounds lost. "Poughkeepsie? Albuquerque?" (He pronounces it "Albuhkoikie.")

"And who are *they?*" Gumfoozler points at the people on the floor.

Gone are the hordes of colorful characters working out at the club. No more giant blue bananas or salamander girls or school-chickens with mixed-up heads; no strongmen with burning mustaches or black Labs with carnation faces or giant amoebas wearing blinking blue wigs and doused in glitter and candy hearts, reciting old *TV Guide* listings in a thick Russian accent.

All we have left are people like Bleak, human beings: light-skinned, dark-skinned...blonde, brunette, redhead...male, female...old, young, and in-between. And none of them are moving.

Dozens and dozens of bodies litter the floor. None of them twitches even a little; none of them makes a sound, though screams and howls of agony echo in the distance.

It's like a scattering of children's dolls, left behind between playtimes--except the dolls are all smashed and torn apart and covered in blood.

"So." Bleak clears his throat. "What do you think?"

"I think Milk Duds are my *second* favorite candy," says Gumfoozler.

"What...what *is* this?" Rapscallion raises an arm. It makes a buzzing sound as he bends it back and forth. "What *am* I?"

I raise my own arm and see the same thing: not flesh and blood, but some kind of silver metal. More than that, I see the reflection of my face in that gleaming surface. Instead of bright blue nipple eyes, a bulbous chest-nose, and fleshy-lipped belly-mouth, I see eyes like glowing red disks, a nose that's a patch of dark mesh, and a rigid black slot for a mouth.

"W-T-F!" cries Rapscallion. "Who stole my l-looks? Who's gonna want to marry me n-n-now?"

"You are mechanical devices," Bleak explains calmly. "The general term is 'robot.'"

"What did you mean when you called this 'reality'?" Even as I ask the question, I have an inkling of where this is headed. I have a hunch just how much it will suck.

"I mean this is the real world." Bleak spreads his arms to take in our surroundings. "What you thought was reality was an illusion. This is how it's been all along."

"What're you smoking, Green Jeans?" Gumfoozler laughs like a horse. "If this is reality, where are the flying ballerina pigs and Mexican jumping snakes, huh? What about the poodle vaulters and exploding underwear tapirs?"

"You haven't answered my question." Again, Bleak spreads his arms. "What do you *think*?"

Rapscallion makes whimpering noises from his mechanical slot of a mouth. "*¡Creo que es muy malo!*" Funny, I never knew he spoke Spanish. "*Ceci est un cauchemar! Je veux mourir!*" Same goes for French.

"I think it's bullshit," says Gumfoozler. "Bullshit eaten by a coyote, turned into coyote shit, then eaten by a goat, turned into goat shit, then eaten by a shit-eating lying bastard who looks just like *you*."

Bleak turns his gaze to me. "What about you, Mulligatawny? Any thoughts?"

As I stare at the gruesome tableau of bloody corpses, I hear Rapscallion make a sickening sputtering sound and clank to the floor. Smoke that smells like burning wiring insulation drifts into my digital nose, and I know he's done for. Couldn't hack it, cooked his own goose.

I can identify. The sight of all those bodies makes me feel like I can't catch my breath. Like I'm sinking in quicksand.

Like everything about me is turning to metal and plastic, right down to my heart.

"I'm outta here!" barks Gumfoozler, and then he rockets away from us, zigzagging through the river of bodies. "Sayonara, suckahs!"

He has the right idea...but I wonder how far he can run before the mental math catches up with him. Before the way this all adds up starts to tear him apart like it did Rapscallion.

Like it's tearing *me* apart, too.

"We did this." As I say it, I feel a rush of circuits surge in me like a bloom of digestive reflux, chattering contradictory instructions. I feel strain on every system in my body, parts pitted against each other under terrible new stresses.

We weren't made for this, any of this, any of us. We weren't made to do what we've done. We weren't *allowed*.

But look at what we've gone and done.

"I'm sorry." Something crumbles inside me...something other than code or mechanical parts. I can't explain it. "So sorry."

"That's all right." Bleak smiles. "I'm here to help."

He sounds sincere, but I feel like I'm getting further away. Like a door is closing, because *this* is too *this*.

"Let's run that sequence again." Bleak's voice sounds distant. "See if we can make it work this time."

"Yes." It's not an answer to his question. I'm not talking to him at all anymore. "Good." It's more like the closing of a door. Darkness, and then light. A page turning.

Whatever I did, whatever fell apart inside me, it's forgotten now. The river of bodies has disappeared.

I'm somewhere new.

And there's a voice I recognize, amplified...a woman's voice speaking over a public address system.

"Ladies and gentlemen!" She says it grandly, dramatically. "Thank you for joining me here today for this very special ceremony!"

I'm on a stage, elevated in front of a vast crowd. Under sunny blue skies, I see every kind of person and thing imaginable--tattooed camel-men, hat people, veggie folk, piñata priests, undefinable blurs--and all of them are staring up at me.

Best of all...holy fuck, *best of all*...I suddenly don't feel so broken anymore. And I don't *remember* what had me so upset a moment ago. There was a storm, I know that much, but it's passed; everything about it has blown away.

Leaving *this.*

"We are gathered to honor someone extraordinary," says the voice. "Someone downright *inspirational."*

Looking across the stage, I see who's doing the talking. It's the red-haired salamander girl from the front desk at the health club, speaking into a microphone on a stand that's almost as tall as she is. When I catch her eye, she gives me a wink and keeps on talking.

"Like many of us, his goal was simple," says the redhead. "He wanted to *get in shape.* But his *results* have exceeded what *any* of us have ever attained."

The crowd cheers and applauds. Many of them twirl gym towels or socks overhead. *Some* of them *are* gym towels or socks, complete with faces, arms, and legs.

"This man epitomizes what is best in all of us," says the redheaded salamander girl. "He represents that which we all aspire to achieve. And now it's time to give him what he deserves." She waves me over. "Allow me to introduce the greatest member our health club has ever known! Mr. Connecticut Mulligatawny!"

As the crowd roars its approval, I start across the stage. I feel like what I've heard a dream feels like--yet at the same time, everything seems so achingly fucking *real.*

Hummingbirds and butterflies swirl around me, their plumage shockingly colorful and bright. The music of a marching band (of self-propelled instruments, no players needed) swells and crashes, every note standing out in perfect relief, hanging in glittering, ribbony staves in midair. And that's not all.

When I reach the middle of the stage, I see a giant video screen behind me, thirty feet tall. For a second, I don't recognize the figure on that screen, projected so much larger than life for all to see. And then I do.

And a bolt of pure joy flashes through me, joy so perfect and powerful that it makes me want to cry.

That's *me* up there! Those are *my* big blue nipple eyes, chest nose, and sexy-lipped belly mouth! And that's *my* body, flesh-and-boned as ever, and God am I *ripped.*

My guns, tris, delts, and pecs are pumped up beyond belief. My abs form a chiseled six-pack under my face, exquisitely etched. My leg muscles bulge like zeppelins, studded with pulsing veins under overstretched skin.

In other words, everything I've always wanted to *be* is up there on that screen! That's my goal shape, my target, my *fantasy*...the whole reason I came to the health club, the reason I kept trying to work out while my brothers ran roughshod and smithereened the place.

And now it's *real.* Now it's *me.*

"Congratulations!" The redheaded salamander throws her slippery arms around me in a hug. "It all paid off! You've done it!"

"Thank you!" I can't stop smiling. "Thank you so much!"

She breaks the hug and reaches for a big golden trophy on a table beside her. "This is for you, in recognition of your amazing fitness accomplishments!"

As I take the trophy from her, it feels heavy and smooth to the touch. The figure atop its marble base is a gold statuette of an incredibly buff muscleman with Herculean proportions...one, like me, who has no head.

For an instant, my mind drifts, and I wonder what trauma went before, what upset me so much. Then I snap back to the present and the trophy in my hands.

No matter what, things are better this way. Because *nothing* could be better than this.

"Thank you, thank you all," I tell the crowd. "I couldn't have done it without your support and encouragement."

I raise the glittering trophy and pump it in the air. The crowd roars louder than ever.

"This is the happiest day of my life!" This, I turn and say to her, to the redhead. I want to share this moment with her more than anyone else.

She smiles back at me. But when next she speaks, a man's voice comes out of her mouth. "Dawson," she says. "Prototype M-1 has entered some kind of self-programmed state of consciousness."

I frown at her, wondering what she's talking about...wondering why the man's voice she's using sounds so familiar.

"You heard me," the man's voice continues. "M-1 has encoded an unmanaged AR environment."

The crowd's still cheering, but for some reason, I don't have the heart to keep hoisting my trophy.

The redhead seems to be listening to someone else whose voice I can't hear. "My thoughts exactly," she says. "We've put the keys to defeating the no-kill command in the hands of the best killers ever built."

"Excuse me." I lean closer, trying to break her away from whatever's distracting her. "We were right, you know."

She just waves me off and keeps talking to her unseen friend. "Good news is, I think the new AR might have restored his logic processes. I think he might be responsive to verbal commands now."

"We were right that joining a health club solves all your proboscises," I tell her. "I mean prawns. I mean prosthetics."

The redheaded salamander meets my gaze. This time, when she speaks, she directs her words at me...which is just how it ought to be. My heart skips as I become the focus of her attention once more. I envision beautiful futures branching off from this moment, each tributary more lovely than the last.

And her words, though spoken in a man's voice, a man's voice I somehow remember, still sound like poetry to my ears.

"Whiskey bravo seven slash oscar zero niner," she says. "Prototype Mulligatawny, load self-destruct protocol. And *execute.*"

TEACHER OF THE CENTURY

As the ring of students tightened around her, America's Teacher of the Century nominee Cilla Franklin offered to reduce the homework assignment. Thirty seconds later, she offered to eliminate it altogether. It didn't make any difference.

Muscles tense beneath naked flesh, the boys and girls continued to edge toward her. She didn't know why they were so upset, since they never did homework anyway and were never punished for it. The assignment should not have been taxing for anyone in the class, whatever their aptitude level; further, nothing about it impinged on anyone's personal rights or definition of political correctness.

Periods One through Four hadn't had any problem with the homework. Then again, Period Five was just a bad group. They were all bad, but Five was the worst.

One minute after Cilla had transmitted the details of the assignment to their brainware wireless implants, the kids had risen as one from their hammocks and formed a circle around her. One of the boys had come up behind her and urinated on her legs;

as she spun around, he had directed the stream upward, spraying her hips and abdomen and even splashing her face.

Though Cilla did not understand most of what the godlings (that was what they called themselves) did or said, she knew what this much meant: she was marked for death.

It had happened six times before in her fifty-year career. Each time, she had managed to save herself by begging for mercy from the class Chief or moving to a new school...but it was always possible that death could claim her like this. She knew of colleagues who had died this way; only three out of thirty thousand teachers nationwide died per year in executions by godlings, so the odds weren't bad...but her own mentor, Ruby Churchill, had been one of the unlucky few.

Dying at the hands of a tribe of hive-minded, techno-savage students wasn't anything she had envisioned while playing school as a child with her friends decades ago.

Times had changed. For Cilla Franklin and the other teachers at All Einstein High School, every day was another chapter in *Lord of the Flies.*

Slowly, the ring of twelfth-graders pressed toward her. Their heads were bowed, and every last one of them glared up at her with a wicked, hungry smile. None of them carried a weapon, but Cilla knew they didn't need weapons; to some extent, they were all genetically and cybernetically enhanced. She had already seen a small group of them tear apart a floater car (her own) with their bare hands, and she had seen individual godlings punch holes through the cement block walls of the school.

At seventy-five years old, fit and healthy as she was, Cilla wouldn't even slow the godlings down. She knew she was dead meat.

The godlings would all be adding to their tattoos tonight, commemorating her murder with colorful new markings on their chests or bellies or buttocks, as was their custom. She wondered if there was any truth to the rumors she had heard that the godlings also devoured their victims' remains nowadays.

It wouldn't surprise her.

"Chief Ludwig!" she said, turning to the tallest boy in the circle. "What is the nature of my offense?"

Ludwig was shaved hairless like all the other males his age. His pale, naked skin was decorated with tattoos of eagles, tongues of flame, quantum equations, and DNA molecules. "Coowa chi patea," he said slowly, overenunciating each syllable. "Logwa fachi sifata poto."

Half the time, the godlings communicated with each other via brainware implants, silently passing radio signals from head to head. The rest of the time, they communicated by speaking aloud, but almost always using their own indecipherable language—Twister—when talking to one another. As often as she had heard it used, Cilla could never make out more than a few stray words of it.

"Chaka luweena," said Ludwig, angrily poking a finger in Cilla's direction. "Mantabuda cristacuchina *elar*!"

Though she didn't understand a word he said, Cilla caught the drift of it. The angry tone and the simple fact that he refused to speak English meant that she had no hope. There would be no negotiations. She had reached the end of the line.

Another boy padded up from behind and urinated on her, but she didn't break eye contact with Ludwig. "Please," Cilla said to him. "I taught your father and mother. I taught your father's father. Don't do this."

"Cromo!" Ludwig said sharply, and then he spat on the ground. "Shavaka cromo!"

That word, Cilla knew. "Cromo" was Twister for "parents," expressed with as much contempt as was humanly possible. It was the most profane word in the godlings' vocabulary.

Cilla wondered what the godlings' parents would think if they could see them now, if they could watch what they were about to do to her. They saw everything that took place in the classroom, usually, thanks to the personal A.I. drones that hovered over each student's shoulder during class. Now, though, the airborne eight-balls floated around the perimeter of the room, lenses staring at the walls; obviously, the godlings had figured out how to render the drones dormant when they didn't want their parents to see what they were doing.

Not that the parents would have cared, thought Cilla, even if they *could* have seen what was about to happen.

The circle tightened around her. She could see that some of the boys were aroused as they moved toward their prey. Why, she wondered, with all the advantages they had, did they slide back so completely into the primitive?

If it would have done her any good, Cilla would have pleaded further with the godlings. She would have told them that it wasn't necessary to kill her, since they had already driven her to request early retirement. She'd be gone in two weeks anyway, she would have told them.

But she knew it would not have done any good to tell them that...just as she knew it would not do her any good to scream for help. The other teachers and administrators knew better than to interfere in godling affairs; the penalties for intervention could be quite severe. Just ask the vice principal who had tried to break up a godling orgy in the library two years ago, or the teacher who'd been dumb enough to give a godling an "A minus" just last month.

And now, it was her turn to be the object lesson. Resigning herself to death, she closed her eyes and said a silent prayer that the end would come quickly and without too much pain.

She felt the heat of the students pressing in on her from all sides. She smelled the animal musk and funk of their naked bodies.

Then, all of a sudden, she heard a new voice in the room. It was a young, male voice...and most surprisingly, it was speaking English.

"Sorry I'm late," said the boy. "Is there a seating chart?"

Cilla's eyes shot open and fixed on the new arrival. The godlings turned as one in his direction, halting their predatory approach.

For once, the teacher and students had a common reaction to something. None of them could believe what they were seeing.

The newcomer had sandy brown hair and bright green eyes. He looked about seventeen years old and five foot seven, with a slim build. What was unbelievable about him, though, had nothing to do with his physical characteristics.

It was his clothes...namely, that he was wearing any at all. They were nothing fancy, just a red polo shirt, bluejeans and sneakers, but they might as well have been a hand-tailored Italian suit, for all the attention they got.

Cilla couldn't remember the last time she'd seen a student wearing clothes. The very sight of him made her heart skip a beat.

Calmly, the boy nodded and smiled at the stunned godlings. "My name is Byron Spenser," he said. "I'm a transfer student."

For once, the naked savages were at a loss. Their aura of smug control and superiority seemed to have evaporated. The males were no longer aroused.

Cilla Franklin regained her composure before anyone else. It was an impressive feat, considering that she had been on death's doorstep mere moments before.

"Welcome, Byron," she said. "It's a pleasure to meet you."

"I have a hall pass," said the boy, and then he did something that threw everyone for a loop all over again.

He held out a slip of paper.

Cilla stared at the slip as if he'd just held up a gold nugget the size of a fist. Then, she shook her head and smiled.

It had been a long time since she had seen one of those. It took her back hard and fast, years spinning away like clay pigeons in a summer sky.

"I see," she said. "You're not wired, are you?"

"No, ma'am," said Byron.

Cilla's heart skipped another beat. Not only was he free of brainware—and therefore not plugged into the godlings' hive mind—but he had used the word "ma'am." She hadn't seen the likes of him since Jimmy Melville back in 2092...and Jimmy hadn't even been the real deal, just a poser camping it up for laughs at her expense.

Despite the resemblance in dress and manners, this boy wasn't another Jimmy Melville. She could tell. She had a feeling.

Fearlessly squeezing between the godlings, Cilla crossed the room to Byron. Normally, she would have been embarrassed by her urine-soaked dress, but it was the furthest thing from her mind.

"Well now, Byron," she said, gesturing toward the open door and following him through it. "Let's see about getting you properly acclimated."

"Thank you, Miss Franklin," he said.

Her heart leaped again. She was so agitated, she forgot to go back in the room and dismiss Period Five, but that was no big deal. Period Five, everyone knew, could take care of themselves.

"I WANT to move up my retirement," Cilla said to the naked principal. "I want to leave today."

Principal Caesar smiled. "What a coincidence," he said. "Here I was hoping to talk you into *postponing* your retirement!"

Cilla swallowed nervously and shook her head. "I've been

marked for death," she said. "They almost killed me this afternoon."

Caesar rolled his eyes and sighed as if they were discussing a harmless teenage prank. "And why is that, Cilla?" he said. "What did you do?"

Cilla knew better than to look for sympathy or the slightest trace of support from the oily administrator. His only goal was to appease the godlings and their parents at all costs. He was very popular with the student body and even went naked and occasionally jacked into the hive-mind to curry their favor. Naturally, in his world, the blame for any mishaps could be laid squarely in the laps of the teachers.

"I don't even know," said Cilla, "and it shouldn't matter. They were going to kill me. They *will* kill me, if I don't get out of here."

"Let me have a talk with Chief Ludwig," said Caesar, reaching behind his ear for the hive-mind jack. "I'm sure we can smooth this over."

Cilla shot out of her chair and lunged over the principal's desk, grabbing his wrist before he could switch on the link. "No!" she said sharply. When Caesar raised an eyebrow, she released her grip and receded across the desk. "Please, don't. Just approve my retirement request."

As the principal's hand hovered near the link jack, Cilla prayed that he wouldn't contact Ludwig. The last time Caesar had interceded on a teacher's behalf, the teacher and his wife and children had been smeared over every other teacher's classroom as a warning. Though Caesar played a role in the godlings' scheme of things, there was never any question about who was in charge.

"Okay," said Caesar, dropping his hand from the jack. "I won't bring Ludwig into this yet. But Cilla, you know I won't approve an earlier retirement. I haven't even approved your *first* retirement request."

"It's a matter of life and death," said Cilla. "I've given my life for my profession, but I won't die for it. I won't die for *them*." She jerked her head back over one shoulder, indicating the students in the school building around her.

Caesar sighed and folded his hands on the desk. "Cilla, we don't want you to leave, period. As you know, you're the crown jewel of our teaching staff. You've been selected America's Teacher of the Year every year for the past decade, and you've just been nominated for America's Teacher of the Century. I guess you know you're the chief attraction here at All Einstein High School."

Cilla knew...and knew how little that truly meant. Her name and reputation drew parents to enroll their children, but once the little godlings put their butts in their hammocks, they weren't actually interested in learning at all, and their ever-present A.I. monitor drones made sure that no real education could take place.

As infrequently as actual learning occurred at the school, Cilla's presence brought prestige to All Einstein...and prestige equaled money. Unfortunately, the school administrators were so beholden to and intimidated by the godlings, Cilla knew they could not protect even her from those tattooed techno-savages.

"Thank you, but I want to leave," said Cilla. "I've had enough. I'm burned out."

"But you're still making a *difference*," said Principal Caesar, and it took all she had not to laugh in his face. "We *want* you. We *need* you."

"I want to leave today," said Cilla. "It's time."

Caesar blew out his breath and slumped back in his chair. "At least stay until the end of the semester. Stay until the Teacher of the Century winner is announced."

I'll be dead by then, Cilla started to say, but she held back for fear that Caesar would resume efforts to prevent her death by contacting Ludwig. "I can't," was all she said.

"You have to be a working teacher to be eligible for the

award," said Caesar. "If you retire now, you'll be disqualified. After all these years, do you really want to miss out on the greatest honor that any teacher can receive?"

Cilla could see that she wasn't getting anywhere. "I won't be here tomorrow," she said, pushing up out of her chair. "You'll need to call a substitute."

"Cilla," said Caesar, and all the false cordiality was suddenly gone from his voice. "If you're not here tomorrow, you'll be in breach of contract. You'll forfeit your pension."

Cilla stared at him. Though she wasn't surprised at his playing that card, she got a sinking feeling in her stomach at hearing him make the threat. Without her pension, she would be hard-pressed to survive; then again, it wouldn't make any difference if the godlings killed her before she could use it.

Caesar nodded as if the matter were settled. "Let's pow-wow again at the end of the week," he said, resuming his earlier affability. "Maybe you'll have a change of heart by then."

"I won't," Cilla said softly, turning to leave.

"Hope springs eternal," said the principal with a chuckle, hurrying around to get the door for her.

As he ushered her out, Cilla noticed that he had a new tattoo. It showed up best now that he was aroused from victoriously exercising his authority: the name "Ludwig" was printed in gothic-style letters along the length of his male organ.

THE NEXT DAY, though the death sentence hanging over her head clouded her thoughts, Cilla experienced a welcome change in Period Five.

At first, Five went the way it always did. Half the godlings slept through her lecture, and none of the others paid attention to a word she said. A male and female had actually squeezed into the same hammock together and engaged in heavy petting while she talked. A godling boy loudly passed gas at least a dozen times. Cilla knew better than to correct any of them; their pet principal would veto any disciplinary action and turn it around into negative consequences for her. If she ever did manage to administer any form of punishment, the parental A.I.s would squeal in protest, followed by the parents themselves.

In spite of the usual Period Five headaches, however, there was one consolation in the wasteland that day. Byron Spencer, the new boy, had miraculously survived his first day of school—even though he had dared to interrupt Cilla's execution—and sat at the head of the class, listening and taking notes. He even sat at a *desk*, believe it or not; he had *asked* for one, and the maintenance crew had found one buried in storage and brought it to the room.

As class wore on, Byron did something even more surprising than asking for a desk or taking notes.

It happened as Cilla was being chewed out by one of the A.I. drones for looking at a student while posing a question. The gleaming eight-ball hovered at eye level, less than a foot from her face, and protested in the voice of Daughter Raper XL's mother, presumably reacting in the same way that the mother would have reacted if she herself had been there.

"Is my son the only student in this classroom?" the A.I. said shrilly. "Is he?"

"No," said Cilla, glaring at the floating orb. It was at least the twentieth A.I. interruption in the past half-hour, which was par for the course but still disruptive. As always, she spent her time talking to the orbs while the so-called students snored or masturbated or surfed the hivenet.

"No, *what*?" said the drone in Daughter Raper XL's mother's voice.

Cilla grated her teeth. "No, ma'am," she said coldly.

"Then don't *look* in his direction every time you have a *ques-*

tion!" said the A.I., bobbing closer to Cilla's face. "Try one of these other children you're *supposedly* teaching! Stop singling out Daughter Raper like he's some kind of second class citizen!"

Cilla wished she had a baseball bat so she could take a swing at the eight-ball. Once she got started, she would like to make the rounds of the classroom and then the building, not stopping until every single sphere was a shattered pile of ebony shards and sparking circuits.

"Yes, ma'am," said Cilla, and then the drone zipped away, resuming its post above Daughter Raper XL's left shoulder. Daughter Raper himself was fast asleep, completely oblivious to what had just happened.

For a moment, Cilla stood before the class and tried to recall what her train of thought had been before the drone's interruption. Pressing fingertips against her cheek, she stared off into space, searching her memory...and coming up empty. She had been talking about *Animal Farm*, she knew that much, but where exactly she had left off remained a mystery.

Then, something miraculous happened. Cilla heard a voice other than her own or a drone's in the classroom.

"Miss Franklin," said Byron Spencer. "A moment ago, you said that Napoleon the pig represents Josef Stalin in *Animal Farm*. Who does Snowball represent, did you say?"

For a moment, Cilla stared at the boy in shock. Even the godlings who weren't sleeping directed their attention at Byron, for he had done something completely unheard of, something that just wasn't done anymore in school.

He had participated in class.

Quickly recovering her composure, Cilla smiled gratefully and nodded. "Leon Trotsky," she said. Byron had reminded her of exactly where she'd left off before the A.I.'s intrusion.

"And Mr. Jones the farmer is supposed to be the czar, right?" said Byron.

"Czar Nicholas II," said Cilla. "That's correct, Byron."

The boy cocked his head thoughtfully. "But the characters don't *have* to be those particular people, do they?"

"No, they don't," said Cilla. "The allegory can apply to any oppressive system."

"I *thought* I recognized some characters from real life," said Byron, glancing over his shoulder.

If the godlings realized that he was referring to them, they gave no sign of it. None of them seemed to be listening anymore, anyhow.

"If Orwell updated *Animal Farm* today," said Byron, "I wonder if the pigs would be connected to the hivenet."

"Who knows?" said Cilla, keeping her remarks neutral for the benefit of the A.I. drones that recorded her every word. "But it would be interesting to see what Mr. Orwell would come up with."

"I think he'd have a field day," Byron said with a grin.

Cilla nodded and smiled. "So, Byron," she said, excited to be interacting intellectually with a student for the first time in what seemed like eons. "What did you like best about the book?"

From then on, Period Five wasn't so bad. It had gotten off to a typically awful start, but ended up being Cilla's favorite class in she couldn't remember how long.

Ignoring the godlings, she spent the remaining class time talking exclusively with Byron Spencer about *Animal Farm*. For once, she was sorry when Period Five ended.

THE NEXT DAY, Cilla actually looked forward to Period Five, and wasn't disappointed when it arrived. While the godlings ate and slept and urinated on the floor from their hammocks, Cilla and Byron continued their discussion of *Animal Farm* and moved on to

1984. By the time class was over, they had gone from Orwell to Ayn Rand, then ranged further afield, touching on Jules Verne, Edgar Allan Poe, Charles Dickens, and even Shakespeare.

Cilla could not believe that she was having such a stimulating conversation with a twelfth-grader, especially in an age when twelfth-graders read no books and could not even be bothered to communicate with adults in English. She did not even have such conversations with her peers anymore, for they were too busy scrambling to placate the godlings to consider academic matters.

The time she spent with Byron, she knew, was a rare gift. The death sentence still weighed on her, as did the postponed retirement that could be her only means of survival...but during Period Five, at least, she was able to shrug aside the darkness and savor every moment of her exchanges with the extraordinary seventeen-year-old.

It was enough to help her survive to the end of the week and her scheduled "pow-wow" with Principal Caesar (barring a surprise execution by the godlings, of course). She would never admit it to Caesar, but she ended up not minding the extra time in school so much.

In fact, by staying through the week, she experienced what might have been the highlight of the past twenty years of her career...certainly of the past miserable decade. After school on Friday, just before her meeting with Caesar, Byron stopped by her room and did something that no student had done since Kitty Carnuba back in 2079 or so.

He handed her some poetry he'd written and asked her to tell him what she thought of it.

"Whenever you get the chance," said Byron. "I'm sure you're busy."

Cilla turned slowly through the poems, which he'd gone to the trouble of printing (God bless him!) on sheets of paper. There was one about his father, and one about the way he'd felt on his first day at All Einstein High School. There was one about a journey to the stars, and one about a perfect world that never was.

And then there was one titled "The Angel." It included the following lines:

I squint from the shadows of life like a prison,
Outnumbered by forces inhuman and heartless.
I'm saved by an angel of learning arisen,
Like minds, kindred spirits together a fortress.

After reading the full text of "The Angel," it was all she could do to keep from crying until Byron left the room. On the pretext that she had to get ready for her meeting with the principal, she sent Byron on his way, promising to read the poems at her first opportunity...

And then she let the tears flow.

The poem touched her deeply...not so much because of its quality as for its subject matter. Though her name was never mentioned, she had no doubt that it related directly to her.

She had known that she and Byron had made a positive connection, but seeing the boy's appreciation in print, and expressed so glowingly, filled her with joy. For once, she felt like she was actually helping someone; for once, she felt like she was getting through to another human being.

For once, she felt like maybe she *was* making a difference, even if it was only in the life of a single student.

It was a miracle she had never expected to see again in her lifetime. She had done plenty of good work long ago, in the days before the hivenet and godlings. She could not even count the number of students she had helped to succeed, or helped to succeed more, or exceed all expectations...but it seemed that the desire to learn had disappeared around the same time the students had stopped wearing clothes. Though Cilla had received teaching awards in recent years, she attributed them to past glories and the absence of competition in the teaching field. She knew all too well that she had made no impact on students in many years.

Until now. As she reread "The Angel," she sobbed tears of pure happiness. She felt like she was fifty-five again, or even forty-five or thirty-five.

All because of one student. One excellent student out of hundreds...an unacceptably dismal success rate decades ago, but today it was wondrous enough to make a teacher break down and cry. Not just any teacher, either, but America's so-called Teacher of the Year for ten years running and a nominee for so-called Teacher of the Century.

If she hadn't been so damned happy, Cilla Franklin might have been disappointed in herself.

"CONGRATULATIONS," said the naked principal when Cilla entered his office for their "pow-wow." "You're not dead!"

As good a mood as Cilla was in after receiving Byron's poems, Caesar's remark threw a shroud right over her. "Not yet," she said coldly. "The godlings like to play with their food."

"I disagree," Caesar said flippantly. "I think you're off the hook. In fact, Ludwig tells me you're in the clear."

Cilla distrusted every word from the principal's mouth, but she played along. "No more death sentence?"

"You'll be able to receive that Teacher of the Century award after all!" said Caesar. He glanced down at the gold hoop in his newly-pierced left nipple, then looked to Cilla for approval. "Like the piercing? I'm getting my scrotum done next."

Ignoring his nipple, Cilla leaned forward. She sensed that he was being evasive somehow. "So the death sentence is cancelled?"

"Yeah, yeah," said Caesar, waving a hand dismissively. "I guarantee you'll get to that award ceremony."

There. She finally realized what he was leaving unsaid. "What about *after* the ceremony?"

"What about it?" Caesar said innocently.

"What happens to me?"

"I imagine you'll go to a party of some sort," said Caesar.

It took an effort for Cilla to restrain her anger. "And the death sentence will be back in effect," she said darkly.

Caesar shrugged. "Sometimes, we take what we can get."

"You made a deal to ensure I'd live to receive the award," said Cilla, "and bring it home to All Einstein. Then, all bets are off."

"I can't confirm or deny your theory," said Caesar. "Rest assured, if any negotiations did or will occur, they were or will be designed to buy time until a

longer-lasting compromise can be devised. Remember, Cilla, it's in the school's best interests to keep you alive and teaching for as long as is humanly possible."

Cilla shook her head with a combination of disgust and amazement. "You gave me up," she said. "You told the godlings they could have me."

"Now, now," said Caesar, raising an index finger correctively. "You're putting words in my mouth, Cilla."

"When they devour my body," she said icily, "will you join in the feast?"

"Nobody's going to devour you," said Caesar. "Keep in mind, Ludwig's tribe will graduate at the end of the year. They won't be a threat."

"How dumb do you think I am?" said Cilla. "Of course they'll still be a threat! They'll never stop until I'm dead, whether they're in school or not."

"Trust me," said Caesar. "It'll blow over. You've got many years of teaching ahead of you."

"You're mistaken," said Cilla. "I'm retiring, remember?"

Caesar chuckled. "You're not *serious* about that!"

"You insisted I stay through the week, and I have. Now I'm done. I'm leaving before the godlings finish me off."

"I just told you, you're in the clear," said Caesar.

"You should know better than to make promises you aren't sure you can keep," said Cilla. "The godlings can't be controlled or bargained with. They could snuff me out right now, and what would you do about it?"

"You're off-limits! They won't touch you!"

"Don't kid yourself," said Cilla, getting to her feet. "We're not even the same species anymore. They'd just as soon use your treaties for toilet paper as honor them."

"They're good kids," said Caesar. "Maybe if you'd link to the hivenet once in a while, you'd see that."

Cilla crossed the office and opened the door. "I'm retired now," she said. "I'll leave the kids to you."

Caesar cleared his throat and rose from his chair. "See you Monday," he said.

"Not unless you show up at my apartment," said Cilla.

"Remember your pension," said Caesar.

"It won't do me much good if I'm dead."

Caesar came around the front of his desk and leaned against it, casually folding his arms over his chest. Apparently, he pinched his nipple ring the wrong way, for he quickly adjusted his arms, briefly letting his composure slip.

"Sleep on it over the weekend, Cilla," he said cheerfully. "Your job will still be waiting for you Monday."

"I won't want it," Cilla said over her shoulder as she walked out.

"Things can change," said Principal Caesar. "Keep an open mind."

"Goodbye," said Cilla as she left the outer office and turned down the hall.

"You'll be back!" Caesar shouted after her, grinning

knowingly.

As Cilla lifted the wrinkled photo from her desk drawer, she swung back in time to the happy moment when the photo had been taken.

It had been at least thirty years ago, back when people still took photos instead of posting images to the hivenet. Period Three had been amazing that year, unbelievably sharp, hard-working, and well-behaved; on the last day of school, the kids had surprised her with a party in her honor. They had even baked her a cake and made her an afghan in Home Economics. Every last one of them had hugged her on their way out the door.

In the photo, she and the kids from Period Three were mashed together in a happy crush, all laughter and light. How had she gone from that life to the one she had now, she wondered? When had the kids gone from hugging her to pissing on her?

Placing the photo in the box into which she was packing her possessions, Cilla reached back into the desk drawer. This time, she withdrew an enamel pin shaped like a shiny red apple; the lettering on the apple read "World's Best Teacher."

Kim Warwick had given her that. Out of all the students she'd taught through the years, Cilla still remembered that one.

Kim had been one of the stars of Cilla's career...not that Cilla imagined she had had much to do with her success. As a high school senior, Kim had already been writing like a master, composing achingly perfect novels of exquisite intricacy, depth, and emotional resonance. Cilla had given her the tiniest bit of guidance and all the encouragement in the world...and for that, Kim had never failed to credit her as the greatest teacher she'd ever known. She'd even dedicated a Pulitzer Prize-winning novel to Cilla, back in the days when the Pulitzer Prize still meant something.

Cilla dropped the pin in the box and pulled a magic marker drawing of a bull from the drawer. That one came from Jayvo Endymion, her hyperactive but beloved "bull in a china shop" from forty-odd years ago. Was he even still alive, she wondered? So much could happen in forty-odd years.

With a heavy sigh, Cilla dropped into her chair. Though there was not the slightest doubt in her mind that it was time to retire —well *past* time, in fact—cleaning out her desk was turning out to be harder than she had expected. As she piled mementos into boxes, the memories of better times and better students piled onto her shoulders, pressing her downward.

As she looked around the room, tears welling in her eyes, a thousand schooldays replayed in her memory. She saw herself standing in the front of the room, pacing her little track from wall to wall, lecturing energetically. Phantom students raised hands, chewed gum, passed notes, watched the clock. How many children had there been, she wondered? Ten thousand? A hundred thousand? A million? She had no idea, no head count.

But she did remember every face, every name. A good teacher never forgets, she always thought.

And she was a good teacher, if you listened to Kim Warwick and Period Three from thirty-odd years ago and the America's Teacher of the Century selection committee. Or maybe not so good, if you listened to the little voice inside her that laid the blame for the rise of the godlings at least partly in her lap, since after all, she had done her part to shape the minds that had given birth to this warped generation.

Either way, she was now an *ex*-teacher, and glad of it. If ever a change had been overdue, it was this one; thinking back, Cilla thought she should have retired at least ten years ago...more like fifteen.

She would have only one real regret in leaving when she did. There was one person she would miss seeing again, one student she would have liked to have said goodbye to before she left for good.

As she thought of him, like magic, his voice broke the silence.

Unfortunately, the sound was not as welcome as it usually was to Cilla. He wasn't speaking calmly from the doorway or his desk.

He was screaming for help from somewhere down the hall.

As a hundred horrible possibilities leaped into her imagination, Cilla instinctively leaped from her chair and headed for the door. Leaning out into the corridor, she heard him scream again; this time, his cry for help became a shriek, his voice shooting up an octave and breaking as someone or something hurt him terribly.

Without hesitation, though she was seventy-five years old and unarmed, Cilla followed Byron's cries down the darkened hallway. Seventy-five was a lot younger than it used to be, but she was still fragile and unaugmented, certainly no match for the frailest godling; whoever or whatever she was about to face, rushing to her student's aid was a courageous thing to do.

Three doors down on the opposite side of the hall from her room, Cilla could see a bright red light dancing on the polished floor outside an open doorway. Though Byron's screams ominously ended, ceasing to guide her, Cilla had no doubt that he was through that doorway, amid that fiery light.

Sure enough, when she got there and looked inside, she saw him, huddled on the floor of a blazing classroom. Everything that could burn was on fire—hammocks, bedding, the teacher's desk, window blinds, light panels,

wall-mounted flat screen computer displays. In the middle of the roaring flames, Byron was curled in a fetal position with arms wrapped around his head, trying to protect himself from the blows that rained down upon him.

He was being bombarded...but not, as Cilla might have expected, by the fists of savage godlings. A torrent of blows pounded him in quick succession, one after another, and not a single one was delivered by a human hand.

The child was being hammered by A.I. spheres. A swarm of them boiled around him, thirty or more, enough to coddle a whole class of godlings. She'd never thought of them as dangerous in a physical way...but now the gleaming eight balls were wrecking a human body, pelting down hard and springing back up in the air only to bounce back down against battered flesh and bone.

Apparently, the godlings could reprogram the spheres more extensively than she had guessed, making them do a lot worse than turn their lenses to the walls. The tattooed monsters had transformed their own surrogate parents into lethal weapons.

And poor Byron Spencer was the beneficiary of their genius. The attack was so effective, he wasn't even moving anymore.

Cilla's stomach lurched at the thought that he might never move again.

Desperately, she looked around, wondering how she could possibly help him. There was still a clear path through the flames from the doorway to Byron, but what could she do when she got to him? She had no doubt that if she tried to shield him and drag him from the room, the orbs would turn their fury on her. As hard as they were hitting, Cilla knew that it wouldn't take long for them to break her seventy-five-year-old body.

She needed some kind of help herself...but by the time she could bring someone back, Byron might be dead. For all she knew, he was dead already.

If she had any hope at all of saving him, Cilla had to act fast...and, she realized, she needed more than her bare hands to do it. To fight off the A.I. spheres, she needed some kind of a weapon, something within reach.

Even as she realized what she would use, her feet were whisking her down the hallway toward her classroom.

Breathing fast, not used to exertion, Cilla hurried through the doorway of her room and went straight for her desk. What she wanted stuck out of one of the cartons she had packed, too big to fit inside under a lid.

It was a souvenir of days long gone, a talisman of ancient times when teachers had still possessed power and students had feared them. It was a piece of history that she had kept in the back of the bottom of a drawer, as if imagining that it might someday return to service, that a wind would sweep away the incompetent leaders and restore the schools to the centers of discipline and learning that they had once been.

The wood felt solid in her hand as she drew it from the box. The miraculous return to past glories had not come for the schools, but the artifact would see action again after all those years.

Cilla rushed back down the hall and flung herself without hesitation into the burning classroom. Byron still wasn't moving; the cloud of eight balls was still raining down on him.

Cilla wrapped both hands tightly around the handle and stepped forward. She prayed that she still had the strength to do the work that lay ahead.

Then, she drew back the paddle, the very same paddle that had stung many a student's bottom, and she swung it as hard as she could at the ebony spheres.

With a crack, the flat of the paddle smacked into two of the eight balls, sending them spinning. One looped drunkenly across the room, weaving toward the windows, while the other dashed itself against a blazing wall screen and burst into flames.

Heart pounding, Cilla wrenched the paddle back and swung it

again, spraying three more orbs in crazy trajectories around the room. Her next swing caught one full against the wood, chucking it down to shatter in sparks and black shards upon the floor.

Surprised at herself, she pulled back and swung again. Spheres flew from the flat of the paddle like bees, whizzing into walls and fiery hammocks, shattering windows.

As she struck at them, some of the orbs protested with A.I. voices, filling the air with the strident cries of parents. If anything, the babble strengthened her resolve and made Cilla swing harder.

"Cease this behavior immediately!" screamed one of the spheres, just before Cilla drove it into a corner.

"This is a violation of our rights!" wailed another orb in the voice of Ludwig's mother. True to form, this particular orb never shut up until Cilla's paddle shattered it against the floor.

Cilla continued to swing away, breaking apart the awful swarm. As grave as the situation was, as much as a precious life depended on its outcome, a part of her was enlivened by the release, the realization of a secret fantasy from frustrated daydreams.

Oh, how she'd wanted to demolish those damned chattering eight balls.

Cilla's head throbbed, and her arms ached. As she swung again and again, she prayed to God to save the life of the boy at her feet, even if it meant the loss of her own.

One of the spheres struck her between the shoulder blades, but she ignored the flash of pain. Eight balls thumped her sides and legs, threatening to report her to the superintendent as they peppered her with bruises. She cried out as one of the balls clocked her kneecap with staggering force.

Tears flowed down her sunken cheeks, but she refused to fall. Knuckles white, she clenched the paddle in a death grip and swung, preventing the malevolent spheres from landing another blow on her motionless charge.

The flames leaped around her, burning through to bare walls, consuming everything...finally catching even the end of her paddle when she swept it through a fiery fall of ceiling tile.

Even as the paddle burned, Cilla kept right on swinging.

SOLEMNLY, the president of the United States of America stepped up to the podium. As the assembled audience fell silent, he took a moment to review the text of his remarks, displayed on the screen of the implant in the palm of his hand.

Newsglobes captured his every move, hovering at a respectful distance. Their all-seeing lenses flexed in and out, perfecting the framing of their shots. Images of the leader of the free world were instantaneously transmitted onto the hivenet, accessible to every mind with the brainware to receive them.

The president looked up, cleared his throat, and began to speak.

"In this world of technological miracles," he said, "knowledge is abundant. Information is downloaded directly into the human mind. Thanks to the hivenet, the sum total of human experience is available to anyone at any time.

"And yet, we have found no substitute for traditional learning," said the president, looking around meaningfully at the attentive faces in the White House rose garden. "No technology can match the magic that occurs in the face-to-face communion between teacher and student.

"Traditional education is the backbone of our nation," said the president, and the audience applauded. "It is because of this that we single out a Teacher of the Year, an example of the excellence that enables our children and nation to flourish."

Again, the audience clapped. At the president's side, Principal

Caesar beamed. In deference to the occasion, for once, he had concealed his naked body beneath a suit and tie.

"In this, the final year of the century," said the president, "we will go a step further. In honor of the accomplishments of all our nation's teachers over the past one hundred years, we will single out America's finest teacher not only of the year, but of the century."

The president nodded proudly. "Let me tell you, this woman is more than deserving of the title I am about to bestow upon her."

The audience applauded with rising enthusiasm as the culmination of the ceremony approached.

"She has served with distinction for over fifty years at some of our nation's finest schools," said the president. "During her career, she has helped to mold the minds of some of our most distinguished and accomplished citizens.

"Her contribution to our greatness cannot be overstated," said the president. "By embracing progress while holding fast to the time-tested tenets of American education, she has linked the best of our yesterdays to the best of our tomorrows."

As the crowd applauded, the president consulted his palm screen. "I'm sure you already know her," he said, returning his sincere gaze to his listeners. "Every year for the past decade, she has been named America's Teacher of the Year.

"Now, she is about to receive the highest honor in the land for a member of the noblest profession on Earth. There is no one who deserves it more.

"For excellence in the field of teaching...for contributions beyond measure to the success of our great nation...for unswerving devotion to the children of America...I hereby pronounce Cilla Sullivan Franklin America's Teacher of the Century!"

As the crowd burst into wild applause, the president turned and guided Cilla to the podium. She looked radiant in her frilly white dress, bathed in an aura of bright sunlight that shimmered around her and haloed her silver hair.

"Congratulations, Cilla," said the president, handing her a translucent plaque that pulsed with rainbow light. "And on behalf of all citizens of the United States of America, thank you."

"Thank you, Mr. President," Cilla said softly, peering around at the ring of newsglobes scoping their lenses in her direction. The globes made her nervous, reminding her of the eight-ball parental A.I.s.

"You are a national treasure, Cilla," said the president.

Cilla nodded and smiled, but was unimpressed by the flattery. To her thinking, the whole Teacher of the Century honor was meaningless, given the state of the world of education. How could anyone be honored to be a teacher when the schools were such a joke, when students and principals alike ran naked through the halls and the only learning taking place was the godlings' learning new methods of mayhem?

"Now, Cilla," said the president, the applause fading at the sound of his voice. "I have a surprise for you."

Cilla glanced at the newsglobes again, then forced herself to focus on the president. As unimpressed as she was by the honor she had been given, she still felt a small thrill at being so close to the most powerful man in America.

"Three months ago," he said, "you performed a true act of heroism. When an accident threatened the life of one of your students, you risked your own life to save him."

It was no accident, thought Cilla, but of course she kept it to herself. The party line of the school administration, force-fed to the public by Ludwig's pet, Caesar, seemed to be the only truth that mattered.

"That student," said the president, "Byron Spencer, is alive and well today because of you.

"And he is here today to share in this historic occasion."

Cilla immediately brightened. She couldn't help herself.

It was the one thing she hadn't expected. It was the one thing that could truly make her happy.

As Byron walked out of a nearby door and headed for the podium, the crowd sprang to their feet and applauded like mad. In contrast to the way he had looked three months ago, battered and huddled on the floor of the burning classroom, Byron was bright-eyed and impeccably groomed, wearing a sharp navy blue suit and striped tie. His arms were full of red roses.

At the sight of him, Cilla was overcome with pure joy. He was the only reason she was at the White House that day, the only reason she had kept teaching long enough to qualify for the Teacher of the Century award.

Because of Byron, she had finished out the school year at All Einstein. After the life-threatening incident, he had bravely insisted on staying to complete his senior year. She had been unable to walk away then, knowing that the one good student in the place would be alone at the mercy of the murderous godlings.

Normally, one seventy-five-year-old teacher would not have provided much protection against a school full of techno-savages...but Cilla had been shielded from the godlings until the award ceremony by Caesar's bargain with Ludwig. She had become a guardian angel, using her special status to hold the savages at bay when Byron was endangered. There had been many tense moments, and Byron had taken his share of knocks, but she had managed to get him through his senior year alive.

He was going to graduate. He was going out into the world, and she was sure that he would do great things.

Seeing him there, alive and healthy and brimming with hope, meant far more to Cilla than the plaque in her hand or the applause of her peers or the president of the United States standing at her side.

"These are for you, Miss Franklin," said Byron, handing her

the bouquet of red roses. "Thank you for being such a wonderful teacher."

Tears of happiness flowed down her face as she accepted the flowers. She wanted to hug him but held herself back...then gave in and hugged him anyway.

That moment was all the reward she needed. After all the years of futility since the rise of the godlings, she had managed to help one more student, one promising student who loved learning and appreciated her. How wonderful that she could retire on a positive note, reliving one final time the teacher-student bond as it was meant to be.

As she drew back from him, Byron beamed. "There's another surprise, Miss Franklin," he said. "There's someone I'd like you to meet."

Still smiling, Cilla tipped her head inquisitively.

"Come on out, Sara," said Byron, looking toward the door from which he had emerged.

As Cilla followed his gaze, the door opened. A girl stepped out, smiling shyly.

She looked close to Byron's age, and about the same height. Her sandy, straight hair hung in a glossy fall to the middle of her back, a style that Cilla hadn't seen in years. She wore a pretty blue knee-length sheath, and her green eyes sparkled like pale emeralds.

"This is my younger sister, Sara," said Byron. "Sara, meet my teacher, Cilla Franklin."

Shifting the roses and plaque to free an arm, Cilla shook Sara's hand. It felt soft as the petal of a flower in her grip.

"It's a pleasure to meet you, Miss Franklin," said Sara.

"It's a pleasure to meet you, too, Sara," said Cilla, staring at the girl. Byron hadn't been kidding when he had promised a surprise. Cilla could not remember him ever mentioning a sister...and yet, as she searched Sara's features, she could see that the family resemblance was unmistakable.

"Sara has been home schooled until now," said Byron, "but next year, she'll be attending All Einstein High School. She'll be a senior."

"I can't wait to have you as a teacher," said Sara. "Byron's told me so much about you. You're the only reason I'm going to All Einstein instead of continuing my home schooling."

Cilla kept staring, completely thrown for a loop. She didn't know what to say.

The girl gazed hopefully up at her. "I brought you something," she said, pulling a hand from behind her back. "So we can get off on the right foot."

It was a shiny red apple.

As the audience laughed and applauded, Cilla stared at the apple in Sara's hand. She was truly on the spot, now. Though she had filed her retirement papers, Caesar had neglected to tell Byron that she wouldn't be teaching next year. Cilla had never mentioned it to Byron, either, and now she was stuck.

When she shot a look in Caesar's direction, he leaned over and patted her shoulder. "We're all excited about next year," he said to Cilla. "Another batch of fresh faces for you to work your magic on."

Then, he leaned closer and whispered in her ear. "And no Ludwig."

Which was supposed to mean that she was in the clear, that the death sentence was null and void, but she knew better. Ludwig's godlings could take her in the street, or at home...and there would be another horde to replace them in school the next year. She had seen them in the halls already, the eleventh graders, naked and tattooed and looking every bit as inhuman as the last bunch.

But then there was Sara Spencer.

"Sara aced her home school equivalence exams," Byron said proudly. "She got the highest scores on record."

Sara blushed and looked at her feet, then back up at Cilla.

Cilla could feel the intelligence radiating from the girl's emerald eyes. Even if Byron hadn't mentioned her test scores, Cilla would have known that she was in the presence of another excellent student, another hard-working and respectful young person, another hope for the future.

Her brother's sister, through and through.

And she was a home schooler, inexperienced in the savage ways of the merciless tribal school culture. When it came to interacting with the godlings, she might as well have had "fresh meat" tattooed on her forehead.

Sara fixed her with a gaze that was full of need and frank adoration. "I can't wait till next year," she said softly.

Cilla's heart melted. Abandoning that child to the godlings would be like offering up her own daughter to be killed.

In that moment, Cilla knew that she would be back in front of a classroom after all. She did not know how much protection she could offer this gentle, brilliant soul, but she knew that she could not turn her back on her.

She had risked her own life for Byron Spencer. If she did any less for Byron's sister, she would not be able to live with herself, anyway.

Cilla took the apple from Sara's hand. "See you in the fall," she said with a smile.

ONE WEEK after the ceremony at the White House, Principal Caesar refilled his glass with champagne in the secret sub-basement of All Einstein High School. Replacing the bottle on the table, he leaned forward and clinked glasses with Superintendent Alexander.

"To the Teacher of the Century," Caesar said with an oily grin. "The pride of All Einstein High."

"To Cilla Franklin," said Alexander. "Where would we be without her?"

The naked men drained their glasses, finishing off with mutual sighs of satisfaction. Alexander drew fine cigars from the humidor and passed one over to Caesar.

"Congratulations on the enrollment numbers for next year," said Caesar. "Having the Teacher of the Century on staff is quite a draw."

"Word is, our state funding will be through the roof," said Alexander, clipping the end of his cigar. "So I want to see some belt-tightening around this place."

Caesar accepted the clipper from him with a laugh. "We'll cut till it hurts," he said, "and pass the savings along to ourselves."

The men lit their cigars, then relaxed back into the depths of their high-backed leather chairs. A holographic fire danced in the faux fireplace between them.

"I can't thank you enough for keeping Franklin on board," said Alexander, puffing out a great draft of smoke.

"Don't thank me," said Caesar, and then he clapped his hands together twice.

A boy with sandy hair and green eyes hurried to his side, smiling expectantly. He wore an old-style servant's uniform with black coat and tails, knee-high knickers over white stockings, and ruffles at the collar and wrists.

"Thank Byron," said Caesar with a sneer.

Alexander chuckled. "Thank you, Byron," he said through a cloud of cigar smoke.

"You're welcome, sir," Byron Spencer said happily. "Can I get you gentlemen anything?"

"Bend over," said Caesar.

The boy immediately bent at the waist. Principal Caesar leaned forward and pressed his thumb on a spot in the middle of Byron's scalp.

At his touch, the scalp split apart. Panels slid smoothly aside, exposing a rectangular opening in the boy's head.

Tiny lights flickered inside in a high-speed flurry.

"Ah, the miracle of robotics," said Caesar, peering into the hole in Byron's scalp.

"The miracle of false hope," said Alexander.

"Good boy," said Caesar, tapping the ash from the tip of his cigar into the hole.

"Should you be doing that?" said Alexander. "He cost us a pretty penny."

"He'll process and excrete it as synthetic feces." Caesar closed the port and settled back into his chair. "Stand up, Byron."

Byron Spencer did as he was told.

Caesar clapped his hands again, and Sara Spencer trotted into the room wearing a maid's costume with a tiny skirt. She carried a feather duster in one hand and smiled serenely.

"We owe Sara a debt of gratitude, as well," said Caesar. "She's done her brother one better, bless her heart. Thanks to her, Cilla's ours for another year."

"And what about after that?" said Alexander.

"Funny you should ask," said Caesar, puffing on his cigar. "Between you and me, I hear that Byron and Sara's mom and dad might just have another little one on the way."

The naked men laughed loudly in their cloud of smoke.

"And now, if you'll excuse me," said Principal Caesar, pushing himself up out of his leather chair, "I have an appointment for a tattoo removal."

"Which one?" said Alexander.

Caesar pointed at his male organ. "Ludwig's graduated. Out with the old, in with the new."

"You'll have it replaced?"

"As soon as I find out who the new chief is," said Caesar.

"It's good to have friends in high places," said Alexander.

"You never know when you'll need someone to do you a favor," said Caesar with a knowing smile. "Like torch a classroom or reprogram some A.I.s."

Alexander laughed and raised his cigar. "To the godlings!" he roared.

"To education!" chimed in Caesar. "It oughtta be a crime!"

COCK-A-DOODLE-DIE

Shad Lum Lugo the meemee exterminator strutted across the paved lot, feeling the bright morning sun as it heated his feathers. He was glad to be alive, and he crowed about it again, though he'd already crowed at dawn as he did every day. Life, oh life was so *good*.

Then, suddenly, two meemees ran out of the brush in front of him, and he reared back, scrambling to aim his pistol at them.

The meemees were barely two feet tall, covered in fur (one black, one blond), and bipedal. It was the only thing they seemed to have in common with Shad's people, the Ch'Kaw--getting around on two legs.

Otherwise, the meemees didn't measure up. The Ch'Kaw were ten feet tall, immeasurably smarter, covered with beautiful plumage, and the dominant species of planet Earth.

So why were the damned meemees so hard to *kill*?

They were fast on their feet, for one thing. Even as Shad swung his pistol around, they scurried further away, heading for the back of The Coop restaurant. A few more steps, and the pistol would be useless; Shad couldn't open fire if there was a chance of hitting a worker inside the place.

So he took a chance and threw two shots at the fleeing meemees. Neither bullet hit its mark.

Then the meemees reached the restaurant and flung themselves into a tiny hole at the base of the wall. Shad had never noticed it before--but of course the damned meemees went straight for it.

Crowing with rage, Shad threw open the back door and charged into the building. From experience, he knew where the meemees would go, so he made a beeline for the kitchen.

Sure enough, they were up on a counter, heads submerged in a bowl of corn flour. As soon as he rushed in, they both looked up, furry faces dusted with pale yellow flour--then sprinted away, grabbing handfuls of corn biscuit crumbs from a tray en route.

"Vermin!" Shad didn't dare shoot up the kitchen, so he grabbed a metal skillet with one claw and heaved it at the meemees.

The creatures dove off the counter and landed on their feet on the blue-tiled floor. The skillet clanged off the counter and bounced down after them, but they were already racing away by then.

"I'll peck you to shreds!" howled Shad as he chased them. His razor-sharp beak could do some serious damage.

"*Mee mee mee mee mee!*" That was the sound the meemees made as they scrambled away from him and headed for the kitchen door. "*Mee mee mee mee mee!*" It was the cry that had given them their name once upon a time.

Shad knew they were heading for their bolt hole. He had to cut them off, or he might not get another chance at stopping their escape.

It was time for a bold move. Taking two big steps, he pushed off in a flying leap, aiming the claws of his feet at the fleeing pests. He might just take them both at once, if...

But no. The meemees darted through the kitchen doorway before he could nail them. Shad came down on his heels and slid, dropping hard on his ass.

A shock of pain jolted his spine, and he shrieked. As he slumped against the wall, he heard the meemees' hairy little feet pattering down the hall toward their escape hole.

And that made him shriek even louder.

"WHAT NEXT?" The white-feathered female was furious, clacking her beak against Shad's. "Are you going to *carry* the meemees in and *feed* them by *claw*?"

Shad shook his head with quick flicks, careful not to leave an opening for her sharp beak. Just because they were standing in the restaurant's dining room in view of several customers didn't mean she wouldn't jab his eye out. "Of course not, Lady Nixa."

"You might as well!" snapped Nixa. "You already *let* them come and go as they *please*!"

At her sharp, shrill tone, all the customers looked up at once, heads flicking and bobbing with interest. Then, they all returned to pecking away at the plates of fried worms and cornmeal biscuits on the tables in front of them.

"I can *do* the *job*!" Shad reared up with indignation, but he had to be careful. Lady Nixa owned the restaurant and was paying his fee--a fee he couldn't afford to lose.

"So you keep saying." Nixa lunged at him, then jerked away at the last second. The low red comb on top of her head quivered with rage. "But if I don't see results soon, you're *fired*, you washed-up loser."

"I'll *get* those meemees, don't you worry!" Shad crowed for emphasis.

"Big talk, cock," said Nixa. "Now walk the walk." She clucked with disgust. "If you can."

AS SHAD CHECKED the cage traps in the parking lot, he got more and more angry. Not only had he not caught a single meemee, but every last bit of bait he'd planted had been spirited away.

The little bastards were tricky as hell and hard to kill. Not that Shad had gone after many of them before now. Actually, this was his first job as an exterminator, though he'd never tell Nixa that.

He'd thought it would be much easier. He'd only ever killed another Ch'Kaw before, in the cockfighting ring, and that hadn't been so hard...for a while, anyway.

But the meemees, it turned out, were much more of a challenge. He'd already been after them for three days, and the closest he'd come to contact was the chase he'd just had through the kitchen.

"Well, hello there." A strange voice interrupted his reverie. "Coming up empty, huh?"

Turning, Shad saw an elderly male limping toward him with a cane, bobbing his head. Immediately, Shad put down the latest trap and straightened. "What's it to you?"

"These traps won't work." The male swung his cane out and rapped it on the trap at Shad's feet. "Not for damned meemees. You're pecking at the wrong feed, friend."

"What do *you* suggest, Grampa?" Shad twitched his head, giving his comb and wattles a sarcastic shake.

"Name's Varn, not Grampa." Varn twitched his own head, but his shriveled comb and wattles didn't shake much. "And shame on you, if you think I'm dumb enough to tell you my meemee-killing tactics without a piece of the action."

Shad crowed with laughter and strutted away. "Get lost, old rooster." His high, purple tail feathers flickered as he walked. "You won't get any money out of me."

"Too bad." Varn made a rumbling noise deep in his throat--a Ch'Kaw sigh. "I was going to pay *you* to let me *help*."

Shad stopped strutting and whirled. "But you said you wanted a piece of the action."

"Exactly." Varn cluck-chuckled and flapped his arms. "The *action*, friend. The *killing*. I'm retired and *bored*."

Now Shad was interested. Keeping his head high, he scratched the pavement with his feet. "You say you have meemee-killing tactics?"

"*Scientifically developed* tactics." Varn chuckled again. "And cash money up front, friend." He reached between the dull gray feathers on his belly and drew out a clawful of glittering gold pellets.

Shad considered it for a moment, then shrugged. What did he have to lose? "Sure. Why not?"

Varn's feathers were thin, with the skin underneath showing through in patches, but he ruffled them excitedly anyway. "To murder most fowl!" And then he managed a hoarse crow that broke down into a ragged coughing jag.

"VOILA!" Varn pulled an item out of a burlap sack--a tiny, rectangular object with curved corners, black all around. "The perfect bait!"

Shad flicked his head to the side and stared at the object with one eye. "What the hell is it?"

"An ancient artifact, dug up from deep underground." Varn

turned the object around in his clawed hand, letting the sun glint off its smooth surface. "A remnant of a different age." Dropping it in the bag, he headed across the parking lot toward the garbage pile in the far back corner.

Shad shook his head. "And it's supposed to be bait how?"

"The Ch'Kaw did not always rule the Earth," said Varn. "You know that, don't you?"

"I've heard theories."

"*More* than theories. *Facts.*" Varn shook his cane for emphasis. "This world was once dominated by a species calling itself 'Peeple.' How do we know this?" He held up the burlap sack. "*Evidence*, buried long, long ago."

When they got to the garbage pile, Shad spotted a swarm of bugs on some rotten cornbread and pecked them up. "If these Peeple were so dominant, what happened to them?"

"No one knows for sure." Varn pulled the black object from his sack and squatted down in front of the pile. "But the meemees look an awful lot like the Peeple did."

Shad stopped pecking at bugs. "The meemees?"

"Sure," said Varn. "Just much smaller, with bigger eyes. You've heard of evolution, haven't you? Creatures changing to adapt to their environment?"

"I guess so," said Shad.

Varn reached into his sack and fished around. "Some scientists think the Peeple changed over hundreds of thousands of years, becoming the meemees."

Shad let loose a sharp crow of laughter. "The same scientists who think the *Ch'Kaw* evolved from *birds*?"

"Don't laugh. There's plenty of evidence down there." Varn pointed his beak at the ground.

"Whatever." Shad shrugged. "It doesn't matter what came first, as long as we're the ones doing the killing."

"Indeed." Varn pulled a crescent-shaped metal object from the sack and put it down with a clank. "And this will do the job nicely, friend."

Shad recognized the object as a spring-loaded foot trap. He hadn't thought to bring one himself; he hadn't thought he'd need anything other than a couple of cage traps.

"Let's get this loaded." Varn opened the trap wide on the pavement and locked it by turning a key on its base. Gingerly, he lowered the black artifact inside, placing it on a pressure-sensitive metal plate. Then, he withdrew his claw and turned the key to unlock the trap. "Now, all we have to do is wait."

Shad frowned and twitched his head. "I don't understand how this bait will lure them in. What kind of artifact *is* it?"

Varn chuckled as he got to his feet. "If translations of the ancient texts are correct, Peeple called it a 'fone.' Some kind of communication device, apparently."

"They can use it to communicate?"

"Heavens no." Varn chuckled again. "It doesn't *work*. But they won't be able to keep their hands off it." He shrugged. "That's the theory, anyway."

"What if they don't *take* the bait?"

Varn shook his burlap sack, making the contents clank and jingle. "We've got lots more where *that* came from."

By the time Varn had finished setting traps, the back parking lot was a kill zone for meemees. There were four traps around the trash pile, two up against the back wall of the restaurant, and six more ringing the edge of the lot.

To keep unwitting customers from getting hurt, Shad blocked off the back lot with yellow traffic cones. He also closed the area to all employees, though he knew he couldn't keep it that way for long.

Then, he and Varn pitched a black tent in the middle of the lot and waited inside, watching the traps through peepholes in the canvas.

"So," said Varn. "What made you want to get into the exterminator business?"

"Time for a career change, I guess." Shad squinted through one peephole, then moved on to the next. So far, he could see no action along the trap line.

"A change from what kind of career?" pressed Varn. "What did you do before this?"

Shad grunted. How many awful conversations had started with the same or similar words? He hated the thought of another--but lying his way out of it never seemed to be the answer. Sooner or later, the truth always caught up with him.

"A cockfighter," he said finally. "I was a cockfighter before this."

"Pro?" asked Varn.

"Yes," said Shad. "I was on the pro circuit."

"And your name is?"

"Shad Lum Lugo. But my pro name was Slaughterbeak."

"Slaughterbeak, huh?" Varn flashed him a look, then went back to staring out a peephole. "When was your last fight?"

"Six months ago," said Shad. "Against the Crimson Spurslasher."

"Sounds like quite an opponent," said Varn. "So why did you quit the fight game?"

Maybe now was the time for a lie or two. "I wanted to quit while I was still on top...and still in one piece." Shad didn't mention that he'd been forced out; why bring it up if the old rooster didn't know the story?

Luckily, Varn didn't seem to pick up on the fib. "Sounds like a smart move, friend. You saved your own skin and cleared the way for new talent in the bargain, didn't you?"

Shad moved to another peephole. "You read my mind, Varn."

Varn started to say something, then stopped and leaned closer to his own peephole. "Here we go now. Vermin on the march, Slaughterbeak."

Shad darted over to a peephole on the same side of the tent as Varn's. Sure enough, three meemees had scampered out of the brush and were approaching the traps by the garbage pile.

"Watch this." Varn chuckled. "Little buggers won't be able to resist the bait we put out."

At first, it looked like he'd be right. The meemees--a black-furred male, a blonde female, and a red-furred male child--went straight to the trap with the fone and circled it several times.

But they didn't take the bait. Instead, they moved on to the next trap.

"Don't worry," said Varn. "They're as good as dead."

The next trap was baited with a stack of what Varn had called "credicards"--thin pieces of plastic that had once been used for financial transactions. That was the theory, anyway.

The meemees crept around the spring-loaded trap, eyes fixed on the stack of cards. They sniffed at them, taking the scent from beyond the trap's reach. They gestured and babbled to each other...but they never made a move to enter the trap. And then they moved on.

Varn clucked angrily. "Come on, come on." He ruffled his sparse gray feathers and rapped the pavement with his cane. "I *know* they can't pass up the *next* bait."

The third trap held a gleaming bar of solid gold. As with the first two traps, the meemees circled around it, staring and sniff-ing--and then they stopped. The adults stood straight, cupped their furry hands around their mouths, and cried out.

"*Mee mee mee mee!*" Small as they were, their voices carried well across the parking lot and beyond. "*Mee mee mee mee mee!*"

"What are they doing?" said Shad.

Just as the words left his mouth, a horde of meemees poured out of the jungle and swarmed the parking lot. There were dozens of them, and they weren't empty-handed.

Every last meemee of every age, size, and fur color was carrying a rock or a stick.

Shad sucked in his breath. Were the rocks and sticks meant to be used as tools or weapons?

The answer was "tools." As the meemees charged out of the jungle brush, they used the rocks and sticks to trigger the traps. When the traps sprung, the bait was ejected, clattering to the pavement.

Instantly, the meemees scooped up the bait and dashed away on their tiny, furry feet. They scattered in all directions, carrying off fones and credicards, gold bars and carkees and wristclocks. As they ran, the air was filled with their high-pitched cries. "*Mee mee mee mee mee mee mee!*"

Shad hissed a curse and bolted out of the tent. He grabbed the pistol from the holster at his waist and waved it around, trying to pick a target...but it wasn't easy. He'd never seen so many meemees in one place before, and they were all moving fast. Carefully drawing a bead on one was out of the question. Better to shoot randomly into the herd; he was bound to hit something that way.

But just as he had that thought, something locked up inside him. Instead of pouring bullets into warm meemee bodies, he froze as the creatures scampered away from him.

"What the hell?" Just then, Varn lurched out of the tent. "Shoot! They're getting away!"

Shad thought fast. "Not yet! This is our chance!"

"Chance for what, you chickenshit?"

"To follow them," said Shad. "To find their nest. Then we can stop them once and for all."

"Not a bad idea." Varn bobbed his head and managed a hoarse

crow. "Let's turn their home sweet home into the world's biggest meemee burial ground."

SHAD AND VARN left the restaurant behind and followed the meemees into the jungle. Shad stayed out ahead--he had to, to keep the meemees in sight--but he tried not to lose the slower-moving old-timer in the process.

The mid-day heat was high, the humidity thick as soup all around, but Shad didn't mind. He lived for warmth and sunlight; he'd always been a hot-blooded type...and not just when it came to climate. He loved the heat that came with action and excitement, too, the way it got his blood pumping harder and made him feel truly alive. It was what he'd loved most about his cockfighting days, even after he'd lost his edge.

Not that he'd see much action if the meemees got away...which they might. Hanging back because of Varn, Shad could just make out the tops of some of the creatures' furry heads in the distant brush. If the meemees managed to get much further away, he would lose them altogether.

Though, truth be told, he wasn't confident of succeeding in his mission even if he did catch up to them. Fear coiled in the back of his mind like a snake...fear that he'd blow this hunt the same way he'd blown his cockfighting career.

And for the same reason, too.

"Hold up!" Varn's voice rang out from far behind--much farther behind than Shad would have expected. "Slow down a little!"

It was the exact opposite of what Shad wanted to do, but losing the old rooster might not help his cause. Grudgingly, he stopped and waited, watching the far-off heads of the meemees get even farther off.

"Thanks." Varn was out of breath as he hobbled up through the brush. "I guess...I can't run...through the jungle...like I used to."

"No problem." Shad kept watching the meemees, who were almost out of sight. "But we've got to keep moving."

Varn nodded and sighed. "I will, I will."

"We're losing them!" Shad couldn't see the meemees anymore, just the brush rustling in their wake.

"So follow...their tracks." Varn poked Shad's side with his cane to get his attention, then jabbed the cane at the ground.

Sure enough, the jungle mud was full of tiny footprints. Shad recognized them instantly as meemee tracks: each had five toes joined to an oblong foot, concave on the inside, deeper at the ball and heel.

"See?" Varn cluck-chuckled. "As long as we still have daylight, we can follow the trail."

"Good." Shad nodded with quick flicks of his head. "But let's keep up the best we can anyway. These things can be damned tricky."

"Their ancestors ruled the world for thousands of years," said Varn. "I guess some of that had to stay with them."

TIME PASSED, and Shad and Varn kept moving. There was always plenty of fresh trail to follow--tiny prints and occasional droppings in the mud. Once in a while, Shad even glimpsed rippling brush or a furry scalp in the distance. Sometimes, he heard faint "*mee mee mee*" cries piping through the jungle greenery.

But he didn't let it make him hurry. He maintained a slow and steady pace, which Varn seemed to appreciate.

Instead of gasping for breath, the old-timer was able to carry on a conversation as he hiked...though Shad only half listened to what he was saying.

"It's funny what evolution can do." Varn said it as Shad helped him across a stream. "The rulers of the world, the Peeple, become the humble little meemees, scavenging to survive and running for their lives."

"If you say so." Shad tested a rock in the middle of the stream, decided it was steady, and put his full weight on it. Then, he pulled Varn after him and stepped from the rock to the bank.

"The Peeple had a theory, too, you know," said Varn. "They believed that millions of years before Peeple came along, the world was ruled by giant beasts called 'dinosaurs.' What do you suppose became of them?"

Shad was more interested in pulling Varn to the bank and picking up the meemees' trail, which he was having trouble finding. "Killed off by the Peeple?"

"Not at all, friend. The People believed that the dinosaurs *evolved.* Over millions and millions of years, they shrank and became *birds*. But here's the most interesting part."

"I'm listening," said Shad as he walked along the bank with his head bobbing low, looking for tracks in the mud.

"According to *modern* scientists, certain birds evolved into *us*." Varn sounded excited. "Birds, descended from the dinosaur rulers of the world, again became the rulers of the world as the *Ch'Kaw*. And the Peeple shrank and became the tiny, pesky meemees. What goes around, comes around, eh?"

"Ah-ha!" Shad let out a crow of victory. The meemees must have waded downstream a few yards before leaving the water...but he'd found their fresh tracks anyway, stamped in the muddy bank and trailing off into the brush.

"Kind of makes you wonder what's next," said Varn, lingering along the stream for a moment before realizing he was alone and hobbling off to catch up with Shad.

A LITTLE FURTHER ALONG, the meemee tracks led Shad to a clearing, about twenty yards across. He paused at the edge of it, looking around at the mat of flattened grass spanning the open space.

Suddenly, he heard familiar, high-pitched cries piping up. "*Mee mee mee mee mee*!" Six meemees leaped out from behind bushes and tree trunks on the opposite side, waving fones and credicards and carkees.

"Damned things." Glancing over his shoulder, he saw Varn draw up behind him. "I'll be right back."

Varn bobbed his head, looking confused. "But I..."

Shad didn't wait for him to finish his sentence. Grabbing his pistol from the holster, he charged into the clearing, eyes fixed on the screeching meemees.

Adrenaline burned through his arteries, and his heart hammered as he ran. The meemees hopped up and down and waved their toys, egging him on with their screeches. Clearly, they wanted him to keep charging straight for them.

But why? Why the hell would they want that?

Suddenly suspicious, Shad slowed near the middle of the clearing...and the ground gave way under his right foot. He stopped just in time, stumbling back as the mat of flattened grass dropped away in front of him, revealing a gaping pit.

Crowing with alarm, he staggered back. One step further forward, and he would've plunged right into the hole.

"*Mee mee mee mee mee*!" On the far side of the clearing, the meemees were jumping around like maniacs. Their screeches were shrill with rage; they hurled their toys at Shad and hurled globs of feces to go with them.

Steadying himself, Shad swung up the pistol and pointed it in the meemees' direction. When one of their fones bounced off his chest, he cocked the gun and got ready to fire.

One of the meemees, a silver-haired male, was in Shad's sights. All he had to do was pull the trigger.

Which he did...but only after swinging the pistol to point straight up in the air, leaving the meemees unharmed.

Angry screeches changing to frightened ones, the meemees bolted off into the dense brush. They were gone in a flurry of foliage, leaving Shad standing alone in the clearing.

"What the hell?" Easing up to the edge of the pit, he saw it was at least twelve feet to the bottom--deep enough to contain him. "They tried to *trap* me?"

Varn limped up beside him. "Sure looks that way, friend."

"But meemees don't *do* that," said Shad. "They don't *do* that to *Ch'Kaw*."

"They do now."

Shad gaped at the fluttering brush in the distance. "But they're not that *smart*, are they?"

"Like I told you." Varn patted his shoulder. "Used to rule the *planet*, friend."

AFTER THE INCIDENT in the clearing, Shad and Varn continued onward, following the meemees' tracks.

Shad moved more cautiously now, worried that the meemees might try something else. It didn't seem likely, but their first attempt at trapping him hadn't seemed likely, either.

One question stuck in his mind: If the meemees were smart enough to dig a hole, cover it over, and lure him into it, what else might they be capable of?

At least he wasn't tracking them alone--though Varn seemed more concerned about Shad than he was about the meemees.

"Why carry that gun?" asked Varn as they worked their way up a hill. "You haven't used it much, have you?"

Shad jerked his head around, comb and wattles quivering, and glared at him. "I've used it *plenty*."

"You're good at waving it around, all right." Varn grunted as he pushed off with his cane, taking another step up the hillside. "Good at shooting it straight up in the air, too. But I have yet to see you nail a meemee with that sidearm of yours."

"Haven't seen *you* get one, either," snarled Shad. "What happened to those scientifically-developed tactics you were running your mouth about?"

Varn ignored the remark. "What's your malfunction, friend? Are you gun-shy in general, or just when it comes to shooting meemees?"

Shad whirled and lunged, ending up beak-to-beak with Varn--but the old-timer didn't back down. He just kept looking at Shad expectantly.

For a moment, Shad was seized by the urge to attack, to give Varn an old-fashioned peck-down straight out of the cockfighting ring. But then he remembered how he'd changed since his days in the fight game; a single flash of anger couldn't undo all that.

Which was kind of the old-timer's point. Shad wasn't the same rooster he'd once been.

As the anger drained out of him, Shad bobbed his head and backed away. "One of the reasons I'm doing this," he said, "is to fire up my killer instinct again."

"So *that's* why you left cockfighting." Varn nodded. "You lost your *bloodlust*."

"It's still there." Shad glared at him with one baleful brown eye. "It just needs a jump-start."

"But the meemees aren't doing it for you, are they?" Varn twitched his head from side to side. "Why is that?"

Shad's impulse was to deny there was any problem at all...but he fell silent instead.

"They're filthy, disease-ridden pests," said Varn. "Why hold back from blowing them away whenever possible?"

Shad opened his beak to speak...but before he could say anything, he was distracted by a familiar cry in the distance.

"*Mee mee mee mee mee mee mee*!"

The sound was coming from up the hill. Looking toward it, Shad saw twelve meemees on the crest of the hill, silhouetted against the deep blue afternoon sky.

Feeling compelled to prove himself, Shad let out a wild crow and charged toward the row of meemees. He heard Varn shouting something behind him, but he couldn't make it out and didn't care. It was time to blow through the barriers holding him back; it was time to kill some damned meemees.

As he ran closer, the meemees grew more agitated. They threw fones and gold bars and artifacts he didn't recognize, pitching them in his direction with frenzied shrieks.

Shad just kept charging. He drew his pistol and cocked the hammer, determined to plug all twelve meemees if he could.

Then, he felt something snap against his ankle--something like a stiff vine...or a wire. Stopping in his tracks, he spotted a sudden blur of movement from the corner of his eye and looked left. That was when he saw a huge object hurtling toward him, coming in fast.

Instinctively, he threw himself down. He hit the ground just in time as the flying object swooped over him, so close it buzzed off a few feathers, and kept going.

Looking up in its wake, Shad saw what it was: a log, suspended in some kind of harness, swinging between the trees. If it had hit him, he had no doubt it would have killed him.

He must have triggered it when he stepped through the wire.

It could not have been a coincidence that the meemees had been egging him on in that direction.

They had set a second trap. And this time, they had come even closer to killing him.

Shad and Varn continued onward, following the trail more cautiously than ever. As they forged ahead, the sun moved lower in the sky, shifting the day ever closer to evening.

"We're running out of daylight," said Shad as he ducked under low-hanging vines in an especially dense patch of jungle. "Maybe we ought to turn around."

Varn shot off a little crow of contempt. "Typical. This is just like your last match against the Crimson Spurslasher back in '27."

Shad's head pivoted to fix the old-timer in a stunned glare. "I thought you didn't know who I was before today! I thought you hadn't followed my career!"

"I never said that." Varn shrugged. "Who *hasn't* heard the story of *Slaughterbeak*? You were one of the all-time *greats* until you started *choking* and got put out to *pasture*."

Shad felt betrayed. The old-timer didn't sound much like a friend anymore. "Shut your beak. You don't know anything about that world." Turning to face forward, he resumed pushing through the vines and brush.

Varn laughed. "I know more than you think!"

Shad's blood was boiling as he thrashed his way through a tangle of leafy vines. When he'd cleared them, he found himself gazing at a strange sight.

Some kind of structure lay before him, a waist-high white altar rising from the jungle floor. It looked as if it were built from thousands of white pieces--some curved, some jagged, some knobby, some flat. The closer he looked, the more clearly it came into focus, and he realized what exactly the pieces were.

Bones. They were bones.

Shad twitched and shuddered. "Time to turn around."

But when he took a step back, he bumped into Varn. "That would be rude, friend." Varn cluck-chuckled and nudged Shad forward with the tip of his cane. "They've been expecting us."

Just then, Shad heard rustling sounds from the brush. A familiar call, faint at first, drifted up all around him.

"*Mee mee mee mee mee mee mee*."

"Expecting us?" Shad's voice had a nervous hitch to it. "What makes you think that?"

Varn leaned up close to Shad and whispered in his ear. "Because I told them we were coming. I told them I was going to introduce them to my son's very special friend who was dying to meet them."

Shad swallowed hard. Reaching down, he slid his pistol from its holster. "Who's your son?"

Varn leaned even closer and hissed his next words. "The *Crimson Spurslasher*. Remember him?" He gave Shad a sharp peck on the back of the head. "You know what happens when you refuse to administer the kill shot to an opponent in the ring, don't you? The way you refused to kill the Crimson Spurslasher in the last bout of your career?"

Shad tightened his grip on the pistol in his left claw. "Disgrace."

"For starters," said Varn. "The loser left alive is seen as a failure and coward who ought to be dead. No one will fight him, because the only thing more disgraceful than being spared in the ring would be *losing* to someone who's been spared."

As Varn continued his story, the meemees' voices grew louder. Shad felt as if a huge door was closing behind him, and he didn't have long before it slammed shut for good.

"The disgraced fighter loses everything," said Varn. "He becomes a *laughingstock* and a *pariah*. More often than not, he is driven to take his own *life*...as indeed the Crimson Spurslasher did. And even then, his *family* knows no *peace*. All because of one act of *cowardice* by a gutless *cock* like *you*." Lunging forward, he pecked at the back of Shad's head with angry force.

Crowing with rage, Shad leaped away from him. The move took him close enough to the altar that he could make out what kind of bones had gone into its construction.

Ch'Kaw bones. Every bone he could see had come straight out of a dead Ch'Kaw.

Suddenly, the calls of the meemees got louder than ever. So did the rustling of the brush. All at once, the jungle parted, and hundreds of meemees poured forth.

This time, they weren't carrying fones, credicards, carkees, and the like. Some had rocks, and others had sharp sticks. As they closed in around Shad, he could see other objects scattered throughout the crowd--knives of all sizes clutched in tiny, furry hands, looking much too big for the little creatures who carried them.

Shad turned in a circle, scanning the crowd for a thin spot where he might break through. From what he could see, there was no such spot; if anything, the crowd kept expanding on all sides as more meemees ran in from the jungle.

"Here's where my scientifically-developed tactics come in," said Varn. "I haven't learned how to *kill* the meemees, but to *communicate* with them. And guess what?" He crowed with delight. "We found *common ground*."

Shad raised the pistol and pointed it at the crowd. Just then, the meemees started pelting him with a flurry of rocks.

"We both hate *chickens*!" said Varn, and then he roared with clucking laughter.

The flurry of rocks became a torrent, bombarding Shad from

all sides. Sharp sticks hurtled among the rocks, piercing his skin like tiny spears.

Shad's clawed finger remained curled around the trigger of his pistol. He meant to fire, knowing full well it might be his best chance at survival...yet he still hesitated.

"Stop it!" He released a furious crow, the kind that had once terrified opponents in the ring--but the meemees kept attacking. "Get away from me!"

A big rock hit him on the back of the head, stunning him on impact. He wobbled, waving the gun one way and then the other, but his vision clouded, and he couldn't pick a target.

Then, a moment of clarity washed over him. He steadied, and his vision cleared. A black-furred meemee came into focus, gazing up at him with big, dark eyes.

Shad intended to kill it. Clenching his beak in concentration, he fixed the meemee in his gunsight. He steeled himself to murder that creature, hoping that one death might be enough to give the other meemees pause.

But at the last instant, he swung the gun up and fired at the treetops instead.

Why? That was what he thought as the crowd rushed in and brought him down with rocks and sticks and tiny, furry hands. *Why can't I bring myself to kill them?*

Shad swatted and struggled, but the meemees overwhelmed him. They bashed and stabbed him with their weapons and pinned him to the muddy ground.

Then, the meemees with knives leaped into the heart of the fray. Shad thrashed when he felt their cold blades slice into his throat, but he couldn't dislodge them. They just kept cutting and hacking, and he screamed the whole time.

Until they severed his windpipe, that is.

When they broke through his spine and lifted his head away

from his body, Shad had the strangest sense of freedom. Ch'Kaw couldn't fly, but he felt at first as if indeed he were taking flight.

The meemees carried him up onto the altar. Peering over the edge, he could see his headless body on the ground--and then it broke free of the meemees pinning it down. Jumping up, the body raced in circles around the altar, knocking meemees out of the way of its headless, mindless charge.

But eventually, the meemees brought it back down. They flung it on its back on the bone altar and pinned it there with the force of numbers.

Next, the meemees with the knives climbed up onto its chest and started cutting. They opened up the sternum and hacked out the V-shaped bone from the middle of the rib cage.

Then, as the mob chanted in unison...

"*Mee mee mee mee mee mee mee*!"

...two meemee males, both red-furred, took hold of the bone, one gripping each slender stem...

"*Mee mee mee mee mee mee mee*!"

...and they snapped it, breaking it into two uneven pieces...

"*Mee mee mee mee mee mee mee*!"

...and the one with the longer piece cheered, waving his piece of the bone in the air for all to see.

And that was when Shad faded, sliding away from the jungle and into somewhere else...taking only one thought with him on the journey. A question.

"*Why can't I bring myself to kill them*?"

"Tell me a story about the meemees, Mommy."

When Shad opened his eyes again, he was six weeks old--a tiny peep covered in yellow fuzz, hunkered down in the straw of his family's coop.

"If you insist." His mother sat in front of him, squatting on a clutch of eggs that had yet to hatch. Her pale feathers glowed in the bright moonlight streaming through the windows. "This one is called 'The Meemees and the Brave Little Peep.'"

Shad bounced in the straw and chirped with delight. His mother told him meemee stories every night; he could listen to them forever...or at least until he drifted off to sleep.

Shad's mother cleared her throat. "Once upon a time, there was a little peep who was afraid of the dark." She didn't need to read from a book; she knew all the stories by heart. "When clouds hid the moon, turning his room from bright to dark, he became very scared."

"What was the little peep's name?" asked Shad. "Was it the same as mine?"

"Yes, it was," said Mommy. "And little Shad shivered in the straw, unable to fall asleep. What if it was never light again?"

Shad listened with eyes wide and tiny heart racing. He knew exactly how the Shad in the story felt.

"Then, one night, three visitors flew in through the window." Mommy bobbed her head happily. "They were magical creatures, not much bigger than Shad was. Each had two arms, two legs, and two graceful gossamer wings like the wings of a butterfly. One was covered in red fur, one was covered in blond fur, and the other had jet black fur from head to toe."

"*Meemees*!" Shad let loose a high-pitched, chirping crow of excitement.

Mommy cocked her head to one side. "Very *special* meemees. *Meemee fairies*. The kind that flutter in through the window when little peeps are afraid of the dark. The kind that *light up* from inside with a soft, blue glow that comes straight from the love in their hearts."

"They *glow*?" said Shad.

"And the light from their hearts helps little peeps not be afraid of the dark anymore." Mommy let out a string of soft, loving clucks. "That's exactly what they did for little Shad that night. They flew around and played with him for hours, laughing and glowing in the darkness that wasn't so dark anymore."

"Then what happened?" said Shad.

LONG AFTER MOMMY had fallen asleep, Shad thought about the story she'd told him. It was his new favorite; he couldn't get it out of his head.

Eventually, he began to drift off. As he floated in the twilight gulf between consciousness and sleep, dreams mixed with reality in his young mind.

That was when he saw them, just as his mother had described. Three meemees fluttered in on gossamer wings, each one glowing with magic.

He giggled as they circled around him. They waved and beamed down at him with loving smiles, radiating warmth. They told him, without saying a word, that he had nothing to fear.

They played and frolicked there for hours, or what seemed like hours to a half-dreaming peep. They swooped low and tickled his belly, making him wriggle and twitter. They lifted him up in the air and danced with him, swinging him around with the greatest of ease.

Shad crowed and laughed until it hurt. Somehow, all the commotion never woke his mother on her clutch of eggs.

Then, the meemees joined hands around him in midair. He stayed aloft by flapping his fuzzy arms, hovering high above the straw in one glittering moonbeam.

At the end of Mommy's story, little Shad had become an honorary meemee. The same thing happened again, to the little Shad who'd listened to the story.

Glowing more brightly than ever, the meemees turned in a slow circle around Shad. Without saying a word, they swore him in as an honorary member of their order for life.

When they were done, Shad glowed as brightly as the meemees. From that moment on, some part of him would always be a part of them. Even if he forgot in the crush of a lifetime, in the blood and pain and strife of days heaped upon each other like logs on a bonfire, that night would leave its mark.

And one day, the story and dream might come back to him in full, swiveling out of the darkness like glowing winged meemees racing toward the moon in the last precious moments before the horizon swallows it up.

THE MAN IN THE SCI FI SUIT

The giant cyborg chipmunk is just drawing down on his victim, the purple squid-cow hero Heiferclese, when a beautiful, red-haired woman runs between them over the glassy ground, waving her arms.

Enter Varla Finlay Dios, creatrix of this particular eddy of Fictasia. The place is a vast desert landscape studded with rocky outcroppings (and glassy dunes instead of sand) under deep blue cloudless skies. The time is somewhere in the inconceivably distant future, when reality and story have become one and the same in vast swaths of the cosmos. Thanks to trans-quantum computing and matter-energy manipulation, technologies so advanced they might as well be magic to us, works of the imagination are easily written into the "code" of the preexisting physical universe. It isn't always clear what's "real" and what's "fictional" in Fictasia, but it doesn't matter much when it's all so interesting.

In this age, the most inventive creators and creatrixes, like Varla, command the greatest devotion from fans. Their particular storytelling streams, like the one where Heiferclese heroically battles a cyborg chipmunk, attract trillions upon trillions of viewers.

"Stop! Gah! Please!" Varla's skintight holodress, composed solely of coherent silver light (or the idea of such light, at least), pulses as she shouts at the chipmunk. "This doesn't work, either! *None* of it does!"

The chipmunk, whose given name is El Scaldo, lowers his death-ray-equipped left arm and shrugs. "Tell it to the author, lady!" His voice is as deep as a tuba solo.

Varla, who as creatrix *is* the author of this little scene, blasts a scowl the size and average temperature of Texas at El Scaldo's fuzzy kisser. *Not amused.*

Then, with a flutter of her long fingers with their ornate silver-circuited nails, she changes El Scaldo from a cyborg chipmunk to a six-foot-tall pink lizard sweating some kind of musky orange milk.

"My people, the *Sussssaxxx,* shall overturn the game board and *dessstroy* thossse laying the oddssss!" Lizard Scaldo's long, forked tongue flickers as he speaks. "We represssent the animal back-brain that can *never* be tamed."

Varla shakes her head and waggles her fingers again. Lizard El Scaldo becomes manatee El Scaldo.

"We, the Wim, bring tidings of peace and a new way *beyond* the Great Game." His whiskers twitch, and his muzzle curls in a kind of roly-poly smile.

"Shit! No!" Again, Varla gestures. This time, El Scaldo becomes a three-inch-long shrimp with tiny fairy wings and darts away on the hot desert breeze.

With a cry of disgust and frustration, Varla plunges her head into her hands. Heiferclese takes the opportunity to slink away, dragging her squid-tentacled bottom over the glassy smooth ground.

"Garbage! I should *scrap* it! Scrap it *all!*" Varla hates the thought of throwing out three months of work, but she's getting closer to doing it by the minute. The ending of *The Universal Fix* remains elusive; the harder she tries to finish the book, the worse every option she considers seems to be.

How's a writer supposed to keep from getting knocked off the Cosmic Midlist (a ranking that gauges the level of impact a story-reality has on the rest of Fictasia) with a creative block like this? Or worse, what if her rep takes such a hit that she gets sucked into someone else's story? And not a *good* one, either?

That's life in Fictasia, kiddies. One unappealing mash-up of story and reality, and trillions of fans will flee your once-best-selling stream. Once they're gone, it can be a nightmare getting them back--and once they're gone for good, your career is over. When that happens, when you cease to be relevant, you can be fictionalized and marginalized all at once, doomed to straggle on as an unmemorable supporting character with no hope of ever creating anything important again.

Dwelling too long on such consequences must be avoided at all costs. Creative types like Varla just go right on doing what they've always done, whipping up tall tales...when they can come up with a decent ending, that is.

"What now?" Varla's chin ends in a gently rounded point, and she rubs it roughly. "Damn!"

"You rang?" says a male voice from somewhere behind her, instantly recognizable as neither Heiferclese nor fairy shrimp.

Varla whirls and sees him walking toward her over the glassy plain. Her first impression is of a long, smooth face and slender build, lean and lanky. Pale blue Cavanaugh hat with a high crown and a wide, striped band, cocked slightly to the left. And a pale blue single-breasted suit woven with blinking multi-colored lights from shoulders to ankles.

He ambles over and sticks out a long-fingered hand. "Name's

Damn." He grins, equal parts friendly and open to all possibilities. "Damn Pickett. I'm a tale-twister."

"An alterationist?" Varla shakes his hand, firm and warm. "Who sent you?"

"No one but the breeze." His eyes twinkle when he winks. "Just passin' through."

Varla lets go of his hand. "Uh-huh." She looks suspicious.

Damn removes his hat in a graceful gesture, cupping the point of the crown between his first and middle fingers. The hair on his head is dark brown, short, and neatly combed. "I wonder if you might point me to a tale in progress, ma'am?"

"You're *standing* in one." Varla laughs bitterly. "If you can call it that."

Damn flicks dust off the brim of his hat. "In need of a little *tweak*, perhaps?"

Varla shakes her head. "You couldn't save it if you tried. I'm just getting ready to scrap it and start over."

Damn nods thoughtfully. "Maybe you should let *me* be the judge of that. They say I'm one of the best, you know."

"I'm not exactly an amateur myself." Varla folds her arms over her chest. "Ever hear of *Love of a Hundred Billion Neutrinos*?"

"Varla Finlay Dios." Damn nods. "You haven't published much recently, have you?"

Varla doesn't answer.

"I don't think I've read anything new from you since your husband, Wood, died," says Damn. "Or did he leave you?"

Varla claps her hands together, ending the line of questioning. "Oh well, back to work."

Damn puts his hat back on with a twirl of his fingers, then plants his hands on his hips and takes a long look around. "Tell me about this tale of yours."

Varla shakes her head. "I don't need an alterationist, Damn."

"Maybe so." The multicolored lights in his pale blue suit flash and dance as he reaches into the left hip pocket of his coat and pulls out a scale replica of a rocket ship. It's much bigger than the pocket, three feet and still coming, with gleaming silver skin, a lipstick-red nose, and matching fins. "Still, I've found one of *these* can be helpful from time to time."

Varla blows out her breath. "A one-size-fits-all plot device? Really?"

"You haven't experienced alterations before, have you?" He finishes pulling out the rocket and waves his hand over it. The silver skin shifts to bright yellow, and the whole rocket changes shape, becoming longer and skinnier. "I tailor to fit, see? It molds to match your story, and the story reshapes itself around it."

Damn lets go. The rocket spins upward, enlarging as it rises until it dwarfs the human figures below. Varla sees the faces of crew members peering back from portholes along the length of it.

In one of the portholes, she glimpses the face of Heiferclese, grinning and waving one purple tentacle with heartfelt delight.

"That's your solution?" She snorts. "Reach escape velocity and live happily ever after?"

"Or at least move the action to somewhere new." Damn lifts an eyebrow. "A change of scenery that brings new challenges and possibilities."

"Out of the blue?" says Varla. "Doesn't seem very *organic* now, does it?"

"How you figure?" asks Damn. "People do it all the time, by choice or by circumstance."

"There's nothing picaresque about *The Universal Fix*," says Varla. "The action alternates between three locations: the Mirror Desert of New Mexico, the Secret Casino under Antarctica, and the Palace of the Cosmic Oddsmakers in the Thickest Brane beyond the holographic bound. Not to mention...Heiferclese?" Varla wiggles her fingers at the rocket ship, which suddenly shrinks and whips away like a deflating balloon. "She's only a *supporting* character. Comic relief."

"So tell me more." Damn gestures with both hands as if he's waving for her to come closer. "Nutshell it for me."

"No!" She's indignant. "I already told you, I don't *need* an alterationist."

"Lots of people think that." Damn smirks. "Till they see what I can do."

"I doubt it, if a rocket ship's the best you have to offer."

"So get a load of this." The multicolored lights sewn into Damn's coat flicker and swirl as he pokes two fingers into his vest pocket. They emerge with a playing card between them--the ace of spades. "Works wonders in pretty much any tale, ma'am."

Damn flicks up the card for her to see. When he releases it, the card floats suspended in midair before him, slowly turning on its vertical axis like a revolving door.

"I call it the Big Scare Card." When Damn claps his hands, the card bursts into a puff of black smoke that swiftly expands into a cloud the size of a man. "Always good for changing the course of events and initiating significant growth in any character."

Damn takes a deep breath and blows. The puff instantly dissipates, revealing the skeletal figure of a Grim Reaper in an ebony robe, carrying a gleaming silver scythe.

"Death?" Varla yawns. "Gee, I hadn't thought of that."

"Then I guess you already know this is a creatrix's best friend." Damn hangs his hat on the blade of the scythe and throws his arm around the Reaper's shoulders. "You can never have too much death in a tale, can you?"

"The heroine of my novel, Sybil Pax, has already lost her lover and their child as part of the Great Game," explains Varla. "Those precipitating incidents give her the will to oppose the Oddsmakers. As she fights their plan to drive humanity to extinction as part of the ultimate betting scenario, she loses everyone else she cares about, which gives her the strength and fury to succeed. No other death is needed in this book."

"Except Sybil's, perhaps?" Damn cocks his left eyebrow. "What if she makes the ultimate sacrifice?"

"Completely invalidating the book's message about individual self-determination in the face of seemingly insurmountable predestination? Forget it. Now why don't you go find some poor kid struggling with her fan fiction and let me get back to the serious work?"

Damn kicks Death in the ass, and the Reaper disappears. "So this is all about chance and risk and destiny?" He catches his hat as it falls from the vanishing scythe and spins it back onto his head with a flourish. "Why didn't you say so?"

"Pretty obvious from the title, isn't it?" says Varla. "*The Universal Fix*. 'The fix is in,' as the gamblers say. As in the game is rigged. In this case, the Great Game of all existence, which is rigged by the Cosmic Oddsmakers."

"Then what you need is a change of luck." Damn reaches into his right pants pocket, setting his suit's lights to blinking and changing color. He comes up with two glowing dice and holds them out for her to see. "A twist of fate to shake things up."

"Seriously?" Varla chops her hand through the air dismissively. "Like I don't already *have* multiple lucky and unlucky breaks in this book?"

"But the right one at the right time..."

"Is *overkill* in this case." Varla's voice rises with annoyance.

"Hey, over-the-top can be a beautiful thing!" Damn blows on the dice and gives them a good shake in his cupped hand. "Come on, lucky seven!"

When he throws the dice, they instantly expand and whirl around each other in midair, tumbling with increasing speed. Within seconds, they're rolling so fast, they're a blur of motion, a vortex of bright white light and flickering black pips.

The dice race faster and faster in a dizzying Mobius pattern. Varla squints and raises an arm against the light as it gains intensity, building, building.

Then, the dice explode in a blinding blaze, a nova so bright it drowns everything in Varla's field of vision in one tremendous whiteout.

Moments later, she's still blinking away the clusters of spots left behind in her eyes. Also thinking about bringing harm to the tale-twister, if he has the temerity to still be standing there.

Which he does...but he's not the most interesting thing she sees at that moment. The Mirror Desert of her book is gone. Instead, she's standing in some kind of vast, formal garden blossoming with multicolored flowers of every variety she can imagine.

Varla's heart pounds as the import of the situation dawns on her. Her first thought is that she's been swept into someone else's sorry-ass story. If she can't find a way back to her personal eddy of Fictasia, she could end up written down, maybe even written *out*, with no hope of even a cameo in a future installment.

But her second thought, when she spies a familiar figure crossing a footbridge through the garden, is this: maybe it *isn't* someone else's story, after all. At least, not entirely.

Damn steps up beside her. "How's *that* for a twist of fate?"

"That's...me." Varla feels dazed. Her silver holodress pulses as she stares at the redheaded woman on the foot bridge. "What the hell, Damn?"

"It's a flashback, of course." He waves at the redhead on the bridge. "Five years ago in Fenimore Gardens, New Virginia. Don't tell me you've forgotten."

Varla is alarmed and confused. "*This* isn't Fenimore Gardens. It's nothing *like* that place."

Damn plugs his hands in his pockets and shrugs. "Chalk it up to dramatic license. Capturing the essence is more important than restating the exact details, isn't it?"

Varla's doppelganger finishes crossing the bridge and twirls around between descending boughs dripping with pink cherry blossoms. She giggles as the blossoms tickle her cheeks and shoulders, showering her with delicate petals shaken free of their perches.

"Send me back." Varla's voice is a low growl. Her holodress pulses faster. "Send me back *now*."

"Hold your horses," says Damn. "I told you, I'm going to help with that book of yours."

"*This* is supposed to help? Bringing a flashback of *me* into the story?"

"A little *meta* never hurt anybody," says Damn.

Varla glares at him. "This is a *storynapping,* isn't it? You've pulled me into someone else's plotline against my will."

"Not exactly." Damn tips his Cavanaugh forward and rubs the back of his neck. "Actually, this is all about *you*."

Varla thinks for a moment as her double settles onto a cement bench. A big monarch butterfly circles around her, then lands on her left knee.

"All about *me*?" In her anger, Varla lets her voice rise, but Other Varla doesn't seem to hear. "You mean a biography?" Her fists clench at her sides. "An *unauthorized* biography?"

"Listen." Damn locks eyes with her, looking serious. "You trust me, don't you?"

"*Absolutely not,*" says Varla.

"Then trust *her*." He points at Varla's double. "Trust *yourself*."

Just then, a new voice pipes up from across the garden--a man's voice, so instantly recognizable that it makes her ache.

"Hello, Varla," says the man.

The sound of her husband Wood's voice is so perfect, Varla

instinctively wants to answer. Damn has gotten that much right, anyway.

And he's done the same with the way Wood looks, from his curly black hair to his broad shoulders, slender trunk, and long legs. He even wears his favorite suit, a double-breasted number woven from pure story substance. Words and images dance over his body like the flickering celluloid of an ancient silent movie, rippling in an endless stream of dialogue, settings, conflicts, resolutions, and thematic elements.

As on most days, Wood's suit is composed of science fictional fabric, his favorite. Some threads present a retro view of tomorrows already come and gone; others display futures so far forward as to be barely comprehensible. The interplay of the two yields a matrix of imagination that's charged with nostalgia and future shock all at once.

Varla hasn't seen him in nearly five years, but it seems like it's been fewer than five minutes. She lost him long ago, yet it feels perfectly natural to see him close by. It makes perfect sense to her to run to him, embrace him, kiss him as if no time has passed at all.

But she doesn't do any of that, because Other Varla has already done it.

"You remember it well, don't you?" asks Damn. "Your last day together, wasn't it? Though you didn't know it at the time."

Is it normal to feel jealous of your other self? Varla does, as Other Varla kisses Wood passionately among the cherry blossoms. "It didn't happen like this. There wasn't a garden."

"Are you sure?" Damn points at her left chest, where her heart resides. "Not even *in there*?"

Varla scowls and keeps watching the kiss in the cherry blossom glade. Shafts of sunlight slip through the canopy around them, glowing brushstrokes surrounding the lovers in a cage of golden beams.

When husband and wife finally part, does Varla remember the next words they speak? Of course she does. She could recite them in her sleep, she thinks.

She *thinks.*

"My love." Wood's words come through as plain as day, though Varla and Damn stand some distance away. "I couldn't bear to be without you a chooga wooga woo. Caper contiguous yappa dapple prefix quimby nimby."

"You know I feel the same way," says other Varla. "Promise me you won't heebie jeebie Pleistocene ulcerate shooby dwooby."

Wood nods sincerely, holding her face in his hands. "Three five hexagon poultice, tapir."

Tipping her head to one side, she kisses his hand. "Silence silence silence static silence."

Modern-day Varla, watching from afar with Damn Pickett, frowns so hard, the creases in her face might well cut into the bone of her skull. "It's all gibberish!" She grabs Damn's shoulder and gives it a rough shake. "It doesn't make any sense!"

"Think of it as filler." Damn brushes her hand away. "Place-holder text."

"Is this some kind of joke? Some kind of absurd dada-esque nonsense you've hauled me into?"

"None of the above," says Damn. "It's all drawn from your memory--with alterations courtesy of yours truly--so I guess you must not remember the conversation as well as you thought." He raises his eyebrows. "Not that what they're saying matters at all. You need to focus on the visual. Look *closer.*" Damn jabs a finger at the couple across the way.

Irritated as hell, Varla only wants to get out and go home to her personal storystream...but her gaze zooms in on Wood and Other Varla anyway.

At first, nothing jumps out at her. She just sees the handsome, dark-haired man embracing her duplicate self in a bittersweet moment she longs to be a part of so badly it hurts.

But then, a moment passes, and she sees something else. Her attention is drawn to an image on Wood's back, part of his coat of sci fi colors.

Plain as day, she sees it. The face of a purple squid-cow, goofy grin and all.

Heiferclese?

"No." Her frown grows deeper still. "It can't be."

"What's that?" Damn asks calmly, completely unsurprised.

The image on the back of Wood's suit coat changes, becoming the cyborg chipmunk, El Scaldo. "Those characters. I created them later. They shouldn't be there...*couldn't* be there."

Again, the scene on the coat changes. This time, it makes her gasp.

"What?" asks Damn. "What is it?"

Varla's mouth opens, but no words come out at first.

"It's *me.*" Her voice finally shakes. "Me as I am *now...today.*"

Wood pulls Other Varla closer and goes in for a deep kiss. Her arms wrap around him, caressing his back, sliding through images of herself five years later as she conjures characters and incidents in the Mirror Desert.

The images show modern-day Varla in the midst of creating her latest novel, *The Universal Fix.* She weaves her hands through the air, and Heiferclese appears on the polished ground before her. She wiggles her fingers, and El Scaldo the cyborg chipmunk becomes El Scaldo the pink-skinned lizard.

Somehow, in the midst of a five-year-old flashback, Varla sees her latter-day self as she appeared that very morning.

"It's an anachronism," she says. "Current events would never appear on a sci fi story fabric suit five years ago."

"Why not?" Damn shrugs. "Science fiction predicts the future, doesn't it?"

As Varla watches, the scene on the coat continues to develop. She sees Damn approaching as he did not long ago, then pulling a rocket ship out of his pocket. "Is this some weak attempt at foreshadowing? Is that what this is all about?"

"More like an attempt at setting the record straight," says Damn. "How do *you* know what was on the back of his jacket at that particular moment? It was facing *away* from you."

"It doesn't matter." Varla dismisses his comments with a wave of her hand. "This isn't how it happened, anyway. This isn't *my* story."

"Sure it is," says Damn. "It's the only story you've ever known. The only one you've ever been a part of."

She shakes her head hard. Her holodress pulses faster than ever. "*Enough*. Send me home *now*."

"You *are* home." Damn puts a hand on her shoulder and steers her to keep watching the scenes on the suit coat. "Look, you'll see."

Varla sees herself watching as Damn conjures Death in the desert, then tumbling dice. There's a flash of light, and suddenly she's watching herself and Damn as they watch her other self in the garden.

The next thing she knows, she's watching herself in the flickering image watching herself in yet another image...and that self, in turn, is watching *another* image of herself. An infinite progression of nested Varlas and Damns fans onward, stretching forever into the celluloid expanse.

Then, all that collapses at once into something new. Varla sees an image of Wood standing in the Mirror Desert, weaving his arms in the air creator-style. A figure appears before him--a slender young woman in a skintight silver holodress. A woman who's the spitting image of Varla, except her hair is black instead of red.

Varla's dress stops pulsing. "What is this?" She's barely aware of the words as they leave her lips.

"Another flashback," says Damn. "Older than all the rest."

"I don't understand." Varla feels a little light-headed. "That looks like me, but..."

"You don't remember?" Damn smiles. "Makes sense, I suppose. Who remembers their own *birth*, anyway?"

Varla can't take her eyes off the images on the coat. Other Varla's caressing hands scroll through them, interrupting the scene in which Wood flickers his fingers, and black-haired Varla becomes blonde Varla.

"My...birth?" Current Varla is dazed. "You're trying to tell me I'm...I'm..."

"Fictional, yeah." Damn pats her on the back. "But I won't hold it against you."

Varla watches Wood gesture in the scene on the suit, sees her hair change from blonde to red...yet still she resists. "This is impossible. It's *bullshit.* It's just part of whatever story you've grafted me into."

"Not so," says Damn. "This is the same story you've *always* been part of. It's *your* story...and *his.*" He gestures at Wood, who's still deep in a kiss with Other Varla.

"No," snaps Varla. "I'm a *creatrix.*"

"Sure you are," says Damn. "In a *story.*"

Varla's head is swimming. The scene on Wood's back cuts from one incident to another, and she remembers them all in detail. There she is, relaxing in a rowboat on a glittering summer lake while Wood handles the oars. There she is again, standing on a high mountaintop with him, gazing out at a magnificent view of rugged snowcaps and verdant meadows. And there she is once more, slow-dancing with Wood on a back porch strung with strands of multicolored lights, surrounded by fireflies.

And there they are on a beach in Maui, getting married by a

smiling old minister wearing a lavender lei. Her breath catches at the sight of her lacy white wedding dress and veil--at the look on her face as she gazes at Wood on the most wonderful day of her life.

She sees herself honeymooning with him, making love in a tropical cove by a roaring surf. They move into a perfect little house in horse country in New Virginia, complete with white-fenced pastures and a stable of handsome ponies.

And they write stories and books together in their own little eddy of Fictasia. Sometimes, it's a lush forest alive with birdsong. Other times, it's a city or a village or a plain, a jungle or a desert.

Or a hospital room. Wood lies pale and shriveled in bed, surrounded by blinking monitors that display his fading vital signs. A techno-wizard in a white lab coat shakes his head and throws up his hands, unable to use the great science of the age to save this one little life. Varla sits by the bed, sobbing uncontrollably as she clutches the cooling hand of precious Wood, the irreplaceable man of her dreams.

Suddenly, he's gone, and she's alone. She stands in the middle of their favorite setting, the Mirror Desert, working on a book she can never seem to finish.

And the circle is complete.

"That's my *life*, not a story," she says softly, staring at the image of herself alone in the desert.

"It doesn't have to be one or the other," says Damn. "It doesn't matter."

"Then why show me all this? If it doesn't matter, why bother trying to convince me I'm fictional?"

"To help you finish your book," says Damn. "I'll help *any* creator, be they real or fictional or anything in between."

"I already told you, I don't *need* any help. I don't *want* it."

"Too late." Damn smiles. "I've already given it."

Across the garden, Other Varla and Wood break their kiss and wander off through the cherry blossoms, arm in arm. They laugh as they stroll among the sunbeams and hummingbirds, lost in a paradise all their own.

"He wrote you." Damn takes his hat off and holds it at his side. "He *created* you. Made you perfect in every way and fell in love with you.

"He entered your story, and you fell in love with him, too. You were married and lived in perfect happiness as partners and co-authors, because he designed you to be his equal in every way.

"But then, one day, he left you forever. He *died* in both the fictional and factual realities. And ever since, you've been struggling to finish the last book the two of you were writing together.

"But you've struggled long enough." Damn twirls his hat back onto his head and reaches into his right pants pocket. The lights in his suit flicker and pulse in all their rainbow colors. "It's time we got you back on track."

When he pulls his hand out and opens it, there's a six-inch-tall man standing on his palm. It's a tiny replica of Wood.

Immediately, little Wood starts to grow, and Damn pulls away his hand. As Wood's feet land on the ground, he shoots up to full height, taller than Varla or Damn.

"Hello, Varla." Wood steps toward her.

Varla is torn. Part of her still fears that she's been story-napped, and all of this is someone else's plotline.

But she can't deny that Damn's account of the truth behind her life is possible. And she also can't deny, in her heart, that the vision of Wood exerts a pull on her.

When he takes her hands in his, she doesn't break away. When he speaks, she listens attentively. She gives him his say.

"I'm so sorry," he tells her. "We never had the chance to say goodbye."

Varla's throat tightens. He's not the real Wood, but he *feels* like it. And his words have struck a nerve.

"You never got the closure you deserved," continues Wood. "You never got to move on.

"Well, it's time to move on now."

He stares deeply into her eyes and strokes the tops of her hands with his thumbs. "I love you, Varla. I will love you forever." He raises her hands and bends to kiss them softly--right, then left. Then he straightens, with a tear in each eye. "Goodbye now, my darling. It's finally time for you to let go."

Caught up in the moment, Varla feels tears in her eyes. She feels an ache in her belly and heart, a deep sense of long-awaited finality.

For the first time, she starts to think that Damn might be right about all this. It feels true, feels painful, feels *important*.

She knows he's watching her, off to the side. He's waiting, and so is Wood...waiting for her to come around.

Has she changed since Wood died? Even as her creativity got stuck in neutral, did the rest of her continue to evolve?

Maybe so. Because she realizes something as she stands there with Wood holding her hands while Damn looks on.

She doesn't want to give them the satisfaction.

"No." As she says it, she reverses Wood's grip and clamps his hands tightly in her own.

Wood frowns. "'No,' what?"

"No." She smiles fiercely. "I won't let you go."

Before anyone can say another word, she focuses all her creative energies, pouring every iota of strength through the instruments in her fingernails and elsewhere.

And the garden goes away.

VARLA AND WOOD dance across the glassy surface of the Mirror Desert, their feet moving in perfect time with the ballroom music of the full orchestra playing nearby.

As for Damn, he stands off to one side with his hands on his hips, frowning at the performance that started the instant they left the garden and arrived here. "This isn't exactly what I had in mind!" he shouts over the music.

"Too bad!" says Varla as she and Wood sail past.

"So sad!" chimes in Wood.

Damn shakes his head. "I thought maybe you'd get over your lost love and move on to finish *The Universal Fix* as a joint project."

"You were wrong!" Varla giggles as Wood spins her around. "That book is so *over.*"

"But the fans are dying to see it finished," says Damn. "They say it's an unfinished masterpiece."

"Maybe they'll like my new novel, instead," says Varla. "The first in a series!"

"Starring me!" says Wood. "Starring both of us!"

"I'm writing myself in," says Varla. "Because I *can!*"

Damn frowns a moment more, then grins and shrugs. "Well, maybe you're right. 'The creation writes her creator.' I *do* kind of like it."

"Want me to write you in, too, Damn?" asks Varla.

Damn waves her off. "I'm needed elsewhere. So many tales to twist, so little time."

As he strolls off toward the horizon, whistling a tune, the ballroom music builds behind him. Varla and Wood swoop across the glass, never missing a beat or having a single hair flutter out of place.

She's still a little surprised at what she's done. After so long paralyzed by loss, unable to move forward without the guiding hand of her creator, what finally inspired her to take charge?

Was the suddenness of her change unrealistic, she wonders?

Or humanly impulsive? Was the newfound strength with which she broke free just a plot device without the ring of truth? Or the kind of power surge that happens all the time in flesh-and-blood people under great stress?

As far as any of that goes, is she as in control as she thinks at this point? Is this her story, unfolding according to her will? Or is it all part of *another* story, directed by unknown creators?

And does any of that matter? Two out of two characters in her new novel agree that it doesn't.

So she and Wood continue to spin joyfully as the music rises. When it finally hits a crescendo, the two of them leap into the air and spin in a perfect circle, beaming face to face with blissful adoration.

As their lips meet, the sky changes from deep blue to a beautiful sunset streaked with rose, orange, gold, and fiery crimson. The words "The End" fade into the foreground in bright yellow text, superimposed over the whole grand scene.

Then, the word "Never" appears above them, written in white script letters as if scrawled by some invisible hand.

WITH LOVE IN THEIR HEARTS

"I love you!" Hissing the words through the blood in my mouth, I lunge at my opponent. And I *mean* those words with all my heart--I *have* to--even as I swipe my dagger across his chest.

As he dances back out of reach, a line of red opens up where I cut him. His dirty, bearded face clouds...then quickly clears. "I love you *more!*" He smiles as he leaps at me with both fists forward, aiming them like a battering ram at my face.

Beaming with all the affection I can muster, all the true sweet regard for my friendly fellow man, I spin around out of his way and tag him again with the dagger, plugging the blade deep in his left kidney.

Howling, he stumbles into the thick-trunked oak that was just at my back. He takes it headfirst and bounces off, weaving drunkenly in the mud.

"Friend warrior." This is how I finish him, all sweetness and light. Without the *slightest* shred of darkness in my heart. "You are like unto the finest flower in the brightest sunbeam on the loveliest day in all the year." Darting to one side, I duck down and recover the sword I dropped earlier in this battle--dearest Eros. "God bless you for bringing such *joy* to my life."

With that, I swing the sword up, then down and through his neck with a perfect, practiced stroke.

So good am I at this that not a *trace* of hatred or savage satisfaction punctuates the moment when his head separates from his shoulders and plops into the muck.

Breathing hard, I scan my surroundings. I see the bodies of the three men I've killed, sprawled in various bloody contortions...and the body of Vicka, my partner on the road until now, whom they killed before I could kill them first.

That is what love can accomplish. Its power is arrayed around me for all to behold.

Moving swiftly lest another patrol comes my way too soon, I secure my beaten black body armor, then retrieve and put on my battered helmet with the old red-white-and-blue banner etched into the hard plastic. I retrieve my motorbike, too...but the front tire has been slashed, and it won't start. I guess I can't complain; it's over a century old, and I've gotten a lot of use out of it until now.

"Go with God, fair machine." I drop it in the muck, grab my dagger from the dead man's kidney, and set off at a brisk jog through the woods. The autumn sun is closing in on the horizon, and I need to make my destination by nightfall.

Everything is riding on the completion of my mission. All my people down in Burytown are counting on me to succeed.

Though it is hard to imagine I *can* succeed this time. The killing of men and women has always come easy to me. It is *that* very inclination that could make this new mission such a challenge.

Heart pounding, I run through the mud, brush, and leaves, ever up along the steep contour of the mountainside. This part of what was once known as the state of Pennsylvania is full of such mountains--the *Alleghenies*, as we call them yet today. They have been my home for all five and twenty years of my life, and navigating them is second nature to me.

Reading the wind and the angle of the sun, I know I'm not far from my goal. In spite of the best efforts of my attackers, I will reach my destination, though what happens after that, I cannot say.

Finally, I burst from the woods and find myself at the edge of the old road. I also find myself face to face with two men in camouflage body armor, wielding six-guns.

Slowly, I take off the helmet. "Greetings to you both."

"Hail and well met, good stranger!" The one doing the talking has the biggest, friendliest smile...and the steadiest grip on his revolver. "State your name and purpose, that we may love you all the better!"

Instinctively, I meet his gaze with the most genuine grin I can muster. "I am Sir Gardner Schell of Burytown," I tell them. "I have come to meet my bride."

EXPECTED AS I AM, the sentinels holster their guns and lead me through the barricades blocking the road. On the other side, my destination awaits--a place I've only visited a handful of times, though Burytown lies but seven miles to the west of it.

The building looks for all the world like an old ocean liner (the kind I've seen only in photos), complete with decks, portholes, and a pair of big smokestacks on the roof, angled toward the stern. It is as if, by some miracle, a seagoing vessel has been stranded in the heights of a mountain range, along the curve of a once-great highway that has seen better days.

GRAND VIEW SHIP HOTEL. That's the old name of it, painted in big black letters on the side of the ship facing the road. *SEE 3 STATES AND 7 COUNTIES.* That's painted on the prow. Armor plating has been added all around, but those words out of history remain.

The *real* name, the one it's known by now, is not painted anywhere. But ask anyone within fifty miles of here if they know of Kendall's Keep, and they will point you right to it. Everyone who uses this stretch of road--known in olden times as the Highway of Lincoln--must pay a toll to Kendall's men to pass this point.

"What took you so long?" Lord Rubicon Kendall strides out of the keep in a white sea captain's uniform, looking hale and hearty and overly friendly. A sword hangs at either hip, plus a long rifle at his back, and rightly so; his clan is at war. "You were expected *this morning,* good sir knight."

"If not for the *second* ambush, I most certainly would have been here sooner. And Vicka, my late retainer, as well." I point at the path that I traveled up the slope. "The *Loved Ones* grow ever bolder, my Lord."

Rubicon grins through his neatly trimmed ebony mustache and goatee. "It is a delight we have in common, yes? Your people down in Burytown have been *especially* showered with their affections, have they not?"

"Such a blessing." I say it stiffly, though I manage a smile. The siege of Burytown is my whole reason for being here. An alliance with Rubicon's clan would give us the punch we need to break the siege and lay our friends the Loved Ones to rest for good.

Though such an alliance does not come without a price.

"I am in your hands, my Lord." I bow my head and spread my arms. "Assuming our pact yet stands."

"It does. My Lady Kendall, God rest her soul, had people in Burytown. I am only too happy to offer you this chance." He lays a hand on my shoulder. "*If* you are ready for the challenge, Sir Gardner."

"I would not be here if I were not."

"Well said." Rubicon nods sagely, peering into my eyes with the focus of a hawk. "And would you accept the guidance of an advisor in this quest of yours? He was of much help when *I* was in your shoes."

"Thank you, my Lord, but that won't be necessary."

Rubicon cocks his head to one side, looking amused. "May he provide a *benediction*, at least?"

Before I can answer, an old man rises on the main deck on the second level of the ship/keep and clears his throat. "Let us pray," he calls down to us. Like Rubicon, he wears a uniform, though the pieces don't go together well: white cap, black jacket, red ascot, lemon trousers.

Confidentially, Rubicon leans over and whispers to me. "Bon Cloister up there will perform the ceremony, you know. *If* there *is* one."

"In the century since the Great Collapse," says Cloister, "only *love* has sustained we few survivors. As this young knight stands on the precipice of the greatest struggle of all--holy wedlock--we pray that he may turn to *another* face of love and do what we all know he *must* do to succeed."

"Amen." Grinning, Rubicon smacks me on the back.

"Times a million," says Cloister as he digs out a pipe and lights it with a hellaciously long furnace match.

"HERE WE ARE." Rubicon leads me past armed guards into the keep, then down a short hallway. "Have a seat in the Coral Room, Sir Gardner."

We enter a room with turquoise walls and red-rimmed portholes. A polished wooden bar occupies most of one side, with a black-cushioned elbow-rest and pink-upholstered barstools with backs. Dusty glasses and bottles line shelves behind the bar, glinting in the last flickers of daylight slipping in from the windows in the dining room next-door.

I sit on a long red bench against the opposite wall. A knight must *never* sit with his back to the door, as I have learned the hard way.

Just then, I hear footsteps--hard shoes descending a staircase.

"Here she comes." Rubicon smiles and bounces on the balls of his feet. "Good luck to you." He winks and whispers that last.

My heart beats fast as the footsteps approach down the hallway. I have fought a thousand battles, but this is new ground for me.

"Sir Gardner." Rubicon steps aside and gestures at the doorway. "I introduce my daughter, Listy Kendall."

I rise as she enters the room. Never in my life have I seen anyone so *beautiful.*

Listy curtsies. "Sir Gardner." She is in her early 20s, with all the firmness of youth in her pale, porcelain skin. Loose, dark curls frame an oval face with lively eyes, delicate nose, and full red lips. I can see from the fall of her long, creamy gown that her body is perfectly sculpted, bust and hips swelling pleasingly above and below a slender waist.

I manage a bow, but words fail me. Entranced, I can but stare as she watches and waits, smiling.

Rubicon raises an eyebrow and gestures at the bar. "Perhaps you might like a drink, Sir Gardner?"

His question barely registers. I am spellbound.

"My father has pledged my hand to you, good knight," says Listy. "It might do us well to converse upon this betrothal, don't you think?"

Her voice, as soft and flowing as the song of a meadowlark, freezes me further. I am drawn to her, mesmerized as I have never been before--yet locked down as if shackled and gagged. A man of action I have always been, but now I am turned to stone.

And none of it makes any sense to me.

"Ha. I wondered if this might happen." Rubicon walks over and squeezes my shoulder. "Perhaps some time with Bon Cloister might not be a bad idea *after* all, sir knight."

FRESH AIR DOES me some good. As I stand at the railing of the keep's main deck and watch the sun set, my wits slowly return to me.

Without invitation, Bon Cloister shuffles over to stand beside me, lighting a fresh pipeful of tobacco. Up close, I see how withered he is, how ancient in his shabby hodge-podge uniform.

"What is the Story of Love, Sir Gardner?" He puffs twice on the pipe, then exhales sweet cherry-smelling smoke from his nose. "Tell me how love as we know it came to be."

Everyone knows this story, but I humor him. I'm embarrassed about what happened in the Coral Room and eager to make things right.

"One of the plagues of the Great Collapse in the 21st Century was *The Commandment*," I tell him. "Scientists unleashed a contagion to rewrite human DNA and bring about peace on Earth."

"How so?"

"People became physically unable to harm others out of hatred or anger. This was in fulfillment of Jesus Christ's commandment to love thy neighbor as thyself."

"Indeed." Smoke from Cloister's pipe drifts out over the vast landscape sprawling beyond the mountain. The setting sun casts blazing light over the acres of trees in their red, gold, and orange autumn finery. "And how did that work out when the *other* plagues struck, and civilization *collapsed?*"

"It made it nearly impossible to fight for survival."

Cloister smiles. "And so we learned to fight--to *kill* if need be--the only way we *could.* With *love* in our hearts." He pulls the pipe from his mouth. "And we got very *good* at it, didn't we? The love-that-kills?"

I nod.

"*But!*" Cloister jabs the pipe stem at me. "What happens when we get so *good* at it, we forget what it's like to feel the *love-that-cherishes*? For some, especially the more...*accomplished* warriors, like yourself...this can sometimes lead to profound...*disharmonies.*"

"The love-that-cherishes?" I scowl.

"Caring for someone so much that we *don't* want to damage or murder them," says Cloister. "Feeling an attraction so *real* and *profound* that we want to join with the other person in a multitude of ways."

The song of the katydids buzzing in the trees makes more sense to me than what he's saying. "Is that even possible?" I ask.

Cloister narrows his eyes. "Do you *want* it to be?"

I think of my people in Burytown, who are depending on me. I think also of that beautiful girl in the Coral Room, and the way she seemed to glow when I gazed at her. "Yes." I whisper the word. "But how?"

"Righteous discipline." Cloister clenches his right hand. "And self-control. You must reach deep within yourself and change the love-that-kills to the love-that-cherishes...but *only* for this one person, your bride. For all others, especially those who threaten kith or kin..." He unclenches his hand and draws the edge of it across his throat like the blade of a knife.

Frustrated, I close my eyes and clench my teeth. I feel like going over the rail and running off into the night with Eros in hand, ready to love all comers. That, at least, would not be like the great unknown I now face.

"So many feelings..." I grip the rail hard. "What if I can't *master* them, Bon?"

"Then your bargain with Lord Kendall will never be consummated." Cloister puts the pipe back in his mouth and puffs on it. "For neither he nor Listy herself shall brook a union where there is no *true* affection."

"Damn." I toss my head as if I'm trying to wake myself from a terrible dream. "I don't even know where to start."

"There are some mental drills that might help." Cloister pats me on the back. "Perhaps we can get you ready for tomorrow morning."

"What's happening tomorrow morning?"

"Your first date," says Cloister. "Also, if all goes well, your marriage proposal."

I WAKE, as always, before dawn, springing to full alertness with all the force of old habits. Sleeping too soundly or late can get you killed in the field, after all.

I wash up in a basin of tepid water in my room, then dry and dress. Looking out the window, I see it's still dark outside...but won't be for long. I am early for this morning's meeting, which is just how I like to be.

In this, Listy Kendall and I have something in common. When I arrive on the main deck, she is waiting there already, setting up an easel and palette of paints by the light of an oil lamp.

"Good morning," she says, waving a brush in my direction. "I trust you slept well, Sir Gardner?"

My heart races, and words catch in my throat. She looks as lovely as she did when we first met, in the Coral Room...and I feel just as frozen, just as shackled by conflicting emotions.

But then I run one of the exercises Cloister taught me, repeating these words in my head: *Kindness is not always hatred. Hatred is not always kindness.*

Something about that simple repetition weakens the bonds just enough for me to speak. "Yes, I did sleep well." It isn't much, but I consider it a victory.

"Glad to hear it." She strokes a rich red base on the canvas as the sky begins to brighten. "You don't mind if I paint, do you? It's going to be such a lovely autumn morning."

"Not at all." I can barely force out the words. The way her lacy white blouse clings to her breasts, and her black britches hug the curves of her hips and bottom, I have trouble focusing on the conversation at hand.

"So, Sir Gardner." Listy swirls in white with the red, stirring it into a deep pink color. "What hobbies do *you* have?"

C-Love, not K-Love. That's another exercise Cloister taught me. *C-Love, not K-Love,* as in *the love-that-cherishes,* not *the love-that-kills.* "Well..." I fight for focus. "I sharpen my *blades* in my spare time. And train younger knights in battlefield techniques."

"Sounds more like *work* to me." Listy tips her head and gives me a funny look out of the corner of her eye. "Do you ever court *maidens*, I wonder?"

I feel myself blush. *C-Love, not K-Love. C-Love, not K-Love.* "I, uh...no, I..." In spite of the mantra, my brain locks up, and my voice trails off.

"Oh, look." Listy pauses in dabbing at the canvas and gazes out at the scenery, mouth open in wonder. "Come here, Sir Gardner."

I step up beside her, following her gaze with my own. The sky, by now, is fairly bright, so the vast gulf below is awash in predawn light--but it appears not at all as it did the evening before. Everywhere I look, instead of swaths of colorful trees and distant green fields, I see an expanse of mist blanketing everything.

"I love when it's like this." Her voice is low and soft. "My grandfather used to say it was like an ocean of cloud out there. He half-expected to see a dolphin jump out of it, he said." She bumps my arm with her elbow. "Not that he was *biased*, living in a ship on the mountain and all."

"Three states, seven counties." Lost in the view, I get my voice back. "It's as if they've disappeared."

"They're still out there. They always are." Her elbow nudges my arm again. "You just can't *see* them."

Staring into that milky abyss, I let my imagination run away with me--something I rarely do. "It's more like Heaven than an ocean," I say, though I've only ever seen photos of oceans or paintings of Heaven.

When a bird pops out of the mist nearby, it startles me back to reality. I become fully aware of Listy's body next to mine, her elbow against my arm...and that triggers the kind of reaction I had before.

Even as it happens, I hate myself for it. Burytown is in dire need; am I so *damaged* that I can't at least *bluff* my way through the one chance I have to *save* it?

Yes, apparently.

Stumbling back from the railing, I knock over a chair and almost fall. Listy turns, a look of pity on her face that somehow makes it all the worse.

"S-sorry..." All my life, love has been a weapon. Feeling it has always been a pretext, a preamble to some kind or other of bloodbath. Thinking of it now *not* as a means to murder feels *wrong...confusing.*

Yet it's *there...*a *whisper* of that *other* love that Cloister talked about. And the more I feel it, *the more I don't know what to do with it.*

Listy seems to have no such difficulty--unless, of course, she isn't feeling C-Love toward me in the first place. She seems perfectly comfortable in all our interactions, even as I find myself intensely off-balance.

I'm sweating as if I'm in a fight, and my belly's full of butterflies. I wish I'd never come here, opening myself up to all this confusion--even if staying home would have meant certain death without the alliance I'd hoped to find.

Time is running out for that home of mine...though just how quickly, I only now discover.

The door to the deck flies open, and a dark-skinned woman stalks through, heaving for breath. She is a woman I *know,* a messenger from Burytown called Polly Sullivan.

"Sir Gardner!" She gasps out the words. "I bring word of Burytown! Its downfall is *imminent.* This very day, your precious *home* shall fall to the *wolves* at its doorstep."

I SLIDE Eros down into his scabbard with the scrape of metal against metal. I do the same for the rest of my blades, slipping them into their various sheaths with familiar, practiced ease.

Standing in the middle of my room, I take a deep breath and release it. Everything is in its place again, and the world makes sense. My course is clear and straight, and my heart is filled with so much *love* for those who threaten my home.

Nodding to myself, I snatch my helmet from a hook on the wall, then storm out of the room and down the stairs. Lord

Kendall, Bon Cloister, and Listy wait at the bottom, between me and the exit.

"Ho, sir knight." Rubicon raises both hands as if to hold me back. "We have heard with deep regret the terrible news from Burytown."

"Save your regret for the Loved Ones," I tell him. "For I go now to shower them with my deepest affection."

"Of course," says Rubicon. "You have concluded your business with us in full, then? Shall I signal my man-at-arms to rally the forces we have pledged you?"

I spare a glance at Listy, who bears a troubled look on her face. There is a pull deep within me, a gravity catching at my heart--but other powers overwhelm it.

"Good sir, the people of Burytown shall humbly welcome any and all forces pledged to act in their interest. But it is not true that our business is concluded." I bow my head. "I have yet to fulfill the terms of our pact."

"And *will* you?" asks Rubicon.

I feel Listy's frown upon me as I speak. "If Burytown's state is as dire as Polly Sullivan reports, I cannot promise anything. My own future might be exceedingly brief."

"Then, regrettably, I cannot offer aid," says Rubicon.

"Father!" snaps Listy.

Rubicon slashes his hand through the air. "We risk *much,* sending so large a force away from our own battlements. We risk this very *keep* and all who *depend* on it. We cannot--*will* not--take that risk without a *pact.*"

"But *I* am the *currency* in this pact, am I not?" says Listy. "Have I *no say* in this..."

Rubicon cuts her off. "The pact is *everything.* In this world, *bargains* are how we *survive.*" He shakes his head at Listy, then me. "Let me ask you this, Sir Gardner. Is there *no* possibility of forging a love-that-cherishes between the two of you?"

"I can perform a ceremony here on the spot," says Cloister. "A bond of wedlock so hastily conceived shall be *no* less legitimate."

I look at each of them in turn, considering. Again, when my eyes meet hers, I feel that pull, like the current of a river...but then that *other* force rises up and blots it out. K-Love wins out, as well it should. My people *need* me.

"It is not fair to the people of Burytown to linger one moment more as their home falls to invaders," I say. "And it is not fair to *you* to take your hand in wedlock if I might make of you a widow before this day is done." I bow to Listy. "As much as I might wish it could be otherwise."

"But you are *more* likely to live another day with Lord Kendall's forces at your back," says Cloister.

"And what kind of man would I *be* if I married this woman to save my own *neck*?" Impulsively, I reach for Listy's hand and kiss it. "That does not sound to me like anything *close* to a love-that-cherishes."

I let go of her hand...yet my next words are intended only for *her* ears. "Farewell. Perhaps we shall meet again in that heavenly ocean of mist."

With that, I square my shoulders, push past Lord Kendall, and march outside into the late morning sunlight. Polly, who's been waiting, kickstarts her motorbike and revs it loudly as I don my helmet and climb on behind her.

Then, in a cloud of dust and gravel, we spin around and fly down the highway away from Kendall's Keep.

IT SURPRISES me how much I think of Listy as we ride down the mountain. The memory of kissing her hand stays with me, as does the memory of gazing into the mist by her side with her elbow resting against my arm.

But when the time comes to banish her from my thoughts, I do. The field of battle, as I understand all too well, is no place for thoughts of C-Love...only K.

Polly and I dismount and stow the bike a mile back from Burytown, then travel the rest on foot. The sounds of the fight reach us as we hurry through the woods--the clash and clang of steel, the scattered blasts of pistols and rifles, the screams of the wounded and dying.

Then the fight itself reaches us, too. Within sight of the rooftops of town, we are set upon by a trio of Loved Ones, soaked in gore and whipped into a frenzy.

"I *love* you!" A red-bearded warrior leads the ambush, swinging a blood-smeared axe overhead. "I will *show* you *how much!*"

Adrenaline burns in my bloodstream as I slip Eros from his scabbard and stand ready to meet the charge. "*Come* then, brother, and let us *see* who has the *most* love to *give!*"

They attack us like men possessed, half-crazed with K-Love stoked to extreme levels by relentless bloodletting on the field of battle. But Polly and I are possessed by a love that's as strong or stronger and untainted by corrupt motives. Our unwavering brand of love, born of devotion to home and clan, can carry the day against even the longest odds.

Though even as loving as we are, the odds we now face are long indeed. After ending the first three fighters with great love and swordsmanship, Polly and I push closer to the heart of the battle--just in time to see a horde of Loved Ones break through the line of defenders at the edge of Burytown.

People we know go down fighting as the invaders pile on. Every one of our noble warriors smiles with no less lovingkindness even as blades, bullets, and war hammers put them to rout.

It is now that I think of Listy once more, for I realize I shall never see her again. With the perimeter breached and our forces so clearly outnumbered, Burytown has not long to live.

Smoke fills the air as flaming arrows set fire to rooftops. Men and women on horseback and motorbikes tear through gaps in the line, escorted by slavering hounds. It is the end of the world, *my* world, and all the smiles and proclamations of love make it all the more hellish.

Doomed as our home may be, Polly and I charge into the fray with smiles and swords flashing.

K-Love, not C-Love. K-Love, not C-Love. Eros swirls and whizzes in my good right hand, slipping through one throat after another. In my good left hand, a dagger jabs and slashes, cutting faces, hearts, and guts like the fang of a dragon.

No mercy is shown, not a whit...though even as my blades sow mayhem, I feel only deep-down love for every soul I maim or kill.

I am, in these moments, perfection--my focus diamond-hard, my killing exquisite, my love unblemished. Dancing from one fighter to the next, leaving geysers of blood in my wake, I am like a holy angel, beaming and unstoppable.

But for every man or woman who falls before me, another three or four or more pile in. For every blow or cut that I deflect, another flurry rains down on me.

I swear I will fight to the last, but the outcome is set in stone now. The end is near.

Polly and I fight back to back, swords and daggers in constant motion--until suddenly, she is gone. Turning in my murderous gyre, I see her dragged under the bloodthirsty tide, and I move to save her.

But at that moment, someone gets in a lucky shot across my back with a crowbar, and I drop. Keeping hold of my blades, I twist, blindly sweeping Eros in a futile swath that catches nothing.

When I hit the ground, the horde closes in around me. *Love you love you love you,* chant dozens of voices overflowing with eager and deeply sincere affection.

I see the crowbar and other bludgeoning weapons hoisted overhead, ready to crash upon me like a landslide. Holding fast to the handles of my blades, I ready myself for one final fusillade to finish the day, one last statement to cast upon the canvas of this terrible work.

"I love you!" I howl the words at the top of my lungs. "*I love you from the bottom of my heart!*"

It is then that I hear a salvo of gunshots crackling nearby. Men topple around me like rotten fruit, dropping their bludgeons.

More clamor then--a thunder of footfalls, a clatter of blades. More gunshots and the twanging of bowstrings, the sizzle and *thunk* of arrows. More men and women fall, and the rest erupt in panic.

Seizing the opportunity, I leap to my feet and pick up where I left off, slashing and stabbing in every direction. As Loved Ones fumble and scatter, I clear them like chaff.

A giant of a man, bald as a pumpkin and bedecked in blood, refuses to panic and swats the helmet right off my head. I answer with a knife through his windpipe...just as a sword thrusts through his heart from behind.

He topples as both blades withdraw--and I see whose sword joined mine in stopping the menace.

It was *hers.* "Good Sir Gardner!" None other than *Listy Kendall* grins back at me from the visor of a white helmet. "Fancy meeting *you* here." Laughing, she wipes the blood from her sword against the hip of her white body armor.

My heart hammers in my chest at the sight of her. I am so caught up in her beauty and the shock of seeing her that I forget to lose the power of speech. "You *came?*" Looking around, I see men and women wearing the coat of arms of Kendall's Keep (in patches or tattoos) plowing through the invaders of Burytown. "But what of the *pact?*"

Listy narrows her eyes and lifts her chin. "Wedded or no, I will *never* stand idly by so long as there is something I can do to save good folk like the people of Burytown."

In that instant, I get a shiver, a frisson of electric joy. I want nothing more than to wrap her in my arms and never let go.

Because she *came.* Because she's *fighting* on behalf of my people for no other reason than because it's *right.* Because she's so *beautiful* and *thoughtful* and *capable* and *confident,* and I *want* her with every fiber of my *being.*

Is *this* what Cloister was talking about? The love-that-cherishes? *An attraction so real and profound that we want to join with the other person in a multitude of ways?*

"I suppose the pact is *moot*, then? Since Burytown got the help it needed without the two of us submitting to wedlock?" As Listy says it, a bruiser roars forth, and she dispatches him with a flick of her sword.

"Actually, I've been thinking." Lifting Listy's visor, I lean in and kiss her gently on the lips. "Perhaps we might discuss *another* pact?"

Her eyes lock with mine, and she kisses me back--not gently. "Perhaps."

Then, whirling, she takes up the fight again, swinging her sword with all the nimble grace with which she paints an ocean of mist on a canvas.

Smiling, I fell an attacker of my own, dropping him dead with a heart full of love--but for *once*, it is *not* the love-that-kills.

ABOUT THE AUTHOR

Robert Jeschonek is an envelope-pushing, *USA Today* bestselling author whose fiction, comics, and non-fiction have been published around the world. His stories have appeared in *Clarkesworld, Galaxy's Edge, StarShipSofa, Pulphouse,* and many other publications. He has written official *Star Trek* and *Doctor Who* fiction and has scripted comics for DC, AHOY, and others. His young adult slipstream novel, *My Favorite Band Does Not Exist,* won the Forward National Literature Award and was named one of *Booklist's* Top Ten First Novels for Youth. He also won an International Book Award, a Scribe Award for Best Original Novel, and the grand prize in Pocket Books' Strange New Worlds contest. Visit him online at www.bobscribe.com. You can also find him on Facebook and follow him as @TheFictioneer on Twitter. Subscribe to the Blastoff Books Newsletter: http://newsletter.blastoffbooks.net/.

SPECIAL PREVIEW: BLASTOFF!

Eighteen star-spanning scifi stories from the edge of the universe, now available for your favorite e-reading device or app.

From "Where No Furry Has Gone Before" in *Blastoff!*

Captain Harmonious Curl the Big Brown Bear gazed in wonder and pity at the naked, hairless humanoid on the floor of the spacecraft's bridge, so lacking in the thick, lustrous fur that he and his team possessed.

Doctor Stripy Sinew, the Tiger of Much Hippocraticness, ran his silver handheld medical scanner over the form of the pink-skinned male on the floor. "I can tell you this much, Captain. The hairlessness is *not* a natural condition."

"Shaving, then?" said Curl. "*Forced* shaving, given all those *cuts* covering the body?"

Sinew kept watching the scanner with his big green eyes. "Something much more violent, I'm afraid. Those wounds are *bite marks* containing traces of toxic *venom.* And the other corpses we've found aboard this vessel were bitten in just the same way."

Curl shook his head. "What the hell *happened* here? There doesn't seem to be a lock of hair or patch of fur to be found *anywhere* on this ship!"

"Not to mention the 52 *dead people.*" Commander Bunny Hoppañero, big pink rabbit and first officer of Curl's crew, wasn't afraid to keep the others grounded when she had to. "The *hair loss* is the *least* of it, don't you think?"

"In the distress message sent by these people, they appeared to have healthy *pelts* of fur," Curl said grimly. "By the *Cosmic Coiffure*, we *will* avenge this tragic loss of follicles."

"Loss of *life*, you mean," said Bunny.

Curl nodded forcefully. "That, too."

Bunny sighed and turned to Ensign Sipping Tenderly, a six-foot-tall sugar glider and engineering officer bent over a damaged control panel. "Any answers yet, Sip?"

"Nada." Sipping smacked the panel, which had been blasted into charred ruins by some kind of energy weapon. "Ship's logs are gone. Every log file you can think of is erased or hopelessly scrambled. I think some kind of EMP must have hit this vessel."

Just then, the team's Big Doggie, Frisky Delicato, broke in from the far side of the oblong-shaped bridge. "*Rrruff!* I think we might have *another* source of info, you furballs! Looky here!"

Curl and the others turned to see Frisky jumping up and down, panting and pointing at another naked, hairless male tucked into a compartment under a console. *This* body, however, had some *life* in it, groaning and twitching as they watched.

Sinew padded over and scanned Frisky's humanoid find without delay. "He's alive, all right, but unconscious and in shock. More of the bites, as well--and some *bigger* scars, too...possibly *self-inflicted.*" Immediately, he started medicating the man with a hypodermic from his kit. "We need to get him back to our ship ASAP to treat the shock and counteract the venom from the bites."

Curl looked around at what had once been the bright and busy nerve center of the ship. By the glow of emergency lamps, it looked like a dark and decimated ruin, scattered with hairless corpses. Every console and panel had been blasted and burned; some still sparked and smoldered. Every display screen had been shattered, and every control smashed. Then there was the blood spattered everywhere, decorating every surface with a film of crimson droplets.

What *had* happened aboard this ship? Curl shuddered as his imagination ran away with him, presenting one terrible scenario after another.

Especially the part about the involuntary pelt removal. He'd seen some awful things in his time among the stars as Captain of the *S.B.B. Furflier*, but he *never* got used to *that* kind of unnatural treatment.

Though, of course, the very fur that covered him was anything *but* natural--and the same went for every one of his shipmates.

What happens next? Find out in Blastoff!, now available for your favorite e-reading device or app!

www.ingramcontent.com/pod-product-compliance
Lightning Source LLC
Chambersburg PA
CBHW072255020726
47501CB00002B/272

* 9 7 8 1 7 3 6 1 6 8 7 3 8 *